The Complete
Short Stories

BOOKS BY AGATHA CHRISTIE

The ABC Murders
The Adventure of the Christmas
  Pudding
After the Funeral
And Then There Were None
Appointment with Death
At Bertram's Hotel
The Big Four
The Body in the Library
By the Pricking of My Thumbs
Cards on the Table
A Caribbean Mystery
Cat Among the Pigeons
The Clocks
Crooked House
Curtain: Poirot's Last Case
Dead Man's Folly
Death Comes as the End
Death in the Clouds
Death on the Nile
Destination Unknown
Dumb Witness
Elephants Can Remember
Endless Night
Evil Under the Sun
Five Little Pigs
4.50 from Paddington
Hallowe'en Party
Hercule Poirot's Christmas
Hickory Dickory Dock
The Hollow
The Hound of Death
The Labours of Hercules
The Listerdale Mystery
Lord Edgware Dies
The Man in the Brown Suit
The Mirror Crack'd from Side
  to Side
Miss Marple's Final Cases
The Moving Finger
Mrs McGinty's Dead
The Murder at the Vicarage
Murder in Mesopotamia
Murder in the Mews
A Murder is Announced
Murder is Easy
The Murder of Roger Ackroyd
Murder on the Links
Murder on the Orient Express

The Mysterious Affair at Styles
The Mysterious Mr Quin
The Mystery of the Blue Train
Nemesis
N or M?
One, Two, Buckle My Shoe
Ordeal by Innocence
The Pale Horse
Parker Pyne Investigates
Partners in Crime
Passenger to Frankfurt
Peril at End House
A Pocket Full of Rye
Poirot Investigates
Poirot's Early Cases
Postern of Fate
Problem at Pollensa Bay
Sad Cypress
The Secret Adversary
The Secret of Chimneys
The Seven Dials Mystery
The Sittaford Mystery
Sleeping Murder
Sparkling Cyanide
Taken at the Flood
They Came to Baghdad
They Do It With Mirrors
Third Girl
The Thirteen Problems
Three-Act Tragedy
Towards Zero
Why Didn't They Ask Evans

*Novels under the Nom de Plume
of 'Mary Westmacott'*
Absent in the Spring
The Burden
A Daughter's A Daughter
Giant's Bread
The Rose and the Tew Tree
Unfinished Portrait

*Books under the name of
Agatha Christie Mallowan*
Come Tell me How You Live
Star Over Bethlehem

Autobiography
Agatha Christie: An Autobiography

AGATHA CHRISTIE

MISS MARPLE

The Complete
Short Stories

HarperCollins*Publishers*

HarperCollins*Publishers*
77–85 Fulham Palace Road,
Hammersmith, London w6 8jb

This edition first published 1997
11 13 15 17 16 14 12 10

The Thirteen Problems copyright © Agatha Christie Mallowan 1932
The Adventures of the Christmas Pudding copyright © Agatha Christie
Limited 1960
Miss Marple's Final Cases copyright © Agatha Christie Limited 1979
This collection copyright © Agatha Christie Limited 1997

ISBN 0 00 649962 7

Set in Baskerville by
Rowland Phototypesetting Ltd,
Bury St Edmunds, Suffolk

Printed and bound in Great Britain by
Clays Ltd, St Ives plc

CONTENTS

INTRODUCTION

Enter Miss Marple

Miss Marple insinuated herself so quickly into my life that I hardly noticed her arrival. I wrote a series of six short stories for a magazine, and chose six people whom I thought might meet once a week in a small village and describe some unsolved crime. I started with Miss Jane Marple, the sort of old lady who would have been rather like some of my grandmother's Ealing cronies – old ladies whom I have met in so many villages where I have gone to stay as a girl. Miss Marple was not in any way a picture of my grandmother; she was far more fussy and spinsterish than my grandmother ever was. But one thing she did have in common with her – though a cheerful person, she always expected the worst of everyone and everything, and was, with almost frightening accuracy, usually proved right . . .

Anyway, I endowed my Miss Marple with something of Grannie's powers of prophecy. There was no unkindness in Miss Marple, she just did not trust people. Though she expected the worst, she often accepted people kindly in spite of what they were.

Miss Marple was born at the age of sixty-five to seventy – which, as with Poirot, proved most unfortunate, because she was going to have to last a long time in my life. If *I* had had any second sight, I would have provided myself with a precocious schoolboy as my first detective; then he could have grown old with me.

I gave Miss Marple five colleagues for the series of six stories First was her nephew; a modern novelist who dealt in strong meat in his books, incest, sex, and sordid descriptions of bedrooms and lavatory equipment – the stark side of life was what Raymond West saw. His dear, pretty, old fluffy Aunt Jane he treated with an indulgent kindness as one who knew nothing of the world. Secondly, I produced a young woman who was a modern painter, and was just getting on very special terms with Raymond West. Then there were Mr Petherick, a local solicitor, dry, shrewd, elderly; the local doctor – a useful person to know of cases which would make a suitable story for an evening's problem; and a clergyman.

Some time later I wrote another six Miss Marple stories, and the twelve, with an extra story, were published in England under the title of *The Thirteen Problems*, and in America as *The Tuesday Club Murders*.

AGATHA CHRISTIE
from *An Autobiography*

The Thirteen Problems

TO
LEONARD AND KATHERINE
WOOLLEY

The Tuesday Night Club

'Unsolved mysteries.'

Raymond West blew out a cloud of smoke and repeated the words with a kind of deliberate self-conscious pleasure.

'Unsolved mysteries.'

He looked round him with satisfaction. The room was an old one with broad black beams across the ceiling and it was furnished with good old furniture that belonged to it. Hence Raymond West's approving glance. By profession he was a writer and he liked the atmosphere to be flawless. His Aunt Jane's house always pleased him as the right setting for her personality. He looked across the hearth to where she sat erect in the big grandfather chair. Miss Marple wore a black brocade dress, very much pinched in round the waist. Mechlin lace was arranged in a cascade down the front of the bodice. She had on black lace mittens, and a black lace cap surmounted the piled-up masses of her snowy hair. She was knitting – something white and soft and fleecy. Her faded blue eyes, benignant and kindly, surveyed her nephew and her nephew's guests with gentle pleasure. They rested first on Raymond himself, self-consciously debonair, then on Joyce Lemprière, the artist, with her close-cropped black head and queer hazel-green eyes, then on that well-groomed man of the world, Sir Henry Clithering. There were two other people in the room, Dr Pender, the elderly clergyman of the parish, and Mr Petherick, the solicitor, a dried-up little man with eyeglasses which he looked over and not through. Miss Marple gave a brief moment of attention to all these people and returned to her knitting with a gentle smile upon her lips.

Mr Petherick gave the dry little cough with which he usually prefaced his remarks.

'What is that you say, Raymond? Unsolved mysteries? Ha – and what about them?'

'Nothing about them,' said Joyce Lemprière. 'Raymond just likes the sound of himself saying them.'

Raymond West threw her a glance of reproach at which she threw back her head and laughed.

'He is a humbug, isn't he, Miss Marple?' she demanded. 'You know that, I am sure.'

Miss Marple smiled gently at her but made no reply.

'Life itself is an unsolved mystery,' said the clergyman gravely.

Raymond sat up in his chair and flung away his cigarette with an impulsive gesture.

'That's not what I mean. I was not talking philosophy,' he said. 'I was thinking of actual bare prosaic facts, things that have happened and that no one has ever explained.'

'I know just the sort of thing you mean, dear,' said Miss Marple. 'For instance Mrs Carruthers had a very strange experience yesterday morning. She bought two gills of picked shrimps at Elliot's. She called at two other shops and when she got home she found she had not got the shrimps with her. She went back to the two shops she had visited but these shrimps had completely disappeared. Now that seems to me very remarkable.'

'A very fishy story,' said Sir Henry Clithering gravely.

'There are, of course, all kinds of possible

4

explanations,' said Miss Marple, her cheeks growing slightly pinker with excitement. 'For instance, somebody else –'

'My dear Aunt,' said Raymond West with some amusement, 'I didn't mean that sort of village incident. I was thinking of murders and disappearances – the kind of thing that Sir Henry could tell us about by the hour if he liked.'

'But I never talk shop,' said Sir Henry modestly. 'No, I never talk shop.'

Sir Henry Clithering had been until lately Commissioner of Scotland Yard.

'I suppose there are a lot of murders and things that never are solved by the police,' said Joyce Lemprière.

'That is an admitted fact, I believe,' said Mr Petherick.

'I wonder,' said Raymond West, 'what class of brain really succeeds best in unravelling a mystery? One always feels that the average police detective must be hampered by lack of imagination.'

'That is the layman's point of view,' said Sir Henry dryly.

'You really want a committee,' said Joyce, smiling. 'For psychology and imagination go to the writer –'

She made an ironical bow to Raymond but he remained serious.

'The art of writing gives one an insight into human nature,' he said gravely. 'One sees, perhaps, motives that the ordinary person would pass by.'

'I know, dear,' said Miss Marple, 'that your books are very clever. But do you think that people are really so unpleasant as you make them out to be?'

'My dear Aunt,' said Raymond gently, 'keep your beliefs. Heaven forbid that *I* should in any way shatter them.'

'I mean,' said Miss Marple, puckering her brow a

little as she counted the stitches in her knitting, 'that so many people seem to me not to be either bad or good, but simply, you know, very silly.'

Mr Petherick gave his dry little cough again.

'Don't you think, Raymond,' he said, 'that you attach too much weight to imagination? Imagination is a very dangerous thing, as we lawyers know only too well. To be able to sift evidence impartially, to take the facts and look at them as facts – that seems to me the only logical method of arriving at the truth. I may add that in my experience it is the only one that succeeds.'

'Bah!' cried Joyce, flinging back her black head indignantly. 'I bet I could beat you all at this game. I am not only a woman – and say what you like, women have an intuition that is denied to men – I am an artist as well. I see things that you don't. And then, too, as an artist I have knocked about among all sorts and conditions of people. I know life as darling Miss Marple here cannot possibly know it.'

'I don't know about that, dear,' said Miss Marple. 'Very painful and distressing things happen in villages sometimes.'

'May I speak?' said Dr Pender smiling. 'It is the fashion nowadays to decry the clergy, I know, but we hear things, we know a side of human character which is a sealed book to the outside world.'

'Well,' said Joyce, 'it seems to me we are a pretty representative gathering. How would it be if we formed a Club? What is today? Tuesday? We will call it The Tuesday Night Club. It is to meet every week, and each member in turn has to propound a problem. Some mystery of which they have personal knowledge, and to which, of course, they know the answer. Let me see, how many are we? One, two, three, four, five. We ought really to be six.'

6

'You have forgotten me, dear,' said Miss Marple, smiling brightly.

Joyce was slightly taken aback, but she concealed the fact quickly.

'That would be lovely, Miss Marple,' she said. 'I didn't think you would care to play.'

'I think it would be very interesting,' said Miss Marple, 'especially with so many clever gentlemen present. I am afraid I am not clever myself, but living all these years in St Mary Mead does give one an insight into human nature.'

'I am sure your co-operation will be very valuable,' said Sir Henry, courteously.

'Who is going to start?' said Joyce.

'I think there is no doubt as to that,' said Dr Pender, 'when we have the great good fortune to have such a distinguished man as Sir Henry staying with us –'

He left his sentence unfinished, making a courtly bow in the direction of Sir Henry.

The latter was silent for a minute or two. At last he sighed and recrossed his legs and began:

'It is a little difficult for me to select just the kind of thing you want, but I think, as it happens, I know of an instance which fits these conditions very aptly. You may have seen some mention of the case in the papers of a year ago. It was laid aside at the time as an unsolved mystery, but, as it happens, the solution came into my hands not very many days ago.

'The facts are very simple. Three people sat down to a supper consisting, amongst other things, of tinned lobster. Later in the night, all three were taken ill, and a doctor was hastily summoned. Two of the people recovered, the third one died.'

'Ah!' said Raymond approvingly.

'As I say, the facts as such were very simple. Death

was considered to be due to ptomaine poisoning, a certificate was given to that effect, and the victim was duly buried. But things did not rest at that.'

Miss Marple nodded her head.

'There was talk, I suppose,' she said, 'there usually is.'

'And now I must describe the actors in this little drama. I will call the husband and wife Mr and Mrs Jones, and the wife's companion Miss Clark. Mr Jones was a traveller for a firm of manufacturing chemists. He was a good-looking man in a kind of coarse, florid way, aged about fifty. His wife was a rather common-place woman, of about forty-five. The companion, Miss Clark, was a woman of sixty, a stout cheery woman with a beaming rubicund face. None of them, you might say, very interesting.

'Now the beginning of the troubles arose in a very curious way. Mr Jones had been staying the previous night at a small commercial hotel in Birmingham. It happened that the blotting paper in the blotting book had been put in fresh that day, and the chambermaid, having apparently nothing better to do, amused herself by studying the blotter in the mirror just after Mr Jones had been writing a letter there. A few days later there was a report in the papers of the death of Mrs Jones as the result of eating tinned lobster, and the chamber-maid then imparted to her fellow servants the words that she had deciphered on the blotting pad. They were as follows: *Entirely dependent on my wife . . . when she is dead I will . . . hundreds and thousands . . .*

'You may remember that there had recently been a case of a wife being poisoned by her husband. It needed very little to fire the imagination of these maids. Mr Jones had planned to do away with his wife and inherit hundreds of thousands of pounds! As it happened one of the maids had relations living in the small market town where the Joneses resided. She wrote to them, and they in return wrote to her. Mr Jones, it seemed, had been very attentive to the local doctor's daughter, a good-looking young woman of thirty-three. Scandal began to hum. The Home Secretary was petitioned. Numerous anonymous letters poured into Scotland Yard all accusing Mr Jones of having murdered his wife. Now I may say that not for one moment did we think there was anything in it except idle village talk and gossip. Nevertheless, to quiet public opinion an exhumation order was granted. It was one of these cases of popular superstition based on nothing solid whatever, which proved to be so surprisingly justified. As a result of the autopsy sufficient arsenic was found to make it quite clear that the deceased lady had died of arsenical poisoning. It was for Scotland Yard working with the local authorities to prove how that arsenic had been administered, and by whom.'

'Ah!' said Joyce. 'I like this. This is the real stuff.'

'Suspicion naturally fell on the husband. He benefited by his wife's death. Not to the extent of the hundreds of thousands romantically imagined by the hotel chambermaid, but to the very solid amount of £8000. He had no money of his own apart from what he earned, and he was a man of somewhat extravagant habits with a partiality for the society of women. We investigated as delicately as possible the rumour of his attachment to the doctor's daughter; but while it seemed clear that there had been a strong friendship between them at one time, there had been a most abrupt break two months previously, and they did not appear to have seen each other since. The doctor himself, an elderly man of a straightforward and unsuspicious type, was dumbfounded at the result of the autopsy. He had been called in about midnight to find all three people suffering. He had realized immediately the serious condition of Mrs Jones, and had sent back to his dispensary for some opium pills, to allay the pain. In spite of all his efforts, however, she succumbed, but not for a moment did he suspect that anything was amiss. He was convinced that her death was due to a form of botulism. Supper that night had consisted of tinned lobster and salad, trifle and bread and cheese. Unfortunately none of the lobster remained – it had all been eaten and the tin thrown away. He had interrogated the young maid, Gladys Linch. She was terribly upset, very tearful and agitated, and he found it hard to get her to keep to the point, but she declared again and again that the tin had not been distended in any way and that the lobster had appeared to her in a perfectly good condition.

'Such were the facts we had to go upon. If Jones had feloniously administered arsenic to his wife, it seemed clear that it could not have been done in any of the things eaten at supper, as all three persons had partaken of the meal. Also – another point – Jones himself had returned from Birmingham just as supper was being brought in to table, so that he would have had no opportunity of doctoring any of the food beforehand.'

'What about the companion?' asked Joyce. 'The stout woman with the good-humoured face.'

Sir Henry nodded.

'We did not neglect Miss Clark, I can assure you. But it seemed doubtful what motive she could have had for the crime. Mrs Jones left her no legacy of any kind and the net result of her employer's death was that she had to seek for another situation.'

'That seems to leave her out of it,' said Joyce thoughtfully..

'Now one of my inspectors soon discovered a significant fact,' went on Sir Henry. 'After supper on that evening Mr Jones had gone down to the kitchen and had demanded a bowl of cornflour for his wife who had complained of not feeling well. He had waited in the kitchen until Gladys Linch prepared it, and then carried it up to his wife's room himself. That, I admit, seemed to clinch the case.'

The lawyer nodded.

'Motive,' he said, ticking the points off on his fingers. 'Opportunity. As a traveller for a firm of druggists, easy access to the poison.'

'And a man of weak moral fibre,' said the clergyman.

Raymond West was staring at Sir Henry.

'There is a catch in this somewhere,' he said. 'Why did you not arrest him?'

Sir Henry smiled rather wryly.

'That is the unfortunate part of the case. So far all had gone swimmingly, but now we come to the snags. Jones was not arrested because on interrogating Miss Clark she told us that the whole of the bowl of cornflour was drunk not by Mrs Jones but by her.

'Yes, it seems that she went to Mrs Jones's room as was her custom. Mrs Jones was sitting up in bed and the bowl of cornflour was beside her.

' "I am not feeling a bit well, Milly," she said. "Serves me right, I suppose, for touching lobster at night. I asked Albert to get me a bowl of cornflour, but now that I have got it I don't seem to fancy it."

' "A pity," commented Miss Clark, "it is nicely made too, no lumps. Gladys is really quite a nice cook. Very few girls nowadays seem to be able to make a bowl of cornflour nicely. I declare I quite fancy it myself, I am that hungry."

' "I should think you were with your foolish ways," said Mrs Jones.

11

'I must explain,' broke off Sir Henry, 'that Miss Clark, alarmed at her increasing stoutness, was doing a course of what is popularly known as "banting".

'"It is not good for you, Milly, it really isn't," urged Mrs Jones. "If the Lord made you stout he meant you to be stout. You drink up that bowl of cornflour. It will do you all the good in the world."

'And straight away Miss Clark set to and did in actual fact finish the bowl. So, you see, that knocked our case against the husband to pieces. Asked for an explanation of the words on the blotting book Jones gave one readily enough. The letter, he explained, was in answer to one written from his brother in Australia who had applied to him for money. He had written, pointing out that he was entirely dependent on his wife. When his wife was dead he would have control of money and would assist his brother if possible. He regretted his inability to help but pointed out that there were hundreds and thousands of people in the world in the same unfortunate plight.'

'And so the case fell to pieces?' said Dr Pender.

'And so the case fell to pieces,' said Sir Henry gravely. 'We could not take the risk of arresting Jones with nothing to go upon.'

There was a silence and then Joyce said, 'And that is all, is it?'

'That is the case as it has stood for the last year. The true solution is now in the hands of Scotland Yard, and in two or three days' time you will probably read of it in the newspapers.'

'The true solution,' said Joyce thoughtfully. 'I wonder. Let's all think for five minutes and then speak.'

Raymond West nodded and noted the time on his watch. When the five minutes were up he looked over at Dr Pender.

'Will you speak first?' he said.

The old man shook his head. 'I confess,' he said, 'that I am utterly baffled. I can but think that the husband in some way must be the guilty party, but how he did it I cannot imagine. I can only suggest that he must have given her the poison in some way that has not yet been discovered, although how in that case it should have come to light after all this time I cannot imagine.'

'Joyce?'

'The companion!' said Joyce decidedly. 'The companion every time! How do we know what motive she may have had? Just because she was old and stout and ugly it doesn't follow that she wasn't in love with Jones herself. She may have hated the wife for some other reason. Think of being a companion – always having to be pleasant and agree and stifle yourself and bottle yourself up. One day she couldn't bear it any longer and then she killed her. She probably put the arsenic in the bowl of cornflour and all that story about eating it herself is a lie.'

'Mr Petherick?'

The lawyer joined the tips of his fingers together professionally. 'I should hardly like to say. On the facts I should hardly like to say.'

'But you have got to, Mr Petherick,' said Joyce. 'You can't reserve judgement and say "without prejudice", and be legal. You have got to play the game.'

'On the facts,' said Mr Petherick, 'there seems nothing to be said. It is my private opinion, having seen, alas, too many cases of this kind, that the husband was guilty. The only explanation that will cover the facts seems to be that Miss Clark for some reason or other deliberately sheltered him. There may have been some financial arrangement made between them. He might realize that he would be suspected, and she, seeing only a future of poverty before her, may have agreed to tell the story of drinking the cornflour in return for a substantial sum to be paid to her privately. If that was the case it was of course most irregular. Most irregular indeed.'

'I disagree with you all,' said Raymond. 'You have forgotten the one important factor in the case. *The doctor's daughter.* I will give you my reading of the case. The tinned lobster was bad. It accounted for the poisoning symptoms. The doctor was sent for. He finds Mrs Jones, who has eaten more lobster than the others, in great pain, and he sends, as you told us, for some opium pills. He does not go himself, he sends. Who will give the messenger the opium pills? Clearly his daughter. Very likely she dispenses his medicines for him. She is in love with Jones and at this moment all the worst instincts in her nature rise and she realizes that the means to procure his freedom are in her hands. The pills she sends contain pure white arsenic. That is my solution.'

'And now, Sir Henry, tell us,' said Joyce eagerly.

'One moment,' said Sir Henry. 'Miss Marple has not yet spoken.'

Miss Marple was shaking her head sadly.

'Dear, dear,' she said. 'I have dropped another stitch. I have been so interested in the story. A sad case, a very sad case. It reminds me of old Mr Hargraves who lived up at the Mount. His wife never had the least suspicion – until he died, leaving all his money to a woman he had been living with and by whom he had five children. She had at one time been their housemaid. Such a nice girl, Mrs Hargraves always said – thoroughly to be relied upon to turn the mattresses every day – except Fridays, of course. And there was old Hargraves keeping this woman in a house in the neighbouring town and continuing to be a churchwarden and to hand round the plate every Sunday.'

'My dear Aunt Jane,' said Raymond with some impatience. 'What has dead and gone Hargraves got to do with the case?'

'This story made me think of him at once,' said Miss Marple. 'The facts are so very alike, aren't they? I suppose the poor girl has confessed now and that is how you know, Sir Henry.'

'What girl?' said Raymond. 'My dear Aunt, what *are* you talking about?'

'That poor girl, Gladys Linch, of course – the one who was so terribly agitated when the doctor spoke to her – and well she might be, poor thing. I hope that wicked Jones is hanged, I am sure, making that poor girl a murderess. I suppose they will hang her too, poor thing.'

'I think, Miss Marple, that you are under a slight misapprehension,' began Mr Petherick.

But Miss Marple shook her head obstinately and looked across at Sir Henry.

'I am right, am I not? It seems so clear to me. The hundreds and thousands – and the trifle – I mean, one cannot miss it.'

'What about the trifle and the hundreds and thousands?' cried Raymond.

His aunt turned to him.

'Cooks nearly always put hundreds and thousands on trifle, dear,' she said. 'Those little pink and white sugar things. Of course when I heard that they had trifle for supper and that the husband had been writing to someone about hundreds and thousands, I naturally connected the two things together. That is where the arsenic was – in the hundreds and thousands. He left it with the girl and told her to put it on the trifle.'

'But that is impossible,' said Joyce quickly. 'They all ate the trifle.'

'Oh, no,' said Miss Marple. 'The companion was banting, you remember. You never eat anything like trifle if you are banting; and I expect Jones just scraped the hundreds and thousands off his share and left them at the side of his plate. It was a clever idea, but a very wicked one.'

The eyes of the others were all fixed upon Sir Henry.

'It is a very curious thing,' he said slowly, 'but Miss Marple happens to have hit upon the truth. Jones had got Gladys Linch into trouble, as the saying goes. She was nearly desperate. He wanted his wife out of the way and promised to marry Gladys when his wife was dead. He doctored the hundreds and thousands and gave them to her with instructions how to use them. Gladys Linch died a week ago. Her child died at birth and Jones had deserted her for another woman. When she was dying she confessed the truth.'

There was a few moments' silence and then Raymond said:

'Well, Aunt Jane, this is one up to you. I can't think how on earth you managed to hit upon the truth. I should never have thought of the little maid in the kitchen being connected with the case.'

'No, dear,' said Miss Marple, 'but you don't know as much of life as I do. A man of that Jones's type – coarse and jovial. As soon as I heard there was a pretty young girl in the house I felt sure that he would not have left her alone. It is all very distressing and painful, and not a very nice thing to talk about. I can't tell you the shock it was to Mrs Hargraves, and a nine days' wonder in the village.'

The Idol House of Astarte

'And now, Dr Pender, what are you going to tell us?'

The old clergyman smiled gently.

'My life has been passed in quiet places,' he said. 'Very few eventful happenings have come my way. Yet once, when I was a young man, I had one very strange and tragic experience.'

'Ah!' said Joyce Lemprière encouragingly.

'I have never forgotten it,' continued the clergyman. 'It made a profound impression on me at the time, and to this day by a slight effort of memory I can feel again the awe and horror of that terrible moment when I saw a man stricken to death by apparently no mortal agency.'

'You make me feel quite creepy, Pender,' complained Sir Henry.

'It made me feel creepy, as you call it,' replied the other. 'Since then I have never laughed at the people who use the word atmosphere. There is such a thing. There are certain places imbued and saturated with good or evil influences which can make their power felt.'

'That house, The Larches, is a very unhappy one,' remarked Miss Marple. 'Old Mr Smithers lost all his money and had to leave it, then the Carslakes took it and Johnny Carslake fell downstairs and broke his leg and Mrs Carslake had to go away to the South of France for her health, and now the Burdens have got it and I hear that poor Mr Burden has got to have an operation almost immediately.'

'There is, I think, rather too much superstition about such matters,' said Mr Petherick. 'A lot of damage is done to property by foolish reports heedlessly circulated.'

'I have known one or two "ghosts" that have had a very robust personality,' remarked Sir Henry with a chuckle.

'I think,' said Raymond, 'we should allow Dr Pender to go on with his story.'

Joyce got up and switched off the two lamps, leaving the room lit only by the flickering firelight.

'Atmosphere,' she said. 'Now we can get along.'

Dr Pender smiled at her and, leaning back in his chair and taking off his pince-nez, he began his story in a gentle reminiscent voice.

'I don't know whether any of you know Dartmoor at all. The place I am telling you about is situated on the borders of Dartmoor. It was a very charming property, though it had been on the market without finding a purchaser for several years. The situation was perhaps a little bleak in winter, but the views were magnificent and there were certain curious and original features about the property itself. It was bought by a man called Haydon – Sir Richard Haydon. I had known him in his college days, and though I had lost sight of him for some years, the old ties of friendship still held, and I accepted with pleasure his invitation to go down to Silent Grove, as his new purchase was called.

'The house party was not a very large one. There was Richard Haydon himself, and his cousin, Elliot Haydon. There was a Lady Mannering with a pale, rather inconspicuous daughter called Violet. There was a Captain Rogers and his wife, hard riding, weatherbeaten people, who lived only for horses and hunting. There was also a young Dr Symonds and there was Miss Diana Ashley. I knew something about the last named. Her picture was very often in the Society papers and she was one of the notorious beauties of the Season. Her appearance was indeed very striking. She was dark and tall, with a beautiful skin of an even tint of pale cream, and her half closed dark eyes set slantways in her head gave her a curiously piquant oriental appearance. She had, too, a wonderful speaking voice, deep-toned and bell-like.

'I saw at once that my friend Richard Haydon was very much attracted by her, and I guessed that the whole party was merely arranged as a setting for her. Of her own feelings I was not so sure. She was capricious in her favours. One day talking to Richard and excluding everyone else from her notice, and another day she would favour his cousin, Elliot, and appear hardly to notice that such a person as Richard existed, and then again she would bestow the most bewitching smiles upon the quiet and retiring Dr Symonds.

'On the morning after my arrival our host showed us all over the place. The house itself was unremarkable, a good solid house built of Devonshire granite. Built to withstand time and exposure. It was unromantic but very comfortable. From the windows of it one looked out over the panorama of the moor, vast rolling hills crowned with weather-beaten tors.

'On the slopes of the tor nearest to us were various hut circles, relics of the bygone days of the late Stone Age. On another hill was a barrow which had recently been excavated, and in which certain bronze implements had been found. Haydon was by way of being interested in antiquarian matters and he talked to us with a great deal of energy and enthusiasm. This particular spot, he explained, was particularly rich in relics of the past.

'Neolithic hut dwellers, Druids, Romans, and even traces of the early Phoenicians were to be found.

'"But this place is the most interesting of all," he said "You know its name – Silent Grove. Well, it is easy enough to see what it takes its name from."

'He pointed with his hand. That particular part of the country was bare enough – rocks, heather and bracken, but about a hundred yards from the house there was a densely planted grove of trees.

'"That is a relic of very early days," said Haydon. "The trees have died and been replanted, but on the whole it has been kept very much as it used to be – perhaps in the time of the Phoenician settlers. Come and look at it."

'We all followed him. As we entered the grove of trees a curious oppression came over me. I think it was the silence. No birds seemed to nest in these trees. There was a feeling about it of desolation and horror. I saw Haydon looking at me with a curious smile.

'"Any feeling about this place, Pender?" he asked me. "Antagonism now? Or uneasiness?"

'"I don't like it," I said quietly.

'"You are within your rights. This was a stronghold of one of the ancient enemies of your faith. This is the Grove of Astarte."

'"Astarte?"

'"Astarte, or Ishtar, or Ashtoreth, or whatever you choose to call her. I prefer the Phoenician name of Astarte. There is, I believe, one known Grove of Astarte in this country – in the North on the Wall. I have no evidence, but I like to believe that we have a true and authentic Grove of Astarte here. Here, within this dense circle of trees, sacred rites were performed."

'"Sacred rites," murmured Diana Ashley. Her eyes had a dreamy faraway look. "What were they, I wonder?"

'"Not very reputable by all accounts," said Captain Rogers with a loud unmeaning laugh. "Rather hot stuff, I imagine."

'Haydon paid no attention to him.

'"In the centre of the grove there should be a temple," he said. "I can't run to temples, but I have indulged in a little fancy of my own."

'We had at that moment stepped out into a little clearing in the centre of the trees. In the middle of it was something not unlike a summerhouse made of stone. Diana Ashley looked inquiringly at Haydon.

'"I call it The Idol House," he said. "It is the Idol House of Astarte."

'He led the way up to it. Inside, on a rude ebony pillar, there reposed a curious little image representing a woman with crescent horns, seated on a lion.

'"Astarte of the Phoenicians," said Haydon, "the Goddess of the Moon."

'"The Goddess of the Moon," cried Diana. "Oh, do let us have a wild orgy tonight. Fancy dress. And we will come out here in the moonlight and celebrate the rites of Astarte."

'I made a sudden movement and Elliot Haydon, Richard's cousin, turned quickly to me.

'"You don't like all this, do you, Padre?" he said.

'"No," I said gravely. "I don't."

'He looked at me curiously. "But it is only tomfoolery. Dick can't know that this really is a sacred grove. It is just a fancy of his; he likes to play with the idea. And anyway, if it were –"

' "If it were?"

' "Well –" he laughed uncomfortably. "You don't believe in that sort of thing, do you? You, a parson."

' "I am not sure that as a parson I ought not to believe in it."

' "But that sort of thing is all finished and done with."

' "I am not so sure," I said musingly. "I only know this: I am not as a rule a sensitive man to atmosphere, but ever since I entered this grove of trees I have felt a curious impression and sense of evil and menace all round me."

'He glanced uneasily over his shoulder.

' "Yes," he said, "it is – it is queer, somehow. I know what you mean but I suppose it is only our imagination makes us feel like that. What do you say, Symonds?"

'The doctor was silent a minute or two before he replied. Then he said quietly:

' "I don't like it. I can't tell you why. But somehow or other, I don't like it."

'At that moment Violet Mannering came across to me.

' "I hate this place," she cried. "I hate it. Do let's get out of it."

'We moved away and the others followed us. Only Diana Ashley lingered. I turned my head over my shoulder and saw her standing in front of the idol house gazing earnestly at the image within it.

'The day was an unusually hot and beautiful one and Diana Ashley's suggestion of a fancy dress party that evening was received with general favour. The usual laughing and whispering and frenzied secret sewing took place and when we all made our appearance for dinner there were the usual outcries of merriment. Rogers and his wife were Neolithic hut dwellers –

explaining the sudden lack of hearth rugs. Richard Haydon called himself a Phoenician sailor, and his cousin was a brigand chief, Dr Symonds was a chef, Lady Mannering was a hospital nurse, and her daughter was a Circassian slave. I myself was arrayed somewhat too warmly as a monk. Diana Ashley came down last and was somewhat of a disappointment to all of us, being wrapped in a shapeless black domino.

'"The Unknown," she declared airily. "That is what I am. Now for goodness' sake let's go in to dinner."

'After dinner we went outside. It was a lovely night, warm and soft, and the moon was rising.

'We wandered about and chatted and the time passed quickly enough. It must have been an hour later when we realized that Diana Ashley was not with us.

'"Surely she has not gone to bed," said Richard Haydon.

'Violet Mannering shook her head.

'"Oh, no," she said. "I saw her going off in that direction about a quarter of an hour ago." She pointed as she spoke towards the grove of trees that showed black and shadowy in the moonlight.

'"I wonder what she is up to," said Richard Haydon. "Some devilment, I swear. Let's go and see."

'We all trooped off together, somewhat curious as to what Miss Ashley had been up to. Yet I, for one, felt a curious reluctance to enter that dark foreboding belt of trees. Something stronger than myself seemed to be holding me back and urging me not to enter. I felt more definitely convinced than ever of the essential evilness of the spot. I think that some of the others experienced the same sensations that I did, though they would have been loath to admit it. The trees were so closely planted that the moonlight could not penetrate. There were a dozen soft sounds all round us, whisper-

23

ings and sighings. The feeling was eerie in the extreme, and by common consent we all kept close together.

'Suddenly we came out into the open clearing in the middle of the grove and stood rooted to the spot in amazement, for there, on the threshold of the Idol House, stood a shimmering figure wrapped tightly round in diaphanous gauze and with two crescent horns rising from the dark masses of her hair.

'"My God!" said Richard Haydon, and the sweat sprang out on his brow.

'But Violet Mannering was sharper.

'"Why, it's Diana," she exclaimed. "What has she done to herself? Oh, she looks quite different somehow!"

'The figure in the doorway raised her hands. She took a step forward and chanted in a high sweet voice.

'"I am the Priestess of Astarte," she crooned. "Beware how you approach me, for I hold death in my hand."

'"Don't do it, dear," protested Lady Mannering. "You give us the creeps, you really do."

'Haydon sprang forward towards her.

'"My God, Diana!" he cried. "You are wonderful."

'My eyes were accustomed to the moonlight now and I could see more plainly. She did, indeed, as Violet had said, look quite different. Her face was more definitely oriental, and her eyes more of slits with something cruel in their gleam, and the strange smile on her lips was one that I had never seen there before.

'"Beware," she cried warningly. "Do not approach the Goddess. If anyone lays a hand on me it is death."

'"You are wonderful, Diana," cried Haydon, "but do stop it. Somehow or other I – I don't like it."

'He was moving towards her across the grass and she flung out a hand towards him.

'"Stop," she cried. "One step nearer and I will smite you with the magic of Astarte."

'Richard Haydon laughed and quickened his pace, when all at once a curious thing happened. He hesitated for a moment, then seemed to stumble and fall headlong.

'He did not get up again but lay where he had fallen prone on the ground.

'Suddenly Diana began to laugh hysterically. It was a strange horrible sound breaking the silence of the glade.

'With an oath Elliot sprang forward.

'"I can't stand this," he cried, "get up, Dick, get up, man."

'But still Richard Haydon lay where he had fallen. Elliot Haydon reached his side, knelt by him and turned him gently over. He bent over him, peering in his face.

'Then he rose sharply to his feet and stood swaying a little.

'"Doctor," he said. "Doctor, for God's sake come. I – I think he is dead."

'Symonds ran forward and Elliot rejoined us walking very slowly. He was looking down at his hands in a way I didn't understand.

'At that moment there was a wild scream from Diana.

'"I have killed him," she cried. "Oh, my God! I didn't mean to, but I have killed him."

'And she fainted dead away, falling in a crumpled heap on the grass.

'There was a cry from Mrs Rogers.

'"Oh, do let us get away from this dreadful place," she wailed, "anything might happen to us here. Oh, it's awful!"

'Elliot got hold of me by the shoulder.

'"It can't be, man," he murmured. "I tell you it can't

be. A man cannot be killed like that. It is – it's against Nature."

'I tried to soothe him.

'"There is some explanation," I said. "Your cousin must have had some unsuspected weakness of the heart. The shock and excitement –"

'He interrupted me.

'"You don't understand," he said. He held up his hands for me to see and I noticed a red stain on them.

'"Dick didn't die of shock, he was stabbed – stabbed to the heart, and *there is no weapon*."

'I stared at him incredulously. At that moment Symonds rose from his examination of the body and came towards us. He was pale and shaking all over.

'"Are we all mad?" he said. "What is this place – that things like this can happen in it?"

'"Then it is true," I said.

'He nodded.

'"The wound is such as would be made by a long thin dagger, but – there is no dagger there."

'We all looked at each other.

'"But it must be there," cried Elliot Haydon. "It must have dropped out. It must be on the ground somewhere. Let us look."

'We peered about vainly on the ground. Violet Mannering said suddenly:

'"Diana had something in her hand. A kind of dagger. I saw it. I saw it glitter when she threatened him."

'Elliot Haydon shook his head.

'"He never even got within three yards of her," he objected.

'Lady Mannering was bending over the prostrate girl on the ground.

26

' "There is nothing in her hand now," she announced, "and I can't see anything on the ground. Are you sure you saw it, Violet? I didn't."

'Dr Symonds came over to the girl.

' "We must get her to the house," he said. "Rogers, will you help?"

'Between us we carried the unconscious girl back to the house. Then we returned and fetched the body of Sir Richard.'

Dr Pender broke off apologetically and looked round.

'One would know better nowadays,' he said, 'owing to the prevalence of detective fiction. Every street boy knows that a body must be left where it is found. But in these days we had not the same knowledge, and accordingly we carried the body of Richard Haydon back to his bedroom in the square granite house and the butler was despatched on a bicycle in search of the police – a ride of some twelve miles.

'It was then that Elliot Haydon drew me aside.

' "Look here," he said. "I am going back to the grove. That weapon has got to be found."

' "If there was a weapon," I said doubtfully.

'He seized my arm and shook it fiercely. "You have got that superstitious stuff into your head. You think his death was supernatural; well, I am going back to the grove to find out."

'I was curiously averse to his doing so. I did my utmost to dissuade him, but without result. The mere idea of that thick circle of trees was abhorrent to me and I felt a strong premonition of further disaster. But Elliot was entirely pig-headed. He was, I think, scared himself, but would not admit it. He went off fully armed with determination to get to the bottom of the mystery.

27

'It was a very dreadful night, none of us could sleep, or attempt to do so. The police, when they arrived, were frankly incredulous of the whole thing. They evinced a strong desire to cross-examine Miss Ashley, but there they had to reckon with Dr Symonds, who opposed the idea vehemently. Miss Ashley had come out of her faint or trance and he had given her a long sleeping draught. She was on no account to be disturbed until the following day.

'It was not until about seven o'clock in the morning that anyone thought about Elliot Haydon, and then Symonds suddenly asked where he was. I explained what Elliot had done and Symonds's grave face grew a shade graver. "I wish he hadn't. It is – it is foolhardy," he said.

'"You don't think any harm can have happened to him?"

'"I hope not. I think, Padre, that you and I had better go and see."

'I knew he was right, but it took all the courage in my command to nerve myself for the task. We set out together and entered once more that ill-fated grove of trees. We called him twice and got no reply. In a minute or two we came into the clearing, which looked pale and ghostly in the early morning light. Symonds clutched my arm and I uttered a muttered exclamation. Last night when we had seen it in the moonlight there had been the body of a man lying face downwards on the grass. Now in the early morning light the same sight met our eyes. Elliot Haydon was lying on the exact spot where his cousin had been.

'"My God!" said Symonds. "*It has got him too!*"

'We ran together over the grass. Elliot Haydon was unconscious but breathing feebly and this time there was no doubt of what had caused the tragedy. A long thin bronze weapon remained in the wound.

'"Got him through the shoulder, not through the heart. That is lucky," commented the doctor. "On my soul, I don't know what to think. At any rate he is not dead and he will be able to tell us what happened."

'But that was just what Elliot Haydon was not able to do. His description was vague in the extreme. He had hunted about vainly for the dagger and at last giving up the search had taken up a stand near the Idol House. It was then that he became increasingly certain that someone was watching him from the belt of trees. He fought against this impression but was not able to shake it off. He described a cold strange wind that began to blow. It seemed to come not from the trees but from the interior of the Idol House. He turned round, peering inside it. He saw the small figure of the Goddess and he felt he was under an optical delusion. The figure seemed to grow larger and larger. Then he suddenly received something that felt like a blow between his temples which sent him reeling back, and as he fell he was conscious of a sharp burning pain in his left shoulder.

'The dagger was identified this time as being the identical one which had been dug up in the barrow on the hill, and which had been bought by Richard Haydon. Where he had kept it, in the house or in the Idol House in the grove, none seemed to know.

'The police were of the opinion, and always will be, that he was deliberately stabbed by Miss Ashley, but in view of our combined evidence that she was never within three yards of him, they could not hope to support the charge against her. So the thing has been and remains a mystery.'

There was a silence.

'There doesn't seem anything to say,' said Joyce

Lemprière at length. 'It is all so horrible – and uncanny. Have you no explanation for yourself, Dr Pender?'

The old man nodded. 'Yes,' he said. 'I have an explanation – a kind of explanation, that is. Rather a curious one – but to my mind it still leaves certain factors unaccounted for.'

'I have been to séances,' said Joyce, 'and you may say what you like, very queer things can happen. I suppose one can explain it by some kind of hypnotism. The girl really turned herself into a Priestess of Astarte, and I suppose somehow or other she must have stabbed him. Perhaps she threw the dagger that Miss Mannering saw in her hand.'

'Or it might have been a javelin,' suggested Raymond West. 'After all, moonlight is not very strong. She might have had a kind of spear in her hand and stabbed him at a distance, and then I suppose mass hypnotism comes into account. I mean, you were all prepared to see him stricken down by supernatural means and so you saw it like that.'

'I have seen many wonderful things done with weapons and knives at music halls,' said Sir Henry. 'I suppose it is possible that a man could have been concealed in the belt of trees, and that he might from there have thrown a knife or a dagger with sufficient accuracy – agreeing, of course, that he was a professional. I admit that that seems rather far-fetched, but it seems the only really feasible theory. You remember that the other man was distinctly under the impression that there was someone in the grove of trees watching him. As to Miss Mannering saying that Miss Ashley had a dagger in her hand and the others saying she hadn't, that doesn't surprise me. If you had had my experience you would know that five persons' account of the same thing will differ so widely as to be almost incredible.'

Mr Petherick coughed.

'But in all these theories we seem to be overlooking one essential fact,' he remarked. 'What became of the weapon? Miss Ashley could hardly get rid of a javelin standing as she was in the middle of an open space; and if a hidden murderer had thrown a dagger, then the dagger would still have been in the wound when the man was turned over. We must, I think, discard all far-fetched theories and confine ourselves to sober fact.'

'And where does sober fact lead us?'

'Well, one thing seems quite clear. No one was near the man when he was stricken down, so the only person who *could* have stabbed him was he himself. Suicide, in fact.'

'But why on earth should he wish to commit suicide?' asked Raymond West incredulously.

The lawyer coughed again. 'Ah, that is a question of theory once more,' he said. 'At the moment I am not concerned with theories. It seems to me, excluding the supernatural in which I do not for one moment believe, that that was the only way things could have happened. He stabbed himself, and as he fell his arms flew out, wrenching the dagger from the wound and flinging it far into the zone of the trees. That is, I think, although somewhat unlikely, a possible happening.'

'I don't like to say, I am sure,' said Miss Marple. 'It all perplexes me very much indeed. But curious things do happen. At Lady Sharpley's garden party last year the man who was arranging the clock golf tripped over one of the numbers – quite unconscious he was – and didn't come round for about five minutes.'

'Yes, dear Aunt,' said Raymond gently, 'but he wasn't stabbed, was he?'

'Of course not, dear,' said Miss Marple. 'That is what I am telling you. Of course there is only one way that poor Sir Richard could have been stabbed, but I do wish I knew what caused him to stumble in the first place. Of course, it might have been a tree root. He would be looking at the girl, of course, and when it is moonlight one does trip over things.'

'You say that there is only one way that Sir Richard could have been stabbed, Miss Marple,' said the clergyman, looking at her curiously.

'It is very sad and I don't like to think of it. He was a right-handed man, was he not? I mean to stab himself in the left shoulder he must have been. I was always so sorry for poor Jack Baynes in the War. He shot himself in the foot, you remember, after very severe fighting at Arras. He told me about it when I went to see him in hospital, and very ashamed of it he was. I don't expect this poor man, Elliot Haydon, profited much by his wicked crime.'

'Elliot Haydon,' cried Raymond. 'You think he did it?'

'I don't see how anyone else could have done it,' said Miss Marple, opening her eyes in gentle surprise. 'I mean if, as Mr Petherick so wisely says, one looks at the facts and disregards all that atmosphere of heathen goddesses which I don't think is very nice. He went up to him first and turned him over, and of course to do that he would have to have had his back to them all, and being dressed as a brigand chief he would be sure to have a weapon of some kind in his belt. I remember dancing with a man dressed as a brigand chief when I was a young girl. He had five kinds of knives and daggers, and I can't tell you how awkward and uncomfortable it was for his partner.'

All eyes were turned towards Dr Pender.

'I knew the truth,' said he, 'five years after that tragedy occurred. It came in the shape of a letter written to me by Elliot Haydon. He said in it that he fancied that I had always suspected him. He said it was a sudden temptation. He too loved Diana Ashley, but he was only a poor struggling barrister. With Richard out of the way and inheriting his title and estates, he saw a wonderful prospect opening up before him. The dagger had jerked out of his belt as he knelt down by his cousin, and almost before he had time to think he drove it in and returned it to his belt again. He stabbed himself later in order to divert suspicion. He wrote to me on the eve of starting on an expedition to the South Pole in case, as he said, he should never come back. I do not think that he meant to come back, and I know that, as Miss Marple has said, his crime profited him nothing. "For five years," he wrote, "I have lived in Hell. I hope, at least, that I may expiate my crime by dying honourably."'

There was a pause.

'And he did die honourably,' said Sir Henry. 'You have changed the names in your story, Dr Pender, but I think I recognize the man you mean.'

'As I said,' went on the old clergyman, 'I do not think that explanation quite covers the facts. I still think there was an evil influence in that grove, an influence that directed Elliot Haydon's action. Even to this day I can never think without a shudder of The Idol House of Astarte.'

Ingots of Gold

'I do not know that the story that I am going to tell you is a fair one,' said Raymond West, 'because I can't give you the solution of it. Yet the facts were so interesting and so curious that I should like to propound it to you as a problem. And perhaps between us we may arrive at some logical conclusion.

'The date of these happenings was two years ago, when I went down to spend Whitsuntide with a man called John Newman, in Cornwall.'

'Cornwall?' said Joyce Lemprière sharply.

'Yes. Why?'

'Nothing. Only it's odd. My story is about a place in Cornwall, too – a little fishing village called Rathole. Don't tell me yours is the same?'

'No. My village is called Polperran. It is situated on the west coast of Cornwall; a very wild and rocky spot. I had been introduced a few weeks previously and had found him a most interesting companion. A man of intelligence and independent means, he was possessed of a romantic imagination. As a result of his latest hobby he had taken the lease of Pol House. He was an authority on Elizabethan times, and he described to me in vivid and graphic language the rout of the Spanish Armada. So enthusiastic was he that one could almost imagine that he had been an eyewitness at the scene.

Is there anything in reincarnation? I wonder – I very much wonder.'

'You are so romantic, Raymond dear,' said Miss Marple, looking benignantly at him.

'Romantic is the last thing that I am,' said Raymond West, slightly annoyed. 'But this fellow Newman was chock-full of it, and he interested me for that reason as a curious survival of the past. It appears that a certain ship belonging to the Armada, and known to contain a vast amount of treasure in the form of gold from the Spanish Main, was wrecked off the coast of Cornwall on the famous and treacherous Serpent Rocks. For some years, so Newman told me, attempts had been made to salvage the ship and recover the treasure. I believe such stories are not uncommon, though the number of mythical treasure ships is largely in excess of the genuine ones. A company had been formed, but had gone bankrupt, and Newman had been able to buy the rights of the thing – or whatever you call it – for a mere song. He waxed very enthusiastic about it all. According to him it was merely a question of the latest scientific, up-to-date machinery. The gold was there, and he had no doubt whatever that it could be recovered.

'It occurred to me as I listened to him how often things happen that way. A rich man such as Newman succeeds almost without effort, and yet in all probability the actual value in money of his find would mean little to him. I must say that his ardour infected me. I saw galleons drifting up the coast, flying before the storm, beaten and broken on the black rocks. The mere word galleon has a romantic sound. The phrase "Spanish Gold" thrills the schoolboy – and the grown-up man also. Moreover, I was working at the time upon a novel, some scenes of which were laid in the sixteenth century,

35

and I saw the prospect of getting valuable local colour from my host.

'I set off that Friday morning from Paddington in high spirits, and looking forward to my trip. The carriage was empty except for one man, who sat facing me in the opposite corner. He was a tall, soldierly-looking man, and I could not rid myself of the impression that somewhere or other I had seen him before. I cudgelled my brains for some time in vain; but at last I had it. My travelling companion was Inspector Badgworth, and I had run across him when I was doing a series of articles on the Everson disappearance case.

'I recalled myself to his notice, and we were soon chatting pleasantly enough. When I told him I was going to Polperran he remarked that that was a rum coincidence, because he himself was also bound for that place. I did not like to seem inquisitive, so was careful not to ask him what took him there. Instead, I spoke of my own interest in the place, and mentioned the wrecked Spanish galleon. To my surprise the inspector seemed to know all about it. "That will be the *Juan Fernandez*," he said. "Your friend won't be the first who has sunk money trying to get money out of her. It is a romantic notion."

'"And probably the whole story is a myth," I said. "No ship was ever wrecked there at all."

'"Oh, the ship was sunk there right enough," said the inspector, "along with a good company of others. You would be surprised if you knew how many wrecks there are on that part of the coast. As a matter of fact, that is what takes me down there now. That is where the *Otranto* was wrecked six months ago."

'"I remember reading about it," I said. "No lives were lost, I think?"

'"No lives were lost," said the inspector; "but something else was lost. It is not generally known, but the *Otranto* was carrying bullion."

' "Yes?" I said, much interested.

' "Naturally we have had divers at work on salvage operations, but – *the gold has gone, Mr West.*"

' "Gone!" I said, staring at him. "How can it have gone?"

' "That is the question," said the inspector. "The rocks tore a gaping hole in her strongroom. It was easy enough for the divers to get in that way, but they found the strongroom empty. The question is, was the gold stolen before the wreck or afterwards? Was it ever in the strongroom at all?"

' "It seems a curious case," I said.

' "It is a very curious case, when you consider what bullion is. Not a diamond necklace that you could put into your pocket. When you think how cumbersome it is and how bulky – well, the whole thing seems absolutely impossible. There may have been some hocus-pocus before the ship sailed; but if not, it must have been removed within the last six months – and I am going down to look into the matter."

'I found Newman waiting to meet me at the station. He apologized for the absence of his car, which had gone to Truro for some necessary repairs. Instead, he met me with a farm lorry belonging to the property.

'I swung myself up beside him, and we wound carefully in and out of the narrow streets of the fishing village. We went up a steep ascent, with a gradient, I should say, of one in five, ran a little distance along a winding lane, and turned in at the granite-pillared gates of Pol House.

'The place was a charming one; it was situated high up the cliffs, with a good view out to sea. Part of it was some three or four hundred years old, and a modern wing had been added. Behind it farming land of about seven or eight acres ran inland.

'"Welcome to Pol House," said Newman. "And to the Sign of the Golden Galleon." And he pointed to where, over the front door, hung a perfect reproduction of a Spanish galleon with all sails set.

'My first evening was a most charming and instructive one. My host showed me the old manuscripts relating to the *Juan Fernandez*. He unrolled charts for me and indicated positions on them with dotted lines, and he produced plans of diving apparatus, which, I may say, mystified me utterly and completely.

'I told him of my meeting with Inspector Badgworth, in which he was much interested.

'"They are a queer people round this coast," he said reflectively. "Smuggling and wrecking is in their blood. When a ship goes down on their coast they cannot help regarding it as lawful plunder meant for their pockets. There is a fellow here I should like you to see. He is an interesting survival."

'Next day dawned bright and clear. I was taken down into Polperran and there introduced to Newman's diver, a man called Higgins. He was a wooden-faced individual, extremely taciturn, and his contributions to the conversation were mostly monosyllables. After a discussion between them on highly technical matters, we adjourned to the Three Anchors. A tankard of beer somewhat loosened the worthy fellow's tongue.

'"Detective gentleman from London has come down," he grunted. "They do say that that ship that went down there last November was carrying a mortal lot of gold. Well, she wasn't the first to go down, and she won't be the last."

'"Hear, hear," chimed in the landlord of the Three

Anchors. "That is a true word you say there, Bill Higgins."

'"I reckon it is, Mr Kelvin," said Higgins.

'I looked with some curiosity at the landlord. He was a remarkable-looking man, dark and swarthy, with curiously broad shoulders. His eyes were bloodshot, and he had a curiously furtive way of avoiding one's glance. I suspected that this was the man of whom Newman had spoken, saying he was an interesting survival.

'"We don't want interfering foreigners on this coast," he said, somewhat truculently.

'"Meaning the police?" asked Newman, smiling.

'"Meaning the police – *and others*," said Kelvin significantly. "And don't you forget it, mister."

'"Do you know, Newman, that sounded to me very like a threat," I said as we climbed the hill homewards.

'My friend laughed.

'"Nonsense; I don't do the folk down here any harm."

'I shook my head doubtfully. There was something sinister and uncivilized about Kelvin. I felt that his mind might run in strange, unrecognized channels.

'I think I date the beginning of my uneasiness from that moment. I had slept well enough that first night, but the next night my sleep was troubled and broken. Sunday dawned, dark and sullen, with an overcast sky and the threatenings of thunder in the air. I am always a bad hand at hiding my feelings, and Newman noticed the change in me.

'"What is the matter with you, West? You are a bundle of nerves this morning."

'"I don't know," I confessed, "but I have got a horrible feeling of foreboding."

'"It's the weather."

'"Yes, perhaps."

39

'I said no more. In the afternoon we went out in Newman's motor boat, but the rain came on with such vigour that we were glad to return to shore and change into dry clothing.

'And that evening my uneasiness increased. Outside the storm howled and roared. Towards ten o'clock the tempest calmed down. Newman looked out of the window.

'"It is clearing," he said. "I shouldn't wonder if it was a perfectly fine night in another half-hour. If so, I shall go out for a stroll."

'I yawned. "I am frightfully sleepy," I said. "I didn't get much sleep last night. I think that tonight I shall turn in early."

'This I did. On the previous night I had slept little. Tonight I slept heavily. Yet my slumbers were not restful. I was still oppressed with an awful foreboding of evil. I had terrible dreams. I dreamt of dreadful abysses and vast chasms, amongst which I was wandering, knowing that a slip of the foot meant death. I waked to find the hands of my clock pointing to eight o'clock. My head was aching badly, and the terror of my night's dreams was still upon me.

'So strongly was this so that when I went to the window and drew it up I started back with a fresh feeling of terror, for the first thing I saw, or thought I saw – was a man digging an open grave.

'It took me a minute or two to pull myself together; then I realized that the grave-digger was Newman's gardener, and the "grave" was destined to accommodate three new rose trees which were lying on the turf waiting for the moment they should be securely planted in the earth.

'The gardener looked up and saw me and touched his hat.

'"Good morning, sir. Nice morning, sir."

'"I suppose it is," I said doubtfully, still unable to shake off completely the depression of my spirits.

'However, as the gardener had said, it was certainly a nice morning. The sun was shining and the sky a clear pale blue that promised fine weather for the day. I went down to breakfast whistling a tune. Newman had no maids living in the house. Two middle-aged sisters, who lived in a farm-house near by, came daily to attend to his simple wants. One of them was placing the coffee-pot on the table as I entered the room.

'"Good morning, Elizabeth," I said. "Mr Newman not down yet?"

'"He must have been out very early, sir," she replied. "He wasn't in the house when we arrived."

'Instantly my uneasiness returned. On the two previous mornings Newman had come down to breakfast somewhat late; and I didn't fancy that at any time he was an early riser. Moved by those forebodings, I ran up to his bedroom. It was empty, and, moreover, his bed had not been slept in. A brief examination of his room showed me two other things. If Newman had gone out for a stroll he must have gone out in his evening clothes, for they were missing.

'I was sure now that my premonition of evil was justified. Newman had gone, as he had said he would do, for an evening stroll. For some reason or other he had not returned. Why? Had he met with an accident? Fallen over the cliffs? A search must be made at once.

'In a few hours I had collected a large band of helpers, and together we hunted in every direction along the cliffs and on the rocks below. But there was no sign of Newman.

'In the end, in despair, I sought out Inspector Badgworth. His face grew very grave.

41

' "It looks to me as if there has been foul play," he said. "There are some not over-scrupulous customers in these parts. Have you seen Kelvin, the landlord of the Three Anchors?"

'I said that I had seen him.

' "Did you know he did a turn in gaol four years ago? Assault and battery."

' "It doesn't surprise me," I said.

' "The general opinion in this place seems to be that your friend is a bit too fond of nosing his way into things that do not concern him. I hope he has come to no serious harm."

'The search was continued with redoubled vigour. It was not until late that afternoon that our efforts were rewarded. We discovered Newman in a deep ditch in a corner of his own property. His hands and feet were securely fastened with rope, and a handkerchief had been thrust into his mouth and secured there so as to prevent him crying out.

'He was terribly exhausted and in great pain; but after some frictioning of his wrists and ankles, and a long draught from a whisky flask, he was able to give his account of what had occurred.

'The weather having cleared, he had gone out for a stroll about eleven o'clock. His way had taken him some distance along the cliffs to a spot commonly known as Smugglers' Cove, owing to the large number of caves to be found there. Here he had noticed some men landing something from a small boat, and had strolled down to see what was going on. Whatever the stuff was it seemed to be a great weight, and it was being carried into one of the farthermost caves.

'With no real suspicion of anything being amiss, nevertheless Newman had wondered. He had drawn quite near them without being observed. Suddenly there was a cry of alarm, and immediately two powerful seafaring men had set upon him and rendered him unconscious. When next he camé to himself he found himself lying on a motor vehicle of some kind, which was proceeding, with many bumps and bangs, as far as he could guess, up the lane which led from the coast to the village. To his great surprise, the lorry turned in at the gate of his own house. There, after a whispered conversation between the men, they at length drew him forth and flung him into a ditch at a spot where the depth of it rendered discovery unlikely for some time. Then the lorry drove on, and, he thought, passed out through another gate some quarter of a mile nearer the village. He could give no description of his assailants except that they were certainly seafaring men and, by their speech, Cornishmen.

'Inspector Badgworth was very interested.

'"Depend upon it that is where the stuff has been hidden," he cried. "Somehow or other it has been salvaged from the wreck and has been stored in some lonely cave somewhere. It is known that we have searched all the caves in Smugglers' Cove, and that we are now going farther afield, and they have evidently been moving the stuff at night to a cave that has been already searched and is not likely to be searched again. Unfortunately they have had at least eighteen hours to dispose of the stuff. If they got Mr Newman last night I doubt if we will find any of it by now."

'The inspector hurried off to make a search. He found definite evidence that the bullion had been stored as supposed, but the gold had been once more removed, and there was no clue as to its fresh hiding-place.

'One clue there was, however, and the inspector himself pointed it out to me the following morning.

' "That lane is very little used by motor vehicles," he said, "and in one or two places we get the traces of the tyres very clearly. There is a three-cornered piece out of one tyre, leaving a mark which is quite unmistakable. It shows going into the gate; here and there is a faint mark of it going out of the other gate, so there is not much doubt that it is the right vehicle we are after. Now, why did they take it out through the farther gate? It seems quite clear to me that the lorry came from the village. Now, there aren't many people who own a lorry in the village – not more than two or three at most. Kelvin, the landlord of the Three Anchors, has one."

' "What was Kelvin's original profession?" asked Newman.

' "It is curious that you should ask me that, Mr Newman. In his young days Kelvin was a professional diver."

'Newman and I looked at each other. The puzzle seemed to be fitting itself together piece by piece.

' "You didn't recognize Kelvin as one of the men on the beach?" asked the inspector.

'Newman shook his head.

' "I am afraid I can't say anything as to that," he said regretfully. "I really hadn't time to see anything."

' "The inspector very kindly allowed me to accompany him to the Three Anchors. The garage was up a side street. The big doors were closed, but by going up a little alley at the side we found a small door that led into it, and the door was open. A very brief examination of the tyres sufficed for the inspector. "We have got him, by Jove!" he exclaimed. "Here is the mark as large as life on the rear left wheel. Now, Mr Kelvin, I don't think you will be clever enough to wriggle out of this." '

Raymond West came to a halt.

'Well?' said Joyce. 'So far I don't see anything to

make a problem about – unless they never found the gold.'

'They never found the gold certainly,' said Raymond. 'And they never got Kelvin either. I expect he was too clever for them, but I don't quite see how he worked it. He was duly arrested – on the evidence of the tyre mark. But an extraordinary hitch arose. Just opposite the big doors of the garage was a cottage rented for the summer by a lady artist.'

'Oh, these lady artists!' said Joyce, laughing.

'As you say, "Oh, these lady artists!" This particular one had been ill for some weeks, and, in consequence, had two hospital nurses attending her. The nurse who was on night duty had pulled her armchair up to the window, where the blind was up. She declared that the motor lorry could not have left the garage opposite without her seeing it, and she swore that in actual fact it never left the garage that night.'

'I don't think that is much of a problem,' said Joyce. 'The nurse went to sleep, of course. They always do.'

'That has – er – been known to happen,' said Mr Petherick, judiciously; 'but it seems to me that we are accepting facts without sufficient examination. Before accepting the testimony of the hospital nurse, we should inquire very closely into her bona fides. The alibi coming with such suspicious promptness is inclined to raise doubts in one's mind.'

'There is also the lady artist's testimony,' said Raymond. 'She declared that she was in pain, and awake most of the night, and that she would certainly have heard the lorry, it being an unusual noise, and the night being very quiet after the storm.'

'H'm,' said the clergyman, 'that is certainly an additional fact. Had Kelvin himself any alibi?'

'He declared that he was at home and in bed from

ten o'clock onwards, but he could produce no witnesses in support of that statement.'

'The nurse went to sleep,' said Joyce, 'and so did the patient. Ill people always think they have never slept a wink all night.'

Raymond West looked inquiringly at Dr Pender.

'Do you know, I feel very sorry for that man Kelvin. It seems to me very much a case of "Give a dog a bad name." Kelvin had been in prison. Apart from the tyre mark, which certainly seems too remarkable to be coincidence, there doesn't seem to be much against him except his unfortunate record.'

'You, Sir Henry?'

Sir Henry shook his head.

'As it happens,' he said, smiling, 'I know something about this case. So clearly I mustn't speak.'

'Well, go on, Aunt Jane; haven't you got anything to say?'

'In a minute, dear,' said Miss Marple. 'I am afraid I have counted wrong. Two purl, three plain, slip one, two purl – yes, that's right. What did you say, dear?'

'What is your opinion?'

'You wouldn't like my opinion, dear. Young people never do, I notice. It is better to say nothing.'

'Nonsense, Aunt Jane; out with it.'

'Well, dear Raymond,' said Miss Marple, laying down her knitting and looking across at her nephew. 'I do think you should be more careful how you choose your friends. You are so credulous, dear, so easily gulled. I suppose it is being a writer and having so much imagination. All that story about a Spanish galleon! If you were older and had more experience of life you would have been on your guard at once. A man you had known only a few weeks, too!'

46

Sir Henry suddenly gave vent to a great roar of laughter and slapped his knee.

'Got you this time, Raymond,' he said. 'Miss Marple, you are wonderful. Your friend Newman, my boy, has another name – several other names in fact. At the present moment he is not in Cornwall but in Devonshire – Dartmoor, to be exact – a convict in Princetown prison. We didn't catch him over the stolen bullion business, but over the rifling of the strongroom of one of the London banks. Then we looked up his past record and we found a good portion of the gold stolen buried in the garden at Pol House. It was rather a neat idea. All along that Cornish coast there are stories of wrecked galleons full of gold. It accounted for the diver and it would account later for the gold. But a scapegoat was needed, and Kelvin was ideal for the purpose. Newman played his little comedy very well, and our friend Raymond, with his celebrity as a writer, made an unimpeachable witness.'

'But the tyre mark?' objected Joyce.

'Oh, I saw that at once, dear, although I know nothing about motors,' said Miss Marple. 'People change a wheel, you know – I have often seen them doing it – and, of course, they could take a wheel off Kelvin's lorry and take it out through the small door into the alley and put it on to Mr Newman's lorry and take the lorry out of one gate down to the beach, fill it up with the gold and bring it up through the other gate, and then they must have taken the wheel back and put it back on Mr Kelvin's lorry while, I suppose, someone else was tying up Mr Newman in a ditch. Very uncomfortable for him and probably longer before he was found than he expected. I suppose the man who called himself the gardener attended to that side of the business.'

'Why do you say, "called himself the gardener," Aunt Jane?' asked Raymond curiously.

'Well, he can't have been a real gardener, can he?' said Miss Marple. 'Gardeners don't work on Whit Monday. Everybody knows that.'

She smiled and folded up her knitting.

'It was really that little fact that put me on the right scent,' she said. She looked across at Raymond.

'When you are a householder, dear, and have a garden of your own, you will know these little things.'

The Bloodstained Pavement

'It's curious,' said Joyce Lemprière, 'but I hardly like telling you my story. It happened a long time ago – five years ago to be exact – but it's sort of haunted me ever since. The smiling, bright, top part of it – and the hidden gruesomeness underneath. And the queer thing is that the sketch I painted at the time has become tinged with the same atmosphere. When you look at it first it is just a rough sketch of a little steep Cornish street with the sunlight on it. But if you look long enough at it something sinister creeps in. I have never sold it but I never look at it. It lives in the studio in a corner with its face to the wall.

'The name of the place was Rathole. It is a queer little Cornish fishing village, very picturesque – too picturesque perhaps. There is rather too much of the atmosphere of "Ye Olde Cornish Tea House" about it. It has shops with bobbed-headed girls in smocks doing hand-illuminated mottoes on parchment. It is pretty and it is quaint, but it is very self-consciously so.'

'Don't I know,' said Raymond West, groaning. 'The curse of the charabanc, I suppose. No matter how narrow the lanes leading down to them no picturesque village is safe.'

Joyce nodded.

'They are narrow lanes that lead down to Rathole and very steep, like the side of a house. Well, to get

49

on with my story. I had come down to Cornwall for a fortnight, to sketch. There is an old inn in Rathole, the Polharwith Arms. It was supposed to be the only house left standing by the Spaniards when they shelled the place in fifteen hundred and something.'

'Not shelled,' said Raymond West, frowning. 'Do try to be historically accurate, Joyce.'

'Well, at all events they landed guns somewhere along the coast and they fired them and the houses fell down. Anyway that is not the point. The inn was a wonderful old place with a kind of porch in front built on four pillars. I got a very good pitch and was just settling down to work when a car came creeping and twisting down the hill. Of course, it *would* stop before the inn – just where it was most awkward for me. The people got out – a man and a woman – I didn't notice them particularly. She had a kind of mauve linen dress on and a mauve hat.

'Presently the man came out again and to my great thankfulness drove the car down to the quay and left it there. He strolled back past me towards the inn. Just at that moment another beastly car came twisting down, and a woman got out of it dressed in the brightest chintz frock I have ever seen, scarlet poinsettias, I think they were, and she had on one of those big native straw hats – Cuban, aren't they? – in very bright scarlet.

'This woman didn't stop in front of the inn but drove the car farther down the street towards the other one. Then she got out and the man seeing her gave an astonished shout. "Carol," he cried, "in the name of all that is wonderful. Fancy meeting you in this out-of-the-way spot. I haven't seen you for years. Hello, there's Margery – my wife, you know. You must come and meet her."

'They went up the street towards the inn side by side,

50

and I saw the other woman had just come out of the door and was moving down towards them. I had had just a glimpse of the woman called Carol as she passed by me. Just enough to see a very white powdered chin and a flaming scarlet mouth and I wondered – I just wondered – if Margery would be so very pleased to meet her. I hadn't seen Margery near to, but in the distance she looked dowdy and extra prim and proper.

'Well, of course, it was not any of my business but you get very queer little glimpses of life sometimes, and you can't help speculating about them. From where they were standing I could just catch fragments of their conversation that floated down to me. They were talking about bathing. The husband, whose name seemed to be Denis, wanted to take a boat and row round the coast. There was a famous cave well worth seeing, so he said, about a mile along. Carol wanted to see the cave too but suggested walking along the cliffs and seeing it from the land side. She said she hated boats. In the end they fixed it that way. Carol was to go along the cliff path and meet them at the cave, and Denis and Margery would take a boat and row round.

'Hearing them talk about bathing made me want to bathe too. It was a very hot morning and I wasn't doing particularly good work. Also, I fancied that the afternoon sunlight would be far more attractive in effect. So I packed up my things and went off to a little beach that I knew of – it was quite the opposite direction from the cave, and was rather a discovery of mine. I had a ripping bathe there and I lunched off a tinned tongue and two tomatoes, and I came back in the afternoon full of confidence and enthusiasm to get on with my sketch.

'The whole of Rathole seemed to be asleep. I had been right about the afternoon sunlight, the shadows were far more telling. The Polharwith Arms was the principal note of my sketch. A ray of sunlight came slanting obliquely down and hit the ground in front of it and had rather a curious effect. I gathered that the bathing party had returned safely, because two bathing dresses, a scarlet one and a dark blue one, were hanging from the balcony, drying in the sun.

'Something had gone a bit wrong with one corner of my sketch and I bent over it for some moments doing something to put it right. When I looked up again there was a figure leaning against one of the pillars of the Polharwith Arms, who seemed to have appeared there by magic. He was dressed in seafaring clothes and was, I suppose, a fisherman. But he had a long dark beard, and if I had been looking for a model for a wicked Spanish captain I couldn't have imagined anyone better. I got to work with feverish haste before he should move away, though from his attitude he looked as though he was perfectly prepared to prop up the pillars through all eternity.

'He did move, however, but luckily not until I had got what I wanted. He came over to me and he began to talk. Oh, how that man talked.

'"Rathole," he said, "was a very interesting place."

'I knew that already but although I said so that didn't save me. I had the whole history of the shelling – I mean the destroying – of the village, and how the landlord of the Polharwith Arms was the last man to be killed. Run through on his own threshold by a Spanish captain's sword, and of how his blood spurted out on the pavement and no one could wash out the stain for a hundred years.

'It all fitted in very well with the languorous drowsy feeling of the afternoon. The man's voice was very suave and yet at the same time there was an undercurrent in it of something rather frightening. He was very obsequious in his manner, yet I felt underneath he was cruel. He made me understand the Inquisition and the terrors of all the things the Spaniards did better than I have ever done before.

'All the time he was talking to me I went on painting, and suddenly I realized that in the excitement of listening to his story I had painted in something that was not there. On that white square of pavement where the sun fell before the door of the Polharwith Arms, I had painted in bloodstains. It seemed extraordinary that the mind could play such tricks with the hand, but as I looked over towards the inn again I got a second shock. My hand had only painted what my eyes saw – drops of blood on the white pavement.

'I stared for a minute or two. Then I shut my eyes, said to myself, "Don't be so stupid, there's nothing there, really," then I opened them again, but the bloodstains were still there.

'I suddenly felt I couldn't stand it. I interrupted the fisherman's flood of language.

'"Tell me," I said, "my eyesight is not very good. Are those bloodstains on that pavement over there?"

'He looked at me indulgently and kindly.

'"No bloodstains in these days, lady. What I am telling you about is nearly five hundred years ago."

'"Yes," I said, "but now – on the pavement" – the words died away in my throat. I *knew – I knew* that he wouldn't see what I was seeing. I got up and with shaking hands began to put my things together. As I did so the young man who had come in the car that morning came out of the inn door. He looked up and down the street perplexedly. On the balcony above his wife came out and collected the bathing things. He walked down towards the car but suddenly swerved and came across the road towards the fisherman.

'"Tell me, my man," he said. "You don't know whether the lady who came in that second car there has got back yet?"

'"Lady in a dress with flowers all over it? No, sir, I haven't seen her. She went along the cliff towards the cave this morning."

'"I know, I know. We all bathed there together, and then she left us to walk home and I have not seen her since. It can't have taken her all this time. The cliffs round here are not dangerous, are they?"

'"It depends, sir, on the way you go. The best way is to take a man what knows the place with you."

'He very clearly meant himself and was beginning to enlarge on the theme, but the young man cut him short unceremoniously and ran back towards the inn calling up to his wife on the balcony.

'"I say, Margery, Carol hasn't come back yet. Odd, isn't it?"

'I didn't hear Margery's reply, but her husband went on. "Well, we can't wait any longer. We have got to push on to Penrithar. Are you ready? I will turn the car."

'He did as he had said, and presently the two of them drove off together. Meanwhile I had deliberately been nerving myself to prove how ridiculous my fancies were. When the car had gone I went over to the inn and examined the pavement closely. Of course there were no bloodstains there. No, all along it had been the result of my distorted imagination. Yet, somehow, it seemed to make the thing more frightening. It was while I was standing there that I heard the fisherman's voice.

'He was looking at me curiously. "You thought you saw bloodstains here, eh, lady?"

'I nodded.

'"That is very curious, that is very curious. We have got a superstition here, lady. If anyone sees those bloodstains –"

'He paused.

'"Well?" I said.

'He went on in his soft voice, Cornish in intonation, but unconsciously smooth and well-bred in its pronunciation, and completely free from Cornish turns of speech.

'"They do say, lady, that if anyone sees those bloodstains that there will be a death within twenty-four hours."

'Creepy! It gave me a nasty feeling all down my spine.

'He went on persuasively. "There is a very interesting tablet in the church, lady, about a death –"

'"No thanks," I said decisively, and I turned sharply on my heel and walked up the street towards the cottage where I was lodging. Just as I got there I saw in the distance the woman called Carol coming along the cliff path. She was hurrying. Against the grey of the rocks she looked like some poisonous scarlet flower. Her hat was the colour of blood . . .

'I shook myself. Really, I had blood on the brain.

'Later I heard the sound of her car. I wondered whether she too was going to Penrithar; but she took the road to the left in the opposite direction. I watched the car crawl up the hill and disappear, and I breathed somehow more easily. Rathole seemed its quiet sleepy self once more.'

'If that is all,' said Raymond West as Joyce came to a stop, 'I will give my verdict at once. Indigestion, spots before the eyes after meals.'

'It isn't all,' said Joyce. 'You have got to hear the sequel. I read it in the paper two days later under the heading of "Sea Bathing Fatality". It told how Mrs Dacre, the wife of Captain Denis Dacre, was unfortunately drowned at Landeer Cove, just a little farther along the coast. She and her husband were staying at the time at the hotel there, and had declared their intention of bathing, but a cold wind sprang up. Captain Dacre had declared it was too cold, so he and some other people in the hotel had gone off to the golf links near by. Mrs Dacre, however, had said it was not too cold for her and she went off alone down to the cove. As she didn't return her husband became alarmed, and in company with his friends went down to the beach. They found her clothes lying beside a rock, but no trace of the unfortunate lady. Her body was not found until nearly a week later when it was washed ashore at a point some distance down the coast. There was a bad blow on her head which had occurred before death, and the theory was that she must have dived into the sea and hit her head on a rock. As far as I could make out her death would have occurred just twenty-four hours after the time I saw the bloodstains.'

'I protest,' said Sir Henry. 'This is not a problem – this is a ghost story. Miss Lemprière is evidently a medium.'

Mr Petherick gave his usual cough.

'One point strikes me –' he said, 'that blow on the head. We must not, I think, exclude the possibility of foul play. But I do not see that we have any data to go upon. Miss Lemprière's hallucination, or vision, is interesting certainly, but I do not see clearly the point on which she wishes us to pronounce.'

'Indigestion and coincidence,' said Raymond, 'and anyway you can't be sure that they were the same people. Besides, the curse, or whatever it was, would only apply to the actual inhabitants of Rathole.'

'I feel,' said Sir Henry, 'that the sinister seafaring man has something to do with this tale. But I agree with Mr Petherick, Miss Lemprière has given us very little data.'

Joyce turned to Dr Pender who smilingly shook his head.

'It is a most interesting story,' he said, 'but I am afraid I agree with Sir Henry and Mr Petherick that there is very little data to go upon.'

Joyce then looked curiously at Miss Marple, who smiled back at her.

'I, too, think you are just a little unfair, Joyce dear,' she said. 'Of course, it is different for me. I mean, we, being women, appreciate the point about clothes. I don't think it is a fair problem to put to a man. It must have meant a lot of rapid changing. What a wicked woman! And a still more wicked man.'

Joyce stared at her.

'Aunt Jane,' she said. 'Miss Marple, I mean, I believe – I do really believe you know the truth.'

'Well, dear,' said Miss Marple, 'it is much easier for me sitting here quietly than it was for you – and being an artist you are so susceptible to atmosphere, aren't you? Sitting here with one's knitting, one just sees the facts. Bloodstains dropped on the pavement from the bathing dress hanging above, and being a red bathing dress, of course, the criminals themselves did not realize it was bloodstained. Poor thing, poor young thing!'

'Excuse me, Miss Marple,' said Sir Henry, 'but you do know that I am entirely in the dark still. You and Miss Lemprière seem to know what you are talking about, but we men are still in utter darkness.'

'I will tell you the end of the story now,' said Joyce. 'It was a year later. I was at a little east coast seaside resort, and I was sketching, when suddenly I had that queer feeling one has of something having happened before. There were two people, a man and a woman, on the pavement in front of me, and they were greeting a third person, a woman dressed in a scarlet poinsettia chintz dress. "Carol, by all that is wonderful! Fancy meeting you after all these years. You don't know my wife? Joan, this is an old friend of mine, Miss Harding."

'I recognized the man at once. It was the same Denis I had seen at Rathole. The wife was different – that is, she was a Joan instead of a Margery; but she was the same type, young and rather dowdy and very inconspicuous. I thought for a minute I was going mad. They began to talk of going bathing. I will tell you what I did. I marched straight then and there to the police station. I thought they would probably think I was off my head, but I didn't care. And as it happened everything was quite all right. There was a man from Scotland Yard there, and he had come down just about this very thing. It seems – oh, it's horrible to talk about – that the police had got suspicions of Denis Dacre. That wasn't his real name – he took different names on different occasions. He got to know girls, usually quiet inconspicuous girls without many relatives or friends, he married them and insured their lives for large sums and then – oh, it's horrible! The woman called Carol was his real wife, and they always carried out the same plan. That is really how they came to catch him. The insurance companies became suspicious. He would come to some quiet seaside place with his new wife, then the other woman would turn up and they would all go bathing together. Then the wife would be murdered and Carol would put on her clothes and go back in the boat with him. Then they would leave the place, wherever it was, after inquiring for the supposed Carol and when they got outside the village Carol would hastily change back into her own flamboyant clothes and her vivid make-up and would go back there and drive off in her own car. They would find out which way the current was flowing and the supposed death would take place at the next bathing place along the coast that way. Carol would play the part of the wife and would go down to some lonely beach and would leave the wife's clothes there by a rock and depart in her flowery chintz dress to wait quietly until her husband could rejoin her.

'I suppose when they killed poor Margery some of the blood must have spurted over Carol's bathing suit, and being a red one they didn't notice it, as Miss Marple says. But when they hung it over the balcony it dripped. Ugh!' she gave a shiver. 'I can see it still.'

'Of course,' said Sir Henry, 'I remember very well now. Davis was the man's real name. It had quite slipped my memory that one of his many aliases was Dacre. They were an extraordinarily cunning pair. It always seemed so amazing to me that no one spotted the change of identity. I suppose, as Miss Marple says, clothes are more easily identified than faces; but it was a very clever scheme, for although we suspected Davis it was not easy to bring the crime home to him as he always seemed to have an unimpeachable alibi.'

'Aunt Jane,' said Raymond, looking at her curiously, 'how do you do it? You have lived such a peaceful life and yet nothing seems to surprise you.'

'I always find one thing very like another in this world,' said Miss Marple. 'There was Mrs Green, you know, she buried five children – and every one of them insured. Well, naturally, one began to get suspicious.'

She shook her head.

'There is a great deal of wickedness in village life. I hope you dear young people will never realize how very wicked the world is.'

Motive *v* Opportunity

Mr Petherick cleared his throat rather more importantly than usual.

'I am afraid my little problem will seem rather tame to you all,' he said apologetically, 'after the sensational stories we have been hearing. There is no bloodshed in mine, but it seems to me an interesting and rather ingenious little problem, and fortunately I am in the position to know the right answer to it.'

'It isn't terribly legal, is it?' asked Joyce Lemprière. 'I mean points of law and lots of Barnaby *v* Skinner in the year 1881, and things like that.'

Mr Petherick beamed appreciatively at her over his eyeglasses.

'No, no, my dear young lady. You need have no fears on that score. The story I am about to tell is a perfectly simple and straightforward one and can be followed by any layman.'

'No legal quibbles, now,' said Miss Marple, shaking a knitting needle at him.

'Certainly not,' said Mr Petherick.

'Ah well, I am not so sure, but let's hear the story.'

'It concerns a former client of mine. I will call him Mr Clode – Simon Clode. He was a man of considerable wealth and lived in a large house not very far from here. He had had one son killed in the War and this son had left one child, a little girl. Her mother had died at her

61

birth, and on her father's death she had come to live with her grandfather who at once became passionately attached to her. Little Chris could do anything she liked with her grandfather. I have never seen a man more completely wrapped up in a child, and I cannot describe to you his grief and despair when, at the age of eleven, the child contracted pneumonia and died.

'Poor Simon Clode was inconsolable. A brother of his had recently died in poor circumstances and Simon Clode had generously offered a home to his brother's children – two girls, Grace and Mary, and a boy, George. But though kind and generous to his nephew and nieces, the old man never expended on them any of the love and devotion he had accorded to his little grandchild. Employment was found for George Clode in a bank near by, and Grace married a clever young research chemist of the name of Philip Garrod. Mary, who was a quiet, self-contained girl, lived at home and looked after her uncle. She was, I think, fond of him in her quiet undemonstrative way. And to all appearances things went on very peacefully. I may say that after the death of little Christobel, Simon Clode came to me and instructed me to draw up a new will. By this will, his fortune, a very considerable one, was divided equally between his nephew and nieces, a third share to each.

'Time went on. Chancing to meet George Clode one day I inquired for his uncle, whom I had not seen for some time. To my surprise George's face clouded over. "I wish you could put some sense into Uncle Simon," he said ruefully. His honest but not very brilliant countenance looked puzzled and worried. "This spirit business is getting worse and worse."

' "What spirit business?" I asked, very much surprised.

'Then George told me the whole story. How Mr Clode

had gradually got interested in the subject and how on the top of this interest he had chanced to meet an American medium, a Mrs Eurydice Spragg. This woman, whom George did not hesitate to characterize as an out and out swindler, had gained an immense ascendency over Simon Clode. She was practically always in the house and many séances were held in which the spirit of Christobel manifested itself to the doting grandfather.

'I may say here and now that I do not belong to the ranks of those who cover spiritualism with ridicule and scorn. I am, as I have told you, a believer in evidence. And I think that when we have an impartial mind and weigh the evidence in favour of spiritualism there remains much that cannot be put down to fraud or lightly set aside. Therefore, as I say, I am neither a believer nor an unbeliever. There is certain testimony with which one cannot afford to disagree.

'On the other hand, spiritualism lends itself very easily to fraud and imposture, and from all young George Clode told me about this Mrs Eurydice Spragg I felt more and more convinced that Simon Clode was in bad hands and that Mrs Spragg was probably an imposter of the worst type. The old man, shrewd as he was in practical matters, would be easily imposed on where his love for his dead grandchild was concerned.

'Turning things over in my mind I felt more and more uneasy. I was fond of the young Clodes, Mary and George, and I realized that this Mrs Spragg and her influence over their uncle might lead to trouble in the future.

'At the earliest opportunity I made a pretext for calling on Simon Clode. I found Mrs Spragg installed as an honoured and friendly guest. As soon as I saw her my worst apprehensions were fulfilled. She was a stout woman of middle age, dressed in a flamboyant style. Very full of cant phrases about "Our dear ones who have passed over", and other things of the kind.

'Her husband was also staying in the house, Mr Absalom Spragg, a thin lank man with a melancholy expression and extremely furtive eyes. As soon as I could, I got Simon Clode to myself and sounded him tactfully on the subject. He was full of enthusiasm. Eurydice Spragg was wonderful! She had been sent to him directly in answer to a prayer! She cared nothing for money, the joy of helping a heart in affliction was enough for her. She had quite a mother's feeling for little Chris. He was beginning to regard her almost as a daughter. Then he went on to give me details – how he had heard his Chris's voice speaking – how she was well and happy with her father and mother. He went on to tell other sentiments expressed by the child, which in my remembrance of little Christobel seemed to me highly unlikely. She laid stress on the fact that 'Father and Mother loved dear Mrs Spragg".

'"But, of course," he broke off, "you are a scoffer, Petherick."

'"No, I am not a scoffer. Very far from it. Some of the men who have written on the subject are men whose testimony I would accept unhesitatingly, and I should accord any medium recommended by them respect and credence. I presume that this Mrs Spragg is well vouched for?"

'Simon went into ecstasies over Mrs Spragg. She had been sent to him by Heaven. He had come across her at the watering place where he had spent two months in the summer. A chance meeting, with what a wonderful result!

'I went away very dissatisfied. My worst fears were realized, but I did not see what I could do. After a good deal of thought and deliberation I wrote to Philip Garrod who had, as I mentioned, just married the eldest Clode girl, Grace. I set the case before him – of course, in the most carefully guarded language. I pointed out the danger of such a woman gaining ascendency over the old man's mind. And I suggested that Mr Clode should be brought into contact if possible with some reputable spiritualistic circles. This, I thought, would not be a difficult matter for Philip Garrod to arrange.

'Garrod was prompt to act. He realized, which I did not, that Simon Clode's health was in a very precarious condition, and as a practical man he had no intention of letting his wife or her sister and brother be despoiled of the inheritance which was so rightly theirs. He came down the following week, bringing with him as a guest no other than the famous Professor Longman. Longman was a scientist of the first order, a man whose association with spiritualism compelled the latter to be treated with respect. Not only a brilliant scientist; he was a man of the utmost uprightness and probity.

'The result of the visit was most unfortunate. Longman, it seemed, had said very little while he was there. Two séances were held – under what conditions I do not know. Longman was non-committal all the time he was in the house, but after his departure he wrote a letter to Philip Garrod. In it he admitted that he had not been able to detect Mrs Spragg in fraud, nevertheless his private opinion was that the phenomena were not genuine. Mr Garrod, he said, was at liberty to show this letter to his uncle if he thought fit, and he suggested that he himself should put Mr Clode in touch with a medium of perfect integrity.

'Philip Garrod had taken this letter straight to his uncle, but the result was not what he had anticipated. The old man flew into a towering rage. It was all a plot to discredit Mrs Spragg who was a maligned and injured saint! She had told him already what bitter jealousy there was of her in this country. He pointed out that Longman was forced to say he had not detected fraud. Eurydice Spragg had come to him in the darkest hour of his life, had given him help and comfort, and he was prepared to espouse her cause even if it meant quarrelling with every member of his family. She was more to him than anyone else in the world.

'Philip Garrod was turned out of the house with scant ceremony; but as a result of his rage Clode's own health took a decided turn for the worse. For the last month he had kept to his bed pretty continuously, and now there seemed every possibility of his being a bedridden invalid until such time as death should release him. Two days after Philip's departure I received an urgent summons and went hurriedly over. Clode was in bed and looked even to my layman's eye very ill indeed. He was gasping for breath.

'"This is the end of me," he said. "I feel it. Don't argue with me, Petherick. But before I die I am going to do my duty by the one human being who has done more for me than anyone else in the world. I want to make a fresh will."

'"Certainly," I said, "if you will give me your instructions now I will draft out a will and send it to you."

'"That won't do," he said. "Why, man, I might not live through the night. I have written out what I want here," he fumbled under his pillow, "and you can tell me if it is right."

'He produced a sheet of paper with a few words roughly scribbled on it in pencil. It was quite simple and clear. He left £5000 to each of his nieces and nephew, and the residue of his vast property outright to Eurydice Spragg "in gratitude and admiration".

'I didn't like it, but there it was. There was no question of unsound mind, the old man was as sane as anybody.

'He rang the bell for two of the servants. They came promptly. The housemaid, Emma Gaunt, was a tall middle-aged woman who had been in service there for many years and who had nursed Clode devotedly. With her came the cook, a fresh buxom young woman of thirty. Simon Clode glared at them both from under his bushy eyebrows.

'"I want you to witness my will. Emma, get me my fountain pen."

'Emma went over obediently to the desk.

'"Not that left-hand drawer, girl," said old Simon irritably. "Don't you know it is in the right-hand one?"

'"No, it is here, sir," said Emma, producing it.

'"Then you must have put it away wrong last time," grumbled the old man. "I can't stand things not being kept in their proper places."

'Still grumbling he took the pen from her and copied his own rough draught, amended by me, on to a fresh piece of paper. Then he signed his name. Emma Gaunt and the cook, Lucy David, also signed. I folded the will up and put it into a long blue envelope. It was necessarily, you understand, written on an ordinary piece of paper.

'Just as the servants were turning to leave the room Clode lay back on the pillows with a gasp and a distorted face. I bent over him anxiously and Emma Gaunt came quickly back. However, the old man recovered and smiled weakly.

'"It is all right, Petherick, don't be alarmed. At any rate I shall die easy now having done what I wanted to."

'Emma Gaunt looked inquiringly at me as if to know

67

whether she could leave the room. I nodded reassuringly and she went out – first stopping to pick up the blue envelope which I had let slip to the ground in my moment of anxiety. She handed it to me and I slipped it into my coat pocket and then she went out.

'"You are annoyed, Petherick," said Simon Clode. "You are prejudiced, like everybody else."

'"It is not a question of prejudice," I said. "Mrs Spragg may be all that she claims to be. I should see no objection to you leaving her a small legacy as a memento of gratitude; but I tell you frankly, Clode, that to disinherit your own flesh and blood in favour of a stranger is wrong."

'With that I turned to depart. I had done what I could and made my protest.

'Mary Clode came out of the drawing-room and met me in the hall.

'"You will have tea before you go, won't you? Come in here," and she led me into the drawing-room.

'A fire was burning on the hearth and the room looked cosy and cheerful. She relieved me of my overcoat just as her brother, George, came into the room. He took it from her and laid it across a chair at the far end of the room, then he came back to the fireside where we drank tea. During the meal a question arose about some point concerning the estate. Simon Clode said he didn't want to be bothered with it and had left it to George to decide. George was rather nervous about trusting to his own judgment. At my suggestion, we adjourned to the study after tea and I looked over the papers in question. Mary Clode accompanied us.

'A quarter of an hour later I prepared to take my departure. Remembering that I had left my overcoat in the drawing-room, I went there to fetch it. The only occupant of the room was Mrs Spragg, who was kneeling by the chair on which the overcoat lay. She seemed to be doing something rather unnecessary to the cretonne cover. She rose with a very red face as we entered.

'"That cover never did sit right," she complained. "My! I could make a better fit myself."

'I took up my overcoat and put it on. As I did so I noticed that the envelope containing the will had fallen out of the pocket and was lying on the floor. I replaced it in my pocket, said goodbye, and took my departure.

'On arrival at my office, I will describe my next actions carefully. I removed my overcoat and took the will from the pocket. I had it in my hand and was standing by the table when my clerk came in. Somebody wished to speak to me on the telephone, and the extension to my desk was out of order. I accordingly accompanied him to the outer office and remained there for about five minutes engaged in conversation over the telephone.

'When I emerged, I found my clerk waiting for me.

'"Mr Spragg has called to see you, sir. I showed him into your office.'

'I went there to find Mr Spragg sitting by the table. He rose and greeted me in a somewhat unctuous manner, then proceeded to a long discursive speech. In the main it seemed to be an uneasy justification of himself and his wife. He was afraid people were saying etc., etc. His wife had been known from her babyhood upwards for the pureness of her heart and her motives . . . and so on and so on. I was, I am afraid, rather curt with him. In the end I think he realized that his visit was not being a success and he left somewhat abruptly. I then remembered that I had left the will lying on the table. I took it, sealed the envelope, and wrote on it and put it away in the safe.

'Now I come to the crux of my story. Two months

later Mr Simon Clode died. I will not go into long-winded discussions, I will just state the bare facts. *When the sealed envelope containing the will was opened it was found to contain a sheet of blank paper.'*

He paused, looking round the circle of interested faces. He smiled himself with a certain enjoyment.

'You appreciate the point, of course? For two months the sealed envelope had lain in my safe. It could not have been tampered with then. No, the time limit was a very short one. Between the moment the will was signed and my locking it away in the safe. Now who had had the opportunity, and to whose interests would it be to do so?

'I will recapitulate the vital points in a brief summary: The will was signed by Mr Clode, placed by me in an envelope – so far so good. It was then put by me in my overcoat pocket. That overcoat was taken from me by Mary and handed by her to George, who was in full sight of me whilst handling the coat. During the time that I was in the study Mrs Eurydice Spragg would have had plenty of time to extract the envelope from the coat pocket and read its contents and, as a matter of fact, finding the envelope on the ground and not in the pocket seemed to point to her having done so. But here we come to a curious point: she had the *opportunity* of substituting the blank paper, but no *motive.* The will was in her favour, and by substituting a blank piece of paper she despoiled herself of the heritage she had been so anxious to gain. The same applied to Mr Spragg. He, too, had the opportunity. He was left alone with the document in question for some two or three minutes in my office. But again, it was not to his advantage to do so. So we are faced with this curious problem: the two people who had the *opportunity* of substituting a blank piece of paper had no *motive* for doing so, and the two people who had a *motive* had no *opportunity*. By the way, I would not exclude the housemaid, Emma Gaunt, from suspicion. She was devoted to her young master and mistress and detested the Spraggs. She would, I feel sure, have been quite equal to attempting the substitution if she had thought of it. But although she actually handled the envelope when she picked it up from the floor and handed it to me, she certainly had no opportunity of tampering with its contents and she could not have substituted another envelope by some sleight of hand (of which anyway she would not be capable) because the envelope in question was brought into the house by me and no one there would be likely to have a duplicate.'

He looked round, beaming on the assembly.

'Now, there is my little problem. I have, I hope, stated it clearly. I should be interested to hear your views.'

To everyone's astonishment Miss Marple gave vent to a long and prolonged chuckle. Something seemed to be amusing her immensely.

'What *is* the matter, Aunt Jane? Can't we share the joke?' said Raymond.

'I was thinking of little Tommy Symonds, a naughty little boy, I am afraid, but sometimes very amusing. One of those children with innocent childlike faces who are always up to some mischief or other. I was thinking how last week in Sunday School he said, "Teacher, do you say yolk of eggs *is* white or yolk of eggs *are* white?" And Miss Durston explained that anyone would say "yolks of eggs *are* white, or yolk of egg *is* white" – and naughty Tommy said: "Well, *I* should say yolk of egg is yellow!" Very naughty of him, of course, and as old as the hills. I knew that one as a child.'

'Very funny, my dear Aunt Jane,' Raymond said gently, 'but surely that has nothing to do with the very

71

interesting story that Mr Petherick has been telling us.'

'Oh yes, it has,' said Miss Marple. 'It is a catch! And so is Mr Petherick's story a catch. So like a lawyer! Ah, my dear old friend!' She shook a reproving head at him.

'I wonder if you really know,' said the lawyer with a twinkle.

Miss Marple wrote a few words on a piece of paper, folded them up and passed them across to him.

Mr Petherick unfolded the paper, read what was written on it and looked across at her appreciatively.

'My dear friend,' he said, 'is there anything you do not know?'

'I knew that as a child,' said Miss Marple. 'Played with it too.'

'I feel rather out of this,' said Sir Henry. 'I feel sure that Mr Petherick has some clever legerdemain up his sleeve.'

'Not at all,' said Mr Petherick. 'Not at all. It is a perfectly fair straightforward proposition. You must not pay any attention to Miss Marple. She has her own way of looking at things.'

'We *should* be able to arrive at the truth,' said Raymond West a trifle vexedly. 'The facts certainly seem plain enough. Five persons actually touched that envelope. The Spraggs clearly could have meddled with it but equally clearly they did not do so. There remains the other three. Now, when one sees the marvellous ways that conjurers have of doing a thing before one's eyes, it seems to me that the paper could have been extracted and another substituted by George Clode during the time he was carrying the overcoat to the far end of the room.'

'Well, *I* think it was the girl,' said Joyce. 'I think the

72

housemaid ran down and told her what was happening and she got hold of another blue envelope and just substituted the one for the other.'

Sir Henry shook his head. 'I disagree with you both,' he said slowly. 'These sort of things are done by conjurers, and they are done on the stage and in novels, but I think they would be impossible to do in real life, especially under the shrewd eyes of a man like my friend Mr Petherick here. But I have an idea – it is only an idea and nothing more. We know that Professor Longman had just been down for a visit and that he said very little. It is only reasonable to suppose that the Spraggs may have been very anxious as to the result of that visit. If Simon Clode did not take them into his confidence, which is quite probable, they may have viewed his sending for Mr Petherick from quite another angle. They may have believed that Mr Clode had already made a will which benefited Eurydice Spragg and that this new one might be made for the express purpose of cutting her out as a result of Professor Longman's revelations, or alternatively, as you lawyers say, Philip Garrod had impressed on his uncle the claims of his own flesh and blood. In that case, suppose Mrs Spragg prepared to effect a substitution. This she does, but Mr Petherick coming in at an unfortunate moment she had no time to read the real document and hastily destroys it by fire in case the lawyer should discover his loss.'

Joyce shook her head very decidedly.

'She would never burn it without reading it.'

'The solution is rather a weak one,' admitted Sir Henry. 'I suppose – er – Mr Petherick did not assist Providence himself.'

The suggestion was only a laughing one, but the little lawyer drew himself up in offended dignity.

'A most improper suggestion,' he said with some asperity.

'What does Dr Pender say?' asked Sir Henry.

'I cannot say I have any very clear ideas. I think the substitution must have been effected by either Mrs Spragg or her husband, possibly for the motive that Sir Henry suggests. If she did not read the will until after Mr Petherick had departed, she would then be in somewhat of a dilemma, since she could not own up to her action in the matter. Possibly she would place it among Mr Clode's papers where she thought it would be found after his death. But why it wasn't found I don't know. It *might* be a mere speculation this – that Emma Gaunt came across it – and out of misplaced devotion to her employers deliberately destroyed it.'

'I think Dr Pender's solution is the best of all,' said Joyce. 'Is it right, Mr Petherick?'

The lawyer shook his head.

'I will go on where I left off. I was dumbfounded and quite as much at sea as all of you are. I don't think I should ever have guessed the truth – probably not – but I was enlightened. It was cleverly done too.

'I went and dined with Philip Garrod about a month later and in the course of our after dinner conversation he mentioned an interesting case that had recently come to his notice.'

'"I should like to tell you about it, Petherick, in confidence, of course."

'"Quite so," I replied.

'"A friend of mine who had expectations from one of his relatives was greatly distressed to find that that relative had thoughts of benefiting a totally unworthy person. My friend, I am afraid, is a trifle unscrupulous in his methods. There was a maid in the house who was greatly devoted to the interests of what I may call

74

the legitimate party. My friend gave her very simple instructions. He gave her a fountain pen, duly filled. She was to place this in a drawer in the writing table in her master's room, but not the usual drawer where the pen was generally kept. If her master asked her to witness his signature to any document and asked her to bring him his pen, she was to bring him not the right one, but this one which was an exact duplicate of it. That was all she had to do. He gave her no other information. She was a devoted creature and she carried out his instructions faithfully."

'He broke off and said:

' "I hope I am not boring you, Petherick."

' "Not at all," I said. "I am keenly interested."

'Our eyes met.

' "My friend is, of course, not known to you," he said.

' "Of course not," I replied.

' "Then that is all right," said Philip Garrod.

'He paused then said smilingly, "You see the point? The pen was filled with what is commonly known as evanescent ink – a solution of starch in water to which a few drops of iodine has been added. This makes a deep blue-black fluid, but the writing disappears entirely in four or five days."

Miss Marple chuckled.

'Disappearing ink,' she said. 'I know it. Many is the time I have played with it as a child.'

And she beamed round on them all, pausing to shake a finger once more at Mr Petherick.

'But all the same it's a catch, Mr Petherick,' she said. 'Just like a lawyer.'

The Thumb Mark of St Peter

'And now, Aunt Jane, it is up to you,' said Raymond West.

'Yes, Aunt Jane, we are expecting something really spicy,' chimed in Joyce Lemprière.

'Now, you are laughing at me, my dears,' said Miss Marple placidly. 'You think that because I have lived in this out-of-the-way spot all my life I am not likely to have had any very interesting experiences.'

'God forbid that I should ever regard village life as peaceful and uneventful,' said Raymond with fervour. 'Not after the horrible revelations we have heard from you! The cosmopolitan world seems a mild and peaceful place compared with St Mary Mead.'

'Well, my dear,' said Miss Marple, 'human nature is much the same everywhere, and, of course, one has opportunities of observing it at close quarters in a village.'

'You really are unique, Aunt Jane,' cried Joyce. 'I hope you don't mind me calling you Aunt Jane?' she added. 'I don't know why I do it.'

'Don't you, my dear?' said Miss Marple.

She looked up for a moment or two with something quizzical in her glance, which made the blood flame to the girl's cheeks. Raymond West fidgeted and cleared his throat in a somewhat embarrassed manner.

Miss Marple looked at them both and smiled again,

and bent her attention once more to her knitting.

'It is true, of course, that I have lived what is called a very uneventful life, but I have had a lot of experience in solving different little problems that have arisen. Some of them have been really quite ingenious, but it would be no good telling them to you, because they are about such unimportant things that you would not be interested – just things like: Who cut the meshes of Mrs Jones's string bag? and why Mrs Sims only wore her new fur coat once. Very interesting things, really, to any student of human nature. No, the only experience I can remember that would be of interest to you is the one about my poor niece Mabel's husband.

'It is about ten or fifteen years ago now, and happily it is all over and done with, and everyone has forgotten about it. People's memories are very short – a lucky thing, I always think.'

Miss Marple paused and murmured to herself:

'I must just count this row. The decreasing is a little awkward. One, two, three, four, five, and then three purl; that is right. Now, what was I saying? Oh, yes, about poor Mabel.

'Mabel was my niece. A nice girl, really a very nice girl, but just a trifle what one might call *silly*. Rather fond of being melodramatic and of saying a great deal more than she meant whenever she was upset. She married a Mr Denman when she was twenty-two, and I am afraid it was not a very happy marriage. I had hoped very much that the attachment would not come to anything, for Mr Denman was a man of very violent temper – not the kind of man who would be patient with Mabel's foibles – and I also learned that there was insanity in his family. However, girls were just as obstinate then as they are now, and as they always will be. And Mabel married him.

77

'I didn't see very much of her after her marriage. She came to stay with me once or twice, and they asked me there several times, but, as a matter of fact, I am not very fond of staying in other people's houses, and I always managed to make some excuse. They had been married ten years when Mr Denman died suddenly. There were no children, and he left all his money to Mabel. I wrote, of course, and offered to come to Mabel if she wanted me; but she wrote back a very sensible letter, and I gathered that she was not altogether overwhelmed by grief. I thought that was only natural, because I knew they had not been getting on together for some time. It was not until about three months afterwards that I got a most hysterical letter from Mabel, begging me to come to her, and saying that things were going from bad to worse, and she couldn't stand it much longer.

'So, of course,' continued Miss Marple, 'I put Clara on board wages and sent the plate and the King Charles tankard to the bank, and I went off at once. I found Mabel in a very nervous state. The house, Myrtle Dene, was a fairly large one, very comfortably furnished. There was a cook and a house-parlourmaid as well as a nurse-attendant to look after old Mr Denman, Mabel's husband's father, who was what is called "not quite right in the head". Quite peaceful and well behaved, but distinctly odd at times. As I say, there was insanity in the family.

'I was really shocked to see the change in Mabel. She was a mass of nerves, twitching all over, yet I had the greatest difficulty in making her tell me what the trouble was. I got at it, as one always does get at these things, indirectly. I asked her about some friends of hers she was always mentioning in her letters, the Gallaghers. She said, to my surprise, that she hardly ever saw them nowadays. Other friends whom I mentioned elicited the same remark. I spoke to her then of the folly of shutting herself up and brooding, and especially of the silliness of cutting herself adrift from her friends. Then she came bursting out with the truth.

'"It is not my doing, it is theirs. There is not a soul in the place who will speak to me now. When I go down the High Street they all get out of the way so that they shan't have to meet me or speak to me. I am like a kind of leper. It is awful, and I can't bear it any longer. I shall have to sell the house and go abroad. Yet why should I be driven away from a home like this? I have done nothing."

'I was more disturbed than I can tell you. I was knitting a comforter for old Mrs Hay at the time, and in my perturbation I dropped two stitches and never discovered it until long after.

'"My dear Mabel," I said, "you amaze me. But what is the cause of all this?"

'Even as a child Mabel was always difficult. I had the greatest difficulty in getting her to give me a straightforward answer to my question. She would only say vague things about wicked talk and idle people who had nothing better to do than gossip, and people who put ideas into other people's heads.

'"That is all quite clear to me," I said. "There is evidently some story being circulated about you. But what that story is you must know as well as anyone. And you are going to tell me."

'"It is so wicked," moaned Mabel.

'"Of course it is wicked," I said briskly. "There is nothing that you can tell me about people's minds that would astonish or surprise me. Now, Mabel, will you tell me in plain English what people are saying about you?"

'Then it all came out.

'It seemed that Geoffrey Denman's death, being quite sudden and unexpected, gave rise to various rumours. In fact – and in plain English as I had put it to her – people were saying that she had poisoned her husband.

'Now, as I expect you know, there is nothing more cruel than talk, and there is nothing more difficult to combat. When people say things behind your back there is nothing you can refute or deny, and the rumours go on growing and growing, and no one can stop them. I was quite certain of one thing: Mabel was quite incapable of poisoning anyone. And I didn't see why life should be ruined for her and her home made unbearable just because in all probability she had been doing something silly and foolish.

'"There is no smoke without fire," I said. "Now, Mabel, you have got to tell me what started people off on this tack. There must have been something."

'Mabel was very incoherent, and declared there was nothing – nothing at all, except, of course, that Geoffrey's death had been very sudden. He had seemed quite well at supper that evening, and had taken violently ill in the night. The doctor had been sent for, but the poor man had died a few minutes after the doctor's arrival. Death had been thought to be the result of eating poisoned mushrooms.

'"Well," I said, "I suppose a sudden death of that kind might start tongues wagging, but surely not without some additional facts. Did you have a quarrel with Geoffrey or anything of that kind?"

'She admitted that she had had a quarrel with him on the preceding morning at breakfast time.

'"And the servants heard it, I suppose?" I asked.

'"They weren't in the room."

' "No, my dear," I said, "but they probably were fairly near the door outside."

'I knew the carrying power of Mabel's high-pitched hysterical voice only too well. Geoffrey Denman, too, was a man given to raising his voice loudly when angry.

' "What did you quarrel about?" I asked.

' "Oh, the usual things. It was always the same things over and over again. Some little thing would start us off, and then Geoffrey became impossible and said abominable things, and I told him what I thought of him."

' "There had been a lot of quarrelling, then?" I asked.

' "It wasn't my fault –"

' "My dear child," I said, "it doesn't matter whose fault it was. That is not what we are discussing. In a place like this everybody's private affairs are more or less public property. You and your husband were always quarrelling. You had a particularly bad quarrel one morning, and that night your husband died suddenly and mysteriously. Is that all, or is there anything else?"

' "I don't know what you mean by anything else," said Mabel sullenly.

' "Just what I say, my dear. If you have done anything silly, don't for Heaven's sake keep it back now. I only want to do what I can to help you."

' "Nothing and nobody can help me," said Mabel wildly, "except death."

' "Have a little more faith in Providence, dear," I said. "Now then, Mabel, I know perfectly well there *is* something else that you are keeping back."

'I always did know, even when she was a child, when she was not telling me the whole truth. It took a long time, but I got it out at last. She had gone down to the

81

chemist's that morning and had bought some arsenic. She had had, of course, to sign the book for it. Naturally, the chemist had talked.

'"Who is your doctor?" I asked.

'"Dr Rawlinson."

'I knew him by sight. Mabel had pointed him out to me the other day. To put it in perfectly plain language he was what I would describe as an old dodderer. I have had too much experience of life to believe in the infallibility of doctors. Some of them are clever men and some of them are not, and half the time the best of them don't know what is the matter with you. I have no truck with doctors and their medicines myself.

'I thought things over, and then I put my bonnet on and went to call on Dr Rawlinson. He was just what I had thought him – a nice old man, kindly, vague, and so short-sighted as to be pitiful, slightly deaf, and, withal, touchy and sensitive to the last degree. He was on his high horse at once when I mentioned Geoffrey Denman's death, talked for a long time about various kinds of fungi, edible and otherwise. He had questioned the cook, and she had admitted that one or two of the mushrooms cooked had been "a little queer", but as the shop had sent them she thought they must be all right. The more she had thought about them since, the more she was convinced that their appearance was unusual.

'"She would be," I said. "They would start by being quite like mushrooms in appearance, and they would end by being orange with purple spots. There is nothing that class cannot remember if it tries."

'I gathered that Denman had been past speech when the doctor got to him. He was incapable of swallowing, and had died within a few minutes. The doctor seemed perfectly satisfied with the certificate he had given. But how much of that was obstinacy and how much of it was genuine belief I could not be sure.

'I went straight home and asked Mabel quite frankly why she had bought arsenic.

'"You must have had some idea in your mind," I pointed out.

'Mabel burst into tears. "I wanted to make away with myself," she moaned. "I was too unhappy. I thought I would end it all."

'"Have you the arsenic still?" I asked.

'"No, I threw it away."

'I sat there turning things over and over in my mind.

'"What happened when he was taken ill? Did he call you?"

'"No." She shook her head. "He rang the bell violently. He must have rung several times. At last Dorothy, the house-parlourmaid, heard it, and she waked the cook up, and they came down. When Dorothy saw him she was frightened. He was rambling and delirious. She left the cook with him and came rushing to me. I got up and went to him. Of course I saw at once he was dreadfully ill. Unfortunately Brewster, who looks after old Mr Denman, was away for the night, so there was no one who knew what to do. I sent Dorothy off for the doctor, and cook and I stayed with him, but after a few minutes I couldn't bear it any longer; it was too dreadful. I ran away back to my room and locked the door."

'"Very selfish and unkind of you," I said; "and no doubt that conduct of yours has done nothing to help you since, you may be sure of that. Cook will have repeated it everywhere. Well, well, this is a bad business."

'Next I spoke to the servants. The cook wanted to tell me about the mushrooms, but I stopped her. I was tired of these mushrooms. Instead, I questioned both of them very closely about their master's condition on that night. They both agreed that he seemed to be in great agony, that he was unable to swallow, and he could only speak in a strangled voice, and when he did speak it was only rambling – nothing sensible.

'"What did he say when he was rambling?" I asked curiously.

'"Something about some fish, wasn't it?" turning to the other.

'Dorothy agreed.

'"A heap of fish," she said; "some nonsense like that. I could see at once he wasn't in his right mind, poor gentleman."

'There didn't seem to be any sense to be made out of that. As a last resource I went up to see Brewster, who was a gaunt, middle-aged woman of about fifty.

'"It is a pity that I wasn't here that night," she said. "Nobody seems to have tried to do anything for him until the doctor came."

'"I suppose he was delirious," I said doubtfully; "but that is not a symptom of ptomaine poisoning, is it?"

'"It depends," said Brewster.

'I asked her how her patient was getting on.

'She shook her head.

'"He is pretty bad," she said.

'"Weak?"

'"Oh no, he is strong enough physically – all but his eyesight. That is failing badly. He may outlive all of us, but his mind is failing very fast now. I have already told both Mr and Mrs Denman that he ought to be in an institution, but Mrs Denman wouldn't hear of it at any price."

'I will say for Mabel that she always had a kindly heart.

'Well, there the thing was. I thought it over in every

aspect, and at last I decided that there was only one thing to be done. In view of the rumours that were going about, permission must be applied for to exhume the body, and a proper post-mortem must be made and lying tongues quietened once and for all. Mabel, of course, made a fuss, mostly on sentimental grounds – disturbing the dead man in his peaceful grave, etc., etc. – but I was firm.

'I won't make a long story of this part of it. We got the order and they did the autopsy, or whatever they call it, but the result was not so satisfactory as it might have been. There was no trace of arsenic – that was all to the good – but the actual words of the report were *that there was nothing to show by what means deceased had come to his death.*

'So, you see, that didn't lead us out of trouble altogether. People went on talking – about rare poisons impossible to detect, and rubbish of that sort. I had seen the pathologist who had done the post-mortem, and I had asked him several questions, though he tried his best to get out of answering most of them; but I got out of him that he considered it highly unlikely that the poisoned mushrooms were the cause of death. An idea was simmering in my mind, and I asked him what poison, if any, could have been employed to obtain that result. He made a long explanation to me, most of which, I must admit, I did not follow, but it amounted to this: That death might have been due to some strong vegetable alkaloid.

'The idea I had was this: Supposing the taint of insanity was in Geoffrey Denman's blood also, might he not have made away with himself? He had, at one period of his life, studied medicine, and he would have a good knowledge of poisons and their effects.

'I didn't think it sounded very likely, but it was the

only thing I could think of. And I was nearly at my wits' end, I can tell you. Now, I dare say you modern young people will laugh, but when I am in really bad trouble I always say a little prayer to myself – anywhere, when I am walking along the street, or at a bazaar. And I always get an answer. It may be some trifling thing, apparently quite unconnected with the subject, but there it is. I had that text pinned over my bed when I was a little girl: *Ask and you shall receive.* On the morning that I am telling you about, I was walking along the High Street, and I was praying hard. I shut my eyes, and when I opened them, what do you think was the first thing that I saw?'

Five faces with varying degrees of interest were turned to Miss Marple. It may be safely assumed, however, that no one would have guessed the answer to the question right.

'I saw,' said Miss Marple impressively, '*the window of the fishmonger's shop.* There was only one thing in it, a *fresh haddock.*'

She looked round triumphantly.

'Oh, my God!' said Raymond West. 'An answer to prayer – a fresh haddock!'

'Yes, Raymond,' said Miss Marple severely, 'and there is no need to be profane about it. The hand of God is everywhere. The first thing I saw were the black spots – the marks of St Peter's thumb. That is the legend, you know. St Peter's thumb. And that brought things home to me. I needed faith, the ever true faith of St Peter. I connected the two things together, faith – and fish.'

Sir Henry blew his nose rather hurriedly. Joyce bit her lip.

'Now what did that bring to my mind? Of course, both the cook and house-parlourmaid mentioned fish as being one of the things spoken of by the dying man. I was convinced, absolutely convinced, that there was some solution of the mystery to be found in these words. I went home determined to get to the bottom of the matter.'

She paused.

'Has it ever occurred to you,' the old lady went on, 'how much we go by what is called, I believe, the context? There is a place on Dartmoor called Grey Wethers. If you were talking to a farmer there and mentioned Grey Wethers, he would probably conclude that you were speaking of these stone circles, yet it is possible that you might be speaking of the atmosphere; and in the same way, if you were meaning the stone circles, an outsider, hearing a fragment of the conversation, might think you meant the weather. So when we repeat a conversation, we don't, as a rule, repeat the actual words; we put in some other words that seem to us to mean exactly the same thing.

'I saw both the cook and Dorothy separately. I asked the cook if she was quite sure that her master had really mentioned a heap of fish. She said she was quite sure.

'"Were these his exact words," I asked, "or did he mention some particular kind of fish?"

'"That's it," said the cook; "it was some particular kind of fish, but I can't remember what now. A heap of – now what was it? Not any of the fish you send to table. Would it be a perch now – or pike? No. It didn't begin with a P."

'Dorothy also recalled that her master had mentioned some special kind of fish. "Some outlandish kind of fish it was," she said.

'"A pile of – now what was it?"

'"Did he say heap or pile?" I asked.

'"I think he said pile. But there, I really can't be

87

sure – it's so hard to remember the actual words, isn't it, Miss, especially when they don't seem to make sense. But now I come to think of it, I am pretty sure that it was a pile, and the fish began with C; but it wasn't a cod or a crayfish."

'The next part is where I am really proud of myself,' said Miss Marple, 'because, of course, I don't know anything about drugs – nasty, dangerous things I call them. I have got an old recipe of my grandmother's for tansy tea that is worth any amount of your drugs. But I knew that there were several medical volumes in the house, and in one of them there was an index of drugs. You see, my idea was that Geoffrey had taken some particular poison, and was trying to say the name of it.

'Well, I looked down the list of H's, beginning He. Nothing there that sounded likely; then I began on the P's, and almost at once I came to – what do you think?'

She looked round, postponing her moment of triumph.

'Pilocarpine. Can't you understand a man who could hardly speak trying to drag that word out? What would that sound like to a cook who had never heard the word? Wouldn't it convey the impression "pile of carp"?'

'By Jove!' said Sir Henry.

'I should never have hit upon that,' said Dr Pender.

'Most interesting,' said Mr Petherick. 'Really most interesting.'

'I turned quickly to the page indicated in the index. I read about pilocarpine and its effect on the eyes and other things that didn't seem to have any bearing on the case, but at last I came to a most significant phrase: *Has been tried with success as an antidote for atropine poisoning.*

'I can't tell you the light that dawned upon me then. I never had thought it likely that Geoffrey Denman would commit suicide. No, this new solution was not only possible, but I was absolutely sure it was the correct one, because all the pieces fitted in logically.'

'I am not going to try to guess,' said Raymond. 'Go on, Aunt Jane, and tell us what was so startlingly clear to you.'

'I don't know anything about medicine, of course,' said Miss Marple, 'but I did happen to know this, that when my eyesight was failing, the doctor ordered me drops with atropine sulphate in them. I went straight upstairs to old Mr Denman's room. I didn't beat about the bush.

' "Mr Denman," I said, "I know everything. Why did you poison your son?"

'He looked at me for a minute or two – rather a handsome old man he was, in his way – and then he burst out laughing. It was one of the most vicious laughs I have ever heard. I can assure you it made my flesh creep. I had only heard anything like it once before, when poor Mrs Jones went off her head.

' "Yes," he said, "I got even with Geoffrey. I was too clever for Geoffrey. He was going to put me away, was he? Have me shut up in an asylum? I heard them talking about it. Mabel is a good girl – Mabel stuck up for me, but I knew she wouldn't be able to stand up against Geoffrey. In the end he would have his own way; he always did. But I settled him – I settled my kind, loving son! Ha, ha! I crept down in the night. It was quite easy. Brewster was away. My dear son was asleep; he had a glass of water by the side of his bed; he always woke up in the middle of the night and drank it off. I poured it away – ha, ha! – and I emptied the bottle of eyedrops into the glass. He would wake up and swill it down before he knew what it was. There was only a table-spoonful of it – quite enough, quite enough. And so he did! They came to me in the morning and broke it to me very gently. They were afraid it would upset me. Ha! Ha! Ha! Ha! Ha!''

'Well,' said Miss Marple, 'that is the end of the story. Of course, the poor old man was put in an asylum. He wasn't really responsible for what he had done, and the truth was known, and everyone was sorry for Mabel and could not do enough to make up to her for the unjust suspicions they had had. But if it hadn't been for Geoffrey realizing what the stuff was he had swallowed and trying to get everybody to get hold of the antidote without delay, it might never have been found out. I believe there are very definite symptoms with atropine – dilated pupils of the eyes, and all that; but, of course, as I have said, Dr Rawlinson was very shortsighted, poor old man. And in the same medical book which I went on reading – and some of it was *most* interesting – it gave the symptoms of ptomaine poisoning and atropine, and they are not unlike. But I can assure you I have never seen a pile of fresh haddock without thinking of the thumb mark of St Peter.'

There was a very long pause.

'My dear friend,' said Mr Petherick. 'My very dear friend, you really are amazing.'

'I shall recommend Scotland Yard to come to you for advice,' said Sir Henry.

'Well, at all events, Aunt Jane,' said Raymond, 'there is one thing that you don't know.'

'Oh, yes, I do, dear,' said Miss Marple. 'It happened just before dinner, didn't it? When you took Joyce out to admire the sunset. It is a very favourite place, that. There by the jasmine hedge. That is where the milkman asked Annie if he could put up the banns.'

'Dash it all, Aunt Jane,' said Raymond, 'don't spoil all the romance. Joyce and I aren't like the milkman and Annie.'

'That is where you make a mistake, dear,' said Miss Marple. 'Everybody is very much alike, really. But fortunately, perhaps, they don't realize it.'

The Blue Geranium

'When I was down here last year – ' said Sir Henry Clithering, and stopped.

His hostess, Mrs Bantry, looked at him curiously.

The ex-Commissioner of Scotland Yard was staying with old friends of his, Colonel and Mrs Bantry, who lived near St Mary Mead.

Mrs Bantry, pen in hand, had just asked his advice as to who should be invited to make a sixth guest at dinner that evening.

'Yes?' said Mrs Bantry encouragingly. 'When you were here last year?'

'Tell me,' said Sir Henry, 'do you know a Miss Marple?'

Mrs Bantry was surprised. It was the last thing she had expected.

'Know Miss Marple? Who doesn't! The typical old maid of fiction. Quite a dear, but hopelessly behind the times. Do you mean you would like me to ask *her* to dinner?'

'You are surprised?'

'A little, I must confess. I should hardly have thought you – but perhaps there's an explanation?'

'The explanation is simple enough. When I was down here last year we got into the habit of discussing unsolved mysteries – there were five or six of us – Raymond West, the novelist, started it. We each supplied a story to which we knew the answer, but nobody else did. It was supposed to be an exercise in the deductive faculties – to see who could get nearest the truth.'

'Well?'

'Like in the old story – we hardly realized that Miss Marple was playing; but we were very polite about it – didn't want to hurt the old dear's feelings. And now comes the cream of the jest. The old lady outdid us every time!'

'What?'

'I assure you – straight to the truth like a homing pigeon.'

'But how extraordinary! Why, dear old Miss Marple has hardly ever been out of St Mary Mead.'

'Ah! But according to her, that has given her unlimited opportunities of observing human nature – under the microscope as it were.'

'I suppose there's something in that,' conceded Mrs Bantry. 'One would at least know the petty side of people. But I don't think we have any really exciting criminals in our midst. I think we must try her with Arthur's ghost story after dinner. I'd be thankful if she'd find a solution to that.'

'I didn't know that Arthur believed in ghosts?'

'Oh! he doesn't. That's what worries him so. And it happened to a friend of his, George Pritchard – a most prosaic person. It's really rather tragic for poor George. Either this extraordinary story is true – or else –'

'Or else what?'

Mrs Bantry did not answer. After a minute or two she said irrelevantly:

'You know, I like George – everyone does. One can't believe that he – but people do do such extraordinary things.'

Sir Henry nodded. He knew, better than Mrs Bantry, the extraordinary things that people did.

So it came about that that evening Mrs Bantry looked round her dinner table (shivering a little as she did so, because the dining-room, like most English dining-rooms, was extremely cold) and fixed her gaze on the very upright old lady sitting on her husband's right. Miss Marple wore black lace mittens; an old lace fichu was draped round her shoulders and another piece of lace surmounted her white hair. She was talking animatedly to the elderly doctor, Dr Lloyd, about the Workhouse and the suspected shortcomings of the District Nurse.

Mrs Bantry marvelled anew. She even wondered whether Sir Henry had been making an elaborate joke – but there seemed no point in that. Incredible that what he had said could be really true.

Her glance went on and rested affectionately on her red-faced, broad-shouldered husband as he sat talking horses to Jane Helier, the beautiful and popular actress. Jane, more beautiful (if that were possible) off the stage than on, opened enormous blue eyes and murmured at discreet intervals: 'Really?' 'Oh fancy!' 'How extraordinary!' She knew nothing whatever about horses and cared less.

'Arthur,' said Mrs Bantry, 'you're boring poor Jane to distraction. Leave horses alone and tell her your ghost story instead. You know . . . George Pritchard.'

'Eh, Dolly? Oh! but I don't know –'

'Sir Henry wants to hear it too. I was telling him something about it this morning. It would be interesting to hear what everyone has to say about it.'

'Oh do!' said Jane. 'I love ghost stories.'

'Well –' Colonel Bantry hesitated. 'I've never believed much in the supernatural. But this –

'I don't think any of you know George Pritchard. He's one of the best. His wife – well, she's dead now, poor woman. I'll just say this much: she didn't give George any too easy a time when she was alive. She was one of those semi-invalids – I believe she had really something wrong with her, but whatever it was she played it for all it was worth. She was capricious, exacting, unreasonable. She complained from morning to night. George was expected to wait on her hand and foot, and every thing he did was always wrong and he got cursed for it. Most men, I'm fully convinced, would have hit her over the head with a hatchet long ago. Eh, Dolly, isn't that so?'

'She was a dreadful woman,' said Mrs Bantry with conviction. 'If George Pritchard had brained her with a hatchet, and there had been any woman on the jury, he would have been triumphantly acquitted.'

'I don't quite know how this business started. George was rather vague about it. I gather Mrs Pritchard had always had a weakness for fortune tellers, palmists, clairvoyants – anything of that sort. George didn't mind. If she found amusement in it well and good. But he refused to go into rhapsodies himself, and that was another grievance.

'A succession of hospital nurses was always passing through the house, Mrs Pritchard usually becoming dissatisfied with them after a few weeks. One young nurse had been very keen on this fortune telling stunt, and for a time Mrs Pritchard had been very fond of her. Then she suddenly fell out with her and insisted on her going. She had back another nurse who had been with her previously – an older woman, experienced and tactful in dealing with a neurotic patient. Nurse Copling, according to George, was a very good sort – a sensible woman to talk to. She put up with Mrs Pritchard's tantrums and nervestorms with complete indifference.

'Mrs Pritchard always lunched upstairs, and it was usual at lunch time for George and the nurse to come to some arrangement for the afternoon. Strictly speaking, the nurse went off from two to four, but 'to oblige' as the phrase goes, she would sometimes take her time off after tea if George wanted to be free for the afternoon. On this occasion, she mentioned that she was going to see a sister at Golders Green and might be a little late returning. George's face fell, for he had arranged to play a round of golf. Nurse Copling, however, reassured him.

' "We'll neither of us be missed, Mr Pritchard." A twinkle came into her eye. "Mrs Pritchard's going to have more exciting company than ours."

' "Who's that?"

' "Wait a minute," Nurse Copling's eyes twinkled more than ever. "Let me get it right. *Zarida*, Psychic Reader of the Future."

' "Oh Lord!" groaned George. "That's a new one, isn't it?"

' "Quite new. I believe my predecessor, Nurse Carstairs, sent her along. Mrs Pritchard hasn't seen her yet. She made me write, fixing an appointment for this afternoon."

' "Well, at any rate, I shall get my golf," said George, and he went off with the kindliest feelings towards Zarida, the Reader of the Future.

'On his return to the house, he found Mrs Pritchard in a state of great agitation. She was, as usual, lying on her invalid couch, and she had a bottle of smelling salts in her hand which she sniffed at frequent intervals.

' "George," she exclaimed. "What did I tell you about this house? The moment I came into it, I *felt*

96

there was something wrong! Didn't I tell you so at the time?"

'Repressing his desire to reply, "You always do," George said, "No, I can't say I remember it."

'"You never do remember anything that has to do with me. Men are all extraordinarily callous – but I really believe that you are even more insensitive than most."

'"Oh, come now, Mary dear, that's not fair."

'"Well, as I was telling you, this woman *knew* at once! She – she actually blenched – if you know what I mean – as she came in at the door, and she said: 'There is evil here – evil and danger. I feel it.'"

'Very unwisely George laughed.

'"Well, you have had your money's worth this afternoon."

'His wife closed her eyes and took a long sniff from her smelling bottle.

'"How you hate me! You would jeer and laugh if I were dying."

'George protested and after a minute or two she went on.

'"You may laugh, but I shall tell you the whole thing. This house is definitely dangerous to me – the woman said so."

'George's formerly kind feeling towards Zarida underwent a change. He knew his wife was perfectly capable of insisting on moving to a new house if the caprice got hold of her.

'"What else did she say?" he asked.

'"She couldn't tell me very much. She was so upset. One thing she did say. I had some violets in a glass. She pointed at them and cried out:

'"Take those away. No blue flowers – never have blue flowers. *Blue flowers are fatal to you – remember that.*"'

97

'"And you know," added Mrs Pritchard, "I always have told you that blue as a colour is repellent to me. I feel a natural instinctive sort of warning against it."

'George was much too wise to remark that he had never heard her say so before. Instead he asked what the mysterious Zarida was like. Mrs Pritchard entered with gusto upon a description.

'"Black hair in coiled knobs over her ears – her eyes were half closed – great black rims round them – she had a black veil over her mouth and chin – and she spoke in a kind of singing voice with a marked foreign accent – Spanish, I think –"

'"In fact all the usual stock-in-trade," said George cheerfully.

'His wife immediately closed her eyes.

'"I feel extremely ill," she said. "Ring for nurse. Unkindness upsets me, as you know only too well."

'It was two days later that Nurse Copling came to George with a grave face.

'"Will you come to Mrs Pritchard, please. She has had a letter which upsets her greatly."

'He found his wife with the letter in her hand. She held it out to him.

'"Read it," she said.

'George read it. It was on heavily scented paper, and the writing was big and black.

'*I have seen the future. Be warned before it is too late. Beware of the Full Moon. The Blue Primrose means Warning; the Blue Hollyhock means Danger; the Blue Geranium means Death . . .*

'Just about to burst out laughing, George caught Nurse Copling's eye. She made a quick warning gesture. He said rather awkwardly, "The woman's probably trying to frighten you, Mary. Anyway there aren't such things as blue primroses and blue geraniums."

'But Mrs Pritchard began to cry and say her days were numbered. Nurse Copling came out with George upon the landing.

'"Of all the silly tomfoolery," he burst out.

'"I suppose it is."

'Something in the nurse's tone struck him, and he stared at her in amazement.

'"Surely, nurse, you don't believe –"

'"No, no, Mr Pritchard. I don't believe in reading the future – that's nonsense. What puzzles me is the *meaning* of this. Fortune-tellers are usually out for what they can get. But this woman seems to be frightening Mrs Pritchard with no advantage to herself. I can't see the point. There's another thing –"

'"Yes?"

'"Mrs Prichard says that something about Zarida was faintly familiar to her."

'"Well?"

'"Well, I don't like it, Mr Pritchard, that's all."

'"I didn't know you were so superstitious, nurse."

'"I'm not superstitious; but I know when a thing is fishy."

'It was about four days after this that the first incident happened. To explain it to you, I shall have to describe Mrs Pritchard's room –'

'You'd better let me do that,' interrupted Mrs Bantry. 'It was papered with one of those new wallpapers where you apply clumps of flowers to make a kind of herbaceous border. The effect is almost like being in a garden – though, of course, the flowers are all wrong. I mean they simply couldn't be in bloom all at the same time –'

'Don't let a passion for horticultural accuracy run away with you, Dolly,' said her husband. 'We all know you're an enthusiastic gardener.'

'Well, it *is* absurd,' protested Mrs Bantry. 'To have bluebells and daffodils and lupins and hollyhocks and Michaelmas daisies all grouped together.'

'Most unscientific,' said Sir Henry. 'But to proceed with the story.'

'Well, among these massed flowers were primroses, clumps of yellow and pink primroses and – oh go on, Arthur, this is your story –'

Colonel Bantry took up the tale.

'Mrs Pritchard rang her bell violently one morning. The household came running – thought she was *in extremis*, not at all. She was violently excited and pointing at the wallpaper; and there sure enough was *one blue primrose* in the midst of the others . . .'

'Oh!' said Miss Helier, 'how creepy!'

'The question was: Hadn't the blue primrose always been there? That was George's suggestion and the nurse's. But Mrs Pritchard wouldn't have it at any price. She had never noticed it till that very morning and the night before had been full moon. She was very upset about it.'

'I met George Pritchard that same day and he told me about it,' said Mrs Bantry. 'I went to see Mrs Pritchard and did my best to ridicule the whole thing; but without success. I came away really concerned, and I remember I met Jean Instow and told her about it. Jean is a queer girl. She said, "So she's really upset about it?" I told her that I thought the woman was perfectly capable of dying of fright – she was really abnormally superstitious.

'I remember Jean rather startled me with what she said next. She said, "Well, that might be all for the best, mightn't it?" And she said it so coolly, in so matter-of-fact a tone that I was really – well, shocked. Of course I know it's done nowadays – to be brutal and outspoken;

but I never get used to it. Jean smiled at me rather oddly and said, "You don't like my saying that – but it's true. What use is Mrs Pritchard's life to her? None at all; and it's hell for George Pritchard. To have his wife frightened out of existence would be the best thing that could happen to him." I said, "George is most awfully good to her always." And she said, "Yes, he deserves a reward, poor dear. He's a very attractive person, George Pritchard. The last nurse thought so – the pretty one – what was her name? Carstairs. That was the cause of the row between her and Mrs P."

'Now I didn't like hearing Jean say that. Of course one had *wondered* – '

Mrs Bantry paused significantly.

'Yes, dear,' said Miss Marple placidly. 'One always does. Is Miss Instow a pretty girl? I suppose she plays golf?'

'Yes. She's good at all games. And she's nice looking, attractive-looking, very fair with a healthy skin, and nice steady blue eyes. Of course we always have felt that she and George Pritchard – I mean if things had been different – they are so well suited to one another.'

'And they were friends?' asked Miss Marple.

'Oh yes. Great friends.'

'Do you think, Dolly,' said Colonel Bantry plaintively, 'that I might be allowed to go on with my story?'

'Arthur,' said Mrs Bantry resignedly, 'wants to get back to his ghosts.'

'I had the rest of the story from George himself,' went on the colonel. 'There's no doubt that Mrs Pritchard got the wind up badly towards the end of the next month. She marked off on a calendar the day when the moon would be full, and on that night she had both the nurse and then George into her room and made them study the wallpaper carefully. There were pink hollyhocks and red ones, but there were no blue amongst them. Then when George left the room she locked the door –'

'And in the morning there was a large blue hollyhock,' said Miss Helier joyfully.

'Quite right,' said Colonel Bantry. 'Or at any rate, nearly right. One flower of a hollyhock just above her head had turned blue. It staggered George; and of course the more it staggered him the more he refused to take the thing seriously. He insisted that the whole thing was some kind of practical joke. He ignored the evidence of the locked door and the fact that Mrs Pritchard discovered the change before anyone – even Nurse Copling – was admitted.

'It staggered George; and it made him unreasonable. His wife wanted to leave the house, and he wouldn't let her. He was inclined to believe in the supernatural for the first time, but he wasn't going to admit it. He usually gave in to his wife, but this time he wouldn't. Mary was not to make a fool of herself, he said. The whole thing was the most infernal nonsense.

'And so the next month sped away. Mrs Pritchard made less protest than one would have imagined. I think she was superstitious enough to believe that she couldn't escape her fate. She repeated again and again: "The blue primrose – warning. The blue hollyhock – danger. The blue geranium – *death*." And she would lie looking at the clump of pinky-red geraniums nearest her bed.

'The whole business was pretty nervy. Even the nurse caught the infection. She came to George two days before full moon and begged him to take Mrs Pritchard away. George was angry.

' "If all the flowers on that damned wall turned into blue devils it couldn't kill anyone!" he shouted.

'"It might. Shock has killed people before now."

'"Nonsense," said George.

George has always been a shade pig-headed. You can't drive him. I believe he had a secret idea that his wife worked the changes herself and that it was all some morbid hysterical plan of hers.

'Well, the fatal night came. Mrs Pritchard locked the door as usual. She was very calm – in almost an exalted state of mind. The nurse was worried by her state – wanted to give her a stimulant, an injection of strychnine, but Mrs Pritchard refused. In a way, I believe, she was enjoying herself. George said she was.'

'I think that's quite possible,' said Mrs Bantry. 'There must have been a strange sort of glamour about the whole thing.'

'There was no violent ringing of a bell the next morning. Mrs Pritchard usually woke about eight. When, at eight-thirty, there was no sign from her, nurse rapped loudly on the door. Getting no reply, she fetched George, and insisted on the door being broken open. They did so with the help of a chisel.

'One look at the still figure on the bed was enough for Nurse Copling. She sent George to telephone for the doctor, but it was too late. Mrs Pritchard, he said, must have been dead at least eight hours. Her smelling salts lay by her hand on the bed, *and on the wall beside her one of the pinky-red geraniums was a bright deep blue.*'

'Horrible,' said Miss Helier with a shiver.

Sir Henry was frowning.

'No additional details?'

Colonel Bantry shook his head, but Mrs Bantry spoke quickly.

'The gas.'

'What about the gas?' asked Sir Henry.

'When the doctor arrived there was a slight smell of

gas, and sure enough he found the gas ring in the fireplace very slightly turned on; but so little it couldn't have mattered.'

'Did Mr Pritchard and the nurse not notice it when they first went in?'

'The nurse said she did notice a slight smell. George said he didn't notice gas, but something made him feel very queer and overcome; but he put that down to shock – and probably it was. At any rate there was no question of gas poisoning. The smell was scarcely noticeable.'

'And that's the end of the story?'

'No, it isn't. One way and another, there was a lot of talk. The servants, you see, had overheard things – had heard, for instance, Mrs Pritchard telling her husband that he hated her and would jeer if she were dying. And also more recent remarks. She had said one day, apropos of his refusing to leave the house: "Very well, when I am dead, I hope everyone will realize that you have killed me." And as ill luck would have it, he had been mixing some weed killer for the garden paths the day before. One of the younger servants had seen him and had afterwards seen him taking up a glass of hot milk for his wife.

'The talk spread and grew. The doctor had given a certificate – I don't know exactly in what terms – shock, syncope, heart failure, probably some medical terms meaning nothing much. However the poor lady had not been a month in her grave before an exhumation order was applied for and granted.'

'And the result of the autopsy was nil, I remember,' said Sir Henry gravely. 'A case, for once, of smoke without fire.'

'The whole thing is really very curious,' said Mrs Bantry. 'That fortune-teller, for instance – Zarida. At the address where she was supposed to be, no one had ever heard of any such person!'

'She appeared once – out of the blue,' said her husband, 'and then utterly vanished. Out of the *blue* – that's rather good!'

'And what is more,' continued Mrs Bantry, 'little Nurse Carstairs, who was supposed to have recommended her, had never even heard of her.'

They looked at each other.

'It's a mysterious story,' said Dr Lloyd. 'One can make guesses; but to guess –'

He shook his head.

'Has Mr Pritchard married Miss Instow?' asked Miss Marple in her gentle voice.

'Now why do you ask that?' inquired Sir Henry.

Miss Marple opened gentle blue eyes.

'It seems to me so important,' she said. 'Have they married?'

Colonel Bantry shook his head.

'We – well, we expected something of the kind – but it's eighteen months now. I don't believe they even see much of each other.'

'That is important,' said Miss Marple. 'Very important.'

'Then you think the same as I do,' said Mrs Bantry. 'You think –'

'Now, Dolly,' said her husband. 'It's unjustifiable – what you're going to say. You can't go about accusing people without a shadow of proof.'

'Don't be so – so manly, Arthur. Men are always afraid to say *anything*. Anyway, this is all between ourselves. It's just a wild fantastic idea of mine that possibly – only *possibly* – Jean Instow disguised herself as a fortune-teller. Mind you, she may have done it for a joke. I don't for a minute think that she meant any harm; but if she did do it, and if Mrs Pritchard was foolish enough to die of fright – well, that's what Miss Marple meant, wasn't it?'

'No, dear, not quite,' said Miss Marple. 'You see, if I were going to kill anyone – which, of course, I wouldn't dream of doing for a minute, because it would be very wicked, and besides I don't like killing – not even wasps, though I know it has to be, and I'm sure the gardener does it as humanely as possible. Let me see, what was I saying?'

'If you wished to kill anyone,' prompted Sir Henry.

'Oh yes. Well, if I did, I shouldn't be at all satisfied to trust to *fright.* I know one reads of people dying of it, but it seems a very uncertain sort of thing, and the most nervous people are far more brave than one really thinks they are. I should like something definite and certain, and make a thoroughly good plan about it.'

'Miss Marple,' said Sir Henry, 'you frighten me. I hope you will never wish to remove me. Your plans would be too good.'

Miss Marple looked at him reproachfully.

'I thought I had made it clear that I would never contemplate such wickedness,' she said. 'No, I was try-ing to put myself in the place of – er – a certain person.'

'Do you mean George Pritchard?' asked Colonel Ban-try. 'I'll never believe it of George – though – mind you, even the nurse believes it. I went and saw her about a month afterwards, at the time of the exhumation. She didn't know how it was done – in fact, she wouldn't say anything at all – but it was clear enough that she believed George to be in some way responsible for his wife's death. She was convinced of it.'

'Well,' said Dr Lloyd, 'perhaps she wasn't so far wrong. And mind you, a nurse often *knows.* She can't say – she's got no proof – but she *knows.*'

Sir Henry leant forward.

'Come now, Miss Marple,' he said persuasively. 'You're lost in a daydream. Won't you tell us all about it?'

Miss Marple started and turned pink.

'I beg your pardon,' she said. 'I was just thinking about our district nurse. A most difficult problem.'

'More difficult than the problem of the blue geranium?'

'It really depends on the primroses,' said Miss Marple. 'I mean, Mrs Bantry said they were yellow and pink. If it was a pink primrose that turned blue, of course, that fits in perfectly. But if it happened to be a yellow one –'

'It was a pink one,' said Mrs Bantry.

She stared. They all stared at Miss Marple.

'Then that seems to settle it,' said Miss Marple. She shook her head regretfully. 'And the wasp season and everything. And of course the gas.'

'It reminds you, I suppose, of countless village tragedies?' said Sir Henry.

'Not tragedies,' said Miss Marple. 'And certainly nothing criminal. But it does remind me a little of the trouble we are having with the district nurse. After all, nurses are human beings, and what with having to be so correct in their behaviour and wearing those uncomfortable collars and being so thrown with the family – well, can you wonder that things sometimes happen?'

A glimmer of light broke upon Sir Henry.

'You mean Nurse Carstairs?'

'Oh no. Not Nurse Carstairs. Nurse *Copling*. You see, she had been there before, and very much thrown with Mr Pritchard, who you say is an attractive man. I daresay she thought, poor thing – well, we needn't go into that. I don't suppose she knew about Miss Instow, and of course afterwards, when she found out, it turned her against him and she tried to do all the harm she could. Of course the letter really gave her away, didn't it?'

'What letter?'

'Well, she wrote to the fortune-teller at Mrs Pritchard's request, and the fortune-teller came, apparently in answer to the letter. But later it was discovered that there never had been such a person at that address. So that shows that Nurse Copling was in it. She only pretended to write – so what could be more likely than that *she* was the fortune teller herself?'

'I never saw the point about the letter,' said Sir Henry. 'That's a most important point, of course.'

'Rather a bold step to take,' said Miss Marple, 'because Mrs Pritchard might have recognized her in spite of the disguise – though of course if she had, the nurse could have pretended it was a joke.'

'What did you mean,' said Sir Henry, 'when you said that if you were a certain person you would not have trusted to fright?'

'One couldn't be *sure* that way,' said Miss Marple. 'No, I think that the warnings and the blue flowers were, if I may use a military term,' she laughed self-consciously – '*just camouflage.*'

'And the real thing?'

'I know,' said Miss Marple apologetically, 'that I've got wasps on the brain. Poor things, destroyed in their thousands – and usually on such a beautiful summer's day. But I remember thinking, when I saw the gardener shaking up the cyanide of potassium in a bottle with water, how like smelling-salts it looked. And if it were put in a smelling-salts bottle and substituted for the real one – well, the poor lady was in the habit of using her smelling-salts. Indeed you said they were found by her hand. Then, of course, while Mr Pritchard went to tele-

108

phone to the doctor, the nurse would change it for the real bottle, and she'd just turn on the gas a little bit to mask any smell of almonds and in case anyone felt queer, and I always have heard that cyanide leaves no trace if you wait long enough. But, of course I may be wrong, and it may have been something entirely different in the bottle; but that doesn't really matter, does it?'

Miss Marple paused, a little out of breath.

Jane Helier leant forward and said, 'But the blue geranium, and the other flowers?'

'Nurses always have litmus paper, don't they?' said Miss Marple, 'for – well, for testing. Not a very pleasant subject. We won't dwell on it. I have done a little nursing myself.' She grew delicately pink. 'Blue turns red with acids, and red turns blue with alkalis. So easy to paste some red litmus over a red flower – near the bed, of course. And then, when the poor lady used her smelling-salts, the strong ammonia fumes would turn it blue. Really most ingenious. Of course, the geranium wasn't blue when they first broke into the room – nobody noticed it till afterwards. When nurse changed the bottles, she held the sal ammoniac against the wallpaper for a minute, I expect.'

'You might have been there, Miss Marple,' said Sir Henry.

'What worries me,' said Miss Marple, 'is poor Mr Pritchard and that nice girl, Miss Instow. Probably both suspecting each other and keeping apart – and life so very short.'

She shook her head.

'You needn't worry,' said Sir Henry. 'As a matter of fact I have something up my sleeve. A nurse has been arrested on a charge of murdering an elderly patient who had left her a legacy. It was done with cyanide of potassium substituted for smelling-salts. Nurse Copling trying the same trick again. Miss Instow and Mr Pritchard need have no doubts as to the truth.'

'Now isn't that nice?' cried Miss Marple. 'I don't mean about the new murder, of course. That's very sad, and shows how much wickedness there is in the world, and that if once you give way – which reminds me I *must* finish my little conversation with Dr Lloyd about the village nurse.'

The Companion

'Now, Dr Lloyd,' said Miss Helier. 'Don't *you* know any creepy stories?'

She smiled at him – the smile that nightly bewitched the theatre-going public. Jane Helier was sometimes called the most beautiful woman in England, and jealous members of her own profession were in the habit of saying to each other: 'Of course Jane's not an *artist*. She can't *act* – if you know what I mean. It's those eyes!'

And 'those eyes' were at this minute fixed appealingly on the grizzled elderly bachelor doctor, who, for the last five years, had ministered to the ailments of the village of St Mary Mead.

With an unconscious gesture, the doctor pulled down his waistcoat (inclined of late to be uncomfortably tight) and racked his brains hastily, so as not to disappoint the lovely creature who addressed him so confidently.

'I feel,' said Jane dreamily, 'that I would like to wallow in crime this evening.'

'Splendid,' said Colonel Bantry, her host. 'Splendid, splendid.' And he laughed a loud hearty military laugh. 'Eh, Dolly?'

His wife, hastily recalled to the exigencies of social life (she had been planning her spring border) agreed enthusiastically.

'Of course it's splendid,' she said heartily but vaguely. 'I always thought so.'

'Did you, my dear?' said old Miss Marple, and her eyes twinkled a little.

'We don't get much in the creepy line – and still less in the criminal line – in St Mary Mead, you know, Miss Helier,' said Dr Lloyd.

'You surprise me,' said Sir Henry Clithering. The ex-Commissioner of Scotland Yard turned to Miss Marple. 'I always understood from our friend here that St Mary Mead is a positive hotbed of crime and vice.'

'Oh, Sir Henry!' protested Miss Marple, a spot of colour coming into her cheeks. 'I'm sure I never said anything of the kind. The only thing I ever said was that human nature is much the same in a village as anywhere else, only one has opportunities and leisure for seeing it at closer quarters.'

'But *you* haven't always lived here,' said Jane Helier, still addressing the doctor. 'You've been in all sorts of queer places all over the world – places where things *happen*!'

'That is so, of course,' said Dr Lloyd, still thinking desperately. 'Yes, of course ... Yes ... Ah! I have it!'

He sank back with a sigh of relief.

'It is some years ago now – I had almost forgotten. But the facts were really very strange – very strange indeed. And the final coincidence which put the clue into my hand was strange also.'

Miss Helier drew her chair a little nearer to him, applied some lipstick and waited expectantly. The others also turned interested faces towards him.

'I don't know whether any of you know the Canary Islands,' began the doctor.

'They must be wonderful,' said Jane Helier. 'They're

in the South Seas, aren't they? Or is it the Mediterranean?'

'I've called in there on my way to South Africa,' said the colonel. 'The Peak of Tenerife is a fine sight with the setting sun on it.'

'The incident I am describing happened in the island of Grand Canary, not Tenerife. It is a good many years ago now. I had had a breakdown in health and was forced to give up my practice in England and go abroad. I practised in Las Palmas, which is the principal town of Grand Canary. In many ways I enjoyed the life out there very much. The climate was mild and sunny, there was excellent surf bathing (and I am an enthusiastic bather) and the sea life of the port attracted me. Ships from all over the world put in at Las Palmas. I used to walk along the mole every morning far more interested than any member of the fair sex could be in a street of hat shops.

'As I say, ships from all over the world put in at Las Palmas. Sometimes they stay a few hours, sometimes a day or two. In the principal hotel there, the Metropole, you will see people of all races and nationalities – birds of passage. Even the people going to Tenerife usually come here and stay a few days before crossing to the other island.

'My story begins there, in the Metropole Hotel, one Thursday evening in January. There was a dance going on and I and a friend had been sitting at a small table watching the scene. There were a fair sprinkling of English and other nationalities, but the majority of the dancers were Spanish; and when the orchestra struck up a tango, only half a dozen couples of the latter nationality took the floor. They all danced well and we looked on and admired. One woman in particular excited our lively admiration. Tall, beautiful and sinuous, she moved with the grace of a half-tamed leopardess. There was something dangerous about her. I said as much to my friend and he agreed.

'"Women like that," he said, 'are bound to have a history. Life will not pass them by.'

'"Beauty is perhaps a dangerous possession," I said.

'"It's not only beauty," he insisted. 'There is something else. Look at her again. Things are bound to happen to that woman, or because of her. As I said, life will not pass her by. Strange and exciting events will surround her. You've only got to look at her to know it."

'He paused and then added with a smile:

'"Just as you've only got to look at those two women over there, and know that nothing out of the way could ever happen to either of them! They are made for a safe and uneventful existence."

'I followed his eyes. The two women he referred to were travellers who had just arrived – a Holland Lloyd boat had put into port that evening, and the passengers were just beginning to arrive.

'As I looked at them I saw at once what my friend meant. They were two English ladies – the thoroughly nice travelling English that you do find abroad. Their ages, I should say, were round about forty. One was fair and a little – just a little – too plump; the other was dark and a little – again just a little – inclined to scragginess. They were what is called well-preserved, quietly and inconspicuously dressed in well-cut tweeds, and innocent of any kind of make-up. They had that air of quiet assurance which is the birthright of well-bred Englishwomen. There was nothing remarkable about either of them. They were like thousands of their sisters. They would doubtless see what they wished to see, assisted by Baedeker, and be blind to everything else. They would use the English library and attend the English Church in any place they happened to be, and it was quite likely that one or both of them sketched a little. And, as my friend said, nothing exciting or remarkable would ever happen to either of them, though they might quite likely travel half over the world. I looked from them back to our sinuous Spanish woman with her half-closed smouldering eyes and I smiled.'

'Poor things,' said Jane Helier with a sigh. 'But I do think it's so silly of people not to make the most of themselves. That woman in Bond Street – Valentine – is really wonderful. Audrey Denman goes to her; and have you seen her in "The Downward Step"? As the schoolgirl in the first act she's really marvellous. And yet Audrey is fifty if she's a day. As a matter of fact I happen to know she's really nearer sixty.'

'Go on,' said Mrs Bantry to Dr Lloyd. 'I love stories about sinuous Spanish dancers. It makes me forget how old and fat I am.'

'I'm sorry,' said Dr Lloyd apologetically. 'But you see, as a matter of fact, this story isn't about the Spanish woman.'

'It isn't?'

'No. As it happens my friend and I were wrong. Nothing in the least exciting happened to the Spanish beauty. She married a clerk in a shipping office, and by the time I left the island she had had five children and was getting very fat.'

'Just like that girl of Israel Peters,' commented Miss Marple. 'The one who went on the stage and had such good legs that they made her principal boy in the pantomime. Everyone said she'd come to no good, but she married a commercial traveller and settled down splendidly.'

'The village parallel,' murmured Sir Henry softly.

'No,' went on the doctor. 'My story is about the two English ladies.'

'Something happened to them?' breathed Miss Helier.

'Something happened to them – and the very next day, too.'

'Yes?' said Mrs Bantry encouragingly.

'Just for curiosity, as I went out that evening I glanced at the hotel register. I found the names easily enough. Miss Mary Barton and Miss Amy Durrant of Little Paddocks, Caughton Weir, Bucks. I little thought then how soon I was to encounter the owners of those names again – and under what tragic circumstances.

'The following day I had arranged to go for a picnic with some friends. We were to motor across the island, taking our lunch, to a place called (as far as I remember – it is so long ago) Las Nieves, a well-sheltered bay where we could bathe if we felt inclined. This programme we duly carried out, except that we were somewhat late in starting, so that we stopped on the way and picnicked, going on to Las Nieves afterwards for a bathe before tea.

'As we approached the beach, we were at once aware of a tremendous commotion. The whole population of the small village seemed to be gathered on the shore. As soon as they saw us they rushed towards the car and began explaining excitedly. Our Spanish not being very good, it took me a few minutes to understand, but at last I got it.

'Two of the mad English ladies had gone in to bathe, and one had swum out too far and got into difficulties. The other had gone after her and had tried to bring her in, but her strength in turn had failed and she too would have drowned had not a man rowed out in a boat and brought in rescuer and rescued – the latter beyond help.

'As soon as I got the hang of things I pushed the crowd aside and hurried down the beach. I did not at first recognize the two women. The plump figure in the black stockinet costume and the tight green rubber bathing cap awoke no chord of recognition as she looked up anxiously. She was kneeling beside the body of her friend, making somewhat amateurish attempts at artificial respiration. When I told her that I was a doctor she gave a sigh of relief, and I ordered her off at once to one of the cottages for a rub down and dry clothing. One of the ladies in my party went with her. I myself worked unavailingly on the body of the drowned woman. Life was only too clearly extinct, and in the end I had reluctantly to give in.

'I rejoined the others in the small fisherman's cottage and there I had to break the sad news. The survivor was attired now in her own clothes, and I immediately recognized her as one of the two arrivals of the night before. She received the sad news fairly calmly, and it was evidently the horror of the whole thing that struck her more than any great personal feeling.

' "Poor Amy," she said. "Poor, poor Amy. She had been looking forward to the bathing here so much. And she was a good swimmer too. I can't understand it. What do you think it can have been, doctor?"

' "Possibly cramp. Will you tell me exactly what happened?"

' "We had both been swimming about for some time – twenty minutes, I should say. Then I thought I would go in, but Amy said she was going to swim out once more. She did so, and suddenly I heard her call and realized she was crying for help. I swam out as fast as I could. She was still afloat when I got to her, but she clutched at me wildly and we both went under. If it hadn't been for that man coming out with his boat I should have been drowned too."

'"That has happened fairly often," I said. "To save anyone from drowning is not an easy affair."

'"It seems so awful," continued Miss Barton. "We only arrived yesterday, and were so delighting in the sunshine and our little holiday. And now this – this terrible tragedy occurs."

'I asked her then for particulars about the dead woman, explaining that I would do everything I could for her, but that the Spanish authorities would require full information. This she gave me readily enough.

'The dead woman, Miss Amy Durrant, was her companion and had come to her about five months previously. They had got on very well together, but Miss Durrant had spoken very little about her people. She had been left an orphan at an early age and had been brought up by an uncle and had earned her own living since she was twenty-one.

'And so that was that,' went on the doctor. He paused and said again, but this time with a certain finality in his voice, 'And so that was that.'

'I don't understand,' said Jane Helier. 'Is that all? I mean, it's very tragic, I suppose, but it isn't – well, it isn't what I call *creepy*.'

'I think there's more to follow,' said Sir Henry.

'Yes,' said Dr Lloyd, 'there's more to follow. You see, right at the time there was one queer thing. Of course I asked questions of the fishermen, etc., as to what they'd seen. They were eye-witnesses. And one woman had rather a funny story. I didn't pay any attention to it at the time, but it came back to me afterwards. She insisted, you see, that Miss Durrant wasn't in difficulties when she called out. The other swam out to her and, according to this woman, deliberately held Miss Durrant's head under water. I didn't, as I say, pay much attention. It was such a fantastic story, and these things look so differently from the shore. Miss Barton might have tried to make her friend lose consciousness, realizing that the latter's panic-stricken clutching would drown them both. You see, according to the Spanish woman's story, it looked as though – well, as though Miss Barton was deliberately trying to drown her companion.

'As I say, I paid very little attention to this story at the time. It came back to me later. Our great difficulty was to find out anything about this woman, Amy Durrant. She didn't seem to have any relations. Miss Barton and I went through her things together. We found one address and wrote there, but it proved to be simply a room she had taken in which to keep her things. The landlady knew nothing, had only seen her when she took the room. Miss Durrant had remarked at the time that she always liked to have one place she could call her own to which she could return at any moment. There were one or two nice pieces of old furniture and some bound numbers of Academy pictures, and a trunk full of pieces of material bought at sales, but no personal belongings. She had mentioned to the landlady that her father and mother had died in India when she was a child and that she had been brought up by an uncle who was a clergyman, but she did not say if he was her father's or her mother's brother, so the name was no guide.

'It wasn't exactly mysterious, it was just unsatisfactory. There must be many lonely women, proud and reticent, in just that position. There were a couple of photographs amongst her belongings in Las Palmas – rather old and faded and they had been cut to fit the frames they were in, so that there was no photographer's name upon them, and there was an old daguerreotype which might have been her mother or more probably her grandmother.

'Miss Barton had had two references with her. One she had forgotten, the other name she recollected after an effort. It proved to be that of a lady who was now abroad, having gone to Australia. She was written to. Her answer, of course, was a long time in coming, and I may say that when it did arrive there was no particular help to be gained from it. She said Miss Durrant had been with her as companion and had been most efficient and that she was a very charming woman, but that she knew nothing of her private affairs or relations.

'So there it was – as I say, nothing unusual, really. It was just the two things together that aroused my uneasiness. This Amy Durrant of whom no one knew anything, and the Spanish woman's queer story. Yes, and I'll add a third thing: When I was first bending over the body and Miss Barton was walking away towards the huts, she looked back. Looked back with an expression on her face that I can only describe as one of poignant anxiety – a kind of anguished uncertainty that imprinted itself on my brain.

'It didn't strike me as anything unusual at the time. I put it down to her terrible distress over her friend. But, you see, later I realized that they weren't on those terms. There was no devoted attachment between them, no terrible grief. Miss Barton was fond of Amy Durrant and shocked by her death – that was all.

'But, then, why that terrible poignant anxiety? That was the question that kept coming back to me. I had not been mistaken in that look. And almost against my will, an answer began to shape itself in my mind.

Supposing the Spanish woman's story were true; supposing that Mary Barton wilfully and in cold blood tried to drown Amy Durrant. She succeeds in holding her under water whilst pretending to be saving her. She is rescued by a boat. They are on a lonely beach far from anywhere. And then I appear – the last thing she expects. A doctor! And an English doctor! She knows well enough that people who have been under water far longer than Amy Durrant have been revived by artificial respiration. But she has to play her part – to go off leaving me alone with her victim. And as she turns for one last look, a terrible poignant anxiety shows in her face. Will Amy Durrant come back to life *and tell what she knows?*'

'Oh!' said Jane Helier. 'I'm thrilled now.'

'Viewed in that aspect the whole business seemed more sinister, and the personality of Amy Durrant became more mysterious. Who was Amy Durrant? Why should she, an insignificant paid companion, be murdered by her employer? What story lay behind that fatal bathing expedition? She had entered Mary Barton's employment only a few months before. Mary Barton had brought her abroad, and the very day after they landed the tragedy had occurred. And they were both nice, commonplace, refined Englishwomen! The whole thing was fantastic, and I told myself so. I had been letting my imagination run away with me.'

'You didn't do anything, then?' asked Miss Helier.

'My dear young lady, what could I do? There was no evidence. The majority of the eye-witnesses told the same story as Miss Barton. I had built up my own suspicions out of a fleeting expression which I might possibly have imagined. The only thing I could and did do was to see that the widest inquiries were made for the relations of Amy Durrant. The next time I was in England I even went and saw the landlady of her room, with the results I have told you.'

'But you felt there was something wrong,' said Miss Marple.

Dr Lloyd nodded.

'Half the time I was ashamed of myself for thinking so. Who was I to go suspecting this nice, pleasant-mannered English lady of a foul and cold-blooded crime? I did my best to be as cordial as possible to her during the short time she stayed on the island. I helped her with the Spanish authorities. I did everything I could do as an Englishman to help a compatriot in a foreign country; and yet I am convinced that she knew I suspected and disliked her.'

'How long did she stay out there?' asked Miss Marple.

'I think it was about a fortnight. Miss Durrant was buried there, and it must have been about ten days later when she took a boat back to England. The shock had upset her so much that she felt she couldn't spend the winter there as she had planned. That's what she said.'

'Did it seem to have upset her?' asked Miss Marple.

The doctor hesitated.

'Well, I don't know that it affected her appearance at all,' he said cautiously.

'She didn't, for instance, grow fatter?' asked Miss Marple.

'Do you know – it's a curious thing your saying that. Now I come to think back, I believe you're right. She – yes, she did seem, if anything, to be putting on weight.'

'How horrible,' said Jane Helier with a shudder. 'It's like – it's like fattening on your victim's blood.'

'And yet, in another way, I may be doing her an injustice,' went on Dr Lloyd. 'She certainly said something before she left, which pointed in an entirely different direction. There may be, I think there are, consciences which work very slowly – which take some time to awaken to the enormity of the deed committed.

'It was the evening before her departure from the Canaries. She had asked me to go and see her, and had thanked me very warmly for all I had done to help her. I, of course, made light of the matter, said I had only done what was natural under the circumstances, and so on. There was a pause after that, and then she suddenly asked me a question.

' "Do you think," she asked, "that one is ever justified in taking the law into one's own hands?"

'I replied that that was rather a difficult question, but that on the whole, I thought not. The law was the law, and we had to abide by it.

' "Even when it is powerless?"

' "I don't quite understand."

' "It's difficult to explain; but one might do something that is considered definitely wrong – that is considered a crime, even, for a good and sufficient reason."

'I replied drily that possibly several criminals had thought that in their time, and she shrank back.

' "But that's horrible," she murmured. "Horrible."

'And then with a change of tone she asked me to give her something to make her sleep. She had not been able to sleep properly since – she hesitated – since that terrible shock.

' "You're sure it is that? There is nothing worrying you? Nothing on your mind?"

' "On my mind? What should be on my mind?"

'She spoke fiercely and suspiciously.

' "Worry is a cause of sleeplessness sometimes,' I said lightly.

'She seemed to brood for a moment.

123

' "Do you mean worrying over the future, or worrying over the past, which can't be altered?"

' "Either."

' "Only it wouldn't be any good worrying over the past. You couldn't bring back – Oh! what's the use! One mustn't think. One must not think."

'I prescribed her a mild sleeping draught and made my adieu. As I went away I wondered not a little over the words she had spoken. "You couldn't bring back –" What? Or *who*?

'I think that last interview prepared me in a way for what was to come. I didn't expect it, of course, but when it happened, I wasn't surprised. Because, you see, Mary Barton struck me all along as a conscientious woman – not a weak sinner, but a woman with convictions, who would act up to them, and who would not relent as long as she still believed in them. I fancied that in the last conversation we had she was beginning to doubt her own convictions. I know her words suggested to me that she was feeling the first faint beginnings of that terrible soul-searcher – remorse.

'The thing happened in Cornwall, in a small watering-place, rather deserted at that season of the year. It must have been – let me see – late March. I read about it in the papers. A lady had been staying at a small hotel there – a Miss Barton. She had been very odd and peculiar in her manner. That had been noticed by all. At night she would walk up and down her room, muttering to herself, and not allowing the people on either side of her to sleep. She had called on the vicar one day and had told him that she had a communication of the gravest importance to make to him. She had, she said, committed a crime. Then, instead of proceeding, she had stood up abruptly and said she would call another day. The vicar put her down as being slightly

124

mental, and did not take her self-accusation seriously.

'The very next morning she was found to be missing from her room. A note was left addressed to the coroner. It ran as follows:

'I tried to speak to the vicar yesterday, to confess all, but was not allowed. She would not let me. I can make amends only one way – a life for a life; and my life must go the same way as hers did. I, too, must drown in the deep sea. I believed I was justified. I see now that that was not so. If I desire Amy's forgiveness I must go to her. Let no one be blamed for my death –
Mary Barton

'Her clothes were found lying on the beach in a secluded cove nearby, and it seemed clear that she had undressed there and swum resolutely out to sea where the current was known to be dangerous, sweeping one down the coast.

'The body was not recovered, but after a time leave was given to presume death. She was a rich woman, her estate being proved at a hundred thousand pounds. Since she died intestate it all went to her next of kin – a family of cousins in Australia. The papers made discreet references to the tragedy in the Canary Islands, putting forward the theory that the death of Miss Durrant had unhinged her friend's brain. At the inquest the usual verdict of *Suicide whilst temporarily insane* was returned.

'And so the curtain falls on the tragedy of Amy Durrant and Mary Barton.'

There was a long pause and then Jane Helier gave a great gasp.

'Oh, but you mustn't stop there – just at the most interesting part. Go on.'

'But you see, Miss Helier, this isn't a serial story. This

is real life; and real life stops just where it chooses.'

'But I don't want it to,' said Jane. 'I want to know.'

'This is where we use our brains, Miss Helier,' explained Sir Henry. 'Why did Mary Barton kill her companion? That's the problem Dr Lloyd has set us.'

'Oh, well,' said Miss Helier, 'she might have killed her for lots of reasons. I mean – oh, I don't know. She might have got on her nerves, or else she got jealous, although Dr Lloyd doesn't mention any men, but still on the boat out – well, you know what everyone says about boats and sea voyages.'

Miss Helier paused, slightly out of breath, and it was borne in upon her audience that the outside of Jane's charming head was distinctly superior to the inside.

'I would like to have a lot of guesses,' said Mrs Bantry. 'But I suppose I must confine myself to one. Well, I think that Miss Barton's father made all his money out of ruining Amy Durrant's father, so Amy determined to have her revenge. Oh, no, that's the wrong way round. How tiresome! Why does the rich employer kill the humble companion? I've got it. Miss Barton had a young brother who shot himself for love of Amy Durrant. Miss Barton waits her time. Amy comes down in the world. Miss B. engages her as companion and takes her to the Canaries and accomplishes her revenge. How's that?'

'Excellent,' said Sir Henry. 'Only we don't know that Miss Barton ever had a young brother.'

'We deduce that,' said Mrs Bantry. 'Unless she had a young brother there's no motive. So she must have had a young brother. Do you see, Watson?'

'That's all very fine, Dolly,' said her husband. 'But it's only a guess.'

'Of course it is,' said Mrs Bantry. 'That's all we can do – guess. We haven't got any clues. Go on, dear, have a guess yourself.'

'Upon my word, I don't know what to say. But I think there's something in Miss Helier's suggestion that they fell out about a man. Look here, Dolly, it was probably some high church parson. They both embroidered him a cope or something, and he wore the Durrant woman's first. Depend upon it, it was something like that. Look how she went off to a parson at the end. These women all lose their heads over a good-looking clergyman. You hear of it over and over again.'

'I think I must try to make my explanation a little more subtle,' said Sir Henry, 'though I admit it's only a guess. I suggest that Miss Barton was always mentally unhinged. There are more cases like that than you would imagine. Her mania grew stronger and she began to believe it her duty to rid the world of certain persons – possibly what is termed unfortunate females. Nothing much is known about Miss Durrant's past. So very possibly she *had* a past – an "unfortunate" one. Miss Barton learns of this and decides on extermination. Later, the righteousness of her act begins to trouble her and she is overcome by remorse. Her end shows her to be completely unhinged. Now, do say you agree with me, Miss Marple.'

'I'm afraid I don't, Sir Henry,' said Miss Marple, smiling apologetically. 'I think her end shows her to have been a very clever and resourceful woman.'

Jane Helier interrupted with a little scream.

'Oh! I've been so stupid. May I guess again? Of course it must have been that. Blackmail! The companion woman was blackmailing her. Only I don't see why Miss Marple says it was clever of her to kill herself. I can't see that at all.'

'Ah!' said Sir Henry. 'You see, Miss Marple knew a case just like it in St Mary Mead.'

'You always laugh at me, Sir Henry,' said Miss Marple reproachfully. 'I must confess it does remind me, just a little, of old Mrs Trout. She drew the old age pension, you know, for three old women who were dead, in different parishes.'

'It sounds a most complicated and resourceful crime,' said Sir Henry. 'But it doesn't seem to me to throw any light upon our present problem.'

'Of course not,' said Miss Marple. 'It wouldn't – to you. But some of the families were very poor, and the old age pension was a great boon to the children. I know it's difficult for anyone outside to understand. But what I really meant was that the whole thing hinged upon one old woman being so like any other old woman.'

'Eh?' said Sir Henry, mystified.

'I always explain things so badly. What I mean is that when Dr Lloyd described the two ladies first, he didn't know which was which, and I don't suppose anyone else in the hotel did. They would have, of course, after a day or so, but the very next day one of the two was drowned, and if the one who was left said she was Miss Barton, I don't suppose it would ever occur to anyone that she mightn't be.'

'You think – Oh! I see,' said Sir Henry slowly.

'It's the only natural way of thinking of it. Dear Mrs Bantry began that way just now. Why *should* the rich employer kill the humble companion? It's so much more likely to be the other way about. I mean – that's the way things happen.'

'Is it?' said Sir Henry. 'You shock me.'

'But of course,' went on Miss Marple, 'she would have to wear Miss Barton's clothes, and they would probably be a little tight on her, so that her general appearance would look as though she had got a little fatter. That's why I asked that question. A gentleman would be sure to think it was the lady who had got fatter, and not the clothes that had got smaller – though that isn't quite the right way of putting it.'

'But if Amy Durrant killed Miss Barton, what did she gain by it?' asked Mrs Bantry. 'She couldn't keep up the deception for ever.'

'She only kept it up for another month or so,' pointed out Miss Marple. 'And during that time I expect she travelled, keeping away from anyone who might know her. That's what I meant by saying that one lady of a certain age looks so like another. I don't suppose the different photograph on her passport was ever noticed – you know what passports are. And then in March, she went down to this Cornish place and began to act queerly and draw attention to herself so that when people found her clothes on the beach and read her last letter they shouldn't think of the commonsense conclusion.'

'Which was?' asked Sir Henry.

'No *body*,' said Miss Marple firmly. 'That's the thing that would stare you in the face, if there weren't such a lot of red herrings to draw you off the trail – including the suggestion of foul play and remorse. *No body*. That was the real significant fact.'

'Do you mean –' said Mrs Bantry – 'do you mean that there wasn't any remorse? That there wasn't – that she didn't drown herself?'

'Not she!' said Miss Marple. 'It's just Mrs Trout over again. Mrs Trout was very good at red herrings, but she met her match in me. And I can see through your remorse-driven Miss Barton. Drown herself? Went off to Australia, if I'm any good at guessing.'

'You are, Miss Marple,' said Dr Lloyd. 'Undoubtedly you are. Now it again took me quite by surprise. Why, you could have knocked me down with a feather that day in Melbourne.'

'Was that what you spoke of as a final coincidence?' Dr Lloyd nodded.

'Yes, it was rather rough luck on Miss Barton – or Miss Amy Durrant – whatever you like to call her. I became a ship's doctor for a while, and landing in Melbourne, the first person I saw as I walked down the street was the lady I thought had been drowned in Cornwall. She saw the game was up as far as I was concerned, and she did the bold thing – took me into her confidence. A curious woman, completely lacking, I suppose, in some moral sense. She was the eldest of a family of nine, all wretchedly poor. They had applied once for help to their rich cousin in England and been repulsed, Miss Barton having quarrelled with their father. Money was wanted desperately, for the three youngest children were delicate and wanted expensive medical treatment. Amy Barton then and there seems to have decided on her plan of cold-blooded murder. She set out for England, working her passage over as a children's nurse. She obtained the situation of companion to Miss Barton, calling herself Amy Durrant. She engaged a room and put some furniture into it so as to create more of a personality for herself. The drowning plan was a sudden inspiration. She had been waiting for some opportunity to present itself. Then she staged the final scene of the drama and returned to Australia, and in due time she and her brothers and sisters inherited Miss Barton's money as next of kin.'

'A very bold and perfect crime,' said Sir Henry. 'Almost *the* perfect crime. If it had been Miss Barton who had died in the Canaries, suspicion might attach to Amy Durrant and her connection with the Barton family might have been discovered; but the change of identity and the double crime, as you may call it, effectually did away with that. Yes, almost the perfect crime.'

'What happened to her?' asked Mrs Bantry. 'What did you do in the matter, Dr Lloyd?'

'I was in a very curious position, Mrs Bantry. Of evidence as the law understands it, I still have very little. Also, there were certain signs, plain to me as a medical man, that though strong and vigorous in appearance, the lady was not long for this world. I went home with her and saw the rest of the family – a charming family, devoted to their eldest sister and without an idea in their heads that she might prove to have committed a crime. Why bring sorrow on them when I could prove nothing? The lady's admission to me was unheard by anyone else. I let Nature take its course. Miss Amy Barton died six months after my meeting with her. I have often wondered if she was cheerful and unrepentant up to the last.'

'Surely not,' said Mrs Bantry.

'I expect so,' said Miss Marple. 'Mrs Trout was.'

Jane Helier gave herself a little shake.

'Well,' she said. 'It's very, very thrilling. I don't quite understand now who drowned which. And how does this Mrs Trout come into it?'

'She doesn't, my dear,' said Miss Marple. 'She was only a person – not a very nice person – in the village.'

'Oh!' said Jane. 'In the village. But nothing ever happens in a village, does it?' She sighed. 'I'm sure I shouldn't have any brains at all if I lived in a village.'

The Four Suspects

The conversation hovered round undiscovered and unpunished crimes. Everyone in turn vouchsafed their opinion: Colonel Bantry, his plump amiable wife, Jane Helier, Dr Lloyd, and even old Miss Marple. The one person who did not speak was the one best fitted in most people's opinion to do so. Sir Henry Clithering, ex-Commissioner of Scotland Yard, sat silent, twisting his moustache – or rather stroking it – and half smiling, as though at some inward thought that amused him.

'Sir Henry,' said Mrs Bantry at last. 'If you don't say something I shall scream. Are there a lot of crimes that go unpunished, or are there not?'

'You're thinking of newspaper headlines, Mrs Bantry. SCOTLAND YARD AT FAULT AGAIN. And a list of unsolved mysteries to follow.'

'Which really, I suppose, form a very small percentage of the whole?' said Dr Lloyd.

'Yes; that is so. The hundreds of crimes that are solved and the perpetrators punished are seldom heralded and sung. But that isn't quite the point at issue, is it? When you talk of *undiscovered* crimes and *unsolved* crimes, you are talking of two different things. In the first category come all the crimes that Scotland Yard never hears about, the crimes that no one even knows have been committed.'

'But I suppose there aren't very many of those?' said Mrs Bantry.

'Aren't there?'

'Sir Henry! You don't mean there *are*?'

'I should think,' said Miss Marple thoughtfully, 'that there must be a very large number.'

The charming old lady, with her old-world unruffled air, made her statement in a tone of the utmost placidity.

'My dear Miss Marple,' said Colonel Bantry.

'Of course,' said Miss Marple, 'a lot of people are stupid. And stupid people get found out, whatever they do. But there are quite a number of people who aren't stupid, and one shudders to think of what they might accomplish unless they had very strongly rooted principles.'

'Yes,' said Sir Henry, 'there are a lot of people who aren't stupid. How often does some crime come to light simply by reason of a bit of unmitigated bungling, and each time one asks oneself the question: If this hadn't been bungled, would anyone ever have known?'

'But that's very serious, Clithering,' said Colonel Bantry. 'Very serious, indeed.'

'Is it?'

'What do you mean! It is! Of course it's serious.'

'You say crime goes unpunished; but does it? Unpunished by the law perhaps; but cause and effect works outside the law. To say that every crime brings its own punishment is by way of being a platitude, and yet in my opinion nothing can be truer.'

'Perhaps, perhaps,' said Colonel Bantry. 'But that doesn't alter the seriousness – the – er – seriousness –' He paused, rather at a loss.

Sir Henry Clithering smiled.

'Ninety-nine people out of a hundred are doubtless

of your way of thinking,' he said. 'But you know, it isn't really guilt that is important – it's innocence. That's the thing that nobody will realize.'

'I don't understand,' said Jane Helier.

'I do,' said Miss Marple. 'When Mrs Trent found half a crown missing from her bag, the person it affected most was the daily woman, Mrs Arthur. Of course the Trents thought it was her, but being kindly people and knowing she had a large family and a husband who drinks, well – they naturally didn't want to go to extremes. But they felt differently towards her, and they didn't leave her in charge of the house when they went away, which made a great difference to her; and other people began to get a feeling about her too. And then it suddenly came out that it was the governess. Mrs Trent saw her through a door reflected in a mirror. The purest chance – though I prefer to call it Providence. And that, I think, is what Sir Henry means. Most people would be only interested in who took the money, and it turned out to be the most unlikely person – just like in detective stories! But the real person it was life and death to was poor Mrs Arthur, who had done nothing. That's what you mean, isn't it, Sir Henry?'

'Yes, Miss Marple, you've hit off my meaning exactly. Your charwoman person was lucky in the instance you relate. Her innocence was shown. But some people may go through a lifetime crushed by the weight of a suspicion that is really unjustified.'

'Are you thinking of some particular instance, Sir Henry?' asked Mrs Bantry shrewdly.

'As a matter of fact, Mrs Bantry, I am. A very curious case. A case where we believe murder to have been committed, but with no possible chance of ever proving it.'

'Poison, I suppose,' breathed Jane. 'Something untraceable.'

Dr Lloyd moved restlessly and Sir Henry shook his head.

'No, dear lady. *Not* the secret arrow poison of the South American Indians! I wish it *were* something of that kind. We have to deal with something much more prosaic – so prosaic, in fact, that there is no hope of bringing the deed home to its perpetrator. An old gentleman who fell downstairs and broke his neck; one of those regrettable accidents which happen every day.'

'But what happened really?'

'Who can say?' Sir Henry shrugged his shoulders. 'A push from behind? A piece of cotton or string tied across the top of the stairs and carefully removed afterwards? That we shall never know.'

'But you do think that it – well, wasn't an accident? Now why?' asked the doctor.

'That's rather a long story, but – well, yes, we're pretty sure. As I said there's no chance of being able to bring the deed home to anyone – the evidence would be too flimsy. But there's the other aspect of the case – the one I was speaking about. You see, there were four people who might have done the trick. One's guilty; *but* the other three are innocent. And unless the truth is found out, those three are going to remain under the terrible shadow of doubt.'

'I think,' said Mrs Bantry, 'that you'd better tell us your long story.'

'I needn't make it so very long after all,' said Sir Henry. 'I can at any rate condense the beginning. That deals with a German secret society – the Schwartze Hand – something after the lines of the Camorra or what is most people's idea of the Camorra. A scheme of blackmail and terrorization. The thing started quite suddenly after the War, and spread to an amazing extent. Numberless people were victimized by it. The authorities were not successful in coping with it, for its secrets were jealously guarded, and it was almost impossible to find anyone who could be induced to betray them.

'Nothing much was ever known about it in England, but in Germany it was having a most paralysing effect. It was finally broken up and dispersed through the efforts of one man, a Dr Rosen, who had at one time been very prominent in Secret Service work. He became a member, penetrated its inmost circle, and was, as I say, instrumental in bringing about its downfall.

'But he was, in consequence, a marked man, and it was deemed wise that he should leave Germany – at any rate for a time. He came to England, and we had letters about him from the police in Berlin. He came and had a personal interview with me. His point of view was both dispassionate and resigned. He had no doubts of what the future held for him.

' "They will get me, Sir Henry," he said. "Not a doubt of it." He was a big man with a fine head, and a very deep voice, with only a slight guttural intonation to tell of his nationality. "That is a foregone conclusion. It does not matter, I am prepared. I faced the risk when I undertook this business. I have done what I set out to do. The organization can never be got together again. But there are many members of it at liberty, and they will take the only revenge they can – my life. It is simply a question of time; but I am anxious that that time should be as long as possible. You see, I am collecting and editing some very interesting material – the result of my life's work. I should like, if possible, to be able to complete my task."

'He spoke very simply, with a certain grandeur which I could not but admire. I told him we would take all precautions, but he waved my words aside.

' "Some day, sooner or later, they will get me," he repeated. "When that day comes, do not distress yourself. You will, I have no doubt, have done all that is possible."

'He then proceeded to outline his plans which were simple enough. He proposed to take a small cottage in the country where he could live quietly and go on with his work. In the end he selected a village in Somerset – King's Gnaton, which was seven miles from a railway station, and singularly untouched by civilization. He bought a very charming cottage, had various improvements and alterations made, and settled down there most contentedly. His household consisted of his niece, Greta, a secretary, an old German servant who had served him faithfully for nearly forty years, and an outside handyman and gardener who was a native of King's Gnaton.'

'The four suspects,' said Dr Lloyd softly.

'Exactly. The four suspects. There is not much more to tell. Life went on peacefully at King's Gnaton for five months and then the blow fell. Dr Rosen fell down the stairs one morning and was found dead about half an hour later. At the time the accident must have taken place, Gertrud was in her kitchen with the door closed and heard nothing – so *she* says. Fräulein Greta was in the garden planting some bulbs – again, so *she* says. The gardener, Dobbs, was in the small potting shed having his elevenses – so *he* says; and the secretary was out for a walk, and once more there is only his own word for it. No one has an alibi – no one can corroborate anyone else's story. But one thing *is* certain. No one from outside could have done it, for a stranger in the little village of King's Gnaton would be noticed without fail. Both the back and the front doors were locked, each member of the household having their own key. So you see it narrows down to those four. And yet each one seems to be above suspicion. Greta, his own brother's child. Gertrud, with forty years of faithful service. Dobbs, who has never been out of King's Gnaton. And Charles Templeton, the secretary – '

'Yes,' said Colonel Bantry, 'what about him? He seems the suspicious person to my mind. What do you know about him?'

'It is what I knew about him that put him completely out of court – at any rate at the time,' said Sir Henry gravely. 'You see, Charles Templeton was one of my own men.'

'Oh!' said Colonel Bantry, considerably taken aback.

'Yes. I wanted to have someone on the spot, and at the same I didn't want to cause talk in the village. Rosen really needed a secretary. I put Templeton on the job. He's a gentleman, he speaks German fluently, and he's altogether a very able fellow.'

'But, then, which do you suspect?' asked Mrs Bantry in a bewildered tone. 'They all seem so – well, impossible.'

'Yes, so it appears. But you can look at the thing from another angle. Fräulein Greta was his niece and a very lovely girl, but the War has shown us time and again that brother can turn against sister, or father against son and so on, and the loveliest and gentlest of young girls did some of the most amazing things. The same thing applies to Gertrud, and who knows what other forces might be at work in her case. A quarrel, perhaps, with her master, a growing resentment all the more lasting because of the long faithful years behind her. Elderly women of that class can be amazingly bitter sometimes. And Dobbs? Was he right outside it because he had no connection with the family? Money will do much. In some way Dobbs might have been approached and bought.

'For one thing seems certain: Some message or some order must have come from outside. Otherwise why five months immunity? No, the agents of the society must have been at work. Not yet sure of Rosen's perfidy, they delayed till the betrayal had been traced to him beyond any possible doubt. And then, all doubts set aside, they must have sent their message to the spy within the gates – the message that said, "Kill".'

'How nasty!' said Jane Helier, and shuddered.

'But how did the message come? That was the point I tried to elucidate – the one hope of solving my problem. One of those four people must have been approached or communicated with in some way. There would be no delay – I knew that – as soon as the command came, it would be carried out. That was a peculiarity of the Schwartze Hand.

'I went into the question, went into it in a way that will probably strike you as being ridiculously meticulous. Who had come to the cottage that morning? I eliminated nobody. Here is the list.'

He took an envelope from his pocket and selected a paper from its contents.

'*The butcher*, bringing some neck of mutton. Investigated and found correct.

'*The grocer's assistant*, bringing a packet of cornflour, two pounds of sugar, a pound of butter, and a pound of coffee. Also investigated and found correct.

'*The postman*, bringing two circulars for Fräulein Rosen, a local letter for Gertrud, three letters for Dr Rosen, one with a foreign stamp, and two letters for Mr Templeton, one also with a foreign stamp.'

Sir Henry paused and then took a sheaf of documents from the envelope.

'It may interest you to see these for yourself. They were handed me by the various people concerned, or collected from the waste-paper basket. I need hardly say they've been tested by experts for invisible ink, etc. No excitement of that kind is possible.'

Everyone crowded round to look. The catalogues were respectively from a nurseryman and from a prominent London fur establishment. The two bills addressed to Dr Rosen were a local one for seeds for the garden and one from a London stationery firm. The letter addressed to him ran as follows:

My Dear Rosen – Just back from Dr Helmuth Spath's. I saw Edgar Jackson the other day. He and Amos Perry have just come back from Tsingtau. In all Honesty I can't say I envy them the trip. Let me have news of you soon. As I said before: Beware of a certain person. You know who I mean, though you don't agree. – Yours, Georgine.

'Mr Templeton's mail consisted of this bill, which as you see, is an account rendered from his tailor, and a letter from a friend in Germany,' went on Sir Henry. 'The latter, unfortunately, he tore up whilst out on his walk. Finally we have the letter received by Gertrud.'

'Dear Mrs Swartz,
    We're hoping as how you be able to come the social on friday evening, the vicar says has he hopes you will – one and all being welcome. The resipy for the ham was very good, and I thanks you for it. Hoping as this finds you well and that we shall see you friday I remain –
    Yours faithfully,
    Emma Greene'

Dr Lloyd smiled a little over this and so did Mrs Bantry.

'I think the last letter can be put out of court,' said Dr Lloyd.

'I thought the same,' said Sir Henry; 'but I took the precaution of verifying that there was a Mrs Greene and a church social. One can't be too careful, you know.'

'That's what our friend Miss Marple always says,' said Dr Lloyd, smiling. 'You're lost in a daydream, Miss Marple. What are you thinking out?'

Miss Marple gave a start.

'So stupid of me,' she said. 'I was just wondering why the word Honesty in Dr Rosen's letter was spelt with a capital H.'

Mrs Bantry picked it up.

'So it is,' she said. '*Oh!*'

'Yes, dear,' said Miss Marple. 'I thought you'd notice!'

'There's a definite warning in that letter,' said Colonel Bantry. 'That's the first thing caught my attention. I notice more than you'd think. Yes, a definite warning – against whom?'

'There's rather a curious point about that letter,' said Sir Henry. 'According to Templeton, Dr Rosen opened the letter at breakfast and tossed it across to him saying he didn't know who the fellow was from Adam.'

'But it wasn't a fellow,' said Jane Helier. 'It was signed "Georgina".'

'It's difficult to say which it is,' said Dr Lloyd. 'It might be Georgey; but it certainly looks more like Georgina. Only it strikes me that the writing is a man's.'

'You know, that's interesting,' said Colonel Bantry. 'His tossing it across the table like that and pretending he knew nothing about it. Wanted to watch somebody's face. Whose face – the girl's? or the man's?'

'Or even the cook's?' suggested Mrs Bantry. 'She might have been in the room bringing in the breakfast. But what I don't see is . . . it's most peculiar –'

She frowned over the letter. Miss Marple drew closer to her. Miss Marple's finger went out and touched the sheet of paper. They murmured together.

'But why did the secretary tear up the other letter?' asked Jane Helier suddenly. 'It seems – oh! I don't know – it seems queer. Why should he have letters from Germany? Although, of course, if he's above suspicion, as you say –'

'But Sir Henry didn't say that,' said Miss Marple quickly, looking up from her murmured conference with Mrs Bantry. 'He said *four* suspects. So that shows that he includes Mr Templeton. I'm right, am I not, Sir Henry?'

'Yes, Miss Marple. I have learned one thing through bitter experience. Never say to yourself that *anyone* is above suspicion. I gave you reasons just now why three of these people might after all be guilty, unlikely as it seemed. I did not at that time apply the same process to Charles Templeton. But I came to it at last through pursuing the rule I have just mentioned. And I was forced to recognize this: That every army and every navy and every police force has a certain number of traitors within its ranks, much as we hate to admit the idea. And I examined dispassionately the case against Charles Templeton.

'I asked myself very much the same questions as Miss Helier has just asked. Why should he, alone of all the house, not be able to produce the letter he had received – a letter, moreover, with a German stamp on it. Why should he have letters from Germany?

'The last question was an innocent one, and I actually put it to him. His reply came simply enough. His mother's sister was married to a German. The letter had been from a German girl cousin. So I learned something I did not know before – that Charles Templeton had relations with people in Germany. And that put him definitely on the list of suspects – very much so. He is my own man – a lad I have always liked and trusted; but in common justice and fairness I must admit that he heads that list.

'But there it is – I do not know! I do not *know*. . . And in all probability I never shall know. It is not a question of punishing a murderer. It is a question that to me seems a hundred times more important. It is the blighting, perhaps, of an honourable man's whole career . . . because of suspicion – a suspicion that I dare not disregard.'

Miss Marple coughed and said gently:

'Then, Sir Henry, if I understand you rightly, it is this young Mr Templeton only who is so much on your mind?'

'Yes, in a sense. It should, in theory, be the same for all four, but that is not actually the case. Dobbs, for instance – suspicion may attach to him in my mind, but it will not actually affect his career. Nobody in the village has ever had any idea that old Dr Rosen's death was anything but an accident. Gertrud is slightly more affected. It must make, for instance, a difference in Fräulein Rosen's attitude toward her. But that, possibly, is not of great importance to her.

'As for Greta Rosen – well, here we come to the crux of the matter. Greta is a very pretty girl and Charles Templeton is a good-looking young man, and for five months they were thrown together with no outer distractions. The inevitable happened. They fell in love with each other – even if they did not come to the point of admitting the fact in words.

'And then the catastrophe happens. It is three months ago now and a day or two after I returned, Greta Rosen came to see me. She had sold the cottage and was returning to Germany, having finally settled up her uncle's affairs. She came to me personally, although she knew I had retired, because it was really about a personal matter she wanted to see me. She beat about the bush a little, but at last it all came out. What did I think? That letter with the German stamp – she had worried about it and worried about it – the one Charles had torn up. Was it all right? Surely it *must* be all right. Of course she believed his story, but – oh! if she only *knew*! If she knew – for certain.

'You see? The same feeling: the wish to trust – but the horrible lurking suspicion, thrust resolutely to the back of the mind, but persisting nevertheless. I spoke to her with absolute frankness, and asked her to do the same. I asked her whether she had been on the point of caring for Charles, and he for her.

'"I think so," she said. "Oh, yes, I know it was so. We were so happy. Every day passed so contentedly. We knew – we both knew. There was no hurry – there was all the time in the world. Some day he would tell me he loved me, and I should tell him that I too – Ah! But you can guess! And now it is all changed. A black cloud has come between us – we are constrained, when we meet we do not know what to say. It is, perhaps, the same with him as with me ... We are each saying to ourselves, 'If I were *sure*!' That is why, Sir Henry, I beg of you to say to me, 'You may be sure, whoever killed your uncle, it was not Charles Templeton!' Say it to me! Oh, say it to me! I beg – I beg!"

'And, damn it all,' said Sir Henry, bringing down his fist with a bang on the table, 'I couldn't say it to her. They'll drift farther and farther apart, those two – with suspicion like a ghost between them – a ghost that can't be laid.'

He leant back in his chair, his face looked tired and grey. He shook his head once or twice despondently.

'And there's nothing more can be done, unless –' He sat up straight again and a tiny whimsical smile crossed his face – 'unless Miss Marple can help us. Can't you, Miss Marple? I've a feeling that letter might be in your line, you know. The one about the church social. Doesn't it remind you of something or someone that makes everything perfectly plain? Can't you do something to help two helpless young people who want to be happy?'

Behind the whimsicality there was something earnest in his appeal. He had come to think very highly of the mental powers of this frail old-fashioned maiden lady. He looked across at her with something very like hope in his eyes.

Miss Marple coughed and smoothed her lace.

'It does remind me a little of Annie Poultny,' she admitted. 'Of course the letter is perfectly plain – both to Mrs Bantry and myself. I don't mean the church social letter, but the other one. You living so much in London and not being a gardener, Sir Henry, would not have been likely to notice.'

'Eh?' said Sir Henry. 'Notice what?'

Mrs Bantry reached out a hand and selected a catalogue. She opened it and read aloud with gusto:

'Dr Helmuth Spath. Pure lilac, a wonderfully fine flower, carried on exceptionally long and stiff stem. Splendid for cutting and garden decoration. A novelty of striking beauty.

'Edgar Jackson. Beautifully shaped chrysanthemum-like flower of a distinct brick-red colour.

'Amos Perry. Brilliant red, highly decorative.

'Tsingtau. Brilliant orange-red, showy garden plant and lasting cut flower.

'Honesty –'

'With a capital H, you remember,' murmured Miss Marple.

'Honesty. Rose and white shades, enormous perfect shaped flower.'

Mrs Bantry flung down the catalogue, and said with immense explosive force:

'*Dahlias!*'

'And their initial letters spell "DEATH",' explained Miss Marple.

'But the letter came to Dr Rosen himself,' objected Sir Henry.

'That was the clever part of it,' said Miss Marple. 'That and the warning in it. What would he do, getting a letter from someone he didn't know, full of names he didn't know. Why, of course, toss it over to his secretary.'

'Then, after all –'

'Oh, *no!* said Miss Marple. '*Not* the secretary. Why, that's what makes it so perfectly clear that it *wasn't* him. He'd never have let that letter be found if so. And equally he'd never have destroyed a letter to himself with a German stamp on it. Really, his innocence is – if you'll allow me to use the word – just *shining.*'

'Then who –'

'Well, it seems almost certain – as certain as anything can be in this world. There was another person at the breakfast table, and she would – quite naturally under the circumstances – put out her hand for the letter and read it. And that would be that. You remember that she got a gardening catalogue by the same post –'

'Greta Rosen,' said Sir Henry, slowly. 'Then her visit to me –'

'Gentlemen never see through these things,' said Miss Marple. 'And I'm afraid they often think we old women are – well, cats, to see things the way we do. But there it is. One does know a great deal about one's own sex, unfortunately. I've no doubt there was a barrier between them. The young man felt a sudden inexplicable repulsion. He suspected, purely through instinct, and couldn't hide the suspicion. And I really think that the girl's visit to you was just pure *spite*. She was safe enough really; but she just went out of her way to fix your suspicions definitely on poor Mr Templeton. You weren't nearly so sure about him until after her visit.'

'I'm sure it was nothing that she said –' began Sir Henry.

'Gentlemen,' said Miss Marple calmly, 'never see through these things.'

'And that girl –' he stopped. 'She commits a cold-blooded murder and gets off Scot free!'

'Oh! no, Sir Henry,' said Miss Marple. 'Not Scot free. Neither you nor I believe that. Remember what you said not long ago. No. Greta Rosen will not escape punishment. To begin with, she must be in with a very queer set of people – blackmailers and terrorists – associates who will do her no good, and will probably bring her to a miserable end. As you say, one mustn't waste thoughts on the guilty – it's the innocent who matter. Mr Templeton, who I daresay will marry that German cousin, his tearing up her letter looks – well, it looks *suspicious* – using the word in quite a different sense from the one we've been using all the evening. A little as though he were afraid of the other girl noticing or asking to see it? Yes, I think there must have been some little romance there. And then there's Dobbs – though, as you say, I daresay it won't matter much to him. His elevenses are probably all he thinks about. And then there's that poor old Gertrud – the one who reminded me of Annie Poultny. Poor Annie Poultny. Fifty years faithful service and suspected of making away with Miss Lamb's will, though nothing could be proved. Almost broke the poor creature's faithful heart; and then after she was dead it came to light in the secret drawer of the tea caddy where old Miss Lamb had put it herself for safety. But too late then for poor Annie.

'That's what worries me so about that poor old German woman. When one is old, one becomes embittered very easily. I felt much more sorry for her than for Mr Templeton, who is young and good looking and evidently a favourite with the ladies. You will write to her, won't you, Sir Henry, and just tell her that her innocence is established beyond doubt? Her dear old master dead, and she no doubt brooding and feeling herself suspected of ... Oh! It won't bear thinking about!'

'I will write, Miss Marple,' said Sir Henry. He looked at her curiously. 'You know, I shall never quite understand you. Your outlook is always a different one from what I expect.'

'My outlook, I am afraid, is a very petty one,' said Miss Marple humbly. 'I hardly ever go out of St Mary Mead.'

'And yet you have solved what may be called an International mystery,' said Sir Henry. 'For you *have* solved it. I am convinced of that.'

Miss Marple blushed, then bridled a little.

'I was, I think, well educated for the standard of my day. My sister and I had a German governess – a Fräulein. A very sentimental creature. She taught us the language of flowers – a forgotten study nowadays, but most charming. A yellow tulip, for instance, means hopeless love, whilst a China aster means I die of jealousy at your feet. That letter was signed Georgine, which I seem to remember is dahlia in German, and that of course made the whole thing perfectly clear. I wish I could remember the meaning of dahlia, but alas, that eludes me. My memory is not what it was.'

'At any rate it didn't mean DEATH.'

'No, indeed. Horrible, is it not? There are very sad things in the world.'

'There are,' said Mrs Bantry with a sigh. 'It's lucky one has flowers and one's friends.'

'She puts us last, you observe,' said Dr Lloyd.

'A man used to send me purple orchids every night to the theatre,' said Jane dreamily.

' "I await your favours," – that's what that means,' said Miss Marple brightly.

Sir Henry gave a peculiar sort of cough and turned his head away.

Miss Marple gave a sudden exclamation.

'I've remembered. Dahlias mean "Treachery and Misrepresentation".'

'Wonderful,' said Sir Henry. 'Absolutely wonderful.'

And he sighed.

A Christmas Tragedy

'I have a complaint to make,' said Sir Henry Clithering. His eyes twinkled gently as he looked round at the assembled company. Colonel Bantry, his legs stretched out, was frowning at the mantelpiece as though it were a delinquent soldier on parade, his wife was surreptitiously glancing at a catalogue of bulbs which had come by the late post, Dr Lloyd was gazing with frank admiration at Jane Helier, and that beautiful young actress herself was thoughtfully regarding her pink polished nails. Only that elderly, spinster lady, Miss Marple, was sitting bolt upright, and her faded blue eyes met Sir Henry's with an answering twinkle.

'A complaint?' she murmured.

'A very serious complaint. We are a company of six, three representatives of each sex, and I protest on behalf of the downtrodden males. We have had three stories told tonight – and told by the three men! I protest that the ladies have not done their fair share.'

'Oh!' said Mrs Bantry with indignation. 'I'm sure we have. We've listened with the most intelligent appreciation. We've displayed the true womanly attitude – not wishing to thrust ourselves in the limelight!'

'It's an excellent excuse,' said Sir Henry; 'but it won't do. And there's a very good precedent in the Arabian Nights! So, forward, Scheherazade.'

'Meaning me?' said Mrs Bantry. 'But I don't know

anything to tell. I've never been surrounded by blood or mystery.'

'I don't absolutely insist upon blood,' said Sir Henry. 'But I'm sure one of you three ladies has got a pet mystery. Come now, Miss Marple – the "Curious Coincidence of the Charwoman" or the "Mystery of the Mothers' Meeting". Don't disappoint me in St Mary Mead.'

Miss Marple shook her head.

'Nothing that would interest you, Sir Henry. We have our little mysteries, of course – there was that gill of picked shrimps that disappeared so incomprehensibly; but that wouldn't interest you because it all turned out to be so trivial, though throwing a considerable light on human nature.'

'You have taught me to dote on human nature,' said Sir Henry solemnly.

'What about you, Miss Helier?' asked Colonel Bantry. 'You must have had some interesting experiences.'

'Yes, indeed,' said Dr Lloyd.

'Me?' said Jane. 'You mean – you want me to tell you something that happened to me?'

'Or to one of your friends,' amended Sir Henry.

'Oh!' said Jane vaguely. 'I don't think anything has ever happened to me – I mean not that kind of thing. Flowers, of course, and queer messages – but that's just men, isn't it? I don't think' – she paused and appeared lost in thought.

'I see we shall have to have that epic of the shrimps,' said Sir Henry. 'Now then, Miss Marple.'

'You're so fond of your joke, Sir Henry. The shrimps are only nonsense; but now I come to think of it, I *do* remember one incident – at least not exactly an incident, something very much more serious – a tragedy. And I was, in a way, mixed up in it; and for what I did,

I have never had any regrets – no, no regrets at all. But it didn't happen in St Mary Mead.'

'That disappoints me,' said Sir Henry. 'But I will endeavour to bear up. I knew we should not rely upon you in vain.'

He settled himself in the attitude of a listener. Miss Marple grew slightly pink.

'I hope I shall be able to tell it properly,' she said anxiously. 'I fear I am very inclined to become *rambling*. One wanders from the point – altogether without knowing that one is doing so. And it is so hard to remember each fact in its proper order. You must all bear with me if I tell my story badly. It happened a very long time ago now.

'As I say, it was not connected with St Mary Mead. As a matter of fact, it had to do with a Hydro –'

'Do you mean a seaplane?' asked Jane with wide eyes.

'You wouldn't know, dear,' said Mrs Bantry, and explained. Her husband added his quota:

'Beastly places – absolutely beastly! Got to get up early and drink filthy-tasting water. Lot of old women sitting about. Ill-natured tittle tattle. God, when I think –'

'Now, Arthur,' said Mrs Bantry placidly. 'You know it did you all the good in the world.'

'Lot of old women sitting round talking scandal,' grunted Colonel Bantry.

'That I am afraid is true,' said Miss Marple. 'I myself –'

'My dear Miss Marple,' cried the colonel, horrified. 'I didn't mean for one moment –'

With pink cheeks and a little gesture of the hand, Miss Marple stopped him.

'But it is *true*, Colonel Bantry. Only I should just like to say this. Let me recollect my thoughts. Yes. Talking scandal, as you say – well, it *is* done a good deal. And people are very down on it – especially young people. My nephew, who writes books – and very clever ones, I believe – has said some most *scathing* things about taking people's characters away without any kind of proof – and how wicked it is, and all that. But what I say is that none of these young people ever stop to *think*. They really don't examine the facts. Surely the whole crux of the matter is this: *How often is tittle tattle*, as you call it, *true!* And I think if, as I say, they really examined the facts they would find that it was true nine times out of ten! That's really just what makes people so annoyed about it.'

'The inspired guess,' said Sir Henry.

'No, not that, not that at all! It's really a matter of practice and experience. An Egyptologist, so I've heard, if you show him one of those curious little beetles, can tell you by the look and the feel of the thing what date BC it is, or if it's a Birmingham imitation. And he can't always give a definite rule for doing so. He just *knows*. His life has been spent handling such things.

'And that's what I'm trying to say (very badly, I know). What my nephew calls "superfluous women" have a lot of time on their hands, and their chief interest is usually *people*. And so, you see, they get to be what one might call *experts*. Now young people nowadays – they talk very freely about things that weren't mentioned in my young days, but on the other hand their minds are terribly innocent. They believe in everyone and everything. And if one tries to warn them, ever so gently, they tell one that one has a Victorian mind – and that, they say, is like a *sink*.'

'After all,' said Sir Henry, 'what is wrong with a *sink*?'

'Exactly,' said Miss Marple eagerly. 'It's the most necessary thing in any house; but, of course, not romantic. Now I must confess that I have my *feelings*, like everyone else, and I have sometimes been cruelly hurt by unthinking remarks. I know gentlemen are not interested in domestic matters, but I must just mention my maid Ethel – a very good-looking girl and obliging in every way. Now I realized as soon as I saw her that she was the same type as Annie Webb and poor Mrs Bruitt's girl. If the opportunity arose *mine* and *thine* would mean nothing to her. So I let her go at the month and I gave her a written reference saying she was honest and sober, but privately I warned old Mrs Edwards against taking her; and my nephew, Raymond, was exceedingly angry and said he had never heard of anything so wicked – yes, *wicked*. Well, she went to Lady Ashton, whom I felt no obligation to warn – and what happened? All the lace cut off her underclothes and two diamond brooches taken – and the girl departed in the middle of the night and never heard of since!'

Miss Marple paused, drew a long breath, and then went on.

'You'll be saying this has nothing to do with what went on at Keston Spa Hydro – but it has in a way. It explains why I felt no doubt in my mind the first moment I saw the Sanders together that he meant to do away with her.'

'Eh?' said Sir Henry, leaning forward.

Miss Marple turned a placid face to him.

'As I say, Sir Henry, I felt no doubt in my own mind. Mr Sanders was a big, good-looking, florid-faced man, very hearty in his manner and popular with all. And nobody could have been pleasanter to his wife than he was. But I knew! He meant to make away with her.'

'My dear Miss Marple –'

'Yes, I know. That's what my nephew Raymond West, would say. He'd tell me I hadn't a shadow of proof. But

I remember Walter Hones, who kept the Green Man. Walking home with his wife one night she fell into the river – and *he* collected the insurance money! And one or two other people that are walking about Scot free to this day – one indeed in our own class of life. Went to Switzerland for a summer holiday climbing with his wife. I warned her not to go – the poor dear didn't get angry with me as she might have done – she only laughed. It seemed to her funny that a queer old thing like me should say such things about her Harry. Well, well, there was an accident – and Harry is married to another woman now. But what could I *do*? I *knew*, but there was no proof.'

'Oh! Miss Marple,' cried Mrs Bantry. 'You don't really mean –'

'My dear, these things are very common – very common indeed. And gentlemen are especially tempted, being so much the stronger. So easy if a thing looks like an accident. As I say, I knew at once with the Sanders. It was on a tram. It was full inside and I had had to go on top. We all three got up to get off and Mr Sanders lost his balance and fell right against his wife, sending her headfirst down the stairs. Fortunately the conductor was a very strong young man and caught her.'

'But surely that must have been an accident.'

'Of course it was an accident – nothing could have looked more accidental! But Mr Saunders had been in the Merchant Service, so he told me, and a man who can keep his balance on a nasty tilting boat doesn't lose it on top of a tram if an old woman like me doesn't. Don't tell me!'

'At any rate we can take it that you made up your mind, Miss Marple,' said Sir Henry. 'Made it up then and there.'

The old lady nodded.

'I was sure enough, and another incident in crossing the street not long afterwards made me surer still. Now I ask you, what could I do, Sir Henry? Here was a nice contented happy little married woman shortly going to be murdered.'

'My dear lady, you take my breath away.'

'That's because, like most people nowadays, you won't face facts. You prefer to think such a thing couldn't be. But it was so, and I knew it. But one is so sadly handicapped! I couldn't, for instance, go to the police. And to warn the young woman would, I could see, be useless. She was devoted to the man. I just made it my business to find out as much as I could about them. One has a lot of opportunities doing one's needlework round the fire. Mrs Sanders (Gladys, her name was) was only too willing to talk. It seems they had not been married very long. Her husband had some property that was coming to him, but for the moment they were very badly off. In fact, they were living on her little income. One has heard that tale before. She bemoaned the fact that she could not touch the capital. It seems that somebody had had some sense somewhere! But the money was hers to will away – I found that out. And she and her husband had made wills in favour of each other directly after their marriage. Very touching. Of course, when Jack's affairs came right – That was the burden all day long, and in the meantime they were very hard up indeed – actually had a room on the top floor, all among the servants – and so dangerous in case of fire, though, as it happened, there was a fire escape just outside their window. I inquired carefully if there was a balcony – dangerous things, balconies. One push – you know!

'I made her promise not to go out on the balcony; I

said I'd had a dream. That impressed her – one can do a lot with superstition sometimes. She was a fair girl, rather washed-out complexion, and an untidy roll of hair on her neck. Very credulous. She repeated what I had said to her husband, and I noticed him looking at me in a curious way once or twice. *He* wasn't credulous; and he knew I'd been on that tram.

'But I was very worried – terribly worried – because I couldn't see how to circumvent him. I could prevent anything happening at the Hydro, just by saying a few words to show him I suspected. But that only meant his putting off his plan till later. No, I began to believe that the only policy was a bold one – somehow or other to lay a trap for him. If I could induce him to attempt her life in a way of my own choosing – well, then he would be unmasked, and she would be forced to face the truth however much of a shock it was to her.'

'You take my breath away,' said Dr Lloyd. 'What conceivable plan could you adopt?'

'I'd have found one – never fear,' said Miss Marple. 'But the man was too clever for me. He didn't wait. He thought I might suspect, and so he struck before I could be sure. He knew I would suspect an accident. So he made it murder.'

A little gasp went round the circle. Miss Marple nodded and set her lips grimly together.

'I'm afraid I've put that rather abruptly. I must try and tell you exactly what occurred. I've always felt very bitterly about it – it seems to me that I ought, somehow, to have prevented it. But doubtless Providence knew best. I did what I could at all events.

'There was what I can only describe as a curiously eerie feeling in the air. There seemed to be something weighing on us all. A feeling of misfortune. To begin with, there was George, the hall porter. Had been there

157

for years and knew everybody. Bronchitis and pneumonia, and passed away on the fourth day. Terribly sad. A real blow to everybody. And four days before Christmas too. And then one of the housemaids – such a nice girl – a septic finger, actually died in twenty-four hours.

'I was in the drawing-room with Miss Trollope and old Mrs Carpenter, and Mrs Carpenter was being positively ghoulish – relishing it all, you know.

'"Mark my words," she said. '*This isn't the end.* You know the saying? *Never two without three.* I've proved it true time and again. There'll be another death. Not a doubt of it. And we shan't have long to wait. *Never two without three.*'

'As she said the last words, nodding her head and clicking her knitting needles, I just chanced to look up and there was Mr Sanders standing in the doorway. Just for a minute he was off guard, and I saw the look in his face as plain as plain. I shall believe till my dying day that it was that ghoulish Mrs Carpenter's words that put the whole thing into his head. I saw his mind working.

'He came forward into the room smiling in his genial way.

'"Any Christmas shopping I can do for you ladies?" he asked. "I'm going down to Keston presently."

'He stayed a minute or two, laughing and talking, and then went out. As I tell you, I was troubled, and I said straight away:

'"Where's Mrs Sanders? Does anyone know?"

'Mrs Trollope said she'd gone out to some friends of hers, the Mortimers, to play bridge, and that eased my mind for the moment. But I was still very worried and most uncertain as to what to do. About half an hour later I went up to my room. I met Dr Coles, my doctor, there, coming down the stairs as I was going up, and as I happened to want to consult him about my rheumatism, I took him into my room with me then and there. He mentioned to me then (in confidence, he said) about the death of the poor girl Mary. The manager didn't want the news to get about, he said, so would I keep it to myself. Of course I didn't tell him that we'd all been discussing nothing else for the last hour – ever since the poor girl breathed her last. These things are always known at once, and a man of his experience should know that well enough; but Dr Coles always was a simple unsuspicious fellow who believed what he wanted to believe and that's just what alarmed me a minute later. He said as he was leaving that Sanders had asked him to have a look at his wife. It seemed she'd been seedy of late – indigestion, etc.

'*Now that very self-same day Gladys Sanders had said to me that she'd got a wonderful digestion and was thankful for it.*

'You see? All my suspicions of that man came back a hundredfold. He was preparing the way – for what? Dr Coles left before I could make up my mind whether to speak to him or not – though really if I had spoken I shouldn't have known what to say. As I came out of my room, the man himself – Sanders – came down the stairs from the floor above. He was dressed to go out and he asked me again if he could do anything for me in the town. It was all I could do to be civil to the man! I went straight into the lounge and ordered tea. It was just on half past five, I remember.

'Now I'm very anxious to put clearly what happened next. I was still in the lounge at a quarter to seven when Mr Sanders came in. There were two gentlemen with him and all three of them were inclined to be a little on the lively side. Mr Sanders left his two friends and came right over to where I was sitting with Miss Trollope. He explained that he wanted our advice about a Christmas present he was giving his wife. It was an evening bag.

'"And you see, ladies," he said, "I'm only a rough sailorman. What do I know about such things? I've had three sent to me on approval and I want an expert opinion on them."

'We said, of course, that we would be delighted to help him, and he asked if we'd mind coming upstairs, as his wife might come in any minute if he brought the things down. So we went up with him. I shall never forget what happened next – I can feel my little fingers tingling now.

'Mr Sanders opened the door of the bedroom and switched on the light. I don't know which of us saw it first . . .

'*Mrs Sanders was lying on the floor, face downwards – dead.*

'I got to her first. I knelt down and took her hand and felt for the pulse, but it was useless, the arm itself was cold and stiff. Just by her head was a stocking filled with sand – the weapon she had been struck down with. Miss Trollope, silly creature, was moaning and moaning by the door and holding her head. Sanders gave a great cry of "My wife, my wife," and rushed to her. I stopped him touching her. You see, I was sure at the moment he had done it, and there might have been something that he wanted to take away or hide.

'"Nothing must be touched," I said. "Pull yourself together, Mr Sanders. Miss Trollope, please go down and fetch the manager."

'I stayed there, kneeling by the body. I wasn't going to leave Sanders alone with it. And yet I was forced to admit that if the man was acting, he was acting marvellously. He looked dazed and bewildered and scared out of his wits.

'The manager was with us in no time. He made a quick inspection of the room then turned us all out and locked the door, the key of which he took. Then he went off and telephoned to the police. It seemed a positive age before they came (we learnt afterwards that the line was out of order). The manager had to send a messenger to the police station, and the Hydro is right out of the town, up on the edge of the moor; and Mrs Carpenter tried us all very severely. She was so pleased at her prophecy of "Never two without three" coming true so quickly. Sanders, I hear, wandered out into the grounds, clutching his head and groaning and displaying every sign of grief.

'However, the police came at last. They went upstairs with the manager and Mr Sanders. Later they sent down for me. I went up. The inspector was there, sitting at a table writing. He was an intelligent-looking man and I liked him.

'"Miss Jane Marple?" he said.

'"Yes."

'"I understand, madam, that you were present when the body of the deceased was found?"

'I said I was and I described exactly what had occurred.

I think it was a relief to the poor man to find someone who could answer his questions coherently, having previously had to deal with Sanders and Emily Trollope, who, I gather, was completely demoralized – she would be, the silly creature! I remember my dear mother teaching me that a gentlewoman should always be able to control herself in public, however much she may give way in private.'

'An admirable maxim,' said Sir Henry gravely.

'When I had finished the inspector said:

'"Thank you, madam. Now I'm afraid I must ask you just to look at the body once more. Is that exactly the position in which it was lying when you entered the room? It hasn't been moved in any way?"

'I explained that I had prevented Mr Sanders from doing so, and the inspector nodded approval.

'"The gentleman seems terribly upset," he remarked.

'"He seems so – yes," I replied.

'I don't think I put any special emphasis on the "seems", but the inspector looked at me rather keenly.

'"So we can take it that the body is exactly as it was when found?" he said.

'"Except for the hat, yes," I replied.

'The inspector looked up sharply.

'"What do you mean – the hat?"

'I explained that the hat had been on poor Gladys's head, whereas now it was lying beside her. I thought, of course, that the police had done this. The inspector, however, denied it emphatically. Nothing had, as yet, been moved or touched. He stood looking down at that poor prone figure with a puzzled frown. Gladys was dressed in her outdoor clothes – a big dark-red tweed coat with a grey fur collar. The hat, a cheap affair of red felt, lay just by her head.

'The inspector stood for some minutes in silence, frowning to himself. Then an idea struck him.

'"Can you, by any chance, remember, madam, whether there were earrings in the ears, or whether the deceased habitually wore earrings?"

'Now fortunately I am in the habit of observing closely. I remembered that there had been a glint of pearls just below the hat brim, though I had paid no particular notice to it at the time. I was able to answer his first question in the affirmative.

'"Then that settles it. The lady's jewel case was rifled – not that she had anything much of value, I understand – and the rings were taken from her fingers. The murderer must have forgotten the earrings, and come back for them after the murder was discovered. A cool customer! Or perhaps –" He stared round the room and said slowly, "He may have been concealed here in this room – all the time."

'But I negatived that idea. I myself, I explained, looked under the bed. And the manager had opened the doors of the wardrobe. There was nowhere else where a man could hide. It is true the hat cupboard was locked in the middle of the wardrobe, but as that was only a shallow affair with shelves, no one could have been concealed there.

'The inspector nodded his head slowly whilst I explained all this.

'"I'll take your word for it, madam," he said. "In that case, as I said before, he must have come back. A very cool customer."

'"But the manager locked the door and took the key!"

'"That's nothing. The balcony and the fire escape – that's the way the thief came. Why, as likely as not, you actually disturbed him at work. He slips out of the window, and when you've all gone, back he comes and goes on with his business."

'"You are sure," I said, "that there *was* a thief?"

'He said drily:

'"Well, it looks like it, doesn't it?"

'But something in his tone satisfied me. I felt that he wouldn't take Mr Sanders in the rôle of the bereaved widower too seriously.

'You see, I admit it frankly. I was absolutely under the opinion of what I believe our neighbours, the French, call the *ideé fixe*. I knew that that man, Sanders, intended his wife to die. What I didn't allow for was that strange and fantastic thing, coincidence. My views about Mr Sanders were – I was sure of it – absolutely right and *true*. The man was a scoundrel. But although his hypocritical assumptions of grief didn't deceive me for a minute, I do remember feeling at the time that his *surprise* and *bewilderment were marvellously well done. They seemed absolutely natural* – if you know what I mean. I must admit that after my conversation with the inspector, a curious feeling of doubt crept over me. Because if Sanders had done this dreadful thing, I couldn't imagine any conceivable reason why he should creep back by means of the fire escape and take the earrings from his wife's ears. It wouldn't have been a *sensible* thing to do, and Sanders was such a very sensible man – that's just why I always felt he was so dangerous.'

Miss Marple looked round at her audience.

'You see, perhaps, what I am coming to? It is, so often, the unexpected that happens in this world. I was so *sure*, and that, I think, was what blinded me. The result came as a shock to me. *For it was proved, beyond any possible doubt, that Mr Sanders could not possibly have committed the crime . . .*'

A surprised gasp came from Mrs Bantry. Miss Marple turned to her.

'I know, my dear, that isn't what you expected when I began this story. It wasn't what I expected either. But facts are facts, and if one is proved to be wrong, one must just be humble about it and start again. That Mr Sanders was a murderer at heart I knew – and nothing ever occurred to upset that firm conviction of mine.

'And now, I expect, you would like to hear the actual facts themselves. Mrs Sanders, as you know, spent the afternoon playing bridge with some friends, the Mortimers. She left them at about a quarter past six. From her friends' house to the Hydro was about a quarter of an hour's walk – less if one hurried. She must have come in then about six-thirty. No one saw her come in, so she must have entered by the side door and hurried straight up to her room. There she changed (the fawn coat and skirt she wore to the bridge party were hanging up in the cupboard) and was evidently preparing to go out again, when the blow fell. Quite possibly they say, she never even knew who struck her. The sandbag, I understand, is a very efficient weapon. That looks as though the attackers were concealed in the room, possibly in one of the big wardrobe cupboards – the one she didn't open.

'Now as to the movements of Mr Sanders. He went out, as I have said, at about five-thirty – or a little after. He did some shopping at a couple of shops and at about six o'clock he entered the Grand Spa Hotel where he encountered two friends – the same with whom he returned to the Hydro later. They played billiards and, I gather, had a good many whiskies and sodas together. These two men (Hitchcock and Spender, their names were) were actually with him the whole time from six o'clock onwards. They walked back to the Hydro with him and he only left them to come across to me and Miss Trollope. That, as I told you, was about a quarter to seven – at which time his wife must have been already dead.

'I must tell you that I talked myself to these two friends of his. I did not like them. They were neither pleasant nor gentlemanly men, but I was quite certain of one thing, that they were speaking the absolute truth when they said that Sanders had been the whole time in their company.

'There was just one other little point that came up. It seems that while bridge was going on Mrs Sanders was called to the telephone. A Mr Littleworth wanted to speak to her. She seemed both excited and pleased about something – and incidentally made one or two bad mistakes. She left rather earlier than they had expected her to do.

'Mr Sanders was asked whether he knew the name of Littleworth as being one of his wife's friends, but he declared he had never heard of anyone of that name. And to me that seems borne out by his wife's attitude – she too, did not seem to know the name of Littleworth. Nevertheless she came back from the telephone smiling and blushing, so it looks as though whoever it was did not give his real name, and that in itself has a suspicious aspect, does it not?

'Anyway, that is the problem that was left. The burglar story, which seems unlikely – or the alternative theory that Mrs Sanders was preparing to go out and meet somebody. Did that somebody come to her room by means of the fire escape? Was there a quarrel? Or did he treacherously attack her?'

Miss Marple stopped.

'Well?' said Sir Henry. 'What is the answer?'

'I wondered if any of you could guess.'

'I'm never good at guessing,' said Mrs Bantry. 'It seems a pity that Sanders had such a wonderful alibi; but if it satisfied you it must have been all right.'

Jane Helier moved her beautiful head and asked a question.

'Why,' she said, 'was the hat cupboard locked?'

'How very clever of you, my dear,' said Miss Marple, beaming. 'That's just what I wondered myself. Though the explanation was quite simple. In it were a pair of embroidered slippers and some pocket handkerchiefs that the poor girl was embroidering for her husband for Christmas. That's why she locked the cupboard. The key was found in her handbag.'

'Oh!' said Jane. 'Then it isn't very interesting after all.'

'Oh! but it is,' said Miss Marple. 'It's just the one really interesting thing – the thing that made all the murderer's plans go wrong.'

Everyone stared at the old lady.

'I didn't see it myself for two days,' said Miss Marple. 'I puzzled and puzzled – and then suddenly there it was, all clear. I went to the inspector and asked him to try something and he did.'

'What did you ask him to try?'

'*I asked him to fit that hat on the poor girl's head* – and of course he couldn't. It wouldn't go on. *It wasn't her hat, you see.*'

Mrs Bantry stared.

'But it was on her head to begin with?'

'Not on *her* head –'

Miss Marple stopped a moment to let her words sink in, and then went on.

'We took it for granted that it was poor Gladys's body there; but we never looked at the face. She was face downwards, remember, and the hat hid everything.'

'But she *was* killed?'

'Yes, later. At the moment that we were telephoning to the police, Gladys Sanders was alive and well.'

'You mean it was someone pretending to be her? But surely when you touched her –'

'It was a dead body, right enough,' said Miss Marple gravely.

'But, dash it all,' said Colonel Bantry, 'you can't get

hold of dead bodies right and left. What did they do with the – the first corpse afterwards?'

'He put it back,' said Miss Marple. 'It was a wicked idea – but a very clever one. It was our talk in the drawing-room that put it into his head. The body of poor Mary, the housemaid – why not use it? Remember, the Sanders' room was up amongst the servants' quarters. Mary's room was two doors off. The undertakers wouldn't come till after dark – he counted on that. He carried the body along the balcony (it was dark at five), dressed it in one of his wife's dresses and her big red coat. And then he found the hat cupboard locked! There was only one thing to be done, he fetched one of the poor girl's own hats. No one would notice. He put the sandbag down beside her. Then he went off to establish his alibi.

'He telephoned to his wife – calling himself Mr Littleworth. I don't know what he said to her – she was a credulous girl, as I said just now. But he got her to leave the bridge party early and not to go back to the Hydro, and arranged with her to meet him in the grounds of the Hydro near the fire escape at seven o'clock. He probably told her he had some surprise for her.

'He returns to the Hydro with his friends and arranges that Miss Trollope and I shall discover the crime with him. He even pretends to turn the body over – and I stop him! Then the police are sent for, and he staggers out into the grounds.

'Nobody asked him for an alibi *after* the crime. He meets his wife, takes her up the fire escape, they enter their room. Perhaps he has already told her some story about the body. She stoops over it, and he picks up his sandbag and strikes . . . Oh, dear! It makes me sick to think of, even now! Then quickly he strips off her coat

168

and skirt, hangs them up, and dresses her in the clothes from the other body.

'*But the hat won't go on.* Mary's head is shingled – Gladys Sanders, as I say, had a great bun of hair. He is forced to leave it beside the body and hope no one will notice. Then he carries poor Mary's body back to her own room and arranges it decorously once more.'

'It seems incredible,' said Dr Lloyd. 'The risks he took. The police might have arrived too soon.'

'You remember the line was out of order,' said Miss Marple. 'That was a piece of *his* work. He couldn't afford to have the police on the spot too soon. When they did come, they spent some time in the manager's office before going up to the bedroom. That was the weakest point – the chance that someone might notice the difference between a body that had been dead two hours and one that had been dead just over half an hour; but he counted on the fact that the people who first discovered the crime would have no expert knowledge.'

Dr Lloyd nodded.

'The crime would be supposed to have been committed about a quarter to seven or thereabouts, I suppose,' he said. 'It was actually committed at seven or a few minutes after. When the police surgeon examined the body it would be about half past seven at earliest. He couldn't possibly tell.'

'I am the person who should have known,' said Miss Marple. 'I felt the poor girl's hand and it was icy cold. Yet a short time later the inspector spoke as though the murder must have been committed just before we arrived – and I saw nothing!'

'I think you saw a good deal, Miss Marple,' said Sir Henry. 'The case was before my time. I don't even remember hearing of it. What happened?'

'Sanders was hanged,' said Miss Marple crisply. 'And a good job too. I have never regretted my part in bringing that man to justice. I've no patience with modern humanitarian scruples about capital punishment.'

Her stern face softened.

'But I have often reproached myself bitterly with failing to save the life of that poor girl. But who would have listened to an old woman jumping to conclusions? Well, well – who knows? Perhaps it was better for her to die while life was still happy than it would have been for her to live on, unhappy and disillusioned, in a world that would have seemed suddenly horrible. She loved that scoundrel and trusted him. She never found him out.'

'Well, then,' said Jane Helier, 'she was all right. Quite all right. I wish –' she stopped.

Miss Marple looked at the famous, the beautiful, the successful Jane Helier and nodded her head gently.

'I see, my dear,' she said very gently. 'I see.'

The Herb of Death

'Now then, Mrs B,' said Sir Henry Clithering encouragingly.

Mrs Bantry, his hostess, looked at him in cold reproof.

'I've told you before that I will *not* be called Mrs B. It's not dignified.'

'Scheherazade, then.'

'And even less am I Sche – what's her name! I never can tell a story properly, ask Arthur if you don't believe me.'

'You're quite good at the facts, Dolly,' said Colonel Bantry, 'but poor at the embroidery.'

'That's just it,' said Mrs Bantry. She flapped the bulb catalogue she was holding on the table in front of her. 'I've been listening to you all and I don't know how you do it. "He said, she said, you wondered, they thought, everyone implied" – well, I just couldn't and there it is! And besides I don't know anything to tell a story about.'

'We can't believe that, Mrs Bantry,' said Dr Lloyd. He shook his grey head in mocking disbelief.

Old Miss Marple said in her gentle voice: 'Surely dear –'

Mrs Bantry continued obstinately to shake her head.

'You don't know how banal my life is. What with the servants and the difficulties of getting scullery maids,

171

and just going to town for clothes, and dentists, and Ascot (which Arthur hates) and then the garden –'

'Ah!' said Dr Lloyd. 'The garden. We all know where your heart lies, Mrs Bantry.'

'It must be nice to have a garden,' said Jane Helier, the beautiful young actress. 'That is, if you hadn't got to dig, or to get your hands messed up. I'm ever so fond of flowers.'

'The garden,' said Sir Henry. 'Can't we take that as a starting point? Come, Mrs B. The poisoned bulb, the deadly daffodils, the herb of death!'

'Now it's odd your saying that,' said Mrs Bantry. 'You've just reminded me. Arthur, do you remember that business at Clodderham Court? You know. Old Sir Ambrose Bercy. Do you remember what a courtly charming old man we thought him?'

'Why, of course. Yes, that *was* a strange business. Go ahead, Dolly.'

'You'd better tell it, dear.'

'Nonsense. Go ahead. Must paddle your own canoe. I did my bit just now.'

Mrs Bantry drew a deep breath. She clasped her hands and her face registered complete mental anguish. She spoke rapidly and fluently.

'Well, there's really not much to tell. The Herb of Death – that's what put it into my head, though in my own mind I call it *sage and onions*.'

'Sage and onions?' asked Dr Lloyd.

Mrs Bantry nodded.

'That was how it happened you see,' she explained. 'We were staying, Arthur and I, with Sir Ambrose Bercy at Clodderham Court, and one day, by mistake (though very stupidly, I've always thought) a lot of foxglove leaves were picked with the sage. The ducks for dinner that night were stuffed with it and everyone was very ill, and one poor girl – Sir Ambrose's ward – died of it.'

She stopped.

'Dear, dear,' said Miss Marple, 'how very tragic.'

'Wasn't it?'

'Well,' said Sir Henry, 'what next?'

'There isn't any next,' said Mrs Bantry, 'that's all.'

Everyone gasped. Though warned beforehand, they had not expected quite such brevity as this.

'But, my dear lady,' remonstrated Sir Henry, 'it can't be all. What you have related is a tragic occurrence, but not in any sense of the word a problem.'

'Well, of course there's some more,' said Mrs Bantry. 'But if I were to tell you it, you'd know what it was.'

She looked defiantly round the assembly and said plaintively:

'I told you I couldn't dress things up and make it sound properly like a story ought to do.'

'Ah ha!' said Sir Henry. He sat up in his chair and adjusted an eyeglass. 'Really, you know, Scheherazade, this is most refreshing. Our ingenuity is challenged. I'm not so sure you haven't done it on purpose – to stimulate our curiosity. A few brisk rounds of ''Twenty Questions'' is indicated, I think. Miss Marple, will you begin?'

'I'd like to know something about the cook,' said Miss Marple. 'She must have been a very stupid woman, or else very inexperienced.'

'She was just very stupid,' said Mrs Bantry. 'She cried a great deal afterwards and said the leaves had been picked and brought in to her as sage, and how was she to know?'

'Not one who thought for herself,' said Miss Marple.

'Probably an elderly woman and, I daresay, a very good cook?'

'Oh! excellent,' said Mrs Bantry.

'Your turn, Miss Helier,' said Sir Henry.

'Oh! You mean – to ask a question?' there was a pause while Jane pondered. Finally she said helplessly, 'Really – I don't know what to ask.'

Her beautiful eyes looked appealingly at Sir Henry.

'Why not dramatis personae, Miss Helier?' he suggested smiling.

Jane still looked puzzled.

'Characters in order of their appearance,' said Sir Henry gently.

'Oh, yes,' said Jane. 'That's a good idea.'

Mrs Bantry began briskly to tick people off on her fingers.

'Sir Ambrose – Sylvia Keene (that's the girl who died) – a friend of hers who was staying there, Maud Wye, one of those dark ugly girls who manage to make an effort somehow – I never know how they do it. Then there was a Mr Curle who had come down to discuss books with Sir Ambrose – you know, rare books – queer old things in Latin – all musty parchment. There was Jerry Lorimer – he was a kind of next door neighbour. His place, Fairlies, joined Sir Ambrose's estate. And there was Mrs Carpenter, one of those middle-aged pussies who always seem to manage to dig themselves in comfortably somewhere. She was by way of being *dame de compagnie* to Sylvia, I suppose.'

'If it is my turn,' said Sir Henry, 'and I suppose it is, as I'm sitting next to Miss Helier, I want a good deal. I want a short verbal portrait, please, Mrs Bantry, of all the foregoing.'

'Oh!' Mrs Bantry hesitated.

'Sir Ambrose now,' continued Sir Henry. 'Start with him. What was he like?'

'Oh! he was a very distinguished-looking old man – and not so very old really – not more than sixty, I suppose. But he was very delicate – he had a weak heart,

174

could never go upstairs – he had to have a lift put in, and so that made him seem older than he was. Very charming manners – *courtly* – that's the word that describes him best. You never saw him ruffled or upset. He had beautiful white hair and a particularly charming voice.'

'Good,' said Sir Henry. 'I see Sir Ambrose. Now the girl Sylvia – what did you say her name was?'

'Sylvia Keene. She was pretty – really *very* pretty. Fair haired, you know, and a lovely skin. Not, perhaps, very clever. In fact, rather stupid.'

'Oh! come, Dolly,' protested her husband.

'Arthur, of course, wouldn't think so,' said Mrs Bantry drily. 'But she *was* stupid – she really never said anything worth listening to.'

'One of the most graceful creatures I ever saw,' said Colonel Bantry warmly. 'See her playing tennis – charming, simply charming. And she was full of fun – most amusing little thing. And such a pretty way with her. I bet the young fellows all thought so.'

'That's just where you're wrong,' said Mrs Bantry. 'Youth, as such, has no charms for young men nowadays. It's only old buffers like you, Arthur, who sit maundering on about young girls.'

'Being young's no good,' said Jane. 'You've got to have SA.'

'What,' said Miss Marple, 'is SA?'

'Sex appeal,' said Jane.

'Ah! yes,' said Miss Marple. 'What in my day they used to call "having the come hither in your eye".'

'Not a bad description,' said Sir Henry. 'The *dame de compagnie* you described, I think, as a pussy, Mrs Bantry?'

'I didn't mean a *cat*, you know,' said Mrs Bantry. 'It's quite different. Just a big soft white purry person. Always very sweet. That's what Adelaide Carpenter was like.'

'What sort of aged woman?'

'Oh! I should say fortyish. She'd been there some time – ever since Sylvia was eleven, I believe. A very tactful person. One of those widows left in unfortunate circumstances with plenty of aristocratic relations, but no ready cash. I didn't like her myself – but then I never do like people with very white long hands. And I don't like pussies.'

'Mr Curle?'

'Oh! one of those elderly stooping men. There are so many of them about, you'd hardly know one from the other. He showed enthusiasm when talking about his musty books, but not at any other time. I don't think Sir Ambrose knew him very well.'

'And Jerry next door?'

'A really charming boy. He was engaged to Sylvia. That's what made it so sad.'

'Now I wonder –' began Miss Marple, and then stopped.

'What?'

'Nothing, dear.'

Sir Henry looked at the old lady curiously. Then he said thoughtfully:

'So this young couple were engaged. Had they been engaged long?'

'About a year. Sir Ambrose had opposed the engagement on the plea that Sylvia was too young. But after a year's engagement he had given in and the marriage was to have taken place quite soon.'

'Ah! Had the young lady any property?'

'Next to nothing – a bare hundred or two a year.'

'No rat in that hole, Clithering,' said Colonel Bantry, and laughed.

'It's the doctor's turn to ask a question,' said Sir Henry. 'I stand down.'

'My curiosity is mainly professional,' said Dr Lloyd. 'I should like to know what medical evidence was given at the inquest – that is, if our hostess remembers, or, indeed, if she knows.'

'I know roughly,' said Mrs Bantry. 'It was poisoning by digitalin – is that right?'

Dr Lloyd nodded.

'The active principle of the foxglove – digitalis – acts on the heart. Indeed, it is a very valuable drug in some forms of heart trouble. A very curious case altogether. I would never have believed that eating a preparation of foxglove leaves could possibly result fatally. These ideas of eating poisonous leaves and berries are very much exaggerated. Very few people realize that the vital principle, or alkaloid, has to be extracted with much care and preparation.'

'Mrs MacArthur sent some special bulbs round to Mrs Toomie the other day,' said Miss Marple. 'And Mrs Toomie's cook mistook them for onions, and all the Toomies were very ill indeed.'

'But they didn't die of it,' said Dr Lloyd.

'No. They didn't die of it,' admitted Miss Marple.

'A girl I knew died of ptomaine poisoning,' said Jane Helier.

'We must get on with investigating the crime,' said Sir Henry.

'Crime?' said Jane, startled. 'I thought it was an accident.'

'If it were an accident,' said Sir Henry gently, 'I do not think Mrs Bantry would have told us this story. No, as I read it, this was an accident only in appearance – behind it is something more sinister. I remember a case – various guests in a house party were chatting after dinner. The walls were adorned with all kinds of old-fashioned weapons. Entirely as a joke one of the party seized an ancient horse pistol and pointed it at another man, pretending to fire it. The pistol was loaded and went off, killing the man. We had to ascertain in that case, first, who had secretly prepared and loaded that pistol, and secondly who had so led and directed the conversation that that final bit of horseplay resulted – for the man who had fired the pistol was entirely innocent!

'It seems to me we have much the same problem here. Those digitalis leaves were deliberately mixed with the sage, knowing what the result would be. Since we exonerate the cook – we do exonerate the cook, don't we? – the question arises: Who picked the leaves and delivered them to the kitchen?'

'That's easily answered,' said Mrs Bantry. 'At least the last part of it is. It was Sylvia herself who took the leaves to the kitchen. It was part of her daily job to gather things like salad or herbs, bunches of young carrots – all the sort of things that gardeners never pick right. They hate giving you anything young and tender – they wait for them to be fine specimens. Sylvia and Mrs Carpenter used to see to a lot of these things themselves. And there was foxglove actually growing all amongst the sage in one corner, so the mistake was quite natural.'

'But did Sylvia actually pick them herself?'

'That, nobody ever knew. It was assumed so.'

'Assumptions,' said Sir Henry, 'are dangerous things.'

'But I do know that Mrs Carpenter didn't pick them,' said Mrs Bantry. 'Because, as it happened, she was walking with me on the terrace that morning. We went out there after breakfast. It was unusually nice and warm for early spring. Sylvia went alone down into the garden, but later I saw her walking arm-in-arm with Maud Wye.'

'So they were great friends, were they?' asked Miss Marple.

'Yes,' said Mrs Bantry. She seemed as though about to say something, but did not do so.

'Had she been staying there long?' asked Miss Marple.

'About a fortnight,' said Mrs Bantry.

There was a note of trouble in her voice.

'You didn't like Miss Wye?' suggested Sir Henry.

'I did. That's just it. I did.'

The trouble in her voice had grown to distress.

'You're keeping something back, Mrs Bantry,' said Sir Henry accusingly.

'I wondered just now,' said Miss Marple, 'but I didn't like to go on.'

'When did you wonder?'

'When you said that the young people were engaged. You said that that was what made it so sad. But, if you know what I mean, your voice didn't sound right when you said it – not convincing, you know.'

'What a dreadful person you are,' said Mrs Bantry. 'You always seem to *know*. Yes, I was thinking of something. But I don't really know whether I ought to say it or not.'

'You must say it,' said Sir Henry. 'Whatever your scruples, it mustn't be kept back.'

'Well, it was just this,' said Mrs Bantry. 'One evening – in fact the very evening before the tragedy – I happened to go out on the terrace before dinner. The window in the drawing-room was open. And as it chanced I saw Jerry Lorimer and Maud Wye. He was – well – kissing her. Of course I didn't know whether it was just a sort of chance affair, or whether – well, I mean, one can't *tell*. I knew Sir Ambrose never had really liked Jerry Lorimer – so perhaps he knew he was that kind of young man. But one thing I *am* sure of: that girl, Maud Wye, was *really* fond of him. You'd only to see her looking at him when she was off guard. And I think, too, they were really better suited than he and Sylvia were.'

'I am going to ask a question quickly, before Miss Marple can,' said Sir Henry. 'I want to know whether, after the tragedy, Jerry Lorimer married Maud Wye?'

'Yes,' said Mrs Bantry. 'He did. Six months afterwards.'

'Oh! Scheherezade, Scheherezade,' said Sir Henry. 'To think of the way you told us this story at first! Bare bones indeed – and to think of the amount of flesh we're finding on them now.'

'Don't speak so ghoulishly,' said Mrs Bantry. 'And don't use the word flesh. Vegetarians always do. They say, "I never eat flesh" in a way that puts you right off your little beefsteak. Mr Curle was a vegetarian. He used to eat some peculiar stuff that looked like bran for breakfast. Those elderly stooping men with beards are often faddy. They have patent kinds of underwear, too.'

'What on earth, Dolly,' said her husband, 'do you know about Mr Curle's underwear?'

'Nothing,' said Mrs Bantry with dignity. 'I was just making a guess.'

'I'll amend my former statement,' said Sir Henry. 'I'll say instead that the dramatis personae in your problem are very interesting. I'm beginning to see them all – eh, Miss Marple?'

'Human nature is always interesting, Sir Henry. And it's curious to see how certain types always tend to act in exactly the same way.'

'Two women and a man,' said Sir Henry. 'The old eternal human triangle. Is that the base of our problem here? I rather fancy it is.'

Dr Lloyd cleared his throat.

'I've been thinking,' he said rather diffidently. 'Do you say, Mrs Bantry, that you yourself were ill?'

'Was I not! So was Arthur! So was everyone!'

'That's just it – everyone,' said the doctor. 'You see what I mean? In Sir Henry's story which he told us just now, one man shot another – he didn't have to shoot the whole room full.'

'I don't understand,' said Jane. 'Who shot who?'

'I'm saying that whoever planned this thing went about it very curiously, either with a blind belief in chance, or else with an absolutely reckless disregard for human life. I can hardly believe there is a man capable of deliberately poisoning eight people with the object of removing one amongst them.'

'I see your point,' said Sir Henry, thoughtfully. 'I confess I ought to have thought of that.'   ·

'And mightn't he have poisoned himself too?' asked Jane.

'Was anyone absent from dinner that night?' asked Miss Marple.

Mrs Bantry shook her head.

'Everyone was there.'

'Except Mr Lorimer, I suppose, my dear. He wasn't staying in the house, was he?'

'No; but he was dining there that evening,' said Mrs Bantry.

'Oh!' said Miss Marple in a changed voice. 'That makes all the difference in the world.'

She frowned vexedly to herself.

'I've been very stupid,' she murmured. 'Very stupid indeed.'

'I confess your point worries me, Lloyd,' said Sir Henry.

'How ensure that the girl, and the girl only, should get a fatal dose?'

'You can't,' said the doctor. 'That brings me to the point I'm going to make. *Supposing the girl was not the intended victim after all?*'

'What?'

'In all cases of food poisoning, the result is very uncertain. Several people share a dish. What happens? One or two are slightly ill, two more, say, are seriously indisposed, one dies. That's the way of it – there's no certainty anywhere. But there are cases where another factor might enter in. Digitalin is a drug that acts directly on the heart – as I've told you it's prescribed in certain cases. *Now, there was one person in that house who suffered from a heart complaint.* Suppose he was the victim selected? What would not be fatal to the rest *would* be fatal to him – or so the murderer might reasonably suppose. That the thing turned out differently is only a proof of what I was saying just now – the uncertainty and unreliability of the effects of drugs on human beings.'

'Sir Ambrose,' said Sir Henry, 'you think *he* was the person aimed at? Yes, yes – and the girl's death was a mistake.'

'Who got his money after he was dead?' asked Jane.

'A very sound question, Miss Helier. One of the first we always ask in my late profession,' said Sir Henry.

'Sir Ambrose had a son,' said Mrs Bantry slowly. 'He had quarrelled with him many years previously. The boy was wild, I believe. Still, it was not in Sir Ambrose's power to disinherit him – Clodderham Court was entailed. Martin Bercy succeeded to the title and estate. There was, however, a good deal of other property that Sir Ambrose could leave as he chose, and that he left to his ward Sylvia. I know this because Sir Ambrose died less than a year after the events I am telling you of, and he had not troubled to make a new will after Sylvia's death. I think the money went to the Crown – or perhaps it was to his son as next of kin – I don't really remember.'

'So it was only to the interest of a son who wasn't there and the girl who died herself to make away with him,' said Sir Henry thoughtfully. 'That doesn't seem very promising.'

'Didn't the other woman get anything?' asked Jane. 'The one Mrs Bantry calls the Pussy woman.'

'She wasn't mentioned in the will,' said Mrs Bantry.

'Miss Marple, you're not listening,' said Sir Henry. 'You're somewhere far away.'

'I was thinking of old Mr Badger, the chemist,' said Miss Marple. 'He had a very young housekeeper – young enough to be not only his daughter, but his grand-daughter. Not a word to anyone, and his family, a lot of nephews and nieces, full of expectations. And when he died, would you believe it, he'd been secretly married to her for two years? Of course Mr Badger was a chemist, and a very rude, common old man as well, and Sir Ambrose Bercy was a very courtly gentleman, so Mrs Bantry says, but for all that human nature is much the same everywhere.'

There was a pause. Sir Henry looked very hard at Miss Marple who looked back at him with gently quizzical blue eyes. Jane Helier broke the silence.

'Was this Mrs Carpenter good looking?' she asked.

'Yes, in a very quiet way. Nothing startling.'

'She had a very sympathetic voice,' said Colonel Bantry.

'Purring – that's what I call it,' said Mrs Bantry. 'Purring!'

'You'll be called a cat yourself one of these days, Dolly.'

'I like being a cat in my home circle,' said Mrs Bantry.

'I don't much like women anyway, and you know it. I like men and flowers.'

'Excellent taste,' said Sir Henry. 'Especially in putting men first.'

'That was tact,' said Mrs Bantry. 'Well, now, what about my little problem? I've been quite fair, I think. Arthur, don't you think I've been fair?'

'Yes, my dear. I don't think there'll be any inquiry into the running by the stewards of the Jockey Club.'

'First boy,' said Mrs Bantry, pointing a finger at Sir Henry.

'I'm going to be long winded. Because, you see, I haven't really got any feeling of certainty about the matter. First, Sir Ambrose. Well, he wouldn't take such an original method of committing suicide – and on the other hand he certainly had nothing to gain by the death of his ward. Exit Sir Ambrose. Mr Curle. No motive for death of girl. If Sir Ambrose was intended victim, he might possibly have purloined a rare manuscript or two that no one else would miss. Very thin and most unlikely. So I think that, in spite of Mrs Bantry's suspicions as to his underclothing, Mr Curle is cleared. Miss Wye. Motive for death of Sir Ambrose – none. Motive for death of Sylvia pretty strong. She wanted Sylvia's young man, and wanted him rather badly – from Mrs Bantry's account. She was with Sylvia that morning in the garden, so had opportunity to pick leaves. No, we can't dismiss Miss Wye so easily. Young Lorimer. He's got a motive in either case. If he gets rid of his sweetheart, he can marry the other girl. Still it seems a bit drastic to kill her – what's a broken engagement these days? If Sir Ambrose dies, he will marry a rich girl instead of a poor one. That might be important or not – depends on his financial position. If I find that his estate was heavily mortgaged and that Mrs Bantry has deliberately withheld that fact from us, I shall claim a foul. Now Mrs Carpenter. You know, I have suspicions of Mrs Carpenter. Those white hands, for one thing, and her excellent alibi at the time the herbs were picked – I always distrust alibis. And I've got another reason for suspecting her which I will keep to myself. Still, on the whole, if I've got to plump, I shall plump for Miss Maude Wye, because there's more evidence against her than anyone else.'

'Next boy,' said Mrs Bantry, and pointed at Dr Lloyd.

'I think you're wrong, Clithering, in sticking to the theory that the girl's death was meant. I am convinced that the murderer intended to do away with Sir Ambrose. I don't think that young Lorimer had the necessary knowledge. I am inclined to believe that Mrs Carpenter was the guilty party. She had been a long time with the family, knew all about the state of Sir Ambrose's health, and could easily arrange for this girl Sylvia (who, you said yourself, was rather stupid) to pick the right leaves. Motive, I confess, I don't see; but I hazard the guess that Sir Ambrose had at one time made a will in which she was mentioned. That's the best I can do.'

Mrs Bantry's pointing finger went on to Jane Helier.

'I don't know what to say,' said Jane, 'except this: Why shouldn't the girl herself have done it? She took the leaves into the kitchen after all. And you say Sir Ambrose had been sticking out against her marriage. If he died, she'd get the money and be able to marry at once. She'd know just as much about Sir Ambrose's health as Mrs Carpenter would.'

Mrs Bantry's finger came slowly round to Miss Marple.

'Now then, School Marm,' she said.

'Sir Henry has put it all very clearly – very clearly

indeed,' said Miss Marple. 'And Dr Lloyd was so right in what he said. Between them they seem to have made things so very clear. Only I don't think Dr Lloyd quite realized one aspect of what he said. You see, not being Sir Ambrose's medical adviser, he couldn't know just what kind of heart trouble Sir Ambrose had, could he?'

'I don't quite see what you mean, Miss Marple,' said Dr Lloyd.

'You're assuming – aren't you? – that Sir Ambrose had the kind of heart that digitalin would affect adversely? But there's nothing to prove that that's so. It might be just the other way about.'

'The other way about?'

'Yes, you did say that it was often prescribed for heart trouble?'

'Even then, Miss Marple, I don't see what that leads to?'

'Well, it would mean that he would have digitalin in his possession quite naturally – without having to account for it. What I am trying to say (I always express myself so badly) is this: Supposing you wanted to poison anyone with a fatal dose of digitalin. Wouldn't the simplest and easiest way be to arrange for everyone to be poisoned – actually by digitalis leaves? It wouldn't be fatal in anyone else's case, of course, but no one would be surprised at one victim because, as Dr Lloyd said, these things are so uncertain. No one would be likely to ask whether the girl had actually had a fatal dose of infusion of digitalis or something of that kind. He might have put it in a cocktail, or in her coffee or even made her drink it quite simply as a tonic.'

'You mean Sir Ambrose poisoned his ward, the charming girl whom he loved?'

'That's just it,' said Miss Marple. 'Like Mr Badger and his young housekeeper. Don't tell me it's absurd for a man of sixty to fall in love with a girl of twenty. It happens every day – and I daresay with an old autocrat like Sir Ambrose, it might take him queerly. These things become a madness sometimes. He couldn't bear the thought of her getting married – did his best to oppose it – and failed. His mad jealousy became so great that he preferred killing her to letting her go to young Lorimer. He must have thought of it some time beforehand, because that foxglove seed would have to be sown among the sage. He'd pick it himself when the time came, and send her into the kitchen with it. It's horrible to think of, but I suppose we must take as merciful a view of it as we can. Gentlemen of that age are sometimes very peculiar indeed where young girls are concerned. Our last organist – but there, I mustn't talk scandal.'

'Mrs Bantry,' said Sir Henry. 'Is this so?'

Mrs Bantry nodded.

'Yes. I'd no idea of it – never dreamed of the thing being anything but an accident. Then, after Sir Ambrose's death, I got a letter. He had left directions to send it to me. He told me the truth in it. I don't know why – but he and I always got on very well together.'

In the momentary silence, she seemed to feel an unspoken criticism and went on hastily:

'You think I'm betraying a confidence – but that isn't so. I've changed all the names. He wasn't really called Sir Ambrose Bercy. Didn't you see how Arthur stared stupidly when I said that name to him? He didn't understand at first. I've changed everything. It's like they say in magazines and in the beginning of books: "All the characters in this story are purely fictitious." You never know who they really are.'

The Affair at the Bungalow

'I've thought of something,' said Jane Helier.

Her beautiful face was lit up with the confident smile of a child expecting approbation. It was a smile such as moved audiences nightly in London, and which had made the fortunes of photographers.

'It happened,' she went on carefully, 'to a friend of mine.'

Everyone made encouraging but slightly hypocritical noises. Colonel Bantry, Mrs Bantry, Sir Henry Clithering, Dr Lloyd and old Miss Marple were one and all convinced that Jane's 'friend' was Jane herself. She would have been quite incapable of remembering or taking an interest in anything affecting anyone else.

'My friend,' went on Jane, '(I won't mention her name) was an actress – a very well-known actress.'

No one expressed surprise. Sir Henry Clithering thought to himself: 'Now I wonder how many sentences it will be before she forgets to keep up the fiction, and says "I" instead of "She"?'

'My friend was on tour in the provinces – this was a year or two ago. I suppose I'd better not give the name of the place. It was a riverside town not very far from London. I'll call it –'

She paused, her brows perplexed in thought. The invention of even a simple name appeared to be too much for her. Sir Henry came to the rescue.

'Shall we call it Riverbury?' he suggested gravely.

'Oh, yes, that would do splendidly. Riverbury, I'll remember that. Well, as I say, this – my friend – was at Riverbury with her company, and a very curious thing happened.'

She puckered her brows again.

'It's very difficult,' she said plaintively, 'to say just what you want. One gets things mixed up and tells the wrong things first.'

'You're doing it beautifully,' said Dr Lloyd encouragingly. 'Go on.'

'Well, this curious thing happened. My friend was sent for to the police station. And she went. It seemed there had been a burglary at a riverside bungalow and they'd arrested a young man, and he told a very odd story. And so they sent for her.

'She'd never been to a police station before, but they were very nice to her – very nice indeed.'

'They would be, I'm sure,' said Sir Henry.

'The sergeant – I think it was a sergeant – or it may have been an inspector – gave her a chair and explained things, and of course I saw at once that it was some mistake –'

'Aha,' thought Sir Henry. 'I. Here we are. I thought as much.'

'My friend said so,' continued Jane, serenely unconscious of her self-betrayal. 'She explained she had been rehearsing with her understudy at the hotel and that she'd never even heard of this Mr Faulkener. And the sergeant said, "Miss Hel –"'

She stopped and flushed.

'Miss Helman,' suggested Sir Henry with a twinkle.

'Yes – yes, that would do. Thank you. He said, "Well, Miss Helman, I felt it must be some mistake, knowing that you were stopping at the Bridge Hotel," and he

189

said would I have any objection to confronting – or was it being confronted? I can't remember.'

'It doesn't really matter,' said Sir Henry reassuringly.

'Anyway, with the young man. So I said, "Of course not." And they brought him and said, "This is Miss Helier," and – Oh!' Jane broke off open-mouthed.

'Never mind, my dear,' said Miss Marple consolingly. 'We were bound to guess, you know. And you haven't given us the name of the place or anything that really matters.'

'Well,' said Jane. 'I did mean to tell it as though it happened to someone else. But it *is* difficult, isn't it! I mean one forgets so.'

Everyone assured her that it was very difficult, and soothed and reassured, she went on with her slightly involved narrative.

'He was a nice looking man – quite a nice looking man. Young, with reddish hair. His mouth just opened when he saw me. And the sergeant said, "Is this the lady?" And he said, "No, indeed it isn't. What an ass I have been." And I smiled at him and said it didn't matter.'

'I can picture the scene,' said Sir Henry.

Jane Helier frowned.

'Let me see – how had I better go on?'

'Supposing you tell us what it was all about, dear,' said Miss Marple, so mildly that no one could suspect her of irony. 'I mean what the young man's mistake was, and about the burglary.'

'Oh, yes,' said Jane. 'Well, you see, this young man – Leslie Faulkener, his name was – had written a play. He'd written several plays, as a matter of fact, though none of them had ever been taken. And he had sent this particular play to me to read. I didn't know about it, because of course I have hundreds of plays sent to me and I read very few of them myself – only the ones I know something about. Anyway, there it was, and it seems that Mr Faulkener got a letter from me – only it turned out not to be really from me – you understand –'

She paused anxiously, and they assured her that they understood.

'Saying that I'd read the play, and liked it very much and would he come down and talk it over with me. And it gave the address – The Bungalow, Riverbury. So Mr Faulkener was frightfully pleased and he came down and arrived at this place – The Bungalow. A parlourmaid opened the door, and he asked for Miss Helier, and she said Miss Helier was in and expecting him and showed him into the drawing-room, and there a woman came to him. And he accepted her as me as a matter of course – which seems queer because after all he had seen me act and my photographs are very well known, aren't they?'

'Over the length and breadth of England,' said Mrs Bantry promptly. 'But there's often a lot of difference between a photograph and its original, my dear Jane. And there's a great deal of difference between behind the footlights and off the stage. It's not every actress who stands the test as well as you do, remember.'

'Well,' said Jane slightly mollified, 'that may be so. Anyway, he described this woman as tall and fair with big blue eyes and very good-looking, so I suppose it must have been near enough. He certainly had no suspicions. She sat down and began talking about his play and said she was anxious to do it. Whilst they were talking cocktails were brought in and Mr Faulkener had one as a matter of course. Well – that's all he remembers – having this cocktail. When he woke up, or came to himself, or whatever you call it – he was lying out in the road, by the hedge, of course, so that there would be no danger of his being run over. He felt very queer and shaky – so much so that he just got up and staggered along the road not quite knowing where he was going. He said if he'd had his sense about him he'd have gone back to the bungalow and tried to find out what had happened. But he felt just stupid and mazed and walked along without quite knowing what he was doing. He was just more or less coming to himself when the police arrested him.'

'Why did the police arrest him?' asked Dr Lloyd.

'Oh! didn't I tell you?' said Jane opening her eyes very wide. 'How very stupid I am. The burglary.'

'You mentioned a burglary – but you didn't say where or what or why,' said Mrs Bantry.

'Well, this bungalow – the one he went to, of course – it wasn't mine at all. It belonged to a man whose name was –'

Again Jane furrowed her brows.

'Do you want me to be godfather again?' asked Sir Henry. 'Pseudonyms supplied free of charge. Describe the tenant and I'll do the naming.'

'It was taken by a rich city man – a knight.'

'Sir Herman Cohen,' suggested Sir Henry.

'That will do beautifully. He took it for a lady – she was the wife of an actor, and she was also an actress herself.'

'We'll call the actor Claud Leason,' said Sir Henry, 'and the lady would be known by her stage name, I suppose, so we'll call her Miss Mary Kerr.'

'I think you're awfully clever,' said Jane. 'I don't know how you think of these things so easily. Well, you see this was a sort of week-end cottage for Sir Herman – did you say Herman? – and the lady. And, of course, his wife knew nothing about it.'

'Which is so often the case,' said Sir Henry.

'And he'd given this actress woman a good deal of jewellery including some very fine emeralds.'

'Ah!' said Dr Lloyd. 'Now we're getting at it.'

'This jewellery was at the bungalow, just locked up in a jewel case. The police said it was very careless – anyone might have taken it.'

'You see, Dolly,' said Colonel Bantry. 'What do I always tell you?'

'Well, in my experience,' said Mrs Bantry, 'it's always the people who are so dreadfully careful who lose things. I don't lock mine up in a jewel case – I keep it in a drawer loose, under my stockings. I daresay if – what's her name? – Mary Kerr had done the same, it would never have been stolen.'

'It would,' said Jane, 'because all the drawers were burst open, and the contents strewn about.'

'Then they weren't really looking for jewels,' said Mrs Bantry. 'They were looking for secret papers. That's what always happens in books.'

'I don't know about secret papers,' said Jane doubtfully. 'I never heard of any.'

'Don't be distracted, Miss Helier,' said Colonel Bantry. 'Dolly's wild red-herrings are not to be taken seriously.'

'About the burglary,' said Sir Henry.

'Yes. Well, the police were rung up by someone who said she was Miss Mary Kerr. She said the bungalow had been burgled and described a young man with red hair who had called there that morning. Her maid had thought there was something odd about him and had refused him admittance, but later they had seen him getting out through a window. She described the man so accurately that the police arrested him only an hour later and then he told his story and showed them the letter from me. And as I told you, they fetched me and when he saw me he said what I told you – that it hadn't been me at all!'

'A very curious story,' said Dr Lloyd. 'Did Mr Faulkener know this Miss Kerr?'

'No, he didn't – or he said he didn't. But I haven't told you the most curious part yet. The police went to the bungalow of course, and they found everything as described – drawers pulled out and jewels gone, but the whole place was empty. It wasn't till some hours later that Mary Kerr came back, and when she did she said she'd never rung them up at all and this was the first she'd heard of it. It seemed that she had had a wire that morning from a manager offering her a most important part and making an appointment, so she had naturally rushed up to town to keep it. When she got there, she found that the whole thing was a hoax. No telegram had ever been sent.'

'A common enough ruse to get her out of the way,' commented Sir Henry. 'What about the servants?'

'The same sort of thing happened there. There was only one, and she was rung up on the telephone – apparently by Mary Kerr, who said she had left a most important thing behind. She directed the maid to bring up a certain handbag which was in the drawer of her bedroom. She was to catch the first train. The maid did so, of course locking up the house; but when she arrived at Miss Kerr's club, where she had been told to meet her mistress, she waited there in vain.'

'H'm,' said Sir Henry. 'I begin to see. The house was left empty, and to make an entry by one of the windows would present few difficulties, I should imagine. But I don't quite see where Mr Faulkener comes in. Who did ring up the police, if it wasn't Miss Kerr?'

'That's what nobody knew or ever found out.'

'Curious,' said Sir Henry. 'Did the young man turn out to be genuinely the person he said he was?'

'Oh, yes, that part of it was all right. He'd even got the letter which was supposed to be written by me. It wasn't the least bit like my handwriting – but then, of course, he couldn't be supposed to know that.'

'Well, let's state the position clearly,' said Sir Henry. 'Correct me if I go wrong. The lady and the maid are decoyed from the house. This young man is decoyed down there by means of a bogus letter – colour being lent to this last by the fact that you actually are performing at Riverbury that week. The young man is doped, and the police are rung up and have their suspicions directed against him. A burglary actually has taken place. I presume the jewels were taken?'

'Oh, yes.'

'Were they ever recovered?'

'No, never. I think, as a matter of fact, Sir Herman tried to hush things up all he knew how. But he couldn't manage it, and I rather fancy his wife started divorce proceedings in consequence. Still, I don't really know about that.'

'What happened to Mr Leslie Faulkener?'

'He was released in the end. The police said they hadn't really got enough against him. Don't you think the whole thing was rather odd?'

'Distinctly odd. The first question is whose story to believe? In telling it, Miss Helier, I noticed that you incline towards believing Mr Faulkener. Have you any reason for doing so beyond your own instinct in the matter?'

'No – no,' said Jane unwillingly. 'I suppose I haven't. But he was so very nice, and so apologetic for having mistaken anyone else for me, that I feel sure he *must* have been telling the truth.'

'I see,' said Sir Henry smiling. 'But you must admit that he could have invented the story quite easily. He could write the letter purporting to be from you himself. He could also dope himself after successfully committing the burglary. But I confess I don't see where the *point* of all that would be. Easier to enter the house, help himself, and disappear quietly – unless just possibly he was observed by someone in the neighbourhood and knew himself to have been observed. Then he might hastily concoct this plan for diverting suspicion from himself and accounting for his presence in the neighbourhood.'

'Was he well off?' asked Miss Marple.

'I don't think so,' said Jane. 'No, I believe he was rather hard up.'

'The whole thing seems curious,' said Dr Lloyd. 'I must confess that if we accept the young man's story as true, it seems to make the case very much more difficult. Why should the unknown woman who pretended to be Miss Helier drag this unknown man into the affair? Why should she stage such an elaborate comedy?'

'Tell me, Jane,' said Mrs Bantry. 'Did young Faulkener ever come face to face with Mary Kerr at any stage of the proceedings?'

'I don't quite know,' said Jane slowly, as she puzzled her brows in remembrance.

'Because if he didn't the case is solved!' said Mrs Bantry. 'I'm sure I'm right. What is easier than to pretend you're called up to town? You telephone to your maid from Paddington or whatever station you arrive at, and as she comes up to town, you go down again. The young man calls by appointment, he's doped, you set the stage for the burglary, overdoing it as much as possible. You telephone the police, give a description of your scapegoat, and off you go to town again. Then you arrive home by a later train and do the surprised innocent.'

'But why should she steal her own jewels, Dolly?'

'They always do,' said Mrs Bantry. 'And anyway, I can think of hundreds of reasons. She may have wanted money at once – old Sir Herman wouldn't give her the cash, perhaps, so she pretends the jewels are stolen and then sells them secretly. Or she may have been being blackmailed by someone who threatened to tell her husband or Sir Herman's wife. Or she may have already sold the jewels and Sir Herman was getting ratty and asking to see them, so she had to do something about it. That's done a good deal in books. Or perhaps she was going to have them reset and she'd got paste replicas. Or – here's a very good idea – and not so much done in books – she pretends they are stolen, gets in an awful state and he gives her a fresh lot. So she gets two lots instead of one. That kind of woman, I am sure, is most frightfully artful.'

'You are clever, Dolly,' said Jane admiringly. 'I never thought of that.'

'You may be clever, but she doesn't say you're right,' said Colonel Bantry. 'I incline to suspicion of the city gentleman. He'd know the sort of telegram to get the lady out of the way, and he could manage the rest easily enough with the help of a new lady friend. Nobody seems to have thought of asking *him* for an alibi.'

'What do you think, Miss Marple?' asked Jane, turning towards the old lady who had sat silent, a puzzled frown on her face.

'My dear, I really don't know what to say. Sir Henry will laugh, but I recall no village parallel to help me this time. Of course there are several questions that suggest themselves. For instance, the servant question. In – ahem – an irregular ménage of the kind you describe, the servant employed would doubtless be perfectly aware of the state of things, and a really nice girl would not take such a place – her mother wouldn't let her for a minute. So I think we can assume that the maid was *not* a really trustworthy character. She may have been in league with the thieves. She would leave the house open for them and actually go to London as though sure of the pretence telephone message so as to divert suspicion from herself. I must confess that that seems the most probable solution. Only if ordinary thieves were concerned it seems very odd. It seems to argue more knowledge than a maidservant was likely to have.'

Miss Marple paused and then went on dreamily:

'I can't help feeling that there was some – well, what I must describe as personal feeling about the whole thing. Supposing somebody had a spite, for instance? A young actress that he hadn't treated well? Don't you think that that would explain things better? A deliberate attempt to get him into trouble. That's what it looks like. And yet – that's not entirely satisfactory . . .'

'Why, doctor, you haven't said anything,' said Jane. 'I'd forgotten you.'

'I'm always getting forgotten,' said the grizzled doctor sadly. 'I must have a very inconspicuous personality.'

'Oh, no!' said Jane. 'Do tell us what you think.'

'I'm rather in the position of agreeing with everyone's solutions – and yet with none of them. I myself have a far-fetched and probably totally erroneous theory that the wife may have had something to do with it. Sir Herman's wife, I mean. I've no grounds for thinking so – only you would be surprised if you knew the extraordinary – really *very* extraordinary things that a wronged wife will take it into her head to do.'

'Oh! Dr Lloyd,' cried Miss Marple excitedly. 'How

clever of you. And I never thought of poor Mrs Pebmarsh.'

Jane stared at her.

'Mrs Pebmarsh? Who is Mrs Pebmarsh?'

'Well –' Miss Marple hesitated. 'I don't know that she really comes in. She's a laundress. And she stole an opal pin that was pinned into a blouse and put it in another woman's house.'

Jane looked more fogged than ever.

'And that makes it all perfectly clear to you, Miss Marple?' said Sir Henry, with his twinkle.

But to his surprise Miss Marple shook her head.

'No, I'm afraid it doesn't. I must confess myself completely at a loss. What I do realize is that women must stick together – one should, in an emergency, stand by one's own sex. I think that's the moral of the story Miss Helier has told us.'

'I must confess that that particular ethical significance of the mystery has escaped me,' said Sir Henry gravely. 'Perhaps I shall see the significance of your point more clearly when Miss Helier has revealed the solution.'

'Eh?' said Jane looking rather bewildered.

'I was observing that, in childish language, we "give it up". You and you alone, Miss Helier, have had the high honour of presenting such an absolutely baffling mystery that even Miss Marple has to confess herself defeated.'

'You all give it up?' asked Jane.

'Yes.' After a minute's silence during which he waited for the others to speak, Sir Henry constituted himself spokesman once more. 'That is to say we stand or fall by the sketchy solutions we have tentatively advanced. One each for the mere men, two for Miss Marple, and a round dozen from Mrs B.'

'It was not a dozen,' said Mrs Bantry. 'They were

variations on a main theme. And how often am I to tell you that I will *not* be called Mrs B?'

'So you all give it up,' said Jane thoughtfully. 'That's very interesting.'

She leaned back in her chair and began to polish her nails rather absent-mindedly.

'Well,' said Mrs Bantry. 'Come on, Jane. What is the solution?'

'The solution?'

'Yes. What really happened?'

Jane stared at her.

'I haven't the least idea.'

'*What?*'

'I've always wondered. I thought you were all so clever one of you would be able to tell *me.*'

Everybody harboured feelings of annoyance. It was all very well for Jane to be so beautiful – but at this moment everyone felt that stupidity could be carried too far. Even the most transcendent loveliness could not excuse it.

'You mean the truth was never discovered?' said Sir Henry.

'No. That's why, as I say, I did think you would be able to tell *me.*'

Jane sounded injured. It was plain that she had a grievance.

'Well – I'm – I'm – ' said Colonel Bantry, words failing him.

'You are the most aggravating girl, Jane,' said his wife. 'Anyway, I'm sure and always will be that I was right. If you just tell us the proper names of the people, I shall be *quite* sure.'

'I don't think I could do that,' said Jane slowly.

'No, dear,' said Miss Marple. 'Miss Helier couldn't do that.'

'Of course she could,' said Mrs Bantry. 'Don't be so high minded, Jane. We older folk must have a bit of scandal. At any rate tell us who the city magnate was.'

But Jane shook her head, and Miss Marple, in her old-fashioned way, continued to support the girl.

'It must have been a very distressing business,' she said.

'No,' said Jane truthfully. 'I think – I think rather enjoyed it.'

'Well, perhaps you did,' said Miss Marple. 'I suppose it was a break in the monotony. What play were you acting in?'

'*Smith.*'

'Oh, yes. That's one of Mr Somerset Maugham's, isn't it? All his are very clever, I think. I've seen them nearly all.'

'You're reviving it to go on tour next autumn, aren't you?' asked Mrs Bantry.

Jane nodded.

'Well,' said Miss Marple rising. 'I must go home. Such late hours! But we've had a very entertaining evening. Most unusually so. I think Miss Helier's story wins the prize. Don't you agree?'

'I'm sorry you're angry with me,' said Jane. 'About not knowing the end, I mean. I suppose I should have said so sooner.'

Her tone sounded wistful. Dr Lloyd rose gallantly to the occasion.

'My dear young lady, why should you? You gave us a very pretty problem to sharpen our wits on. I am only sorry we could none of us solve it convincingly.'

'Speak for yourself,' said Mrs Bantry. 'I *did* solve it. I'm convinced I am right.'

'Do you know, I really believe you are,' said Jane. 'What you said sounded so probable.'

'Which of her seven solutions do you refer to?' asked Sir Henry teasingly.

Dr Lloyd gallantly assisted Miss Marple to put on her goloshes. 'Just in case,' as the old lady explained. The doctor was to be her escort to her old-world cottage. Wrapped in several woollen shawls, Miss Marple wished everyone good night once more. She came to Jane Helier last and leaning forward, she murmured something in the actress's ear. A startled 'Oh!' burst from Jane – so loud as to cause the others to turn their heads.

Smiling and nodding, Miss Marple made her exit, Jane Helier staring after her.

'Are you coming to bed, Jane?' asked Mrs Bantry. 'What's the matter with you? You're staring as though you'd seen a ghost.'

With a deep sigh Jane came to herself, shed a beautiful and bewildering smile on the two men and followed her hostess up the staircase. Mrs Bantry came into the girl's room with her.

'Your fire's nearly out,' said Mrs Bantry, giving it a vicious and ineffectual poke. 'They can't have made it up properly. How stupid housemaids are. Still, I suppose we are rather late tonight. Why, it's actually past one o'clock!'

'Do you think there are many people like her?' asked Jane Helier.

She was sitting on the side of the bed apparently wrapped in thought.

'Like the housemaid?'

'No. Like that funny old woman – what's her name – Marple?'

'Oh! I don't know. I suppose she's a fairly common type in a small village.'

'Oh dear,' said Jane. 'I don't know what to do.'

She sighed deeply.

'What's the matter?'

'I'm worried.'

'What about?'

'Dolly,' Jane Helier was portentously solemn. 'Do you know what that queer old lady whispered to me before she went out of the door tonight?'

'No. What?'

'She said: "*I shouldn't do it if I were you, my dear. Never put yourself too much in another woman's power, even if you do think she's your friend at the moment.*" You know, Dolly, that's awfully true.'

'The maxim? Yes, perhaps it is. But I don't see the application.'

'I suppose you can't ever really trust a woman. And I should be in her power. I never thought of that.'

'What woman are you talking about?'

'Netta Greene, my understudy.'

'What on earth does Miss Marple know about your understudy?'

'I suppose she guessed – but I can't see how.'

'Jane, will you kindly tell me at once what you are talking about?'

'The story. The one I told. Oh, Dolly, that woman, you know – the one that took Claud from me?'

Mrs Bantry nodded, casting her mind back rapidly to the first of Jane's unfortunate marriages – to Claud Averbury, the actor.

'He married her; and I could have told him how it would be. Claud doesn't know, but she's carrying on with Sir Joseph Salmon – week-ends with him at the bungalow I told you about. I wanted her shown up – I would like everyone to know the sort of woman she was. And you see, with a burglary, everything would be bound to come out.'

'Jane!' gasped Mrs Bantry. 'Did *you* engineer this story you've been telling us?'

Jane nodded.

'That's why I chose *Smith*. I wear parlourmaid's kit in it, you know. So I should have it handy. And when they sent for me to the police station it's the easiest thing in the world to say I was rehearsing my part with my understudy at the hotel. Really, of course, we would be at the bungalow. I just have to open the door and bring in the cocktails, and Netta to pretend to be me. He'd never see *her* again, of course, so there would be no fear of his recognizing her. And I can make myself look quite different as a parlourmaid; and besides, one doesn't look at parlourmaids as though they were people. We planned to drag him out into the road afterwards, bag the jewel case, telephone the police and get back to the hotel. I shouldn't like the poor young man to suffer, but Sir Henry didn't seem to think he would, did he? And she'd be in the papers and everything – and Claud would see what she was really like.'

Mrs Bantry sat down and groaned.

'Oh! my poor head. And all the time – Jane Helier, you deceitful girl! Telling us that story the way you did!'

'I *am* a good actress,' said Jane complacently. 'I always have been, whatever people choose to say. I didn't give myself away once, did I?'

'Miss Marple was right,' murmured Mrs Bantry. 'The personal element. Oh, yes, the personal element. Jane, my good child, do you realize that theft is theft, and you might have been sent to prison?'

'Well, none of you guessed,' said Jane. 'Except Miss Marple.' The worried expression returned to her face. 'Dolly, do you *really* think there are many like her?'

'Frankly, I don't,' said Mrs Bantry.

Jane sighed again.

'Still, one had better not risk it. And of course I should be in Netta's power – that's true enough. She might turn against me or blackmail me or anything. She helped me think out the details and she professed to be devoted to me, but one never *does* know with women. No, I think Miss Marple was right. I had better not risk it.'

'But, my dear, you have risked it.'

'Oh, no.' Jane opened her blue eyes very wide. 'Don't you understand? *None of this has happened yet!* I was – well, trying it on the dog, so to speak.'

'I don't profess to understand your theatrical slang,' said Mrs Bantry with dignity. 'Do you mean this is a future project – not a past deed?'

'I was going to do it this autumn – in September. I don't know what to do now.'

'And Jane Marple guessed – actually guessed the truth and never told us,' said Mrs Bantry wrathfully.

'I think that was why she said that – about women sticking together. She wouldn't give me away before the men. That was nice of her. I don't mind *your* knowing, Dolly.'

'Well, give the idea up, Jane. I beg of you.'

'I think I shall,' murmured Miss Helier. 'There might be other Miss Marples . . .'

Death by Drowning

Sir Henry Clithering, ex-Commissioner of Scotland Yard, was staying with his friends the Bantrys at their place near the little village of St Mary Mead.

On Saturday morning, coming down to breakfast at the pleasant guestly hour of ten fifteen, he almost collided with his hostess, Mrs Bantry, in the doorway of the breakfast room. She was rushing from the room, evidently in a condition of some excitement and distress.

Colonel Bantry was sitting at the table, his face rather redder than usual.

''Morning, Clithering,' he said. 'Nice day. Help yourself.'

Sir Henry obeyed. As he took his seat, a plate of kidneys and bacon in front of him, his host went on:

'Dolly's a bit upset this morning.'

'Yes – er – I rather thought so,' said Sir Henry mildly.

He wondered a little. His hostess was of a placid disposition, little given to moods or excitement. As far as Sir Henry knew, she felt keenly on one subject only – gardening.

'Yes,' said Colonel Bantry. 'Bit of news we got this morning upset her. Girl in the village – Emmott's daughter – Emmott who keeps the Blue Boar.'

'Oh, yes, of course.'

'Ye-es,' said Colonel Bantry ruminatively. 'Pretty girl.

Got herself into trouble. Usual story. I've been arguing with Dolly about that. Foolish of me. Women never see sense. Dolly was all up in arms for the girl – you know what women are – men are brutes – all the rest of it, etcetera. But it's not so simple as all that – not in these days. Girls know what they're about. Fellow who seduces a girl's not necessarily a villain. Fifty-fifty as often as not. I rather liked young Sandford myself. A young ass rather than a Don Juan, I should have said.'

'It is this man Sandford who got the girl into trouble?'

'So it seems. Of course I don't know anything person-ally,' said the colonel cautiously. 'It's all gossip and chat. You know what this place is! As I say, I *know* nothing. And I'm not like Dolly – leaping to conclusions, flinging accusations all over the place. Damn it all, one ought to be careful in what one says. You know – inquest and all that.'

'Inquest?'

Colonel Bantry stared.

'Yes. Didn't I tell you? Girl drowned herself. That's what all the pother's about.'

'That's a nasty business,' said Sir Henry.

'Of course it is. Don't like to think of it myself. Poor pretty little devil. Her father's a hard man by all accounts. I suppose she just felt she couldn't face the music.'

He paused.

'That's what's upset Dolly so.'

'Where did she drown herself?'

'In the river. Just below the mill it runs pretty fast. There's a footpath and a bridge across. They think she threw herself off that. Well, well, it doesn't bear think-ing about.'

And with a portentous rustle, Colonel Bantry opened his newspaper and proceeded to distract his mind from painful matters by an absorption in the newest iniquities of the government.

Sir Henry was only mildly interested by the village tragedy. After breakfast, he established himself on a comfortable chair on the lawn, tilted his hat over his eyes and contemplated life from a peaceful angle.

It was about half past eleven when a neat parlourmaid tripped across the lawn.

'If you please, sir, Miss Marple has called, and would like to see you.'

'Miss Marple?'

Sir Henry sat up and straightened his hat. The name surprised him. He remembered Miss Marple very well – her gentle quiet old-maidish ways, her amazing penetration. He remembered a dozen unsolved and hypothetical cases – and how in each case this typical 'old maid of the village' had leaped unerringly to the right solution of the mystery. Sir Henry had a very deep respect for Miss Marple. He wondered what had brought her to see him.

Miss Marple was sitting in the drawing-room – very upright as always, a gaily coloured marketing basket of foreign extraction beside her. Her cheeks were rather pink and she seemed flustered.

'Sir Henry – I am so glad. So fortunate to find you. I just happened to hear that you were staying down here . . . I do hope you will forgive me . . .'

'This is a great pleasure,' said Sir Henry, taking her hand. 'I'm afraid Mrs Bantry's out.'

'Yes,' said Miss Marple. 'I saw her talking to Footit, the butcher, as I passed. Henry Footit was run over yesterday – that was his dog. One of those smooth-haired fox terriers, rather stout and quarrelsome, that butchers always seem to have.'

'Yes,' said Sir Henry helpfully.

'I was glad to get here when she wasn't at home,' continued Miss Marple. 'Because it was you I wanted to see. About this sad affair.'

'Henry Footit?' asked Sir Henry, slightly bewildered.

Miss Marple threw him a reproachful glance.

'No, no. Rose Emmott, of course. You've heard?'

Sir Henry nodded.

'Bantry was telling me. Very sad.'

He was a little puzzled. He could not conceive why Miss Marple should want to see him about Rose Emmott.

Miss Marple sat down again. Sir Henry also sat. When the old lady spoke her manner had changed. It was grave, and had a certain dignity.

'You may remember, Sir Henry, that on one or two occasions we played what was really a pleasant kind of game. Propounding mysteries and giving solutions. You were kind enough to say that I – that I did not do too badly.'

'You beat us all,' said Sir Henry warmly. 'You displayed an absolute genius for getting to the truth. And you always instanced, I remember, some village parallel which had supplied you with the clue.'

He smiled as he spoke, but Miss Marple did not smile. She remained very grave.

'What you said has emboldened me to come to you now. I feel that if I say something to you – at least you will not laugh at me.'

He realized suddenly that she was in deadly earnest.

'Certainly, I will not laugh,' he said gently.

'Sir Henry – this girl – Rose Emmott. She did not drown herself – *she was murdered*. . . And I know who murdered her.'

Sir Henry was silent with sheer astonishment for quite three seconds. Miss Marple's voice had been perfectly quiet and unexcited. She might have been making the most ordinary statement in the world for all the emotion she showed.

'This is a very serious statement to make, Miss Marple,' said Sir Henry when he had recovered his breath.

She nodded her head gently several times.

'I know – I know – that is why I have come to you.'

'But, my dear lady, I am not the person to come to. I am merely a private individual nowadays. If you have knowledge of the kind you claim, you must go to the police.'

'I don't think I can do that,' said Miss Marple.

'But why not?'

'Because, you see, I haven't got any – what you call *knowledge.*'

'You mean it's only a guess on your part?'

'You can call it that, if you like, but it's not really that at all. I *know.* I'm in a position to know; but if I gave my reasons for knowing to Inspector Drewitt – well, he'd simply laugh. And really, I don't know that I'd blame him. It's very difficult to understand what you might call specialized knowledge.'

'Such as?' suggested Sir Henry.

Miss Marple smiled a little.

'If I were to tell you that I know because of a man called Peasegood leaving turnips instead of carrots when he came round with a cart and sold vegetables to my niece several years ago – '

She stopped eloquently.

'A very appropriate name for the trade,' murmured Sir Henry. 'You mean that you are simply judging from the facts in a parallel case.'

'I know human nature,' said Miss Marple. 'It's impossible not to know human nature living in a village all these years. The question is, do you believe me, or don't you?'

She looked at him very straight. The pink flush had heightened on her cheeks. Her eyes met his steadily without wavering.

Sir Henry was a man with a very vast experience of life. He made his decisions quickly without beating about the bush. Unlikely and fantastic as Miss Marple's statement might seem, he was instantly aware that he accepted it.

'I *do* believe you, Miss Marple. But I do not see what you want me to do in the matter, or why you have come to me.'

'I have thought and thought about it,' said Miss Marple. 'As I said, it would be useless going to the police without any facts. I have no facts. What I would ask you to do is to interest yourself in the matter – Inspector Drewitt would be most flattered, I am sure. And, of course, if the matter went farther, Colonel Melchett, the Chief Constable, I am sure, would be wax in your hands.'

She looked at him appealingly.

'And what data are you going to give me to work upon?'

'I thought,' said Miss Marple, 'of writing a name – *the* name – on a piece of paper and giving it to you. Then if, on investigation, you decided that the – the *person* – is not involved in any way – well, I shall have been quite wrong.'

She paused and then added with a slight shiver. 'It would be so dreadful – so very dreadful – if an innocent person were to be hanged.'

'What on earth –' cried Sir Henry, startled.

She turned a distressed face upon him.

'I may be wrong about that – though I don't think

so. Inspector Drewitt, you see, is really an intelligent man. But a mediocre amount of intelligence is sometimes most dangerous. It does not take one far enough.'

Sir Henry looked at her curiously.

Fumbling a little, Miss Marple opened a small reticule, took out a little notebook, tore out a leaf, carefully wrote a name on it and folding it in two, handed it to Sir Henry.

He opened it and read the name. It conveyed nothing to him, but his eyebrows lifted a little. He looked across at Miss Marple and tucked the piece of paper in his pocket.

'Well, well,' he said. 'Rather an extraordinary business, this. I've never done anything like it before. But I'm going to back my judgment – of *you*, Miss Marple.'

Sir Henry was sitting in a room with Colonel Melchett, the Chief Constable of the county, and Inspector Drewitt.

The Chief Constable was a little man of aggressively military demeanour. The Inspector was big and broad and eminently sensible.

'I really do feel I'm butting in,' said Sir Henry with his pleasant smile. 'I can't really tell you why I'm doing it.' (Strict truth this!)

'My dear fellow, we're charmed. It's a great compliment.'

'Honoured, Sir Henry,' said the Inspector.

The Chief Constable was thinking: 'Bored to death, poor fellow, at the Bantrys. The old man abusing the government and the old woman babbling on about bulbs.'

The Inspector was thinking: 'Pity we're not up against a real teaser. One of the best brains in England, I've heard it said. Pity it's all such plain sailing.'

Aloud, the Chief Constable said:

'I'm afraid it's all very sordid and straightforward. First idea was that the girl had pitched herself in. She was in the family way, you understand. However, our doctor, Haydock, is a careful fellow. He noticed the bruises on each arm – upper arm. Caused before death. Just where a fellow would have taken her by the arms and flung her in.'

'Would that require much strength?'

'I think not. There would be no struggle – the girl would be taken unawares. It's a footbridge of slippery wood. Easiest thing in the world to pitch her over – there's no handrail that side.'

'You know for a fact that the tragedy occurred there?'

'Yes. We've got a boy – Jimmy Brown – aged twelve. He was in the woods on the other side. He heard a kind of scream from the bridge and a splash. It was dusk you know – difficult to see anything. Presently he saw something white floating down in the water and he ran and got help. They got her out, but it was too late to revive her.'

Sir Henry nodded.

'The boy saw no one on the bridge?'

'No. But, as I tell you, it was dusk, and there's mist always hanging about there. I'm going to question him as to whether he saw anyone about just afterwards or just before. You see he naturally assumed that the girl had thrown herself over. Everybody did to start with.'

'Still, we've got the note,' said Inspector Drewitt. He turned to Sir Henry.

'Note in the dead girl's pocket, sir. Written with a kind of artist's pencil it was, and all of a sop though the paper was we managed to read it.'

'And what did it say?'

'It was from young Sandford. "All right," that's how

213

it ran. "I'll meet you at the bridge at eight-thirty. – R.S." Well, it was near as might be to eight-thirty – a few minutes after – when Jimmy Brown heard the cry and the splash.'

'I don't know whether you've met Sandford at all?' went on Colonel Melchett. 'He's been down here about a month. One of these modern day young architects who build peculiar houses. He's doing a house for Allington. God knows what it's going to be like – full of new-fangled stuff, I suppose. Glass dinner table and surgical chairs made of steel and webbing. Well, that's neither here nor there, but it shows the kind of chap Sandford is. Bolshie, you know – no morals.'

'Seduction,' said Sir Henry mildly, 'is quite an old-established crime though it does not, of course, date back so far as murder.'

Colonel Melchett stared.

'Oh! yes,' he said. 'Quite. Quite.'

'Well, Sir Henry,' said Drewitt, 'there it is – an ugly business, but plain. This young Sandford gets the girl into trouble. Then he's all for clearing off back to London. He's got a girl there – nice young lady – he's engaged to be married to her. Well, naturally this business, if she gets to hear of it, may cook his goose good and proper. He meets Rose at the bridge – it's a misty evening, no one about – he catches her by the shoulders and pitches her in. A proper young swine – and deserves what's coming to him. That's my opinion.'

Sir Henry was silent for a minute or two. He perceived a strong undercurrent of local prejudice. A new fangled architect was not likely to be popular in the conservative village of St Mary Mead.

'There is no doubt, I suppose, that this man, Sandford, was actually the father of the coming child?' he asked.

'He's the father all right,' said Drewitt. 'Rose Emmott let out as much to her father. She thought he'd marry her. Marry her! Not he!'

'Dear me,' thought Sir Henry. 'I seem to be back in mid-Victorian melodrama. Unsuspecting girl, the villain from London, the stern father, the betrayal – we only need the faithful village lover. Yes, I think it's time I asked about him.'

And aloud he said:

'Hadn't the girl a young man of her own down here?'

'You mean Joe Ellis?' said the inspector. 'Good fellow Joe. Carpentering's his trade. Ah! If she'd stuck to Joe – '

Colonel Melchett nodded approval.

'Stick to your own class,' he snapped.

'How did Joe Ellis take this affair?' asked Sir Henry.

'Nobody knew how he was taking it,' said the inspector. 'He's a quiet fellow, is Joe. Close. Anything Rose did was right in his eyes. She had him on a string all right. Just hoped she'd come back to him some day – that was his attitude, I reckon.'

'I'd like to see him,' said Sir Henry.

'Oh! We're going to look him up,' said Colonel Melchett. 'We're not neglecting any line. I thought myself we'd see Emmott first, then Sandford, and then we can go on and see Ellis. That suits you, Clithering?'

Sir Henry said it would suit him admirably.

They found Tom Emmott at the Blue Boar. He was a big burly man of middle age with a shifty eye and a truculent jaw.

'Glad to see you, gentlemen – good morning, Colonel. Come in here and we can be private. Can I offer you anything, gentlemen? No? It's as you please. You've come about this business of my poor girl. Ah! She was a good girl, Rose was. Always was a good girl

215

– till this bloody swine – beg pardon, but that's what he is – till he came along. Promised her marriage, he did. But I'll have the law on him. Drove her to it, he did. Murdering swine. Bringing disgrace on all of us. My poor girl.'

'Your daughter distinctly told you that Mr Sandford was responsible for her condition?' asked Melchett crisply.

'She did. In this very room she did.'

'And what did you say to her?' asked Sir Henry.

'Say to her?' The man seemed momentarily taken aback.

'Yes. You didn't, for example, threaten to turn her out of the house.'

'I was a bit upset – that's only natural. I'm sure you'll agree that's only natural. But, of course, I didn't turn her out of the house. I wouldn't do such a thing.' He assumed virtuous indignation. 'No. What's the law for – that's what I say. What's the law for? He'd got to do the right by her. And if he didn't, by God, he'd got to pay.'

He brought down his fist on the table.

'What time did you last see your daughter?' asked Melchett.

'Yesterday – tea time.'

'What was her manner then?'

'Well, much as usual. I didn't notice anything. If I'd known –'

'But you didn't know,' said the inspector drily.

They took their leave.

'Emmott hardly creates a favourable impression,' said Sir Henry thoughtfully.

'Bit of a blackguard,' said Melchett. 'He'd have bled Sandford all right if he'd had the chance.'

Their next call was on the architect. Rex Sandford

was very unlike the picture Sir Henry had unconsciously formed of him. He was a tall young man, very fair and very thin. His eyes were blue and dreamy, his hair was untidy and rather too long. His speech was a little too ladylike.

Colonel Melchett introduced himself and his companions. Then passing straight to the object of his visit, he invited the architect to make a statement as to his movements on the previous evening.

'You understand,' he said warningly. 'I have no power to compel a statement from you and any statement you make may be used in evidence against you. I want the position to be quite clear to you.'

'I – I don't understand,' said Sandford.

'You understand that the girl Rose Emmott was drowned last night?'

'I know. Oh! it's too, too distressing. Really, I haven't slept a wink. I've been incapable of any work today. I feel responsible – terribly responsible.'

He ran his hands through his hair, making it untidier still.

'I never meant any harm,' he said piteously. 'I never thought. I never dreamt she'd take it that way.'

He sat down at a table and buried his face in his hands.

'Do I understand you to say, Mr Sandford, that you refuse to make a statement as to where you were last night at eight-thirty?'

'No, no – certainly not. I was out. I went for a walk.'

'You went to meet Miss Emmott?'

'No. I went by myself. Through the woods. A long way.'

'Then how do you account for this note, sir, which was found in the dead girl's pocket?'

And Inspector Drewitt read it unemotionally aloud.

'Now, sir,' he finished. 'Do you deny that you wrote that?'

'No – no. You're right. I did write it. Rose asked me to meet her. She insisted. I didn't know what to do. So I wrote that note.'

'Ah, that's better,' said the inspector.

'But I didn't go!' Sandford's voice rose high and excited. 'I didn't go! I felt it would be much better not. I was returning to town tomorrow. I felt it would be better not – not to meet. I intended to write from London and – and make – some arrangement.'

'You are aware, sir, that this girl was going to have a child, and that she had named you as its father?'

Sandford groaned, but did not answer.

'Was that statement true, sir?'

Sandford buried his face deeper.

'I suppose so,' he said in a muffled voice.

'Ah!' Inspector Drewitt could not disguise the satisfaction. 'Now about this "walk" of yours. Is there anyone who saw you last night?'

'I don't know. I don't think so. As far as I can remember, I didn't meet anybody.'

'That's a pity.'

'What do you mean?' Sandford stared wildly at him. 'What does it matter whether I was out for a walk or not? What difference does that make to Rose drowning herself?'

'Ah!' said the inspector. 'But you see, *she didn't.* She was thrown in deliberately, Mr Sandford.'

'She was –' It took him a minute or two to take in all the horror of it. 'My God! Then –'

He dropped into a chair.

Colonel Melchett made a move to depart.

'You understand, Sandford,' he said. 'You are on no account to leave this house.'

The three men left together. The inspector and the Chief Constable exchanged glances.

'That's enough, I think, sir,' said the inspector.

'Yes. Get a warrant made out and arrest him.'

'Excuse me,' said Sir Henry, 'I've forgotten my gloves.'

He re-entered the house rapidly. Sandford was sitting just as they had left him, staring dazedly in front of him.

'I have come back,' said Sir Henry, 'to tell you that I personally, am anxious to do all I can to assist you. The motive of my interest in you I am not at liberty to reveal. But I am going to ask you, if you will, to tell me as briefly as possible exactly what passed between you and this girl Rose.'

'She was very pretty,' said Sandford. 'Very pretty and very alluring. And – and she made a dead set at me. Before God, that's true. She wouldn't let me alone. And it was lonely down here, and nobody liked me much, and – and, as I say she was amazingly pretty and she seemed to know her way about and all that –' His voice died away. He looked up. 'And then this happened. She wanted me to marry her. I didn't know what to do. I'm engaged to a girl in London. If she ever gets to hear of this – and she will, of course – well, it's all up. She won't understand. How could she? And I'm a rotter, of course. As I say, I didn't know what to do. I avoided seeing Rose again. I thought I'd get back to town – see my lawyer – make arrangements about money and so forth, for her. God, what a fool I've been! And it's all so clear – the case against me. But they've made a mistake. She *must* have done it herself.'

'Did she ever threaten to take her life?'

Sandford shook his head.

'Never. I shouldn't have said she was that sort.'

'What about a man called Joe Ellis?'

'The carpenter fellow? Good old village stock. Dull fellow – but crazy about Rose.'

'He might have been jealous?' suggested Sir Henry.

'I suppose he was a bit – but he's the bovine kind. He'd suffer in silence.'

'Well,' said Sir Henry. 'I must be going.'

He rejoined the others.

'You know, Melchett,' he said, 'I feel we ought to have a look at this other fellow – Ellis – before we do anything drastic. Pity if you made an arrest that turned out to be a mistake. After all, jealousy is a pretty good motive for murder – and a pretty common one, too.'

'That's true enough,' said the inspector. 'But Joe Ellis isn't that kind. He wouldn't hurt a fly. Why, nobody's ever seen him out of temper. Still, I agree we'd better just ask him where he was last night. He'll be at home now. He lodges with Mrs Bartlett – very decent soul – a widow, she takes in a bit of washing.'

The little cottage to which they bent their footsteps was spotlessly clean and neat. A big stout woman of middle age opened the door to them. She had a pleasant face and blue eyes.

'Good morning, Mrs Bartlett,' said the inspector. 'Is Joe Ellis here?'

'Came back not ten minutes ago,' said Mrs Bartlett. 'Step inside, will you, please, sirs.'

Wiping her hands on her apron she led them into a tiny front parlour with stuffed birds, china dogs, a sofa and several useless pieces of furniture.

She hurriedly arranged seats for them, picked up a whatnot bodily to make further room and went out calling:

'Joe, there's three gentlemen want to see you.'

A voice from the back kitchen replied:

'I'll be there when I've cleaned myself.'

Mrs Bartlett smiled.

'Come in, Mrs Bartlett,' said Colonel Melchett. 'Sit down.'

'Oh, no, sir, I couldn't think of it.'

Mrs Bartlett was shocked at the idea.

'You find Joe Ellis a good lodger?' inquired Melchett in a seemingly careless tone.

'Couldn't have a better, sir. A real steady young fellow. Never touches a drop of drink. Takes a pride in his work. And always kind and helpful about the house. He put up those shelves for me, and he's fixed a new dresser in the kitchen. And any little thing that wants doing in the house – why, Joe does it as a matter of course, and won't hardly take thanks for it. Ah! there aren't many young fellows like Joe, sir.'

'Some girl will be lucky some day,' said Melchett carelessly. 'He was rather sweet on that poor girl, Rose Emmott, wasn't he?'

Mrs Bartlett sighed.

'It made me tired, it did. Him worshipping the ground she trod on and her not caring a snap of the fingers for him.'

'Where does Joe spend his evenings, Mrs Bartlett?'

'Here, sir, usually. He does some odd piece of work in the evenings, sometimes, and he's trying to learn book-keeping by correspondence.'

'Ah! really. Was he in yesterday evening?'

'Yes, sir.'

'You're sure, Mrs Bartlett?' said Sir Henry sharply.

She turned to him.

'Quite sure, sir.'

'He didn't go out, for instance, somewhere about eight to eight-thirty?'

'Oh, no.' Mrs Bartlett laughed. 'He was fixing the kitchen dresser for me nearly all the evening, and I was helping him.'

Sir Henry looked at her smiling assured face and felt his first pang of doubt.

A moment later Ellis himself entered the room.

He was a tall broad-shouldered young man, very good-looking in a rustic way. He had shy, blue eyes and a good-tempered smile. Altogether an amiable young giant.

Melchett opened the conversation. Mrs Barlett withdrew to the kitchen.

'We are investigating the death of Rose Emmott. You knew her, Ellis.'

'Yes.' He hesitated, then muttered, 'Hoped to marry her one day. Poor lass.'

'You have heard of what her condition was?'

'Yes.' A spark of anger showed in his eyes. 'Let her down, he did. But 'twere for the best. She wouldn't have been happy married to him. I reckoned she'd come to me when this happened. I'd have looked after her.'

'In spite of –'

''Tweren't her fault. He led her astray with fine promises and all. Oh! she told me about it. She'd no call to drown herself. He weren't worth it.'

'Where were you, Ellis, last night at eight-thirty?'

Was it Sir Henry's fancy, or was there really a shade of constraint in the ready – almost too ready – reply?

'I was here. Fixing up a contraption in the kitchen for Mrs B. You ask her. She'll tell you.'

'He was too quick with that,' thought Sir Henry. 'He's a slow thinking man. That popped out so pat that I suspect he'd got it ready beforehand.'

Then he told himself that it was imagination. He was imagining things – yes, even imagining an apprehensive glint in those blue eyes.

A few more questions and answers and they left. Sir Henry made an excuse to go to the kitchen. Mrs Bartlett was busy at the stove. She looked up with a pleasant smile. A new dresser was fixed against the wall. It was not quite finished. Some tools lay about and some pieces of wood.

'That's what Ellis was at work on last night?' said Sir Henry.

'Yes, sir, it's a nice bit of work, isn't it? He's a very clever carpenter, Joe is.'

No apprehensive gleam in her eye – no embarrassment.

But Ellis – had he imagined it? No, there *had* been something.

'I must tackle him,' thought Sir Henry.

Turning to leave the kitchen, he collided with a perambulator.

'Not woken the baby up, I hope,' he said.

Mrs Bartlett's laugh rang out.

'Oh, no, sir. I've no children – more's the pity. That's what I take the laundry on, sir.'

'Oh! I see –'

He paused then said on an impulse:

'Mrs Bartlett. You knew Rose Emmott. Tell me what you really thought of her.'

She looked at him curiously.

'Well, sir, I thought she was flighty. But she's dead – and I don't like to speak ill of the dead.'

'But I have a reason – a very good reason for asking.'

He spoke persuasively.

She seemed to consider, studying him attentively. Finally she made up her mind.

'She was a bad lot, sir,' she said quietly. 'I wouldn't say so before Joe. She took *him* in good and proper. That kind can – more's the pity. You know how it is, sir.'

Yes, Sir Henry knew. The Joe Ellises of the world were peculiarly vulnerable. They trusted blindly. But for that very cause the shock of discovery might be greater.

He left the cottage baffled and perplexed. He was up against a blank wall. Joe Ellis had been working indoors all yesterday evening. Mrs Bartlett had actually been there watching him. Could one possibly get round that? There was nothing to set against it – except possibly that suspicious readiness in replying on Joe Ellis's part – that suggestion of having a story pat.

'Well,' said Melchett, 'that seems to make the matter quite clear, eh?'

'It does, sir,' agreed the inspector. 'Sandford's our man. Not a leg to stand upon. The thing's as plain as daylight. It's my opinion as the girl and her father were out to – well – practically blackmail him. He's no money to speak of – he didn't want the matter to get to his young lady's ears. He was desperate and he acted accordingly. What do you say, sir?' he added, addressing Sir Henry deferentially.

'It seems so,' admitted Sir Henry. 'And yet – I can hardly picture Sandford committing any violent action.'

But he knew as he spoke that that objection was hardly valid. The meekest animal, when cornered, is capable of amazing actions.

'I should like to see the boy, though,' he said suddenly. 'The one who heard the cry.'

Jimmy Brown proved to be an intelligent lad, rather small for his age, with a sharp, rather cunning face. He was eager to be questioned and was rather disappointed when checked in his dramatic tale of what he had heard on the fatal night.

'You were on the other side of the bridge, I understand,' said Sir Henry. 'Across the river from the village. Did you see anyone on that side as you came over the bridge?'

'There was someone walking up in the woods. Mr Sandford, I think it was, the architecting gentleman who's building the queer house.'

The three men exchanged glances.

'That was about ten minutes or so before you heard the cry?'

The boy nodded.

'Did you see anyone else – on the village side of the river?'

'A man came along the path that side. Going slow and whistling he was. Might have been Joe Ellis.'

'You couldn't possibly have seen who it was,' said the inspector sharply. 'What with the mist and its being dusk.'

'It's on account of the whistle,' said the boy. 'Joe Ellis always whistles the same tune – "I wanner be happy" – it's the only tune he knows.'

He spoke with the scorn of the modernist for the old-fashioned.

'Anyone might whistle a tune,' said Melchett. 'Was he going towards the bridge?'

'No. Other way – to village.'

'I don't think we need concern ourselves with this unknown man,' said Melchett. 'You heard the cry and the splash and a few minutes later you saw the body floating downstream and you ran for help, going back to the bridge, crossing it, and making straight for the village. You didn't see anyone near the bridge as you ran for help?'

'I think as there were two men with a wheelbarrow on the river path; but they were some way away and I couldn't tell if they were going or coming and Mr Giles's place was nearest – so I ran there.'

'You did well, my boy,' said Melchett. 'You acted very creditably and with presence of mind. You're a scout, aren't you?'

'Yes, sir.'

'Very good. Very good indeed.'

Sir Henry was silent – thinking. He took a slip of paper from his pocket, looked at it, shook his head. It didn't seem possible – and yet –

He decided to pay a call on Miss Marple.

She received him in her pretty, slightly overcrowded old style drawing-room.

'I've come to report progress,' said Sir Henry. 'I'm afraid that from our point of view things aren't going well. They are going to arrest Sandford. And I must say I think they are justified.'

'You have found nothing in – what shall I say – support of my theory, then?' She looked perplexed – anxious. 'Perhaps I have been wrong – quite wrong. You have such wide experience – you would surely detect it if it were so.'

'For one thing,' said Sir Henry, 'I can hardly believe it. And for another we are up against an unbreakable alibi. Joe Ellis was fixing shelves in the kitchen all the evening and Mrs Bartlett was watching him do it.'

Miss Marple leaned forward, taking in a quick breath.

'But that can't be so,' she said. 'It was Friday night.'

'Friday night?'

'Yes – Friday night. On Friday evenings Mrs Bartlett takes the laundry she has done round to the different people.'

Sir Henry leaned back in his chair. He remembered the boy Jimmy's story of the whistling man and – yes – it would all fit in.

He rose, taking Miss Marple warmly by the hand.

'I think I see my way,' he said. 'At least I can try . . .'

Five minutes later he was back at Mrs Bartlett's cottage and facing Joe Ellis in the little parlour among the china dogs.

'You lied to us, Ellis, about last night,' he said crisply. 'You were not in the kitchen here fixing the dresser between eight and eight-thirty. You were seen walking along the path by the river towards the bridge a few minutes before Rose Emmott was murdered.'

The man gasped.

'She weren't murdered – she weren't. I had naught to do with it. She threw herself in, she did. She was desperate like. I wouldn't have harmed a hair on her head, I wouldn't.'

'Then why did you lie as to where you were?' asked Sir Henry keenly.

The man's eyes shifted and lowered uncomfortably.

'I was scared. Mrs B. saw me around there and when we heard just afterwards what had happened – well, she thought it might look bad for me. I fixed I'd say I was working here, and she agreed to back me up. She's a rare one, she is. She's always been good to me.'

Without a word Sir Henry left the room and walked into the kitchen. Mrs Bartlett was washing up at the sink.

'Mrs Bartlett,' he said, 'I know everything. I think you'd better confess – that is, unless you want Joe Ellis hanged for something he didn't do ... No. I see you don't want that. I'll tell you what happened. You were out taking the laundry home. You came across Rose Emmott. You thought she'd given Joe the chuck and was taking up with this stranger. Now she was in trouble – Joe was prepared to come to the rescue – marry her if need be, and if she'd have him. He's lived in your house for four years. You've fallen in love with him. You want him for yourself. You hated this girl – you couldn't bear that this worthless little slut should take your man from you. You're a strong woman, Mrs Bartlett. You caught the girl by the shoulders and shoved her over into the stream. A few minutes later you met

Joe Ellis. The boy Jimmy saw you together in the distance – but in the darkness and the mist he assumed the perambulator was a wheelbarrow and two men wheeling it. You persuaded Joe that he might be suspected and you concocted what was supposed to be an alibi for him, but which was really an alibi for *you*. Now then, I'm right, am I not?'

He held his breath. He had staked all on this throw.

She stood before him rubbing her hands on her apron, slowly making up her mind.

'It's just as you say, sir,' she said at last, in her quiet subdued voice (a dangerous voice, Sir Henry suddenly felt it to be). 'I don't know what came over me. Shameless – that's what she was. It just came over me – she shan't take Joe from me. I haven't had a happy life, sir. My husband, he was a poor lot – an invalid and cross-grained. I nursed and looked after him true. And then Joe came here to lodge. I'm not such an old woman, sir, in spite of my grey hair. I'm just forty, sir. Joe's one in a thousand. I'd have done anything for him – anything at all. He was like a little child, sir, so gentle and believing. He was mine, sir, to look after and see to. And this – this –' She swallowed – checked her emotion. Even at this moment she was a strong woman. She stood up straight and looked at Sir Henry curiously. 'I'm ready to come, sir. I never thought anyone would find out. I don't know how you knew, sir – I don't, I'm sure.'

Sir Henry shook his head gently.

'It was not I who knew,' he said – and he thought of the piece of paper still reposing in his pocket with the words on it written in neat old-fashioned handwriting.

'*Mrs Bartlett, with whom Joe Ellis lodges at 2 Mill Cottages.*'

Miss Marple had been right again.

Miss Marple's Final Cases

Miss Marple Tells a Story

I don't think I've ever told you, my dears – you, Raymond, and you, Joan, about the rather curious little business that happened some years ago now. I don't want to seem *vain* in any way – of course I know that in comparison with you young people I'm not clever at all – Raymond writes those very modern books all about rather unpleasant young men and women – and Joan paints those very remarkable pictures of square people with curious bulges on them – very clever of you, my dear, but as Raymond always says (only quite kindly, because he is the kindest of nephews) I am hopelessly Victorian. I admire Mr Alma-Tadema and Mr Frederic Leighton and I suppose to you they seem hopelessly *vieux jeu.* Now let me see, what was I saying? Oh, yes – that I didn't want to appear vain – but I couldn't help being just a teeny weeny bit pleased with myself, because, just by applying a little common sense, I believe I really did solve a problem that had baffled cleverer heads than mine. Though really I should have thought the whole thing was *obvious* from the beginning . . .

Well, I'll tell you my little story, and if you think I'm inclined to be conceited about it, you must remember that I did at least help a fellow creature who was in very grave distress.

The first I knew of this business was one evening

about nine o'clock when Gwen – (you remember Gwen? My little maid with red hair) well – Gwen came in and told me that Mr Petherick and a gentleman had called to see me. Gwen had shown them into the drawing-room – quite rightly. I was sitting in the dining-room because in early spring I think it is so wasteful to have two fires going.

I directed Gwen to bring in the cherry brandy and some glasses and I hurried into the drawing-room. I don't know whether you remember Mr Petherick? He died two years ago, but he had been a friend of mine for many years as well as attending to all my legal business. A very shrewd man and a really clever solicitor. His son does my business for me now – a very nice lad and very up to date – but somehow I don't feel quite the *confidence* I had with Mr Petherick.

I explained to Mr Petherick about the fires and he said at once that he and his friend would come into the dining-room – and then he introduced his friend – a Mr Rhodes. He was a youngish man – not much over forty – and I saw at once there was something very wrong. His manner was most *peculiar*. One might have called it *rude* if one hadn't realized that the poor fellow was suffering from *strain*.

When we were settled in the dining-room and Gwen had brought the cherry brandy, Mr Petherick explained the reason for his visit.

'Miss Marple,' he said, 'you must forgive an old friend for taking a liberty. What I have come here for is a consultation.'

I couldn't understand at all what he meant, and he went on:

'In a case of illness one likes two points of view – that of the specialist and that of the family physician. It is the fashion to regard the former as of more value, but

I am not sure that I agree. The specialist has experience only in his own subject – the family doctor has, perhaps, less knowledge – but a wider experience.'

I knew just what he meant, because a young niece of mine not long before had hurried her child off to a very well-known specialist in skin diseases without consulting her own doctor whom she considered an old dodderer, and the specialist had ordered some very expensive treatment, and later found that all the child was suffering from was a rather unusual form of measles.

I just mention this – though I have a horror of *digressing* – to show that I appreciate Mr Petherick's point – but I still hadn't any idea what he was driving at.

'If Mr Rhodes is ill –' I said, and stopped – because the poor man gave a most dreadful laugh.

He said: 'I expect to die of a broken neck in a few months' time.'

And then it all came out. There had been a case of murder lately in Barnchester – a town about twenty miles away. I'm afraid I hadn't paid much attention to it at the time, because we had been having a lot of excitement in the village about our district nurse, and outside occurrences like an earthquake in India and a murder in Barnchester, although of course far more important really – had given way to our own little local excitements. I'm afraid villages are like that. Still, I *did* remember having read about a woman having been stabbed in a hotel, though I hadn't remembered her name. But now it seemed that this woman had been Mr Rhodes's wife – and as if that wasn't bad enough – he was actually under suspicion of having murdered her himself.

All this Mr Petherick explained to me very clearly,

saying that, although the coroner's jury had brought in a verdict of murder by a person or persons unknown, Mr Rhodes had reason to believe that he would probably be arrested within a day or two, and that he had come to Mr Petherick and placed himself in his hands. Mr Petherick went on to say that they had that afternoon consulted Sir Malcolm Olde, K.C., and that in the event of the case coming to trial Sir Malcolm had been briefed to defend Mr Rhodes.

Sir Malcolm was a young man, Mr Petherick said, very up to date in his methods, and he had indicated a certain line of defence. But with that line of defence Mr Petherick was not entirely satisfied.

'You see, my dear lady,' he said, 'it is tainted with what I call the specialist's point of view. Give Sir Malcolm a case and he sees only one point – the most likely line of defence. But even the best line of defence may ignore completely what is, to my mind, the vital point. It takes no account of what actually happened.'

Then he went on to say some very kind and flattering things about my acumen and judgement and my knowledge of human nature, and asked permission to tell me the story of the case in the hopes that I might be able to suggest some explanation.

I could see that Mr Rhodes was highly sceptical of my being of any use and he was annoyed at being brought here. But Mr Petherick took no notice and proceeded to give me the facts of what occurred on the night of March 8th.

Mr and Mrs Rhodes had been staying at the Crown Hotel in Barnchester. Mrs Rhodes who (so I gathered from Mr Petherick's careful language) was perhaps just a shade of a hypochondriac, had retired to bed immediately after dinner. She and her husband occupied adjoining rooms with a connecting door. Mr Rhodes, who is writing a book on prehistoric flints, settled down to work in the adjoining room. At eleven o'clock he tidied up his papers and prepared to go to bed. Before doing so, he just glanced into his wife's room to make sure that there was nothing she wanted. He discovered the electric light on and his wife lying in bed stabbed through the heart. She had been dead at least an hour – probably longer. The following were the points made. There was another door in Mrs Rhodes's room leading into the corridor. This door was locked and bolted on the inside. The only window in the room was closed and latched. According to Mr Rhodes nobody had passed through the room in which he was sitting except a chambermaid bringing hot water bottles. The weapon found in the wound was a stiletto dagger which had been lying on Mrs Rhodes's dressing-table. She was in the habit of using it as a paper knife. There were no fingerprints on it.

The situation boiled down to this – no one but Mr Rhodes and the chambermaid had entered the victim's room.

I enquired about the chambermaid.

'That was our first line of enquiry,' said Mr Petherick. 'Mary Hill is a local woman. She had been chambermaid at the Crown for ten years. There seems absolutely no reason why she should commit a sudden assault on a guest. She is, in any case, extraordinarily stupid, almost half-witted. Her story has never varied. She brought Mrs Rhodes her hot water bottle and says the lady was drowsy – just dropping off to sleep. Frankly, I cannot believe, and I am sure no jury would believe, that she committed the crime.'

Mr Petherick went on to mention a few additional details. At the head of the staircase in the Crown Hotel is a kind of miniature lounge where people sometimes

sit and have coffee. A passage goes off to the right and
the last door in it is the door into the room occupied
by Mr Rhodes. The passage then turns sharply to the
right again and the first door round the corner is the
door into Mrs Rhodes's room. As it happened, both
these doors could be seen by witnesses. The first door
– that into Mr Rhodes's room, which I will call A, could
be seen by four people, two commercial travellers and
an elderly married couple who were having coffee.
According to them nobody went in or out of door A
except Mr Rhodes and the chambermaid. As to the
other door in the passage B, there was an electrician
at work there and he also swears that nobody entered
or left door B except the chambermaid.

It was certainly a very curious and interesting case.
On the face of it, it looked as though Mr Rhodes must
have murdered his wife. But I could see that Mr Petherick was quite convinced of his client's innocence and
Mr Petherick was a very shrewd man.

At the inquest Mr Rhodes had told a hesitating and
rambling story about some woman who had written
threatening letters to his wife. His story, I gathered, had
been unconvincing in the extreme. Appealed to by Mr
Petherick, he explained himself.

'Frankly,' he said, 'I never believed it. I thought Amy
had made most of it up.'

Mrs Rhodes, I gathered, was one of those romantic
liars who go through life embroidering everything that
happens to them. The amount of adventures that,
according to her own account, happened to her in a
year was simply incredible. If she slipped on a bit of
banana peel it was a case of near escape from death. If
a lampshade caught fire she was rescued from a burning
building at the hazard of her life. Her husband got into
the habit of discounting her statements. Her tale as to

some woman whose child she had injured in a motor accident and who had vowed vengeance on her – well – Mr Rhodes had simply not taken any notice of it. The incident had happened before he married his wife and although she had read him letters couched in crazy language, he had suspected her of composing them herself. She had actually done such a thing once or twice before. She was a woman of hysterical tendencies who craved ceaselessly for excitement.

Now, all that seemed to me very natural – indeed, we have a young woman in the village who does much the same thing. The danger with such people is that when anything at all extraordinary really does happen to them, nobody believes they are speaking the truth. It seemed to me that that was what had happened in this case. The police, I gathered, merely believed that Mr Rhodes was making up this unconvincing tale in order to avert suspicion from himself.

I asked if there had been any women staying by themselves in the hotel. It seemed there were two – a Mrs Granby, an Anglo-Indian widow, and a Miss Carruthers, rather a horsey spinster who dropped her g's. Mr Petherick added that the most minute enquiries had failed to elicit anyone who had seen either of them near the scene of the crime and there was nothing to connect either of them with it in any way. I asked him to describe their personal appearance. He said that Mrs Granby had reddish hair rather untidily done, was sallow-faced and about fifty years of age. Her clothes were rather picturesque, being made mostly of native silk, etc. Miss Carruthers was about forty, wore pince-nez, had close-cropped hair like a man and wore mannish coats and skirts.

'Dear me,' I said, 'that makes it very difficult.'

Mr Petherick looked enquiringly at me, but I didn't

want to say any more just then, so I asked what Sir Malcolm Olde had said.

Sir Malcolm was confident of being able to call conflicting medical testimony and to suggest some way of getting over the fingerprint difficulty. I asked Mr Rhodes what he thought and he said all doctors were fools but he himself couldn't really believe that his wife had killed herself. 'She wasn't that kind of woman,' he said simply – and I believed him. Hysterical people don't usually commit suicide.

I thought a minute and then I asked if the door from Mrs Rhodes's room led straight into the corridor. Mr Rhodes said no – there was a little hallway with a bathroom and lavatory. It was the door from the bedroom to the hallway that was locked and bolted on the inside.

'In that case,' I said, 'the whole thing seems remarkably simple.'

And really, you know, it *did* . . . the simplest thing in the world. And yet no one seemed to have seen it that way.

Both Mr Petherick and Mr Rhodes were staring at me so that I felt quite embarrassed.

'Perhaps,' said Mr Rhodes, 'Miss Marple hasn't quite appreciated the difficulties.'

'Yes,' I said, 'I think I have. There are four possibilities. Either Mrs Rhodes was killed by her husband, or by the chambermaid, or she committed suicide, or she was killed by an outsider whom nobody saw enter or leave.'

'And that's impossible,' Mr Rhodes broke in. 'Nobody could come in or go out through my room without my seeing them, and even if anyone did manage to come in through my wife's room without the electrician seeing them, how the devil could they get out again leaving the door locked and bolted on the inside?'

Mr Petherick looked at me and said: 'Well, Miss Marple?' in an encouraging manner.

'I should like,' I said, 'to ask a question. Mr Rhodes, what did the chambermaid look like?'

He said he wasn't sure – she was tallish, he thought – he didn't remember if she was fair or dark. I turned to Mr Petherick and asked the same question.

He said she was of medium height, had fairish hair and blue eyes and rather a high colour.

Mr Rhodes said: 'You are a better observer than I am, Petherick.'

I ventured to disagree. I then asked Mr Rhodes if he could describe the maid in my house. Neither he nor Mr Petherick could do so.

'Don't you see what that means?' I said. 'You both came here full of your own affairs and the person who let you in was only a *parlourmaid*. The same applies to Mr Rhodes at the hotel. He saw her uniform and her apron. He was engrossed by his work. But Mr Petherick has interviewed the same woman in a different capacity. He has looked at her as a *person*.

'That's what the woman who did the murder counted upon.'

As they still didn't see, I had to explain.

'I think,' I said, 'that this is how it went. The chambermaid came in by door A, passed through Mr Rhodes's room into Mrs Rhodes's room with the hot water bottle and went out through the hallway into passage B. X – as I will call our murderess – came in by door B into the little hallway, concealed herself in – well, in a certain apartment, ahem – and waited until the chambermaid had passed out. Then she entered Mrs Rhodes's room, took the stiletto from the dressing table (she had doubtless explored the room earlier in the day) – went up to the bed, stabbed the dozing woman, wiped the handle of the stiletto, locked and bolted the door by which she had entered, and then passed out through the room where Mr Rhodes was working.'

Mr Rhodes cried out: 'But I should have *seen* her. The electrician would have seen her go in.'

'No,' I said. 'That's where you're wrong. You wouldn't see her – *not if she were dressed as a chambermaid.*' I let it sink in, then I went on, 'You were engrossed in your work – out of the tail of your eye you saw a chambermaid come in, go into your wife's room, come back and go out. It was the same *dress* – but not the same woman. That's what the people having coffee saw – a chambermaid go in and a chambermaid come out. The electrician did the same. I dare say if a chambermaid were very pretty a gentleman might notice her face – human nature being what it is – but if she were just an ordinary middle-aged woman – well – it would be the chambermaid's *dress* you would see – not the woman herself.'

Mr Rhodes cried: 'Who was she?'

'Well,' I said, 'that is going to be a little difficult. It must be either Mrs Granby or Miss Carruthers. Mrs Granby sounds as though she might wear a wig normally – so she could wear her own hair as a chambermaid. On the other hand, Miss Carruthers with her close-cropped mannish head might easily put on a wig to play her part. I dare say you will find out easily enough which of them it is. Personally, I incline myself to think it will be Miss Carruthers.'

And really, my dears, that is the end of the story. Carruthers was a false name, but she was the woman all right. There was insanity in her family. Mrs Rhodes, who was a most reckless and dangerous driver, had run over her little girl, and it had driven the poor woman off her head. She concealed her madness very cunningly except for writing distinctly insane latters to her intended victim. She had been following her about for some time, and she laid her plans very cleverly. The false hair and maid's dress she posted in a parcel first thing the next morning. When taxed with the truth she broke down and confessed at once. The poor thing is in Broadmoor now. Completely unbalanced of course, but a very cleverly planned crime.

Mr Petherick came to me afterwards and brought me a very nice letter from Mr Rhodes – really, it made me blush. Then my old friend said to me: 'Just one thing – why did you think it was more likely to be Carruthers than Granby? You'd never seen either of them.'

'Well,' I said. 'It was the g's. You said she dropped her g's. Now, that's done by a lot of hunting people in books, but I don't know many people who do it in reality – and certainly no one under sixty. You said this woman was forty. Those dropped g's sounded to me like a woman who was playing a part and over-doing it.'

I shan't tell you what Mr Petherick said to that – but he was very complimentary – and I really couldn't help feeling just a teeny weeny bit pleased with myself.

And it's extraordinary how things turn out for the best in this world. Mr Rhodes has married again – such a nice, sensible girl – and they've got a dear little baby and – what do you think? – they asked me to be god-mother. Wasn't it nice of them?

Now I do hope you don't think I've been running on too long . . .

Strange Jest

'And this,' said Jane Helier, completing her introductions, 'is Miss Marple!'

Being an actress, she was able to make her point. It was clearly the climax, the triumphant finale! Her tone was equally compounded of reverent awe and triumph.

The odd part of it was that the object thus proudly proclaimed was merely a gentle, fussy-looking, elderly spinster. In the eyes of the two young people who had just, by Jane's good offices, made her acquaintance, there showed incredulity and a tinge of dismay. They were nice-looking people; the girl, Charmian Stroud, slim and dark – the man, Edward Rossiter, a fair-haired, amiable young giant.

Charmian said a little breathlessly. 'Oh! We're awfully pleased to meet you.' But there was doubt in her eyes. She flung a quick, questioning glance at Jane Helier.

'Darling,' said Jane, answering the glance, 'she's absolutely *marvellous*. Leave it all to her. I told you I'd get her here and I have.' She added to Miss Marple, '*You'll* fix it for them, I know. It will be easy for *you.*'

Miss Marple turned her placid, china-blue eyes towards Mr Rossiter. 'Won't you tell me,' she said, 'what all this is about?'

'Jane's a friend of ours,' Charmian broke in impatiently. 'Edward and I are in rather a fix. Jane said if we would come to her party, she'd introduce us to someone who was – who would – who could –'

Edward came to the rescue. 'Jane tells us you're the last word in sleuths, Miss Marple!'

The old lady's eyes twinkled, but she protested modestly. 'Oh, no, no! Nothing of the kind. It's just that living in a village as I do, one gets to know so much about human nature. But really you have made me quite curious. Do tell me your problem.'

'I'm afraid it's terribly hackneyed – just buried treasure,' said Edward.

'Indeed? But that sounds most exciting!'

'I know. Like *Treasure Island*. But our problem lacks the usual romantic touches. No point on a chart indicated by a skull and crossbones, no directions like "four paces to the left, west by north". It's horribly prosaic – just where we ought to dig.'

'Have you tried at all?'

'I should say we'd dug about two solid square acres! The whole place is ready to be turned into a market garden. We're just discussing whether to grow vegetable marrows or potatoes.'

Charmian said rather abruptly, 'May we really tell you all about it?'

'But, of course, my dear.'

'Then let's find a peaceful spot. Come on, Edward.' She led the way out of the overcrowded and smoke-laden room, and they went up the stairs, to a small sitting-room on the second floor.

When they were seated, Charmian began abruptly. 'Well, here goes! The story starts with Uncle Mathew, uncle – or rather, great-great-uncle – to both of us. He was incredibly ancient. Edward and I were his only relations. He was fond of us and always declared that when he died he would leave his money between us.

Well, he died last March and left everything he had to be divided equally between Edward and myself. What I've just said sounds rather callous – I don't mean that it was right that he died – actually we were very fond of him. But he'd been ill for some time.

'The point is that the "everything" he left turned out to be practically nothing at all. And that, frankly, was a bit of a blow to us both, wasn't it, Edward?'

The amiable Edward agreed. 'You see,' he said, 'we'd counted on it a bit. I mean, when you know a good bit of money is coming to you, you don't – well – buckle down and try to make it yourself. I'm in the army – not got anything to speak of outside my pay – and Charmian herself hasn't got a bean. She works as a stage manager in a repertory theatre – quite interesting, and she enjoys it – but no money in it. We'd counted on getting married, but weren't worried about the money side of it because we both knew we'd be jolly well off some day.'

'And now, you see, we're not!' said Charmian. 'What's more, Ansteys – that's the family place, and Edward and I both love it – will probably have to be sold. And Edward and I feel we just can't bear that! But if we don't find Uncle Mathew's money, we shall have to sell.'

Edward said, 'You know, Charmian, we still haven't come to the vital point.'

'Well, you talk, then.'

Edward turned to Miss Marple. 'It's like this, you see. As Uncle Mathew grew older, he got more and more suspicious. He didn't trust anybody.'

'Very wise of him,' said Miss Marple. 'The depravity of human nature is unbelievable.'

'Well, you may be right. Anyway, Uncle Mathew thought so. He had a friend who lost his money in a bank, and another friend who was ruined by an absconding solicitor, and he lost some money himself in a fraudulent company. He got so that he used to hold forth at great length that the only safe and sane thing to do was to convert your money into solid bullion and bury it.'

'Ah,' said Miss Marple. 'I begin to see.'

'Yes. Friends argued with him, pointed out that he'd get no interest that way, but he held that that didn't really matter. The bulk of your money, he said, should be "kept in a box under the bed or buried in the garden". Those were his words.'

Charmian went on. 'And when he died, he left hardly anything at all in securities, though he was very rich. So we think that that's what he must have done.'

Edward explained. 'We found that he had sold securities and drawn out large sums of money from time to time, and nobody knows what he did with them. But it seems probable that he lived up to his principles, and that he did buy gold and bury it.'

'He didn't say anything before he died? Leave any paper? No letter?'

'That's the maddening part of it. He didn't. He'd been unconscious for some days, but he rallied before he died. He looked at us both and chuckled – a faint, weak little chuckle. He said, "*You'll* be all right, my pretty pair of doves." And then he tapped his eye – his right eye – and winked at us. And then – he died. Poor old Uncle Mathew.'

'He tapped his eye,' said Miss Marple thoughtfully.

Edward said eagerly. 'Does that convey anything to you? It made me think of an Arsene Lupin story where there was something hidden in a man's glass eye. But Uncle Mathew didn't have a glass eye.'

Miss Marple shook her head. 'No – I can't think of anything at the moment.'

Charmian said disappointedly, 'Jane told us you'd say *at once* where to dig!'

Miss Marple smiled. 'I'm not quite a conjurer, you know. I didn't know your uncle, or what sort of man he was, and I don't know the house or the grounds.'

Charmian said, 'If you did know them?'

'Well, it must be quite simple, really, mustn't it?' said Miss Marple.

'Simple!' said Charmian. 'You come down to Ansteys and see if it's simple!'

It is possible that she did not mean the invitation to be taken seriously, but Miss Marple said briskly, 'Well, really, my dear, that's very kind of you. I've always wanted to have the chance of looking for buried treasure. And,' she added, looking at them with a beaming, late-Victorian smile, 'with a love interest, too!'

'You see!' said Charmian, gesturing dramatically.

They had just completed a grand tour of Ansteys. They had been round the kitchen garden – heavily trenched. They had been through the little woods, where every important tree had been dug round, and had gazed sadly on the pitted surface of the once smooth lawn. They had been up to the attic, where old trunks and chests had been rifled of their contents. They had been down to the cellars, where flagstones had been heaved unwillingly from their sockets. They had measured and tapped walls, and Miss Marple had been shown every antique piece of furniture that contained or could be suspected of containing a secret drawer.

On a table in the morning-room there was a heap of papers – all the papers that the late Mathew Stroud had left. Not one had been destroyed, and Charmian and

Edward were wont to return to them again and again, earnestly perusing bills, invitations, and business correspondence in the hope of spotting a hitherto unnoticed clue.

'Can you think of anywhere we haven't looked?' demanded Charmian hopefully.

Miss Marple shook her head. 'You seem to have been very thorough, my dear. Perhaps, if I may say so, just a little *too* thorough. I always think, you know, that one should have a plan. It's like my friend, Mrs Eldritch, she had such a nice little maid, polished linoleum beautifully, but she was so thorough that she polished the bathroom floor too much, and as Mrs Eldritch was stepping out of the bath the cork mat slipped from under her, and she had a very nasty fall and actually broke her leg! Most awkward, because the bathroom door was locked, of course, and the gardener had to get a ladder and come in through the window – terribly distressing to Mrs Eldritch, who had always been a very modest woman.'

Edward moved restlessly.

Miss Marple said quickly, 'Please forgive me. So apt, I know, to fly off at a tangent. But one thing does remind one of another. And sometimes that is helpful. All I was trying to say was that perhaps if we tried to sharpen our wits and think of a likely place –'

Edward said crossly, 'You think of one, Miss Marple. Charmian's brains and mine are now only beautiful blanks!'

'Dear, dear. Of course – most tiring for you. If you don't mind I'll just look through all this.' She indicated the papers on the table. 'That is, if there's nothing private – I don't want to appear to pry.'

'Oh, that's all right. But I'm afraid you won't find anything.'

She sat down by the table and methodically worked through the sheaf of documents. As she replaced each one, she sorted them automatically into tidy little heaps. When she had finished she sat staring in front of her for some minutes.

Edward asked, not without a touch of malice, 'Well, Miss Marple?'

Miss Marple came to herself with a little start. 'I beg your pardon. Most helpful.'

'You've found something relevant?'

'Oh, no, nothing like that, but I do believe I know what sort of man your Uncle Mathew was. Rather like my own Uncle Henry, I think. Fond of rather obvious jokes. A bachelor, evidently – I wonder why – perhaps an early disappointment? Methodical up to a point, but not very fond of being tied up – so few bachelors are!'

Behind Miss Marple's back, Charmian made a sign to Edward. It said, *She's ga-ga.*

Miss Marple was continuing happily to talk of her deceased Uncle Henry. 'Very fond of puns, he was. And to some people, puns are most annoying. A mere play upon words may be very irritating. He was a suspicious man, too. Always was convinced the servants were robbing him. And sometimes, of course, they were, but not always. It grew upon him, poor man. Towards the end he suspected them of tampering with his food, and finally refused to eat anything but boiled eggs! Said nobody could tamper with the inside of a boiled egg. Dear Uncle Henry, he used to be such a merry soul at one time – very fond of his coffee after dinner. He always used to say, "This coffee is very Moorish," meaning, you know, that he'd like a little more.'

Edward felt that if he heard any more about Uncle Henry he'd go mad.

'Fond of young people, too,' went on Miss Marple,

'but inclined to tease them a little, if you know what I mean. Used to put bags of sweets where a child just couldn't reach them.'

Casting politeness aside, Charmian said, 'I think he sounds horrible!'

'Oh, no, dear, just an old bachelor, you know, and not used to children. And he wasn't at all stupid, really. He used to keep a good deal of money in the house, and he had a safe put in. Made a great fuss about it – and how very secure it was. As a result of his talking so much, burglars broke in one night and actually cut a hole in the safe with a chemical device.'

'Served him right,' said Edward.

'Oh, but there was nothing in the safe,' said Miss Marple. 'You see, he really kept the money somewhere else – behind some volumes of sermons in the library, as a matter of fact. He said people never took a book of that kind out of the shelf!'

Edward interrupted excitedly. 'I say, that's an idea. What about the library?'

But Charmian shook a scornful head. 'Do you think I hadn't thought of that? I went through all the books Tuesday of last week, when you went off to Portsmouth. Took them all out, shook them. Nothing there.'

Edward sighed. Then, rousing himself, he endeavoured to rid himself tactfully of their disappointing guest. 'It's been awfully good of you to come down as you have and try to help us. Sorry it's been all a wash-out. Feel we trespassed a lot on your time. However – I'll get the car out, and you'll be able to catch the three-thirty –'

'Oh,' said Miss Marple, 'but we've got to find the money, haven't we? You mustn't give up, Mr Rossiter. "If at first you don't succeed, try, try, try again."'

'You mean you're going to – go on trying?'

'Strictly speaking,' said Miss Marple, 'I haven't begun yet. "First catch your hare – "' as Mrs Beaton says in her cookery book – a wonderful book but terribly expensive; most of the recipes begin, "Take a quart of cream and a dozen eggs." Let me see, where was I? Oh, yes. Well, we have, so to speak, caught our hare – the hare being, of course, your Uncle Mathew, and we've only got to decide now where he would have hidden the money. It ought to be quite simple.'

'Simple?' demanded Charmian.

'Oh, yes, dear. I'm sure he would have done the obvious thing. A secret drawer – that's my solution.'

Edward said dryly, 'You couldn't put bars of gold in a secret drawer.'

'No, no, of course not. But there's no reason to believe the money is in gold.'

'He always used to say –'

'So did my Uncle Henry about his safe! So I should strongly suspect that that was just a blind. Diamonds – now they could be in a secret drawer quite easily.'

'But we've looked in all the secret drawers. We had a cabinetmaker over to examine the furniture.'

'Did you, dear? That was clever of you. I should suggest your uncle's own desk would be the most likely. Was it the tall escritoire against the wall there?'

'Yes. And I'll show you.' Charmian went over to it. She took down the flap. Inside were pigeonholes and little drawers. She opened a small door in the centre and touched a spring inside the left-hand drawer. The bottom of the centre recess clicked and slid forward. Charmian drew it out, revealing a shallow well beneath. It was empty.

'Now isn't that a coincidence?' exclaimed Miss Marple. 'Uncle Henry had a desk just like this, only his was burr walnut and this is mahogany.'

'At any rate,' said Charmian, 'there's nothing there, as you can see.'

'I expect,' said Miss Marple, 'your cabinetmaker was a young man. He didn't know everything. People were very artful when they made hiding-places in those days. There's such a thing as a secret inside a secret.'

She extracted a hairpin from her neat bun of grey hair. Straightening it out, she stuck the point into what appeared to be a tiny wormhole in one side of the secret recess. With a little difficulty she pulled out a small drawer. In it was a bundle of faded letters and a folded paper.

Edward and Charmian pounced on the find together. With trembling fingers Edward unfolded the paper. He dropped it with an exclamation of disgust.

'A damned cookery recipe. Baked ham!'

Charmian was untying a ribbon that held the letters together. She drew one out and glanced at it. 'Love letters!'

Miss Marple reacted with Victorian gusto. 'How interesting! Perhaps the reason your uncle never married.'

Charmian read aloud:

'My ever dear Mathew, I must confess that the time seems long indeed since I received your last letter. I try to occupy myself with the various tasks allotted to me, and often say to myself that I am indeed fortunate to see so much of the globe, though little did I think when I went to America that I should voyage off to these far islands!'

Charmian broke off. 'Where is it from? Oh! Hawaii!' She went on:

'Alas, these natives are still far from seeing the light. They are in an unclothed and savage state and spend most of their time swimming and dancing, adorning themselves with garlands of flowers. Mr Gray has made some converts but it is uphill work, and he and Mrs Gray get sadly discouraged. I try to do all I can to cheer and encourage him, but I, too, am often sad for a reason you can guess, dear Mathew. Alas, absence is a severe trial for a loving heart. Your renewed vows and protestations of affection cheered me greatly. Now and always you have my faithful and devoted heart, dear Mathew, and I remain –

Your true love, Betty Martin.

PS – I address my letter under cover to our mutual friend, Matilda Graves, as usual. I hope heaven will pardon this little subterfuge.'

Edward whistled. 'A female missionary! So that was Uncle Mathew's romance. I wonder why they never married?'

'She seems to have gone all over the world,' said Charmian, looking through the letters. 'Mauritius – all sorts of places. Probably died of yellow fever or something.'

A gentle chuckle made them start. Miss Marple was apparently much amused. 'Well, well,' she said. 'Fancy that, now!'

She was reading the recipe for baked ham. Seeing their enquiring glances, she read out: ' "Baked ham with spinach. Take a nice piece of gammon, stuff with cloves, and cover with brown sugar. Bake in a slow oven. Serve with a border of puréed spinach." What do you think of that, now?'

'I think it sounds filthy,' said Edward.

'No, no, actually it would be very good – but what do you think of *the whole thing*?'

A sudden ray of light illuminated Edward's face. 'Do you think it's a code – cryptogram of some kind?' He seized it. 'Look here, Charmian, it might be, you know! No reason to put a cooking-recipe in a secret drawer otherwise.'

'Exactly,' said Miss Marple. 'Very, very significant.'

Charmian said, 'I know what it might be – invisible ink! Let's heat it. Turn on the electric fire.'

Edward did so, but no signs of writing appeared under the treatment.

Miss Marple coughed. 'I really think, you know, that you're making it rather *too* difficult. The recipe is only an indication, so to speak. It is, I think, the letters that are significant.'

'The letters?'

'Especially,' said Miss Marple, 'the signature.'

But Edward hardly heard her. He called excitedly, 'Charmian! Come here! She's right. See – the envelopes are old, right enough, but the letters themselves were written much later.'

'Exactly,' said Miss Marple.

'They're only fake old. I bet anything old Uncle Mat faked them himself –'

'Precisely,' said Miss Marple.

'The whole thing's a sell. There never was a female missionary. It must be a code.'

'My dear, dear children – there's really no need to make it all so difficult. Your uncle was really a very simple man. He had to have his little joke, that was all.'

For the first time they gave her their full attention.

'Just exactly what do you mean, Miss Marple?' asked Charmian.

'I mean, dear, that you're actually holding the money in your hand this minute.'

Charmian stared down.

'The signature, dear. That gives the whole thing away. The recipe is just an indication. Shorn of all the cloves and brown sugar and the rest of it, what is it *actually*? Why, gammon and spinach to be sure! *Gammon and spinach!* Meaning – nonsense! So it's clear that it's the letters that are important. And then, if you take into consideration what your uncle did just before he died. He tapped his eye, you said. Well, there you are – that gives you the clue, you see.'

Charmian said, 'Are we mad, or are you?'

'Surely, my dear, you must have heard the expression meaning that something is not a true picture, or has it quite died out nowadays? "All my eye and Betty Martin."'

Edward gasped, his eyes falling to the letter in his hand. 'Betty Martin –'

'Of course, Mr Rossiter. As you have just said, there isn't – there wasn't any such person. The letters were written by your uncle, and I dare say he got a lot of fun out of writing them! As you say, the writing on the envelopes is much older – in fact, the envelope couldn't belong to the letters, anyway, because the postmark of one you are holding is eighteen fifty-one.'

She paused. She made it very emphatic. 'Eighteen fifty-one. And that explains everything, doesn't it?'

'Not to me,' said Edward.

'Well, of course,' said Miss Marple, 'I dare say it wouldn't to me if it weren't for my great-nephew Lionel. Such a dear little boy and a passionate stamp collector. Knows all about stamps. It was he who told me about the rare and expensive stamps and that a wonderful new find had come up for auction. And I actually remember his mentioning one stamp – an eighteen fifty-one *blue two-cent.* It realized something like twenty-five thousand dollars, I believe. Fancy! I should imagine that the other stamps are something also rare and expensive. No doubt your uncle bought through dealers and was careful to "cover his tracks", as they say in detective stories.'

Edward groaned. He sat down and buried his face in his hands.

'What's the matter?' demanded Charmian.

'Nothing. It's only the awful thought that, but for Miss Marple, we might have burned these letters in a decent, gentlemanly way!'

'Ah,' said Miss Marple, 'that's just what these old gentlemen who are fond of their jokes never realize. Uncle Henry, I remember, sent a favourite niece a five-pound note for a Christmas present. He put it in a Christmas card, gummed the card together, and wrote on it, "Love and best wishes. Afraid this is all I can manage this year."

'She, poor girl, was annoyed at what she thought was his meanness and threw it all straight into the fire; then, of course, he had to give her another.'

Edward's feelings towards Uncle Henry had suffered an abrupt and complete change.

'Miss Marple,' he said, 'I'm going to get a bottle of champagne. We'll all drink the health of your Uncle Henry.'

Tape-Measure Murder

Miss Politt took hold of the knocker and rapped politely on the cottage door. After a discreet interval she knocked again. The parcel under her left arm shifted a little as she did so, and she readjusted it. Inside the parcel was Mrs Spenlow's new green winter dress, ready for fitting. From Miss Politt's left hand dangled a bag of black silk, containing a tape measure, a pincushion, and a large practical pair of scissors.

Miss Politt was tall and gaunt, with a sharp nose, pursed lips, and meagre iron-grey hair. She hesitated before using the knocker for the third time. Glancing down the street, she saw a figure rapidly approaching. Miss Hartnell, jolly, weather-beaten, fifty-five, shouted out in her usual loud bass voice, 'Good afternoon, Miss Politt!'

The dressmaker answered, 'Good afternoon, Miss Hartnell.' Her voice was excessively thin and genteel in its accents. She had started life as a lady's maid. 'Excuse me,' she went on, 'but do you happen to know if by any chance Mrs Spenlow isn't at home?'

'Not the least idea,' said Miss Hartnell.

'It's rather awkward, you see. I was to fit on Mrs Spenlow's new dress this afternoon. Three-thirty, she said.'

Miss Hartnell consulted her wrist watch. 'It's a little past the half-hour now.'

'Yes. I have knocked three times, but there doesn't seem to be any answer, so I was wondering if perhaps Mrs Spenlow might have gone out and forgotten. She doesn't forget appointments as a rule, and she wants the dress to wear the day after tomorrow.'

Miss Hartnell entered the gate and walked up the path to join Miss Politt outside the door of Laburnum Cottage.

'Why doesn't Gladys answer the door?' she demanded. 'Oh, no, of course, it's Thursday – Gladys's day out. I expect Mrs Spenlow has fallen asleep. I don't expect you've made enough noise with this thing.'

Seizing the knocker, she executed a deafening *rat-a-tat-tat*, and in addition thumped upon the panels of the door. She also called out in a stentorian voice, 'What ho, within there!'

There was no response.

Miss Politt murmured, 'Oh, I think Mrs Spenlow must have forgotten and gone out, I'll call round some other time.' She began edging away down the path.

'Nonsense,' said Miss Hartnell firmly. 'She can't have gone out. I'd have met her. I'll just take a look through the windows and see if I can find any signs of life.'

She laughed in her usual hearty manner, to indicate that it was a joke, and applied a perfunctory glance to the nearest window-pane – perfunctory because she knew quite well that the front room was seldom used, Mr and Mrs Spenlow preferring the small back sitting-room.

Perfunctory as it was, though, it succeeded in its object. Miss Hartnell, it is true, saw no signs of life. On the contrary, she saw, through the window, Mrs Spenlow lying on the hearthrug – dead.

'Of course,' said Miss Hartnell, telling the story

afterwards, 'I managed to keep my head. That Politt creature wouldn't have had the least idea of what to do. "Got to keep our heads," I said to her. "*You* stay here, and I'll go for Constable Palk." She said something about not wanting to be left, but I paid no attention at all. One has to be firm with that sort of person. I've always found they enjoy making a fuss. So I was just going off when, at that very moment, Mr Spenlow came round the corner of the house.'

Here Miss Hartnell made a significant pause. It enabled her audience to ask breathlessly, 'Tell me, how did he *look*?'

Miss Hartnell would then go on, 'Frankly, *I* suspected something at once! He was *far* too calm. He didn't seem surprised in the least. And you may say what you like, it isn't natural for a man to hear that his wife is dead and display no emotion whatever.'

Everybody agreed with this statement.

The police agreed with it, too. So suspicious did they consider Mr Spenlow's detachment, that they lost no time in ascertaining how that gentleman was situated as a result of his wife's death. When they discovered that Mrs Spenlow had been the monied partner, and that her money went to her husband under a will made soon after their marriage, they were more suspicious than ever.

Miss Marple, that sweet-faced – and, some said, vinegar-tongued – elderly spinster who lived in the house next to the rectory, was interviewed very early – within half an hour of the discovery of the crime. She was approached by Police Constable Palk, importantly thumbing a notebook. 'If you don't mind, ma'am, I've a few questions to ask you.'

Miss Marple said, 'In connection with the murder of Mrs Spenlow?'

Palk was startled. 'May I ask, madam, how you got to know of it?'

'The fish,' said Miss Marple.

The reply was perfectly intelligible to Constable Palk. He assumed correctly that the fishmonger's boy had brought it, together with Miss Marple's evening meal.

Miss Marple continued gently. 'Lying on the floor in the sitting-room, strangled – possibly by a very narrow belt. But whatever it was, it was taken away.'

Palk's face was wrathful. 'How that young Fred gets to know everything –'

Miss Marple cut him short adroitly. She said, 'There's a pin in your tunic.'

Constable Palk looked down, startled. He said, 'They do say, "See a pin and pick it up, all the day you'll have good luck."'

'I hope that will come true. Now what is it you want me to tell you?'

Constable Palk cleared his throat, looked important, and consulted his notebook. 'Statement was made to me by Mr Arthur Spenlow, husband of the deceased. Mr Spenlow says that at two-thirty, as far as he can say, he was rung up by Miss Marple, and asked if he would come over at a quarter past three as she was anxious to consult him about something. Now, ma'am, is that true?'

'Certainly not,' said Miss Marple.

'You did not ring up Mr Spenlow at two-thirty?'

'Neither at two-thirty nor any other time.'

'Ah,' said Constable Palk, and sucked his moustache with a good deal of satisfaction.

'What else did Mr Spenlow say?'

'Mr Spenlow's statement was that he came over here as requested, leaving his own house at ten minutes past three; that on arrival here he was informed by the maid-servant that Miss Marple was "not at 'ome".'

'That part of it is true,' said Miss Marple. 'He did come here, but I was at a meeting at the Women's Institute.'

'Ah,' said Constable Palk again.

Miss Marple exclaimed, 'Do tell me, Constable, do you suspect Mr Spenlow?'

'It's not for me to say at this stage, but it looks to me as though somebody, naming no names, has been trying to be artful.'

Miss Marple said thoughtfully, 'Mr Spenlow?'

She liked Mr Spenlow. He was a small, spare man, stiff and conventional in speech, the acme of respect-ability. It seemed odd that he should have come to live in the country, he had so clearly lived in towns all his life. To Miss Marple he confided the reason. He said, 'I have always intended, ever since I was a small boy, to live in the country some day and have a garden of my own. I have always been very much attached to flowers. My wife, you know, kept a flower shop. That's where I saw her first.'

A dry statement, but it opened up a vista of romance. A younger, prettier Mrs Spenlow, seen against a back-ground of flowers.

Mr Spenlow, however, really knew nothing about flowers. He had no idea of seeds, of cuttings, of bedding out, of annuals or perennials. He had only a vision – a vision of a small cottage garden thickly planted with sweet-smelling, brightly coloured blossoms. He had asked, almost pathetically, for instruction, and had noted down Miss Marple's replies to questions in a little book.

He was a man of quiet method. It was, perhaps, because of this trait, that the police were interested in him when his wife was found murdered. With patience and perseverance they learned a good deal about the late Mrs Spenlow – and soon all St Mary Mead knew it, too.

The late Mrs Spenlow had begun life as a between-maid in a large house. She had left that position to marry the second gardener, and with him had started a flower shop in London. The shop had prospered. Not so the gardener, who before long had sickened and died.

His widow carried on the shop and enlarged it in an ambitious way. She had continued to prosper. Then she had sold the business at a handsome price and embarked upon matrimony for the second time – with Mr Spenlow, a middled-aged jeweller who had inherited a small and struggling business. Not long afterwards, they had sold the business and came down to St Mary Mead.

Mrs Spenlow was a well-to-do woman. The profits from her florist's establishment she had invested – 'under spirit guidance', as she explained to all and sundry. The spirits had advised her with unexpected acumen.

All her investments had prospered, some in quite a sensational fashion. Instead, however, of this increasing her belief in spiritualism, Mrs Spenlow basely deserted mediums and sittings, and made a brief but whole-hearted plunge into an obscure religion with Indian affinities which was based on various forms of deep breathing. When, however, she arrived at St Mary Mead, she had relapsed into a period of orthodox Church-of-England beliefs. She was a good deal at the vicarage, and attended church services with assiduity. She patron-ized the village shops, took an interest in the local hap-penings, and played village bridge.

A humdrum, everyday life. And – suddenly – murder.

Colonel Melchett, the chief constable, had summoned Inspector Slack.

Slack was a positive type of man. When he had made up his mind, he was sure. He was quite sure now. 'Husband did it, sir,' he said.

'You think so?'

'Quite sure of it. You've only got to look at him. Guilty as hell. Never showed a sign of grief or emotion. He came back to the house knowing she was dead.'

'Wouldn't he at least have tried to act the part of the distracted husband?'

'Not him, sir. Too pleased with himself. Some gentlemen can't act. Too stiff.'

'Any other woman in his life?' Colonel Melchett asked.

'Haven't been able to find any trace of one. Of course, he's the artful kind. He'd cover his tracks. As I see it, he was just fed up with his wife. She'd got the money, and I should say was a trying woman to live with – always taking up with some "ism" or other. He cold-bloodedly decided to do away with her and live comfortably on his own.'

'Yes, that could be the case, I suppose.'

'Depend upon it, that was it. Made his plans careful. Pretended to get a phone call –'

Melchett interrupted him. 'No call been traced?'

'No, sir. That means either that he lied, or that the call was put through from a public telephone booth. The only two public phones in the village are at the station and the post office. Post office it certainly wasn't. Mrs Blade sees everyone who comes in. Station it might be. Train arrives at two twenty-seven and there's a bit of a bustle then. But the main thing is *he* says it was

Miss Marple who called him up, and that certainly isn't true. The call didn't come from her house, and she herself was away at the Institute.'

'You're not overlooking the possibility that the husband was deliberately got out of the way – by someone who wanted to murder Mrs Spenlow?'

'You're thinking of young Ted Gerard, aren't you, sir? I've been working on him – what we're up against there is lack of motive. He doesn't stand to gain anything.'

'He's an undesirable character, though. Quite a pretty little spot of embezzlement to his credit.'

'I'm not saying he isn't a wrong 'un. Still, he did go to his boss and own up to that embezzlement. And his employers weren't wise to it.'

'An Oxford Grouper,' said Melchett.

'Yes, sir. Became a convert and went off to do the straight thing and own up to having pinched money. I'm not saying, mind you, that it mayn't have been astuteness. He may have thought he was suspected and decided to gamble on honest repentance.'

'You have a sceptical mind, Slack,' said Colonel Melchett. 'By the way, have you talked to Miss Marple at all?'

'What's *she* got to do with it, sir?'

'Oh, nothing. But she hears things, you know. Why don't you go and have a chat with her? She's a very sharp old lady.'

Slack changed the subject. 'One thing I've been meaning to ask you, sir. That domestic-service job where the deceased started her career – Sir Robert Abercrombie's place. That's where that jewel robbery was – emeralds – worth a packet. Never got them. I've been looking it up – must have happened when the Spenlow woman was there, though she'd have been quite a girl at the time. Don't think she was mixed up in it, do you, sir? Spenlow, you know, was one of those little tuppenny-ha'penny jewellers – just the chap for a fence.'

Melchett shook his head. 'Don't think there's anything in that. She didn't even know Spenlow at the time. I remember the case. Opinion in police circles was that a son of the house was mixed up in it – Jim Abercrombie – awful young waster. Had a pile of debts, and just after the robbery they were all paid off – some rich woman, so they said, but I don't know – Old Abercrombie hedged a bit about the case – tried to call the police off.'

'It was just an idea, sir,' said Slack.

Miss Marple received Inspector Slack with gratification, especially when she heard that he had been sent by Colonel Melchett.

'Now, really, that is very kind of Colonel Melchett. I didn't know he remembered me.'

'He remembers you, all right. Told me that what you didn't know of what goes on in St Mary Mead isn't worth knowing.'

'Too kind of him, but really I don't know anything at all. About this murder, I mean.'

'You know what the talk about it is.'

'Oh, of course – but it wouldn't do, would it, to repeat just idle talk?'

Slack said, with an attempt at geniality, 'This isn't an official conversation, you know. It's in confidence, so to speak.'

'You mean you really want to know what people are saying? Whether there's any truth in it or not?'

'That's the idea.'

'Well, of course, there's been a great deal of talk and

speculation. And there are really two distinct camps, if you understand me. To begin with, there are the people who think that the husband did it. A husband or a wife is, in a way, the natural person to suspect, don't you think so?'

'Maybe,' said the inspector cautiously.

'Such close quarters, you know. Then, so often, the money angle. I hear that it was Mrs Spenlow who had the money, and therefore Mr Spenlow does benefit by her death. In this wicked world I'm afraid the most uncharitable assumptions are often justified.'

'He comes into a tidy sum, all right.'

'Just so. It would seem quite plausible, wouldn't it, for him to strangle her, leave the house by the back, come across the fields to my house, ask for me and pretend he'd had a telephone call from me, then go back and find his wife murdered in his absence – hoping, of course, that the crime would be put down to some tramp or burglar.'

The inspector nodded. 'What with the money angle – and if they'd been on bad terms lately –'

But Miss Marple interrupted him. 'Oh, but they hadn't.'

'You know that for a fact?'

'Everyone would have known if they'd quarrelled! The maid, Gladys Brent – she'd have soon spread it round the village.'

The inspector said feebly, 'She mightn't have known –' and received a pitying smile in reply.

Miss Marple went on. 'And then there's the other school of thought. Ted Gerard. A good-looking young man. I'm afraid, you know, that good looks are inclined to influence one more than they should. Our last curate but one – quite a magical effect! All the girls came to church evening service as well as morning. And many older women became unusually active in parish work – and the slippers and scarfs that were made for him! Quite embarrassing for the poor young man.

'But let me see, where was I? Oh, yes, this young man, Ted Gerard. Of course, there has been talk about him. He's come down to see her so often. Though Mrs Spenlow told me herself that he was a member of what I think they call the Oxford Group. A religious movement. They are quite sincere and very earnest, I believe, and Mrs Spenlow was impressed by it all.'

Miss Marple took a breath and went on. 'And I'm sure there was no reason to believe that there was anything more in it than that, but you know what people are. Quite a lot of people are convinced that Mrs Spenlow was infatuated with the young man, and that she'd lent him quite a lot of money. And it's perfectly true that he was actually seen at the station that day. In the train – the two twenty-seven down train. But of course it would be quite easy, wouldn't it, to slip out of the other side of the train and go through the cutting and over the fence and round by the hedge and never come out of the station entrance at all. So that he need not have been seen going to the cottage. And, of course, people do think that what Mrs Spenlow was wearing was rather peculiar.'

'Peculiar?'

'A kimono. Not a dress.' Miss Marple blushed. 'That sort of thing, you know, is, perhaps, rather suggestive to some people.'

'You think it was suggestive?'

'Oh, no, I don't think so, I think it was perfectly natural.'

'You think it was natural?'

'Under the circumstances, yes.' Miss Marple's glance was cool and reflective.

Inspector Slack said, 'It might give us another motive for the husband. Jealousy.'

'Oh, no, Mr Spenlow would never be jealous. He's not the sort of man who notices things. If his wife had gone away and left a note on the pincushion, it would be the first he'd know of anything of that kind.'

Inspector Slack was puzzled by the intent way she was looking at him. He had an idea that all her conversation was intended to hint at something he didn't understand. She said now, with some emphasis, 'Didn't *you* find any clues, Inspector – on the spot?'

'People don't leave fingerprints and cigarette ash nowadays, Miss Marple.'

'But this, I think,' she suggested, 'was an old-fashioned crime –'

Slack said sharply, 'Now what do you mean by that?'

Miss Marple remarked slowly, 'I think, you know, that Constable Palk could help you. He was the first person on the – on the "scene of the crime", as they say.'

Mr Spenlow was sitting in a deck chair. He looked bewildered. He said, in his thin, precise voice, 'I may, of course, be imagining what occurred. My hearing is not as good as it was. But I distinctly think I heard a small boy call after me, "Yah, who's a Crippen?" It – it conveyed the impression to me that he was of the opinion that I had – had killed my dear wife.'

Miss Marple, gently snipping off a dead rose head, said, 'That was the impression he meant to convey, no doubt.'

'But what could possibly have put such an idea into a child's head?'

Miss Marple coughed. 'Listening, no doubt, to the opinions of his elders.'

'You – you really mean that other people think that, also?'

'Quite half the people in St Mary Mead.'

'But – my dear lady – what can possibly have given rise to such an idea? I was sincerely attached to my wife. She did not, alas, take to living in the country as much as I had hoped she would do, but perfect agreement on every subject is an impossible idea. I assure you I feel her loss very keenly.'

'Probably. But if you will excuse my saying so, you don't sound as though you do.'

Mr Spenlow drew his meagre frame up to its full height. 'My dear lady, many years ago I read of a certain Chinese philosopher who, when his dearly loved wife was taken from him, continued calmly to beat a gong in the street – a customary Chinese pastime, I presume – exactly as usual. The people of the city were much impressed by his fortitude.'

'But,' said Miss Marple, 'the people of St Mary Mead react rather differently. Chinese philosophy does not appeal to them.'

'But you understand?'

Miss Marple nodded. 'My Uncle Henry,' she explained, 'was a man of unusual self-control. His motto was "Never display emotion". He, too, was very fond of flowers.'

'I was thinking,' said Mr Spenlow with something like eagerness, 'that I might, perhaps, have a pergola on the west side of the cottage. Pink roses and, perhaps, wisteria. And there is a white starry flower, whose name for the moment escapes me –'

In the tone in which she spoke to her grandnephew, aged three, Miss Marple said, 'I have a very nice catalogue here, with pictures. Perhaps you would like to look through it – I have to go up to the village.'

Leaving Mr Spenlow sitting happily in the garden with his catalogue, Miss Marple went up to her room, hastily rolled up a dress in a piece of brown paper, and, leaving the house, walked briskly up to the post office. Miss Politt, the dressmaker, lived in the rooms over the post office.

But Miss Marple did not at once go through the door and up the stairs. It was just two-thirty, and, a minute late, the Much Benham bus drew up outside the post office door. It was one of the events of the day in St Mary Mead. The postmistress hurried out with parcels, parcels connected with the shop side of her business, for the post office also dealt in sweets, cheap books, and children's toys.

For some four minutes Miss Marple was alone in the post office.

Not till the postmistress returned to her post did Miss Marple go upstairs and explain to Miss Politt that she wanted her old grey crepe altered and made more fashionable if that were possible. Miss Politt promised to see what she could do.

The chief constable was rather astonished when Miss Marple's name was brought to him. She came in with many apologies. 'So sorry – so very sorry to disturb you. You are so busy, I know, but then you have always been so very kind, Colonel Melchett, and I felt I would rather come to you instead of Inspector Slack. For one thing, you know, I should hate Constable Palk to get into any trouble. Strictly speaking, I suppose he shouldn't have touched anything at all.'

Colonel Melchett was slightly bewildered. He said, 'Palk? That's the St Mary Mead constable, isn't it? What has he been doing?'

'He picked up a pin, you know. It was in his tunic.

And it occurred to me at the time that it was quite probable he had actually picked it up in Mrs Spenlow's house.'

'Quite, quite. But after all, you know, what's a pin? Matter of fact he did pick the pin up just by Mrs Spenlow's body. Came and told Slack about it yesterday – you put him up to that, I gather? Oughtn't to have touched anything, of course, but as I said, what's a pin? It was only a common pin. Sort of thing any woman might use.'

'Oh, no, Colonel Melchett, that's where you're wrong. To a man's eye, perhaps, it looked like an ordinary pin, but it wasn't. It was a special pin, a very thin pin, the kind you buy by the box, the kind used mostly by dressmakers.'

Melchett stared at her, a faint light of comprehension breaking in on him. Miss Marple nodded her head several times, eagerly.

'Yes, of course. It seems to me so obvious. She was in her kimono because she was going to try on her new dress, and she went into the front room, and Miss Politt just said something about measurements and put the tape measure round her neck – and then all she'd have to do was to cross it and pull – quite easy, so I've heard. And then, of course, she'd go outside and pull the door to and stand there knocking as though she'd just arrived. But the pin shows she'd *already been in the house.*'

'And it was Miss Politt who telephoned to Spenlow?'

'Yes. From the post office at two-thirty – just when the bus comes and the post office would be empty.'

Colonel Melchett said, 'But my dear Miss Marple, why? In heaven's name, why? You can't have a murder without a motive.'

'Well, I think, you know, Colonel Melchett, from all I've heard, that the crime dates from a long time back.

It reminds me, you know, of my two cousins, Antony and Gordon. Whatever Antony did always went right for him, and with poor Gordon it was just the other way about. Race horses went lame, and stocks went down, and property depreciated. As I see it, the two women were in it together.'

'In what?'

'The robbery. Long ago. Very valuable emeralds, so I've heard. The lady's maid and the tweeny. Because one thing hasn't been explained – how, when the tweeny married the gardener, did they have enough money to set up a flower shop?

'The answer is, it was her share of the – the swag, I think is the right expression. Everything she did turned out well. Money made money. But the other one, the lady's maid, must have been unlucky. She came down to being just a village dressmaker. Then they met again. Quite all right at first, I expect, until Mr Ted Gerard came on the scene.

'Mrs Spenlow, you see, was already suffering from conscience, and was inclined to be emotionally religious. This young man no doubt urged her to "face up" and to "come clean" and I dare say she was strung up to do it. But Miss Politt didn't see it that way. All she saw was that she might go to prison for a robbery she had committed years ago. So she made up her mind to put a stop to it all. I'm afraid, you know, that she was always rather a wicked woman. I don't believe she'd have turned a hair if that nice, stupid Mr Spenlow had been hanged.'

Colonel Melchett said slowly, 'We can – er – verify your theory – up to a point. The identity of the Politt woman with the lady's maid at the Abercrombies', but –'

Miss Marple reassured him. 'It will be all quite easy.

She's the kind of woman who will break down at once when she's taxed with the truth. And then, you see, I've got her tape measure. I – er – abstracted it yesterday when I was trying on. When she misses it and thinks the police have got it – well, she's quite an ignorant woman and she'll think it will prove the case against her in some way.'

She smiled at him encouragingly. 'You'll have no trouble, I can assure you.' It was the tone in which his favourite aunt had once assured him that he could not fail to pass his entrance examination into Sandhurst.

And he had passed.

The Case of the Caretaker

'Well,' demanded Doctor Haydock of his patient. 'And how goes it today?'

Miss Marple smiled at him wanly from pillows.

'I suppose, really, that I'm better,' she admitted, 'but I feel so terribly depressed. I can't help feeling how much better it would have been if I had died. After all, I'm an old woman. Nobody wants me or cares about me.'

Doctor Haydock interrupted with his usual brusqueness. 'Yes, yes, typical after-reaction of this type of flu. What you need is something to take you out of yourself. A mental tonic.'

Miss Marple sighed and shook her head.

'And what's more,' continued Doctor Haydock, 'I've brought my medicine with me!'

He tossed a long envelope on to the bed.

'Just the thing for you. The kind of puzzle that is right up your street.'

'A puzzle?' Miss Marple looked interested.

'Literary effort of mine,' said the doctor, blushing a little. 'Tried to make a regular story of it. "He said," "she said," "the girl thought," etc. Facts of the story are true.'

'But why a puzzle?' asked Miss Marple.

Doctor Haydock grinned. 'Because the interpretation

273

is up to you. I want to see if you're as clever as you always make out.'

With that Parthian shot he departed.

Miss Marple picked up the manuscript and began to read.

'And where is the bride?' asked Miss Harmon genially. The village was all agog to see the rich and beautiful young wife that Harry Laxton had brought back from abroad. There was a general indulgent feeling that Harry – wicked young scapegrace – had had all the luck. Everyone had always felt indulgent towards Harry. Even the owners of windows that had suffered from his indiscriminate use of a catapult had found their indignation dissipated by young Harry's abject expression of regret. He had broken windows, robbed orchards, poached rabbits, and later had run into debt, got entangled with the local tobacconist's daughter – been disentangled and sent off to Africa – and the village as represented by various ageing spinsters had murmured indulgently. 'Ah, well! Wild oats! He'll settle down!'

And now, sure enough, the prodigal had returned – not in affliction, but in triumph. Harry Laxton had 'made good' as the saying goes. He had pulled himself together, worked hard, and had finally met and successfully wooed a young Anglo-French girl who was the possessor of a considerable fortune.

Harry might have lived in London, or purchased an estate in some fashionable hunting county, but he preferred to come back to the part of the world that was home to him. And there, in the most romantic way, he purchased the derelict estate in the dower house of which he had passed his childhood.

Kingsdean House had been unoccupied for nearly

seventy years. It had gradually fallen into decay and abandon. An elderly caretaker and his wife lived in the one habitable corner of it. It was a vast, unprepossessing grandiose mansion, the gardens overgrown with rank vegetation and the trees hemming it in like some gloomy enchanter's den.

The dower house was a pleasant, unpretentious house and had been let for a long term of years to Major Laxton, Harry's father. As a boy, Harry had roamed over the Kingsdean estate and knew every inch of the tangled woods, and the old house itself had always fascinated him.

Major Laxton had died some years ago, so it might have been thought that Harry would have had no ties to bring him back – nevertheless it was to the home of his boyhood that Harry brought his bride. The ruined old Kingsdean House was pulled down. An army of builders and contractors swooped down upon the place, and in almost a miraculously short space of time – so marvellously does wealth tell – the new house rose white and gleaming among the trees.

Next came a posse of gardeners and after them a procession of furniture vans.

The house was ready. Servants arrived. Lastly, a costly limousine deposited Harry and Mrs Harry at the front door.

The village rushed to call, and Mrs Price, who owned the largest house, and who considered herself to lead society in the place, sent out cards of invitation for a party 'to meet the bride'.

It was a great event. Several ladies had new frocks for the occasion. Everyone was excited, curious, anxious to see this fabulous creature. They said it was all so like a fairy story!

Miss Harmon, weather-beaten, hearty spinster, threw

out her question as she squeezed her way through the crowded drawing-room door. Little Miss Brent, a thin, acidulated spinster, fluttered out information.

'Oh, my dear, quite charming. Such pretty manners. And quite young. Really, you know, it makes one feel quite envious to see someone who has everything like that. Good looks and money and breeding – most distinguished, nothing in the least common about her – and dear Harry so devoted!'

'Ah,' said Miss Harmon, 'it's early days yet!'

Miss Brent's thin nose quivered appreciatively. 'Oh, my dear, do you really think –'

'We all know what Harry is,' said Miss Harmon.

'We know what he was! But I expect now –'

'Ah,' said Miss Harmon, 'men are always the same. Once a gay deceiver, always a gay deceiver. I know them.'

'Dear, dear. Poor young thing.' Miss Brent looked much happier. 'Yes, I expect she'll have trouble with him. Someone ought really to warn her. I wonder if she's heard anything of the old story?

'It seems so very unfair,' said Miss Brent, 'that she should know nothing. So awkward. Especially with only the one chemist's shop in the village.'

For the erstwhile tobacconist's daughter was now married to Mr Edge, the chemist.

'It would be so much nicer,' said Miss Brent, 'if Mrs Laxton were to deal with Boots in Much Benham.'

'I dare say,' said Miss Harmon, 'that Harry Laxton will suggest that himself.'

And again a significant look passed between them.

'But I certainly think,' said Miss Harmon, 'that she ought to know.'

*　　*　　*

'Beasts!' said Clarice Vane indignantly to her uncle, Doctor Haydock. 'Absolute beasts some people are.'

He looked at her curiously.

She was a tall, dark girl, handsome, warm-hearted and impulsive. Her big brown eyes were alight now with indignation as she said, 'All these cats – saying things – hinting things.'

'About Harry Laxton?'

'Yes, about his affair with the tobacconist's daughter.'

'Oh, that!' The doctor shrugged his shoulders. 'A great many young men have affairs of that kind.'

'Of course they do. And it's all over. So why harp on it? And bring it up years after? It's like ghouls feasting on dead bodies.'

'I dare say, my dear, it does seem like that to you. But you see, they have very little to talk about down here, and so I'm afraid they do tend to dwell upon past scandals. But I'm curious to know why it upsets you so much?'

Clarice Vane bit her lip and flushed. She said, in a curiously muffled voice. 'They – they look so happy. The Laxtons, I mean. They're young and in love, and it's all so lovely for them. I hate to think of it being spoiled by whispers and hints and innuendoes and general beastliness.'

'H'm. I see.'

Clarice went on. 'He was talking to me just now. He's so happy and eager and excited and – yes, thrilled – at having got his heart's desire and rebuilt Kingsdean. He's like a child about it all. And she – well, I don't suppose anything has ever gone wrong in her whole life. She's always had everything. You've seen her. What did you think of her?'

The doctor did not answer at once. For other people, Louise Laxton might be an object of envy. A spoiled darling of fortune. To him she had brought only the refrain of a popular song heard many years ago, *Poor little rich girl* –

A small, delicate figure, with flaxen hair curled rather stiffly round her face and big, wistful blue eyes.

Louise was drooping a little. The long stream of congratulations had tired her. She was hoping it might soon be time to go. Perhaps, even now, Harry might say so. She looked at him sideways. So tall and broad-shouldered with his eager pleasure in this horrible, dull party.

Poor little rich girl –

'Ooph!' It was a sigh of relief.

Harry turned to look at his wife amusedly. They were driving away from the party.

She said, 'Darling, what a frightful party!'

Harry laughed. 'Yes, pretty terrible. Never mind, my sweet. It had to be done, you know. All these old pussies knew me when I lived here as a boy. They'd have been terribly disappointed not to have got a look at you close up.'

Louise made a grimace. She said, 'Shall we have to see a lot of them?'

'What? Oh, no. They'll come and make ceremonious calls with card cases, and you'll return the calls and then you needn't bother any more. You can have your own friends down or whatever you like.'

Louise said, after a minute or two, 'Isn't there anyone amusing living down here?'

'Oh, yes. There's the County, you know. Though you may find them a bit dull, too. Mostly interested in bulbs and dogs and horses. You'll ride, of course. You'll enjoy that. There's a horse over at Eglinton I'd like you to see. A beautiful animal, perfectly trained, no vice in him but plenty of spirit.'

The car slowed down to take the turn into the gates of Kingsdean. Harry wrenched the wheel and swore as a grotesque figure sprang up in the middle of the road and he only just managed to avoid it. It stood there, shaking a fist and shouting after them.

Louise clutched his arm. 'Who's that – that horrible old woman?'

Harry's brow was black. 'That's old Murgatroyd. She and her husband were caretakers in the old house. They were there for nearly thirty years.'

'Why does she shake her fist at you?'

Harry's face got red. 'She – well, she resented the house being pulled down. And she got the sack, of course. Her husband's been dead two years. They say she got a bit queer after he died.'

'Is she – she isn't – starving?'

Louise's ideas were vague and somewhat melodramatic. Riches prevented you coming into contact with reality.

Harry was outraged. 'Good Lord, Louise, what an idea! I pensioned her off, of course – and handsomely, too! Found her a new cottage and everything.'

Louise asked, bewildered, 'Then why does she mind?'

Harry was frowning, his brows drawn together. 'Oh, how should I know? Craziness! She loved the house.'

'But it was a ruin, wasn't it?'

'Of course it was – crumbling to pieces – roof leaking – more or less unsafe. All the same I suppose it meant something to her. She'd been there a long time. Oh, I don't know! The old devil's cracked, I think.'

Louise said uneasily, 'She – I think she cursed us. Oh, Harry, I wish she hadn't.'

It seemed to Louise that her new home was tainted and poisoned by the malevolent figure of one crazy old woman. When she went out in the car, when she rode, when she walked out with the dogs, there was always the same figure waiting. Crouched down on herself, a battered hat over wisps of iron-grey hair, and the slow muttering of imprecations.

Louise came to believe that Harry was right – the old woman was mad. Nevertheless that did not make things easier. Mrs Murgatroyd never actually came to the house, nor did she use definite threats, nor offer violence. Her squatting figure remained always just outside the gates. To appeal to the police would have been useless and, in any case, Harry Laxton was averse to that course of action. It would, he said, arouse local sympathy for the old brute. He took the matter more easily than Louise did.

'Don't worry about it, darling. She'll get tired of this silly cursing business. Probably she's only trying it on.'

'She isn't, Harry. She – she hates us! I can feel it. She – she's ill-wishing us.'

'She's not a witch, darling, although she may look like one! Don't be morbid about it all.'

Louise was silent. Now that the first excitement of settling in was over, she felt curiously lonely and at a loose end. She had been used to life in London and the Riviera. She had no knowledge of or taste for English country life. She was ignorant of gardening, except for the final act of 'doing the flowers'. She did not really care for dogs. She was bored by such neighbours as she met. She enjoyed riding best, sometimes with Harry, sometimes, when he was busy about the estate, by herself. She hacked through the woods and lanes, enjoying the easy paces of the beautiful horse that Harry had bought for her. Yet even Prince Hal, most sensitive of chestnut steeds, was wont to shy and snort as he carried his mistress past the huddled figure of a malevolent old woman.

One day Louise took her courage in both hands. She was out walking. She had passed Mrs Murgatroyd, pretending not to notice her, but suddenly she swerved back and went right up to her. She said, a little breathlessly, 'What is it? What's the matter? What do you want?'

The old woman blinked at her. She had a cunning, dark gypsy face, with wisps of iron-grey hair, and bleared, suspicious eyes. Louise wondered if she drank.

She spoke in a whining and yet threatening voice. 'What do I want, you ask? What, indeed! That which has been took away from me. Who turned me out of Kingsdean House? I'd lived there, girl and woman, for near on forty years. It was a black deed to turn me out and it's black bad luck it'll bring to you and him!'

Louise said, 'You've got a very nice cottage and –'

She broke off. The old woman's arms flew up. She screamed, 'What's the good of that to me? It's my own place I want and my own fire as I sat beside all them years. And as for you and him, I'm telling you there will be no happiness for you in your new fine house. It's the black sorrow will be upon you! Sorrow and death and my curse. May your fair face rot.'

Louise turned away and broke into a little stumbling run. She thought, *I must get away from here! We must sell the house! We must go away.*

At the moment, such a solution seemed easy to her. But Harry's utter incomprehension took her aback. He exclaimed, 'Leave here? Sell the house? Because of a crazy old woman's threats? You must be mad.'

'No, I'm not. But she – she frightens me, I know something will happen.'

Harry Laxton said grimly, 'Leave Mrs Murgatroyd to me. I'll settle her!'

A friendship had sprung up between Clarice Vane and young Mrs Laxton. The two girls were much of an age, though dissimilar both in character and in tastes. In Clarice's company, Louise found reassurance. Clarice was so self-reliant, so sure of herself. Louise mentioned the matter of Mrs Murgatroyd and her threats, but Clarice seemed to regard the matter as more annoying than frightening.

'It's so stupid, that sort of thing,' she said. 'And really very annoying for you.'

'You know, Clarice, I – I feel quite frightened sometimes. My heart gives the most awful jumps.'

'Nonsense, you mustn't let a silly thing like that get you down. She'll soon tire of it.'

She was silent for a minute or two. Clarice said, 'What's the matter?'

Louise paused for a minute, then her answer came with a rush. 'I hate this place! I hate being here. The woods and this house, and the awful silence at night, and the queer noise owls make. Oh, and the people and everything.'

'The people. What people?'

'The people in the village. Those prying, gossiping old maids.'

Clarice said sharply, 'What have they been saying?'

'I don't know. Nothing particular. But they've got nasty minds. When you've talked to them you feel you wouldn't trust anybody – not anybody at all.'

Clarice said harshly, 'Forget them. They've nothing to do but gossip. And most of the muck they talk they just invent.'

Louise said, 'I wish we'd never come here. But Harry adores it so.' Her voice softened.

Clarice thought, *How she adores him.* She said abruptly, 'I must go now.'

'I'll send you back in the car. Come again soon.'

Clarice nodded. Louise felt comforted by her new friend's visit. Harry was pleased to find her more cheerful and from then on urged her to have Clarice often to the house.

Then one day he said, 'Good news for you, darling.'

'Oh, what?'

'I've fixed the Murgatroyd. She's got a son in America, you know. Well, I've arranged for her to go out and join him. I'll pay her passage.'

'Oh, Harry, how wonderful. I believe I might get to like Kingsdean after all.'

'Get to like it? Why, it's the most wonderful place in the world!'

Louise gave a little shiver. She could not rid herself of her superstitious fear so easily.

If the ladies of St Mary Mead had hoped for the pleasure of imparting information about her husband's past to the bride, this pleasure was denied them by Harry Laxton's own prompt action.

Miss Harmon and Clarice Vane were both in Mr Edge's shop, the one buying mothballs and the other a packet of boracic, when Harry Laxton and his wife came in.

After greeting the two ladies, Harry turned to the counter and was just demanding a toothbrush when he stopped in mid-speech and exclaimed heartily, 'Well, well, just see who's here! Bella, I do declare.'

Mrs Edge, who had hurried out from the back parlour to attend to the congestion of business, beamed back cheerfully at him, showing her big white teeth. She had been a dark, handsome girl and was still a reasonably handsome woman, though she had put on weight, and the lines of her face had coarsened; but her large brown eyes were full of warmth as she answered, 'Bella, it is, Mr Harry, and pleased to see you after all these years.'

Harry turned to his wife. 'Bella's an old flame of mine, Louise,' he said. 'Head-over-heels in love with her, wasn't I, Bella?'

'That's what you say,' said Mrs Edge.

Louise laughed. She said, 'My husband's very happy seeing all his old friends again.'

'Ah,' said Mrs Edge, 'we haven't forgotten you, Mr Harry. Seems like a fairy tale to think of you married and building up a new house instead of that ruined old Kingsdean House.'

'You look very well and blooming,' said Harry, and Mrs Edge laughed and said there was nothing wrong with her and what about that toothbrush?

Clarice, watching the baffled look on Miss Harmon's face, said to herself exultantly, *Oh, well done, Harry. You've spiked their guns.*

Doctor Haydock said abruptly to his niece, 'What's all this nonsense about old Mrs Murgatroyd hanging about Kingsdean and shaking her fist and cursing the new regime?'

'It isn't nonsense. It's quite true. It's upset Louise a good deal.'

'Tell her she needn't worry – when the Murgatroyds were caretakers they never stopped grumbling about the place – they only stayed because Murgatroyd drank and couldn't get another job.'

'I'll tell her,' said Clarice doubtfully, 'but I don't

think she'll believe you. The old woman fairly screams with rage.'

'Always used to be fond of Harry as a boy. I can't understand it.'

Clarice said, 'Oh, well – they'll be rid of her soon. Harry's paying her passage to America.'

Three days later, Louise was thrown from her horse and killed.

Two men in a baker's van were witnesses of the accident. They saw Louise ride out of the gates, saw the old woman spring up and stand in the road waving her arms and shouting, saw the horse start, swerve, and then bolt madly down the road, flinging Louise Laxton over his head.

One of them stood over the unconscious figure, not knowing what to do, while the other rushed to the house to get help.

Harry Laxton came running out, his face ghastly. They took off a door of the van and carried her on it to the house. She died without regaining consciousness and before the doctor arrived.

(End of Doctor Haydock's manuscript.)

When Doctor Haydock arrived the following day, he was pleased to note that there was a pink flush in Miss Marple's cheek and decidedly more animation in her manner.

'Well,' he said, 'what's the verdict?'

'What's the problem, Doctor Haydock?' countered Miss Marple.

'Oh, my dear lady, do I have to tell you that?'

'I suppose,' said Miss Marple, 'that it's the curious conduct of the caretaker. Why did she behave in that very odd way? People do mind being turned out of their old homes. But it wasn't her home. In fact, she used to complain and grumble while she was there. Yes, it certainly looks very fishy. What became of her, by the way?'

'Did a bunk to Liverpool. The accident scared her. Thought she'd wait there for her boat.'

'All very convenient for somebody,' said Miss Marple. 'Yes, I think the "Problem of the Caretaker's Conduct" can be solved easily enough. Bribery, was it not?'

'That's your solution?'

'Well, if it wasn't natural for her to behave in that way, she must have been "putting on an act" as people say, and that means that somebody paid her to do what she did.'

'And you know who that somebody was?'

'Oh, I think so. Money again, I'm afraid. And I've always noticed that gentlemen always tend to admire the same type.'

'Now I'm out of my depth.'

'No, no, it all hangs together. Harry Laxton admired Bella Edge, a dark, vivacious type. Your niece Clarice was the same. But the poor little wife was quite a different type – fair-haired and clinging – not his type at all. So he must have married her for her money. And murdered her for her money, too!'

'You use the word "murder"?'

'Well, he sounds the right type. Attractive to women and quite unscrupulous. I suppose he wanted to keep his wife's money and marry your niece. He may have been seen talking to Mrs Edge. But I don't fancy he was attached to her any more. Though I dare say he made the poor woman think he was, for ends of his own. He soon had her well under his thumb, I fancy.'

'How exactly did he murder her, do you think?'

Miss Marple stared ahead of her for some minutes with dreamy blue eyes.

'It was very well timed – with the baker's van as witness. They could see the old woman and, of course, they'd put down the horse's fright to that. But I should imagine, myself, that an air gun, or perhaps a catapult. Yes, just as the horse came through the gates. The horse bolted, of course, and Mrs Laxton was thrown.'

She paused, frowning.

'The fall might have killed her. But he couldn't be sure of that. And he seems the sort of man who would lay his plans carefully and leave nothing to chance. After all, Mrs Edge could get him something suitable without her husband knowing. Otherwise, why would Harry bother with her? Yes, I think he had some powerful drug handy, that could be administered before you arrived. After all, if a woman is thrown from her horse and has serious injuries and dies without recovering consciousness, well – a doctor wouldn't normally be suspicious, would he? He'd put it down to shock or something.'

Doctor Haydock nodded.

'Why did you suspect?' asked Miss Marple.

'It wasn't any particular cleverness on my part,' said Doctor Haydock. 'It was just the trite, well-known fact that a murderer is so pleased with his cleverness that he doesn't take proper precautions. I was just saying a few consolatory words to the bereaved husband – and feeling damned sorry for the fellow, too – when he flung himself down on the settee to do a bit of play-acting and a hypodermic syringe fell out of his pocket.

'He snatched it up and looked so scared that I began to think. Harry Laxton didn't drug; he was in perfect health; what was he doing with a hypodermic syringe? I did the autopsy with a view to certain possibilities. I found strophanthin. The rest was easy. There was strophanthin in Laxton's possession, and Bella Edge, questioned by the police, broke down and admitted to having got it for him. And finally old Mrs Murgatroyd confessed that it was Harry Laxton who had put her up to the cursing stunt.'

'And your niece got over it?'

'Yes, she was attracted by the fellow, but it hadn't gone far.'

The doctor picked up his manuscript.

'Full marks to you, Miss Marple – and full marks to me for my prescription. You're looking almost yourself again.'

The Case of the Perfect Maid

'Oh, if you please, madam, could I speak to you a moment?'

It might be thought that this request was in the nature of an absurdity, since Edna, Miss Marple's little maid, was actually speaking to her mistress at the moment.

Recognizing the idiom, however, Miss Marple said promptly, 'Certainly, Edna, come in and shut the door. What is it?'

Obediently shutting the door, Edna advanced into the room, pleated the corner of her apron between her fingers, and swallowed once or twice.

'Yes, Edna?' said Miss Marple encouragingly.

'Oh, please, ma'am, it's my cousin, Gladdie.'

'Dear me,' said Miss Marple, her mind leaping to the worst – and, alas, the most usual conclusion. 'Not – not in trouble?'

Edna hastened to reassure her. 'Oh, no, ma'am, nothing of that kind. Gladdie's not that kind of girl. It's just that she's upset. You see, she's lost her place.'

'Dear me, I am sorry to hear that. She was at Old Hall, wasn't she, with the Miss – Misses – Skinner?'

'Yes, ma'am, that's right, ma'am. And Gladdie's very upset about it – very upset indeed.'

'Gladys has changed places rather often before, though, hasn't she?'

'Oh, yes, ma'am. She's always one for a change,

Gladdie is. She never seems to get really settled, if you know what I mean. But she's always been the one to give the notice, you see!'

'And this time it's the other way round?' asked Miss Marple dryly.

'Yes, ma'am, and it's upset Gladdie something awful.'

Miss Marple looked slightly surprised. Her recollection of Gladys, who had occasionally come to drink tea in the kitchen on her 'days out', was a stout, giggling girl of unshakably equable temperament.

Edna went on. 'You see, ma'am, it's the way it happened – the way Miss Skinner looked.'

'How,' enquired Miss Marple patiently, 'did Miss Skinner look?'

This time Edna got well away with her news bulletin.

'Oh, ma'am, it was ever such a shock to Gladdie. You see, one of Miss Emily's brooches was missing, and such a hue and cry for it as never was, and of course nobody likes a thing like that to happen; it's upsetting, ma'am, if you know what I mean. And Gladdie's helped search everywhere, and there was Miss Lavinia saying she was going to the police about it, and then it turned up again, pushed right to the back of a drawer in the dressing-table, and very thankful Gladdie was.

'And the very next day as ever was a plate got broken, and Miss Lavinia she bounced out right away and told Gladdie to take a month's notice. And what Gladdie feels is it couldn't have been the plate and that Miss Lavinia was just making an excuse of that, and that it must be because of the brooch and they think as she took it and put it back when the police was mentioned, and Gladdie wouldn't do such a thing, not never she wouldn't, and what she feels is as it will get round and tell against her and it's a very serious thing for a girl, as you know, ma'am.'

Miss Marple nodded. Though having no particular liking for the bouncing, self-opinionated Gladys, she was quite sure of the girl's intrinsic honesty and could well imagine that the affair must have upset her.

Edna said wistfully, 'I suppose, ma'am, there isn't anything you could do about it? Gladdie's in ever such a taking.'

'Tell her not to be silly,' said Miss Marple crisply. 'If she didn't take the brooch – which I'm sure she didn't – then she has no cause to be upset.'

'It'll get about,' said Edna dismally.

Miss Marple said, 'I – er – am going up that way this afternoon. I'll have a word with the Misses Skinner.'

'Oh, thank you, madam,' said Edna.

Old Hall was a big Victorian house surrounded by woods and park land. Since it had been proved unlettable and unsaleable as it was, an enterprising speculator had divided it into four flats with a central hot-water system, and the use of 'the grounds' to be held in common by the tenants. The experiment had been satisfactory. A rich and eccentric old lady and her maid occupied one flat. The old lady had a passion for birds and entertained a feathered gathering to meals every day. A retired Indian judge and his wife rented a second. A very young couple, recently married, occupied the third, and the fourth had been taken only two months ago by two maiden ladies of the name of Skinner. The four sets of tenants were only on the most distant terms with each other, since none of them had anything in common. The landlord had been heard to say that this was an excellent thing. What he dreaded were friendships followed by estrangements and subsequent complaints to him.

Miss Marple was acquainted with all the tenants,

though she knew none of them well. The elder Miss Skinner, Miss Lavinia, was what might be termed the working member of the firm, Miss Emily, the younger, spent most of her time in bed suffering from various complaints which, in the opinion of St Mary Mead, were largely imaginary. Only Miss Lavinia believed devoutly in her sister's martyrdom and patience under affliction, and willingly ran errands and trotted up and down to the village for things that 'my sister had suddenly fancied'.

It was the view of St Mary Mead that if Miss Emily suffered half as much as she said she did, she would have sent for Doctor Haydock long ago. But Miss Emily, when this was hinted to her, shut her eyes in a superior way and murmured that her case was not a simple one – the best specialists in London had been baffled by it – and that a wonderful new man had put her on a most revolutionary course of treatment and that she really hoped her health would improve under it. No humdrum GP could possibly understand her case.

'And it's my opinion,' said the outspoken Miss Hartnell, 'that she's very wise not to send for him. Dear Doctor Haydock, in that breezy manner of his, would tell her that there was nothing the matter with her and to get up and not make a fuss! Do her a lot of good!'

Failing such arbitrary treatment, however, Miss Emily continued to lie on sofas, to surround herself with strange little pill boxes, and to reject nearly everything that had been cooked for her and ask for something else – usually something difficult and inconvenient to get.

The door was opened to Miss Marple by 'Gladdie', looking more depressed than Miss Marple had ever thought possible. In the sitting-room (a quarter of the late drawing-room, which had been partitioned into a dining-room, drawing-room, bathroom, and housemaid's cupboard), Miss Lavinia rose to greet Miss Marple.

Lavinia Skinner was a tall, gaunt, bony female of fifty. She had a gruff voice and an abrupt manner.

'Nice to see you,' she said. 'Emily's lying down – feeling low today, poor dear. Hope she'll see you, it would cheer her up, but there are times when she doesn't feel up to seeing anybody. Poor dear, she's wonderfully patient.'

Miss Marple responded politely. Servants were the main topic of conversation in St Mary Mead, so it was not difficult to lead the conversation in that direction. Miss Marple said she had heard that that nice girl, Gladys Holmes, was leaving.

Miss Lavinia nodded. 'Wednesday week. Broke things, you know. Can't have that.'

Miss Marple sighed and said we all had to put up with things nowadays. It was so difficult to get girls to come to the country. Did Miss Skinner really think it was wise to part with Gladys?

'Know it's difficult to get servants,' admitted Miss Lavinia. 'The Devereuxs haven't got anybody – but then, I don't wonder – always quarrelling, jazz on all night – meals any time – that girl knows nothing of housekeeping. I pity her husband! Then the Larkins have just lost their maid. Of course, what with the judge's Indian temper and his wanting *chota hazri*, as he calls it, at six in the morning and Mrs Larkin always fussing, I don't wonder at that, either. Mrs Carmichael's Janet is a fixture of course – though in my opinion she's the most disagreeable woman, and absolutely bullies the old lady.'

'Then don't you think you might reconsider your

293

decision about Gladys? She really is a nice girl. I know all her family; very honest and superior.'

Miss Lavinia shook her head.

'I've got my reasons,' she said importantly.

Miss Marple murmured, 'You missed a brooch, I understand –'

'Now, who has been talking? I suppose the girl has. Quite frankly, I'm almost certain she took it. And then got frightened and put it back – but, of course, one can't say anything unless one is sure.' She changed the subject. 'Do come and see Emily, Miss Marple. I'm sure it would do her good.'

Miss Marple followed meekly to where Miss Lavinia knocked on a door, was bidden enter, and ushered her guest into the best room in the flat, most of the light of which was excluded by half-drawn blinds. Miss Emily was lying in bed, apparenly enjoying the half-gloom and her own indefinite sufferings.

The dim light showed her to be a thin, indecisive-looking creature, with a good deal of greyish-yellow hair untidily wound around her head and erupting into curls, the whole thing looking like a bird's nest of which no self-respecting bird could be proud. There was a smell in the room of Eau de Cologne, stale biscuits, and camphor.

With half-closed eyes and a thin, weak voice, Emily Skinner explained that this was 'one of her bad days'.

'The worst of ill health is,' said Miss Emily in a melancholy tone, 'that one knows what a burden one is to everyone around one.

'Lavinia is very good to me. Lavvie dear, I do so hate giving trouble but if my hot water bottle could only be filled in the way I like it – too full it weighs on me so – on the other hand, if it is not sufficiently filled, it gets cold immediately!'

'I'm sorry, dear. Give it to me. I will empty a little out.'

'Perhaps, if you're doing that, it might be refilled. There are no rusks in the house, I suppose – no, no, it doesn't matter. I can do without. Some weak tea and a slice of lemon – no lemons? No, really, I couldn't drink tea without lemon. I think the milk was slightly turned this morning. It has put me against milk in my tea. It doesn't matter. I can do without my tea. Only I do feel so weak. Oysters, they say, are nourishing. I wonder if I could fancy a few? No, no, too much bother to get hold of them so late in the day. I can fast until tomorrow.'

Lavinia left the room murmuring something incoherent about bicycling down to the village.

Miss Emily smiled feebly at her guest and remarked that she did hate giving anyone any trouble.

Miss Marple told Edna that evening that she was afraid her embassy had met with no success.

She was rather troubled to find that rumours as to Gladys's dishonesty were already going around the village.

In the post office, Miss Wetherby tackled her. 'My dear Jane, they gave her a written reference saying she was willing and sober and respectable, but saying nothing about honesty. That seems to me most significant! I hear there was some trouble about a brooch. I think there must be something in it, you know, because one doesn't let a servant go nowadays unless it's something rather grave. They'll find it most difficult to get anyone else. Girls simply will not go to Old Hall. They're nervous coming home on their days out. You'll see, the Skinners won't find anyone else, and then, perhaps, that dreadful hypochondriac sister will have to get up and do something!'

Great was the chagrin of the village when it was made

295

known that the Misses Skinner had engaged, from an agency, a new maid who, by all accounts, was a perfect paragon.

'A three years' reference recommending her most warmly, she prefers the country, and actually asks less wages than Gladys. I really feel we have been most fortunate.'

'Well, really,' said Miss Marple, to whom these details were imparted by Miss Lavinia in the fishmonger's shop. 'It does seem too good to be true.'

It then became the opinion of St Mary Mead that the paragon would cry off at the last minute and fail to arrive.

None of these prognostications came true, however, and the village was able to observe the domestic treasure, by name, Mary Higgins, driving through the village in Reed's taxi to Old Hall. It had to be admitted that her appearance was good. A most respectable-looking woman, very neatly dressed.

When Miss Marple next visited Old Hall, on the occasion of recruiting stall-holders for the vicarage fete, Mary Higgins opened the door. She was certainly a most superior-looking maid, at a guess forty years of age, with neat black hair, rosy cheeks, a plump figure discreetly arrayed in black with a white apron and cap – 'quite the good, old-fashioned type of servant,' as Miss Marple explained afterwards, and with the proper, inaudible respectful voice, so different from the loud but adenoidal accents of Gladys.

Miss Lavinia was looking far less harassed than usual and, although she regretted that she could not take a stall owing to her preoccupation with her sister, she nevertheless tendered a handsome monetary contribution, and promised to produce a consignment of pen-wipers and babies' socks.

Miss Marple commented on her air of well-being.

'I really feel I owe a great deal to Mary, I am so thankful I had the resolution to get rid of that other girl. Mary is really invaluable. Cooks nicely and waits beautifully and keeps our little flat scrupulously clean – mattresses turned over every day. And she is really wonderful with Emily!'

Miss Marple hastily enquired after Emily.

'Oh, poor dear, she has been very much under the weather lately. She can't help it, of course, but it really makes things a little difficult sometimes. Wanting certain things cooked and then, when they come, saying she can't eat now – and then wanting them again half an hour later and everything spoiled and having to be done again. It makes, of course, a lot of work – but fortunately Mary does not seem to mind at all. She's used to waiting on invalids, she says, and understands them. It is such a comfort.'

'Dear me,' said Miss Marple. 'You are fortunate.'

'Yes, indeed. I really feel Mary has been sent to us as an answer to prayer.'

'She sounds to me,' said Miss Marple, 'almost too good to be true. I should – well, I should be a little careful if I were you.'

Lavinia Skinner failed to perceive the point of this remark. She said, 'Oh! I assure you I do all I can to make her comfortable. I don't know what I should do if she left.'

'I don't expect she'll leave until she's ready to leave,' said Miss Marple and stared very hard at her hostess.

Miss Lavinia said, 'If one has no domestic worries, it takes such a load off one's mind, doesn't it? How is your little Edna shaping?'

'She's doing quite nicely. Not much head, of course.

Not like your Mary. Still, I do know all about Edna because she's a village girl.'

As she went out into the hall she heard the invalid's voice fretfully raised. 'This compress has been allowed to get quite dry – Doctor Allerton particularly said moisture continually renewed. There, there, leave it. I want a cup of tea and a boiled egg – boiled only three minutes and a half, remember, and send Miss Lavinia to me.'

The efficient Mary emerged from the bedroom and, saying to Lavinia, 'Miss Emily is asking for you, madam,' proceeded to open the door for Miss Marple, helping her into her coat and handing her her umbrella in the most irreproachable fashion.

Miss Marple took the umbrella, dropped it, tried to pick it up, and dropped her bag, which flew open. Mary politely retrieved various odds and ends – a handkerchief, an engagement book, an old-fashioned leather purse, two shillings, three pennies, and a striped piece of peppermint rock.

Miss Marple received the last with some signs of confusion.

'Oh, dear, that must have been Mrs Clement's little boy. He was sucking it, I remember, and he took my bag to play with. He must have put it inside. It's terribly sticky, isn't it?'

'Shall I take it, madam?'

'Oh, would you? Thank you so much.'

Mary stooped to retrieve the last item, a small mirror, upon recovering which Miss Marple exclaimed fervently, 'How lucky, now, that that isn't broken.'

She thereupon departed, Mary standing politely by the door holding a piece of striped rock with a completely expressionless face.

*   *   *

For ten days longer St Mary Mead had to endure hearing of the excellencies of Miss Lavinia's and Miss Emily's treasure.

On the eleventh day, the village awoke to its big thrill.

Mary, the paragon, was missing! Her bed had not been slept in, and the front door was found ajar. She had slipped out quietly during the night.

And not Mary alone was missing! Two brooches and five rings of Miss Lavinia's; three rings, a pendant, a bracelet, and four brooches of Miss Emily's were missing, also!

It was the beginning of a chapter of catastrophe.

Young Mrs Devereux had lost her diamonds which she kept in an unlocked drawer and also some valuable furs given to her as a wedding present. The judge and his wife also had had jewellery taken and a certain amount of money. Mrs Carmichael was the greatest sufferer. Not only had she some very valuable jewels but she also kept in the flat a large sum of money which had gone. It had been Janet's evening out, and her mistress was in the habit of walking round the gardens at dusk calling to the birds and scattering crumbs. It seemed clear that Mary, the perfect maid, had had keys to fit all the flats!

There was, it must be confessed, a certain amount of ill-natured pleasure in St Mary Mead. Miss Lavinia had boasted so much of her marvellous Mary.

'And all the time, my dear, just a common thief!'

Interesting revelations followed. Not only had Mary disappeared into the blue, but the agency who had provided her and vouched for her credentials was alarmed to find that the Mary Higgins who had applied to them and whose references they had taken up had, to all intents and purposes, never existed. It was the name of a bona fide servant who had lived with the bona fide sister of a dean, but the real Mary Higgins was existing peacefully in a place in Cornwall.

'Damned clever, the whole thing,' Inspector Slack was forced to admit. 'And, if you ask me, that woman works with a gang. There was a case of much the same kind in Northumberland a year ago. Stuff was never traced, and they never caught her. However, we'll do better than that in Much Benham!'

Inspector Slack was always a confident man.

Nevertheless, weeks passed, and Mary Higgins remained triumphantly at large. In vain Inspector Slack redoubled that energy that so belied his name.

Miss Lavinia remained tearful. Miss Emily was so upset, and felt so alarmed by her condition that she actually sent for Doctor Haydock.

The whole of the village was terribly anxious to know what he thought of Miss Emily's claims to ill health, but naturally could not ask him. Satisfactory data came to hand on the subject, however, through Mr Meek, the chemist's assistant, who was walking out with Clara, Mrs Price-Ridley's maid. It was then known that Doctor Haydock had prescribed a mixture of asafoetida and valerian which, according to Mr Meek, was the stock remedy for malingerers in the army!

Soon afterwards it was learned that Miss Emily, not relishing the medical attention she had had, was declaring that in the state of her health she felt it her duty to be near the specialist in London who understood her case. It was, she said, only fair to Lavinia.

The flat was put up for subletting.

It was a few days after that that Miss Marple, rather pink and flustered, called at the police station in Much Benham and asked for Inspector Slack.

Inspector Slack did not like Miss Marple. But he was

aware that the Chief Constable, Colonel Melchett, did not share that opinion. Rather grudgingly, therefore, he received her.

'Good afternoon, Miss Marple, what can I do for you?'

'Oh, dear,' said Miss Marple, 'I'm afraid you're in a hurry.'

'Lots of work on,' said Inspector Slack, 'but I can spare a few moments.'

'Oh dear,' said Miss Marple. 'I hope I shall be able to put what I say properly. So difficult, you know, to explain oneself, don't you think? No, perhaps you don't. But you see, not having been educated in the modern style – just a governess, you know, who taught one the dates of the kings of England and general knowledge – Doctor Brewer – three kinds of diseases of wheat – blight, mildew – now what was the third – was it smut?'

'Do you want to talk about smut?' asked Inspector Slack and then blushed.

'Oh, no, no.' Miss Marple hastily disclaimed any wish to talk about smut. 'Just an illustration, you know. And how needles are made, and all that. Discursive, you know, but not teaching one to keep to the point. Which is what I want to do. It's about Miss Skinner's maid, Gladys, you know.'

'Mary Higgins,' said Inspector Slack.

'Oh, yes, the second maid. But it's Gladys Holmes I mean – rather an impertinent girl and far too pleased with herself but really strictly honest, and it's so important that that should be recognized.'

'No charge against her so far as I know,' said the inspector.

'No, I know there isn't a charge – but that makes it worse. Because, you see, people go on thinking things.

Oh, dear – I knew I should explain things badly. What I really mean is that the important thing is to find Mary Higgins.'

'Certainly,' said Inspector Slack. 'Have you any ideas on the subject?'

'Well, as a matter of fact, I have,' said Miss Marple. 'May I ask you a question? Are fingerprints of no use to you?'

'Ah,' said Inspector Slack, 'that's where she was a bit too artful for us. Did most of her work in rubber gloves or housemaid's gloves, it seems. And she'd been careful – wiped off everything in her bedroom and on the sink. Couldn't find a single fingerprint in the place!'

'If you did have fingerprints, would it help?'

'It might, madam. They may be known at the Yard. This isn't her first job, I'd say!'

Miss Marple nodded brightly. She opened her bag and extracted a small cardboard box. Inside it, wedged in cotton wool, was a small mirror.

'From my handbag,' said Miss Marple. 'The maid's prints are on it. I think they should be satisfactory – she touched an extremely sticky substance a moment previously.'

Inspector Slack stared. 'Did you get her fingerprints on purpose?'

'Of course.'

'You suspected her then?'

'Well, you know, it did strike me that she was a little too good to be true. I practically told Miss Lavinia so. But she simply wouldn't take the hint! I'm afraid, you know, Inspector, that I don't believe in paragons. Most of us have our faults – and domestic service shows them up very quickly!'

'Well,' said Inspector Slack, recovering his balance,

'I'm obliged to you, I'm sure. We'll send these up to the Yard and see what they have to say.'

He stopped. Miss Marple had put her head a little on one side and was regarding him with a good deal of meaning.

'You wouldn't consider, I suppose, Inspector, looking a little nearer home?'

'What do you mean, Miss Marple?'

'It's very difficult to explain, but when you come across a peculiar thing you notice it. Although, often, peculiar things may be the merest trifles. I've felt that all along, you know; I mean about Gladys and the brooch. She's an honest girl; she didn't take that brooch. Then why did Miss Skinner think she did? Miss Skinner's not a fool; far from it! Why was she so anxious to let a girl go who was a good servant when servants are hard to get? It was peculiar, you know. So I wondered. I wondered a good deal. And I noticed another peculiar thing! Miss Emily's a hypochondriac, but she's the first hypochondriac who hasn't sent for some doctor or other at once. Hypochondriacs love doctors, Miss Emily didn't!'

'What are you suggesting, Miss Marple?'

'Well, I'm suggesting, you know, that Miss Lavinia and Miss Emily are peculiar people. Miss Emily spends nearly all her time in a dark room. And if that hair of hers isn't a wig I – I'll eat my own back switch! And what I say is this – it's perfectly possible for a thin, pale, grey-haired, whining woman to be the same as a black-haired, rosy-cheeked, plump woman. And nobody that I can find ever saw Miss Emily and Mary Higgins at one and the same time.

'Plenty of time to get impressions of all the keys, plenty of time to find out all about the other tenants, and then – get rid of the local girl. Miss Emily takes a brisk walk across country one night and arrives at the station as Mary Higgins next day. And then, at the right moment, Mary Higgins disappears, and off goes the hue and cry after her. I'll tell you where you'll find her, Inspector. On Miss Emily Skinner's sofa! Get her fingerprints if you don't believe me, but you'll find I'm right! A couple of clever thieves, that's what the Skinners are – and no doubt in league with a clever post and rails or fence or whatever you call it. But they won't get away with it this time! I'm not going to have one of our village girls' character for honesty taken away like that! Gladys Holmes is as honest as the day, and everybody's going to know it! Good afternoon!'

Miss Marple had stalked out before Inspector Slack had recovered.

'Whew?' he muttered. 'I wonder if she's right?'

He soon found out that Miss Marple was right again.

Colonel Melchett congratulated Slack on his efficiency, and Miss Marple had Gladys come to tea with Edna and spoke to her seriously on settling down in a good situation when she got one.

Sanctuary

The vicar's wife came round the corner of the vicarage with her arms full of chrysanthemums. A good deal of rich garden soil was attached to her strong brogue shoes and a few fragments of earth were adhering to her nose, but of that fact she was perfectly unconscious.

She had a slight struggle in opening the vicarage gate which hung, rustily, half off its hinges. A puff of wind caught at her battered felt hat, causing it to sit even more rakishly than it had done before. 'Bother!' said Bunch.

Christened by her optimistic parents Diana, Mrs Harmon had become Bunch at an early age for somewhat obvious reasons and the name had stuck to her ever since. Clutching the chrysanthemums, she made her way through the gate to the churchyard, and so to the church door.

The November air was mild and damp. Clouds scudded across the sky with patches of blue here and there. Inside, the church was dark and cold; it was unheated except at service times.

'Brrrrrh!' said Bunch expressively. 'I'd better get on with this quickly. I don't want to die of cold.'

With the quickness born of practice she collected the necessary paraphernalia: vases, water, flower-holders. 'I wish we had lilies,' thought Bunch to herself. 'I get so tired of these scraggy chrysanthemums.' Her nimble fingers arranged the blooms in their holders.

There was nothing particularly original or artistic about the decorations, for Bunch Harmon herself was neither original nor artistic, but it was a homely and pleasant arrangement. Carrying the vases carefully, Bunch stepped up the aisle and made her way towards the altar. As she did so the sun came out.

It shone through the east window of somewhat crude coloured glass, mostly blue and red – the gift of a wealthy Victorian churchgoer. The effect was almost startling in its sudden opulence. 'Like jewels,' thought Bunch. Suddenly she stopped, staring ahead of her. On the chancel steps was a huddled dark form.

Putting down the flowers carefully, Bunch went up to it and bent over it. It was a man lying there, huddled over on himself. Bunch knelt down by him and slowly, carefully, she turned him over. Her fingers went to his pulse – a pulse so feeble and fluttering that it told its own story, as did the almost greenish pallor of his face. There was no doubt, Bunch thought, that the man was dying.

He was a man of about forty-five, dressed in a dark, shabby suit. She laid down the limp hand she had picked up and looked at his other hand. This seemed clenched like a fist on his breast. Looking more closely she saw that the fingers were closed over what seemed to be a large wad or handkerchief which he was holding tightly to his chest. All round the clenched hand there were splashes of a dry brown fluid which, Bunch guessed, was dry blood. Bunch sat back on her heels, frowning.

Up till now the man's eyes had been closed but at this point they suddenly opened and fixed themselves on Bunch's face. They were neither dazed nor wandering. They seemed fully alive and intelligent. His lips moved, and Bunch bent forward to catch the words, or rather the word. It was only one word that he said:

'*Sanctuary.*'

There was, she thought, just a very faint smile as he breathed out this word. There was no mistaking it, for after a moment he said it again, 'Sanctuary...'

Then, with a faint, long-drawn-out sigh, his eyes closed again. Once more Bunch's fingers went to his pulse. It was still there, but fainter now and more intermittent. She got up with decision.

'Don't move,' she said, 'or try to move. I'm going for help.'

The man's eyes opened again but he seemed now to be fixing his attention on the coloured light that came through the east window. He murmured something that Bunch could not quite catch. She thought, startled, that it might have been her husband's name.

'Julian?' she said. 'Did you come here to find Julian?' But there was no answer. The man lay with eyes closed, his breathing coming in slow, shallow fashion.

Bunch turned and left the church rapidly. She glanced at her watch and nodded with some satisfaction. Dr Griffiths would still be in his surgery. It was only a couple of minutes' walk from the church. She went in, without waiting to knock or ring, passing through the waiting room and into the doctor's surgery.

'You must come at once,' said Bunch. 'There's a man dying in the church.'

Some minutes later Dr Griffiths rose from his knees after a brief examination.

'Can we move him from here into the vicarage? I can attend to him better there – not that it's any use.'

'Of course,' said Bunch. 'I'll go along and get things

ready. I'll get Harper and Jones, shall I? To help you carry him.'

'Thanks. I can telephone from the vicarage for an ambulance, but I'm afraid – by the time it comes . . .' He left the remark unfinished.

Bunch said, 'Internal bleeding?'

Dr Griffiths nodded. He said, 'How on earth did he come here?'

'I think he must have been here all night,' said Bunch, considering. 'Harper unlocks the church in the morning as he goes to work, but he doesn't usually come in.'

It was about five minutes later when Dr Griffiths put down the telephone receiver and came back into the morning-room where the injured man was lying on quickly arranged blankets on the sofa. Bunch was moving a basin of water and clearing up after the doctor's examination.

'Well, that's that,' said Griffiths. 'I've sent for an ambulance and I've notified the police.' He stood, frowning, looking down on the patient who lay with closed eyes. His left hand was plucking in a nervous, spasmodic way at his side.

'He was shot,' said Griffiths. 'Shot at fairly close quarters. He rolled his handkerchief up into a ball and plugged the wound with it so as to stop the bleeding.'

'Could he have gone far after that happened?' Bunch asked.

'Oh, yes, it's quite possible. A mortally wounded man has been known to pick himself up and walk along a street as though nothing had happened, and then suddenly collapse five or ten minutes later. So he needn't have been shot in the church. Oh no. He may have been shot some distance away. Of course, he may have shot himself and then dropped the revolver and staggered blindly towards the church. I don't quite know why he made for the church and not for the vicarage.'

'Oh, I know *that*,' said Bunch. 'He said it: "Sanctuary".'

The doctor stared at her. 'Sanctuary?'

'Here's Julian,' said Bunch, turning her head as she heard her husband's steps in the hall. 'Julian! Come here.'

The Reverend Julian Harmon entered the room. His vague, scholarly manner always made him appear much older than he really was. 'Dear me!' said Julian Harmon, staring in a mild, puzzled manner at the surgical appliances and the prone figure on the sofa.

Bunch explained with her usual economy of words. 'He was in the church, dying. He'd been shot. Do you know him, Julian? I thought he said your name.'

The vicar came up to the sofa and looked down at the dying man. 'Poor fellow,' he said, and shook his head. 'No, I don't know him. I'm almost sure I've never seen him before.'

At that moment the dying man's eyes opened once more. They went from the doctor to Julian Harmon and from him to his wife. The eyes stayed there, staring into Bunch's face. Griffiths stepped forward.

'If you could tell us,' he said urgently.

But with eyes fixed on Bunch, the man said in a weak voice, 'Please – *please* – ' And then, with a slight tremor, he died . . .

Sergeant Hayes licked his pencil and turned the page of his notebook.

'So that's all you can tell me, Mrs Harmon?'

'That's all,' said Bunch. 'These are the things out of his coat pockets.'

On a table at Sergeant Hayes's elbow was a wallet, a rather battered old watch with the initials W. S. and the return half of a ticket to London. Nothing more.

'You've found out who he is?' asked Bunch.

'A Mr and Mrs Eccles phoned up the station. He's her brother, it seems. Name of Sandbourne. Been in a low state of health and nerves for some time. He's been getting worse lately. The day before yesterday he walked out and didn't come back. He took a revolver with him.'

'And he came out here and shot himself with it?' said Bunch. 'Why?'

'Well, you see, he'd been depressed . . .'

Bunch interrupted him. 'I don't mean *that*. I mean, why here?'

Since Sergeant Hayes obviously did not know the answer to that one, he replied in an oblique fashion, 'Come out here, he did, on the five-ten bus.'

'Yes,' said Bunch again. 'But *why*?'

'I don't know, Mrs Harmon,' said Sergeant Hayes. 'There's no accounting. If the balance of the mind is disturbed –'

Bunch finished for him. 'They may do it anywhere. But it still seems to me unnecessary to take a bus out to a small country place like this. He didn't know any-one here, did he?'

'Not so far as can be ascertained,' said Sergeant Hayes. He coughed in an apologetic manner and said, as he rose to his feet, 'It may be as Mr and Mrs Eccles will come out and see you, ma'am – if you don't mind, that is.'

'Of course I don't mind,' said Bunch. 'It's very natural. I only wish I had something to tell them.'

'I'll be getting along,' said Sergeant Hayes.

'I'm only so thankful,' said Bunch, going with him to the front door, 'that it wasn't murder.'

A car had driven up at the vicarage gate. Sergeant Hayes, glancing at it, remarked: 'Looks as though that's Mr and Mrs Eccles come here now, ma'am, to talk with you.'

Bunch braced herself to endure what, she felt, might be rather a difficult ordeal. 'However,' she thought, 'I can always call Julian to help me. A clergyman's a great help when people are bereaved.'

Exactly what she had expected Mr and Mrs Eccles to be like, Bunch could not have said, but she was conscious, as she greeted them, of a feeling of surprise. Mr Eccles was a stout florid man whose natural manner would have been cheerful and facetious. Mrs Eccles had a vaguely flashy look about her. She had a small, mean, pursed-up mouth. Her voice was thin and reedy.

'It's been a terrible shock, Mrs Harmon, as you can imagine,' she said.

'Oh, I know,' said Bunch. 'It must have been. Do sit down. Can I offer you – well, perhaps it's a little early for tea –'

Mr Eccles waved a pudgy hand. 'No, no, nothing for us,' he said. 'It's very kind of you, I'm sure. Just wanted to . . . well . . . what poor William said and all that, you know?'

'He's been abroad a long time,' said Mrs Eccles, 'and I think he must have had some very nasty experiences. Very quiet and depressed he's been, ever since he came home. Said the world wasn't fit to live in and there was nothing to look forward to. Poor Bill, he was always moody.'

Bunch stared at them both for a moment or two without speaking.

'Pinched my husband's revolver, he did,' went on Mrs Eccles. 'Without our knowing. Then it seems he come here by bus. I suppose that was nice feeling on his part. He wouldn't have liked to do it in our house.'

'Poor fellow, poor fellow,' said Mr Eccles, with a sigh. 'It doesn't do to judge.'

There was another short pause, and Mr Eccles said, 'Did he leave a message? Any last words, nothing like that?'

His bright, rather pig-like eyes watched Bunch closely. Mrs Eccles, too, leaned forward as though anxious for the reply.

'No,' said Bunch quietly. 'He came into the church when he was dying, for sanctuary.'

Mrs Eccles said in a puzzled voice. 'Sanctuary? I don't think I quite . . .'

Mr Eccles interrupted. 'Holy place, my dear,' he said impatiently. 'That's what the vicar's wife means. It's a sin – suicide, you know. I expect he wanted to make amends.'

'He tried to say something just before he died,' said Bunch. 'He began, "Please," but that's as far as he got.'

Mrs Eccles put her handkerchief to her eyes and sniffed. 'Oh, dear,' she said. 'It's terribly upsetting, isn't it?'

'There, there, Pam,' said her husband. 'Don't take on. These things can't be helped. Poor Willie. Still, he's at peace now. Well, thank you very much, Mrs Harmon. I hope we haven't interrupted you. A vicar's wife is a busy lady, we know that.'

They shook hands with her. Then Eccles turned back suddenly to say, 'Oh yes, there's just one other thing. I think you've got his coat here, haven't you?'

'His coat?' Bunch frowned.

Mrs Eccles said, 'We'd like all his things, you know. Sentimental-like.'

'He had a watch and a wallet and a railway ticket

in the pockets,' said Bunch. 'I gave them to Sergeant Hayes.'

'That's all right, then,' said Mr Eccles. 'He'll hand them over to us, I expect. His private papers would be in the wallet.'

'There was a pound note in the wallet,' said Bunch. 'Nothing else.'

'No letters? Nothing like that?'

Bunch shook her head.

'Well, thank you again, Mrs Harmon. The coat he was wearing – perhaps the sergeant's got that too, has he?'

Bunch frowned in an effort of remembrance.

'No,' she said. 'I don't think ... let me see. The doctor and I took his coat off to examine his wound.' She looked round the room vaguely. 'I must have taken it upstairs with the towels and basin.'

'I wonder now, Mrs Harmon, if you don't mind ... We'd like his coat, you know, the last thing he wore. Well, the wife feels rather sentimental about it.'

'Of course,' said Bunch. 'Would you like me to have it cleaned first? I'm afraid it's rather – well – stained.'

'Oh, no, no, no, that doesn't matter.'

Bunch frowned. 'Now I wonder where ... excuse me a moment.' She went upstairs and it was some few minutes before she returned.

'I'm so sorry,' she said breathlessly, 'my daily woman must have put it aside with other clothes that were going to the cleaners. It's taken me quite a long time to find it. Here it is. I'll do it up for you in brown paper.'

Disclaiming their protests she did so; then once more effusively bidding her farewell the Eccleses departed.

Bunch went slowly back across the hall and entered the study. The Reverend Julian Harmon looked up and his brow cleared. He was composing a sermon and was fearing that he'd been led astray by the interest of the political relations between Judaea and Persia, in the reign of Cyrus.

'Yes, dear?' he said hopefully.

'Julian,' said Bunch. 'What's *Sanctuary* exactly?'

Julian Harmon gratefully put aside his sermon paper.

'Well,' he said. 'Sanctuary in Roman and Greek temples applied to the *cella* in which stood the statue of a god. The Latin word for altar "ara" also means protection.' He continued learnedly: 'In three hundred and ninety-nine AD the right of sanctuary in Christian churches was finally and definitely recognized. The earliest mention of the right of sanctuary in England is in the Code of Laws issued by Ethelbert in AD six hundred . . .'

He continued for some time with his exposition but was, as often, disconcerted by his wife's reception of his erudite pronouncement.

'Darling,' she said. 'You *are* sweet.'

Bending over, she kissed him on the tip of his nose. Julian felt rather like a dog who has been congratulated on performing a clever trick.

'The Eccleses have been here,' said Bunch.

The vicar frowned. 'The Eccleses? I don't seem to remember . . .'

'You don't know them. They're the sister and her husband of the man in the church.'

'My dear, you ought to have called me.'

'There wasn't any need,' said Bunch. 'They were not in need of consolation. I wonder now . . .' She frowned. 'If I put a casserole in the oven tomorrow, can you manage, Julian? I think I shall go up to London for the sales.'

'The sails?' Her husband looked at her blankly. 'Do you mean a yacht or a boat or something?'

Bunch laughed. 'No, darling. There's a special white sale at Burrows and Portman's. You know, sheets, table cloths and towels and glass-cloths. I don't know what we do with our glass-cloths, the way they wear through. Besides,' she added thoughtfully, 'I think I ought to go and see Aunt Jane.'

That sweet old lady, Miss Jane Marple, was enjoying the delights of the metropolis for a fortnight, comfortably installed in her nephew's studio flat.

'So kind of dear Raymond,' she murmured. 'He and Joan have gone to America for a fortnight and they insisted I should come up here and enjoy myself. And now, dear Bunch, do tell me what it is that's worrying you.'

Bunch was Miss Marple's favourite godchild, and the old lady looked at her with great affection as Bunch, thrusting her best felt hat farther on the back of her head, started her story.

Bunch's recital was concise and clear. Miss Marple nodded her head as Bunch finished. 'I see,' she said. 'Yes, I see.'

'That's why I felt I had to see you,' said Bunch. 'You see, not being clever –'

'But you *are* clever, my dear.'

'No, I'm not. Not clever like Julian.'

'Julian, of course, has a very solid intellect,' said Miss Marple.

'That's it,' said Bunch. 'Julian's got the intellect, but on the other hand, I've got the *sense.*'

'You have a lot of common sense, Bunch, and you're very intelligent.'

'You see, I don't really know what I ought to do. I can't ask Julian because – well, I mean, Julian's so full of rectitude . . .'

This statement appeared to be perfectly understood by Miss Marple, who said, 'I know what you mean, dear. We women – well, it's different.' She went on. 'You told me what happened, Bunch, but I'd like to know first exactly what you think.'

'It's all wrong,' said Bunch. 'The man who was there in the church, dying, knew all about Sanctuary. He said it just the way Julian would have said it. I mean, he was a well-read, educated man. And if he'd shot himself, he wouldn't drag himself to a church afterwards and say "sanctuary". Sanctuary means that you're pursued, and when you get into a church you're safe. Your pursuers can't touch you. At one time even the law couldn't get at you.'

She looked questioningly at Miss Marple. The latter nodded. Bunch went on, 'Those people, the Eccleses, were quite different. Ignorant and coarse. And there's another thing. That watch – the dead man's watch. It had the initials W. S. on the back of it. But inside – I opened it – in very small lettering there was "To Walter from his father" and a date. *Walter.* But the Eccleses kept talking of him as William or Bill.'

Miss Marple seemed about to speak but Bunch rushed on. 'Oh, I know you're not always called the name you're baptized by. I mean, I can understand that you might be christened William and called "Porgy" or "Carrots" or something. But your sister wouldn't call you William or Bill if your name was Walter.'

'You mean that she wasn't his sister?'

'I'm quite sure she wasn't his sister. They were horrid – both of them. They came to the vicarage to get his things and to find out if he'd said anything before he died. When I said he hadn't I saw it in their faces – relief. I think myself,' finished Bunch, 'it was Eccles who shot him.'

'Murder?' said Miss Marple.

'Yes,' said Bunch. 'Murder. That's why I came to you, darling.'

Bunch's remark might have seemed incongruous to an ignorant listener, but in certain spheres Miss Marple had a reputation for dealing with murder.

'He said "please" to me before he died,' said Bunch. 'He wanted me to do something for him. The awful thing is I've no idea what.'

Miss Marple considered for a moment or two, and then pounced on the point that had already occurred to Bunch. 'But why was he there at all?' she asked.

'You mean,' said Bunch, 'if you wanted sanctuary you might pop into a church anywhere. There's no need to take a bus that only goes four times a day and come out to a lonely spot like ours for it.'

'He must have come there for a purpose,' Miss Marple thought. 'He must have come to see someone. Chipping Cleghorn's not a big place, Bunch. Surely you must have some idea of who it was he came to see?'

Bunch reviewed the inhabitants of her village in her mind before rather doubtfully shaking her head. 'In a way,' she said, 'it could be anybody.'

'He never mentioned a name?'

'He said Julian, or I thought he said Julian. It might have been Julia, I suppose. As far as I know, there isn't any Julia living in Chipping Cleghorn.'

She screwed up her eyes as she thought back to the scene. The man lying there on the chancel steps, the light coming through the window with its jewels of red and blue light.

'Jewels,' said Miss Marple thoughtfully.

'I'm coming now,' said Bunch, 'to the most important thing of all. The reason why I've really come here today. You see, the Eccleses made a great fuss about having his coat. We took it off when the doctor was seeing him. It was an old, shabby sort of coat – there was no reason they should have wanted it. They pretended it was sentimental, but that was nonsense.

'Anyway, I went up to find it, and as I was just going up the stairs I remembered how he'd made a kind of picking gesture with his hand, as though he was fumbling with the coat. So when I got hold of the coat I looked at it very carefully and I saw that in one place the lining had been sewn up again with a different thread. So I unpicked it and I found a little piece of paper inside. I took it out and I sewed it up again properly with thread that matched. I was careful and I don't really think that the Eccleses would know I've done it. I don't *think* so, but I can't be sure. And I took the coat down to them and made some excuse for the delay.'

'The piece of paper?' asked Miss Marple.

Bunch opened her handbag. 'I didn't show it to Julian,' she said, 'because he would have said that I ought to have given it to the Eccleses. But I thought I'd rather bring it to you instead.

'A cloakroom ticket,' said Miss Marple, looking at it. 'Paddington Station.'

'He had a return ticket to Paddington in his pocket,' said Bunch.

The eyes of the two women met.

'This calls for action,' said Miss Marple briskly. 'But it would be advisable, I think, to be careful. Would you have noticed at all, Bunch dear, whether you were followed when you came to London today?'

'Followed!' exclaimed Bunch. 'You don't think –'

'Well, I think it's *possible*,' said Miss Marple. 'When anything is possible, I think we ought to take precautions.' She rose with a brisk movement. 'You came up here ostensibly, my dear, to go to the sales. I think the right thing to do, therefore, would be for us to *go* to the sales. But before we set out, we might put one or two little arrangements in hand. I don't suppose,' Miss Marple added obscurely, 'that I shall need the old speckled tweed with the beaver collar just at present.'

It was about an hour and a half later that the two ladies, rather the worse for wear and battered in appearance, and both clasping parcels of hardly-won household linen, sat down at a small and sequestered hostelry called the Apple Bough to restore their forces with steak and kidney pudding followed by apple tart and custard.

'Really a pre-war quality face towel,' gasped Miss Marple, slightly out of breath. 'With a J on it, too. So fortunate that Raymond's wife's name is Joan. I shall put them aside until I really need them and then they will do for her if I pass on sooner than I expect.'

'I really did need the glass-cloths,' said Bunch. 'And they were very cheap, though not as cheap as the ones that woman with the ginger hair managed to snatch from me.'

A smart young woman with a lavish application of rouge and lipstick entered the Apple Bough at that moment. After looking around vaguely for a moment or two, she hurried to their table. She laid down an envelope by Miss Marple's elbow.

'There you are, miss,' she said briskly.

'Oh, thank you, Gladys,' said Miss Marple. 'Thank you very much. So kind of you.'

'Always pleased to oblige, I'm sure,' said Gladys. 'Ernie always says to me, "Everything what's good you learned from that Miss Marple of yours that you were in service with," and I'm sure I'm always glad to oblige you, miss.'

'Such a dear girl,' said Miss Marple as Gladys departed again. 'Always so willing and so kind.'

She looked inside the envelope and then passed it on to Bunch. 'Now be very careful, dear,' she said. 'By the way, is there still that nice young inspector at Melchester that I remember?'

'I don't know,' said Bunch. 'I expect so.'

'Well, if not,' said Miss Marple thoughtfully. 'I can always ring up the Chief Constable. I *think* he would remember me.'

'Of course he'd remember you,' said Bunch. 'Everybody would remember *you.* You're quite unique.' She rose.

Arrived at Paddington, Bunch went to the luggage office and produced the cloakroom ticket. A moment or two later a rather shabby old suitcase was passed across to her, and carrying this she made her way to the platform.

The journey home was uneventful. Bunch rose as the train approached Chipping Cleghorn and picked up the old suitcase. She had just left her carriage when a man, sprinting along the platform, suddenly seized the suitcase from her hand and rushed off with it.

'Stop!' Bunch yelled. 'Stop him, stop him. He's taken my suitcase.'

The ticket collector who, at this rural station, was a man of somewhat slow processes, had just begun to say, 'Now, look here, you can't do that –' when a smart blow on the chest pushed him aside, and the man with the suitcase rushed out from the station. He made his way towards a waiting car. Tossing the suitcase in, he was about to climb after it, but before he could move a hand fell on his shoulder, and the voice of Police Constable Abel said, 'Now then, what's all this?'

Bunch arrived, panting, from the station. 'He

snatched my suitcase. I just got out of the train with it.'

'Nonsense,' said the man. 'I don't know what this lady means. It's my suitcase. I just got out of the train with it.'

He looked at Bunch with a bovine and impartial stare. Nobody would have guessed that Police Constable Abel and Mrs Harmon spent long half-hours in Police Constable Abel's off-time discussing the respective merits of manure and bone meal for rose bushes.

'You say, madam, that this is your suitcase?' said Police Constable Abel.

'Yes,' said Bunch. 'Definitely.'

'And you, sir?'

'I say this suitcase is mine.'

The man was tall, dark and well dressed, with a drawling voice and a superior manner. A feminine voice from inside the car said, 'Of course it's your suitcase, Edwin. I don't know what this woman means.'

'We'll have to get this clear,' said Police Constable Abel. 'If it's your suitcase, madam, what do you say is inside it?'

'Clothes,' said Bunch. 'A long speckled coat with a beaver collar, two wool jumpers and a pair of shoes.'

'Well, that's clear enough,' said Police Constable Abel. He turned to the other.

'I am a theatrical costumier,' said the dark man importantly. 'This suitcase contains theatrical properties which I brought down here for an amateur performance.'

'Right, sir,' said Police Constable Abel. 'Well, we'll just look inside, shall we, and see? We can go along to the police station, or if you're in a hurry we'll take the suitcase back to the station and open it there.'

'It'll suit me,' said the dark man. 'My name is Moss, by the way, Edwin Moss.'

The police constable, holding the suitcase, went back into the station. 'Just taking this into the parcels office, George,' he said to the ticket collector.

Police Constable Abel laid the suitcase on the counter of the parcels office and pushed back the clasp. The case was not locked. Bunch and Mr Edwin Moss stood on either side of him, their eyes regarding each other vengefully.

'Ah!' said Police Constable Abel, as he pushed up the lid.

Inside, neatly folded, was a long rather shabby tweed coat with a beaver fur collar. There were also two wool jumpers and a pair of country shoes.

'Exactly as you say, madam,' said Police Constable Abel, turning to Bunch.

Nobody could have said that Mr Edwin Moss under-did things. His dismay and compunction were magnificent.

'I do apologize,' he said. 'I really *do* apologize. Please believe me, dear lady, when I tell you how very, very sorry I am. Unpardonable – quite unpardonable – my behaviour has been.' He looked at his watch. 'I must rush now. Probably my suitcase has gone on the train.' Raising his hat once more, he said meltingly to Bunch, 'Do, *do* forgive me,' and rushed hurriedly out of the parcels office.

'Are you going to let him get away?' asked Bunch in a conspiratorial whisper to Police Constable Abel.

The latter slowly closed a bovine eye in a wink.

'He won't get too far, ma'am,' he said. 'That's to say he won't get far unobserved, if you take my meaning.'

'Oh,' said Bunch, relieved.

'That old lady's been on the phone,' said Police Constable Abel, 'the one as was down here a few years ago.

Bright she is, isn't she? But there's been a lot cooking up all today. Shouldn't wonder if the inspector or sergeant was out to see you about it tomorrow morning.'

It was the inspector who came, the Inspector Craddock whom Miss Marple remembered. He greeted Bunch with a smile as an old friend.

'Crime in Chipping Cleghorn again,' he said cheerfully. 'You don't lack for sensation here, do you, Mrs Harmon?'

'I could do with rather less,' said Bunch. 'Have you come to ask me questions or are you going to tell me things for a change?'

'I'll tell you some things first,' said the inspector. 'To begin with, Mr and Mrs Eccles have been having an eye kept on them for some time. There's reason to believe they've been connected with several robberies in this part of the world. For another thing, although Mrs Eccles *has* a brother called Sandbourne who has recently come back from abroad, the man you found dying in the church yesterday was definitely not Sandbourne.'

'I knew that he wasn't,' said Bunch. 'His name was Walter, to begin with, not William.'

The inspector nodded. 'His name was Walter St John, and he escaped forty-eight hours ago from Charrington Prison.'

'Of course,' said Bunch softly to herself, 'he was being hunted down by the law, and he took sanctuary.' Then she asked, 'What had he done?'

'I'll have to go back rather a long way. It's a complicated story. Several years ago there was a certain dancer doing turns at the music halls. I don't expect you'll have ever heard of her, but she specialized in an Arabian Night turn, 'Aladdin in the Cave of Jewels' it was called. She wore bits of rhinestone and not much else.

'She wasn't much of a dancer, I believe, but she was well – attractive. Anyway, a certain Asiatic royalty fell for her in a big way. Amongst other things he gave her a very magnificent emerald necklace.'

'The historic jewels of a Rajah?' murmured Bunch ecstatically.

Inspector Craddock coughed. 'Well, a rather more modern version, Mrs Harmon. The affair didn't last very long, broke up when our potentate's attention was captured by a certain film star whose demands were not quite so modest.

'Zobeida, to give the dancer her stage name, hung on to the necklace, and in due course it was stolen. It disappeared from her dressing-room at the theatre, and there was a lingering suspicion in the minds of the authorities that she herself might have engineered its disappearance. Such things have been known as a publicity stunt, or indeed from more dishonest motives.

'The necklace was never recovered, but during the course of the investigation the attention of the police was drawn to this man, Walter St John. He was a man of education and breeding who had come down in the world, and who was employed as a working jeweller with a rather obscure firm which was suspected of acting as a fence for jewel robberies.

'There was evidence that this necklace had passed through his hands. It was, however, in connection with the theft of some other jewellery that he was finally brought to trial and convicted and sent to prison. He had not very much longer to serve, so his escape was rather a surprise.'

'But why did he come here?' asked Bunch.

'We'd like to know that very much, Mrs Harmon.

Following up his trial, it seems that he went first to London. He didn't visit any of his old associates but he visited an elderly woman, a Mrs Jacobs who had formerly been a theatrical dresser. She won't say a word of what he came for, but according to other lodgers in the house he left carrying a suitcase.'

'I see,' said Bunch. 'He left it in the cloakroom at Paddington and then he came down here.'

'By that time,' said Inspector Craddock, 'Eccles and the man who calls himself Edwin Moss were on his trail. They wanted that suitcase. They saw him get on the bus. They must have driven out in a car ahead of him and been waiting for him when he left the bus.'

'And he was murdered?' said Bunch.

'Yes,' said Craddock. 'He was shot. It was Eccles's revolver, but I rather fancy it was Moss who did the shooting. Now, Mrs Harmon, what we want to know is, where is the suitcase that Walter St John actually deposited at Paddington Station?'

Bunch grinned. 'I expect Aunt Jane's got it by now,' she said. 'Miss Marple, I mean. That was her plan. She sent a former maid of hers with a suitcase packed with her things to the cloakroom at Paddington and we exchanged tickets. I collected her suitcase and brought it down by train. She seemed to expect that an attempt would be made to get it from me.'

It was Inspector Craddock's turn to grin. 'So she said when she rang up. I'm driving up to London to see her. Do you want to come, too, Mrs Harmon?'

'Wel-l,' said Bunch, considering. 'Wel-l, as a matter of fact, it's very fortunate. I had a toothache last night so I really ought to go to London to see the dentist, oughtn't I?'

'Definitely,' said Inspector Craddock . . .

* * *

Miss Marple looked from Inspector Craddock's face to the eager face of Bunch Harmon. The suitcase lay on the table. 'Of course, I haven't opened it,' the old lady said. 'I wouldn't dream of doing such a thing till somebody official arrived. Besides,' she added, with a demurely mischievous Victorian smile, 'it's locked.'

'Like to make a guess at what's inside, Miss Marple?' asked the inspector.

'I should imagine, you know,' said Miss Marple, 'that it would be Zobeida's theatrical costumes. Would you like a chisel, Inspector?'

The chisel soon did its work. Both women gave a slight gasp as the lid flew up. The sunlight coming through the window lit up what seemed like an inexhaustible treasure of sparkling jewels, red, blue, green, orange.

'Aladdin's Cave,' said Miss Marple. 'The flashing jewels the girl wore to dance.'

'Ah,' said Inspector Craddock. 'Now, what's so precious about it, do you think, that a man was murdered to get hold of it?'

'She was a shrewd girl, I expect,' said Miss Marple thoughtfully. 'She's dead, isn't she, Inspector?'

'Yes, died three years ago.'

'She had this valuable emerald necklace,' said Miss Marple, musingly. 'Had the stones taken out of their setting and fastened here and there on her theatrical costume, where everyone would take them for merely coloured rhinestones. Then she had a replica made of the real necklace, and that, of course, was what was stolen. No wonder it never came on the market. The thief soon discovered the stones were false.'

'Here is an envelope,' said Bunch, pulling aside some of the glittering stones.

Inspector Craddock took it from her and extracted

two official-looking papers from it. He read aloud, ' "Marriage Certificate between Walter Edmund St John and Mary Moss." That was Zobeida's real name.'

'So they were married,' said Miss Marple. 'I see.'

'What's the other?' asked Bunch.

'A birth certificate of a daughter, Jewel.'

'Jewel?' cried Bunch. 'Why, of course. Jewel! *Jill!* That's it. I see now why he came to Chipping Cleghorn. *That's* what he was trying to say to me. Jewel. The Mundys, you know. Laburnum Cottage. They look after a little girl for someone. They're devoted to her. She's been like their own granddaughter. Yes, I remember now, her name *was* Jewel, only, of course, they call her Jill.

'Mrs Mundy had a stroke about a week ago, and the old man's been very ill with pneumonia. They were both going to go to the infirmary. I've been trying hard to find a good home for Jill somewhere. I didn't want her taken away to an institution.

'I suppose her father heard about it in prison and he managed to break away and get hold of this suitcase from the old dresser he or his wife left it with. I suppose if the jewels really belonged to her mother, they can be used for the child now.'

'I should imagine so, Mrs Harmon. *If* they're here.'

'Oh, they'll be here all right,' said Miss Marple cheerfully . . .

'Thank goodness you're back, dear,' said the Reverend Julian Harmon, greeting his wife with affection and a sigh of content. 'Mrs Burt always tries to do her best when you're away, but she really gave me some *very* peculiar fish-cakes for lunch. I didn't want to hurt her feelings so I gave them to Tiglath Pileser, but even *he* wouldn't eat them so I had to throw them out of the window.'

'Tiglath Pileser,' said Bunch, stroking the vicarage cat, who was purring against her knee, 'is *very* particular about what fish he eats. I often tell him he's got a proud stomach!'

'And your tooth, dear? Did you have it seen to?'

'Yes,' said Bunch. 'It didn't hurt much, and I went to see Aunt Jane again, too . . .'

'Dear old thing,' said Julian. 'I hope she's not failing at all.'

'Not in the least,' said Bunch, with a grin.

The following morning Bunch took a fresh supply of chrysanthemums to the church. The sun was once more pouring through the east window, and Bunch stood in the jewelled light on the chancel steps. She said very softly under her breath, 'Your little girl will be all right. *I'll* see that she is. I promise.'

Then she tidied up the church, slipped into a pew and knelt for a few moments to say her prayers before returning to the vicarage to attack the piled-up chores of two neglected days.

The Adventure of the
Christmas Pudding

Greenshaw's Folly

The two men rounded the corner of the shrubbery.

'Well, there you are,' said Raymond West. 'That's it.'

Horace Bindler took a deep, appreciative breath.

'But my dear,' he cried, 'how wonderful.' His voice rose in a high screech of aesthetic delight, then deepened in reverent awe. 'It's unbelievable. Out of this world! A period piece of the best.'

'I thought you'd like it,' said Raymond West, complacently.

'Like it? My dear —' Words failed Horace. He unbuckled the strap of his camera and got busy. 'This will be one of the gems of my collection,' he said happily. 'I do think, don't you, that it's rather amusing to have a collection of monstrosities? The idea came to me one night seven years ago in my bath. My last real gem was in the Campo Santo at Genoa, but I really think this beats it. What's it called?'

'I haven't the least idea,' said Raymond.

'I suppose it's got a name?'

'It must have. But the fact is that it's never referred to round here as anything but Greenshaw's Folly.'

'Greenshaw being the man who built it?'

'Yes. In eighteen-sixty or seventy or thereabouts. The local success story of the time. Barefoot boy who had risen to immense prosperity. Local opinion is divided as to why he built this house, whether it was sheer

331

exuberance of wealth or whether it was done to impress his creditors. If the latter, it didn't impress them. He either went bankrupt or the next thing to it. Hence the name, Greenshaw's Folly.'

Horace's camera clicked. 'There,' he said in a satisfied voice. 'Remind me to show you No. 310 in my collection. A really incredible marble mantelpiece in the Italian manner.' He added, looking at the house, 'I can't conceive of how Mr Greenshaw thought of it all.'

'Rather obvious in some ways,' said Raymond. 'He had visited the châteaux of the Loire, don't you think? Those turrets. And then, rather unfortunately, he seems to have travelled in the Orient. The influence of the Taj Mahal is unmistakable. I rather like the Moorish wing,' he added, 'and the traces of a Venetian palace.'

'One wonders how he ever got hold of an architect to carry out these ideas.'

Raymond shrugged his shoulders.

'No difficulty about that, I expect,' he said. 'Probably the architect retired with a good income for life while poor old Greenshaw went bankrupt.'

'Could we look at it from the other side?' asked Horace, 'or are we trespassing?'

'We're trespassing all right,' said Raymond, 'but I don't think it will matter.'

He turned towards the corner of the house and Horace skipped after him.

'But who lives here, my dear? Orphans or holiday visitors? It can't be a school. No playing-fields or brisk efficiency.'

'Oh, a Greenshaw lives here still,' said Raymond over his shoulder. 'The house itself didn't go in the crash. Old Greenshaw's son inherited it. He was a bit of a miser and lived here in a corner of it. Never spent a penny. Probably never had a penny to spend. His daughter lives here now. Old lady – very eccentric.'

As he spoke Raymond was congratulating himself on having thought of Greenshaw's Folly as a means of entertaining his guest. These literary critics always professed themselves as longing for a week-end in the country, and were wont to find the country extremely boring when they got there. Tomorrow there would be the Sunday papers, and for today Raymond West congratulated himself on suggesting a visit to Greenshaw's Folly to enrich Horace Bindler's well-known collection of monstrosities.

They turned the corner of the house and came out on a neglected lawn. In one corner of it was a large artificial rockery, and bending over it was a figure at sight of which Horace clutched Raymond delightedly by the arm.

'My dear,' he exclaimed, 'do you see what she's got on? A sprigged print dress. Just like a housemaid – when there were housemaids. One of my most cherished memories is staying at a house in the country when I was quite a boy where a real housemaid called you in the morning, all crackling in a print dress and a cap. Yes, my boy, really – a cap. Muslin with streamers. No, perhaps it was the parlour-maid who had the streamers. But anyway she was a real housemaid and she brought in an enormous brass can of hot water. What an exciting day we're having.'

The figure in the print dress had straightened up and had turned towards them, trowel in hand. She was a sufficiently startling figure. Unkempt locks of iron-grey fell wispily on her shoulders, a straw hat rather like the hats that horses wear in Italy was crammed down on her head. The coloured print dress she wore fell nearly to her ankles. Out of a weatherbeaten, not too clean face, shrewd eyes surveyed them appraisingly.

'I must apologize for trespassing, Miss Greenshaw,' said Raymond West, as he advanced towards her, 'but Mr Horace Bindler who is staying with me –'

Horace bowed and removed his hat.

' – is most interested in – er – ancient history and – er – fine buildings.'

Raymond West spoke with the ease of a well-known author who knows that he is a celebrity, that he can venture where other people may not.

Miss Greenshaw looked up at the sprawling exuberance behind her.

'It *is* a fine house,' she said appreciatively. 'My grandfather built it – before my time, of course. He is reported as having said that he wished to astonish the natives.'

'I'll say he did that, ma'am,' said Horace Bindler.

'Mr Bindler is the well-known literary critic,' said Raymond West.

Miss Greenshaw had clearly no reverence for literary critics. She remained unimpressed.

'I consider it,' said Miss Greenshaw, referring to the house, 'as a monument to my grandfather's genius. Silly fools come here, and ask me why I don't sell it and go and live in a flat. What would *I* do in a flat? It's my home and I live in it,' said Miss Greenshaw. 'Always have lived here.' She considered, brooding over the past. 'There were three of us. Laura married the curate. Papa wouldn't give her any money, said clergymen ought to be unworldly. She died, having a baby. Baby died too. Nettie ran away with the riding master. Papa cut her out of his will, of course. Handsome fellow, Harry Fletcher, but no good. Don't think Nettie was happy with him. Anyway, she didn't live long. They had a son. He writes to me sometimes, but of course he isn't a Greenshaw. *I'm* the last of the Greenshaws.' She drew up her bent shoulders with a certain pride, and readjusted the rakish angle of the straw hat. Then, turning, she said sharply:

'Yes, Mrs Cresswell, what is it?'

Approaching them from the house was a figure that, seen side by side with Miss Greenshaw, seemed ludicrously dissimilar. Mrs Cresswell had a marvellously dressed head of well-blued hair towering upwards in meticulously arranged curls and rolls. It was as though she had dressed her head to go as a French marquise to a fancy dress party. The rest of her middle-aged person was dressed in what ought to have been rustling black silk but was actually one of the shinier varieties of black rayon. Although she was not a large woman, she had a well-developed and sumptuous bust. Her voice, when she spoke, was unexpectedly deep. She spoke with exquisite diction, only a slight hesitation over words beginning with 'h' and the final pronunciation of them with an exaggerated aspirate gave rise to a suspicion that at some remote period in her youth she might have had trouble over dropping her h's.

'The fish, madam,' said Mrs Cresswell, 'the slice of cod. It has not arrived. I have asked Alfred to go down for it and he refuses to do so.'

Rather unexpectedly, Miss Greenshaw gave a cackle of laughter.

'Refuses, does he?'

'Alfred, madam, has been most disobliging.'

Miss Greenshaw raised two earth-stained fingers to her lips, suddenly produced an ear-splitting whistle and at the same time yelled:

'Alfred. Alfred, come here.'

Round the corner of the house a young man appeared in answer to the summons, carrying a spade in his hand. He had a bold, handsome face and as he drew near he cast an unmistakably malevolent glance towards Mrs Cresswell.

'You wanted me, miss?' he said.

'Yes, Alfred. I hear you've refused to go down for the fish. What about it, eh?'

Alfred spoke in a surly voice.

'I'll go down for it if you wants it, miss. You've only got to say.'

'I do want it. I want it for my supper.'

'Right you are, miss. I'll go right away.'

He threw an insolent glance at Mrs Cresswell, who flushed and murmured below her breath:

'Really! It's unsupportable.'

'Now that I think of it,' said Miss Greenshaw, 'a couple of strange visitors are just what we need, aren't they, Mrs Cresswell?'

Mrs Cresswell looked puzzled.

'I'm sorry, madam –'

'For you-know-what,' said Miss Greenshaw, nodding her head. 'Beneficiary to a will mustn't witness it. That's right, isn't it?' She appealed to Raymond West.

'Quite correct,' said Raymond.

'I know enough law to know that,' said Miss Greenshaw. 'And you two are men of standing.'

She flung down her trowel on her weeding-basket.

'Would you mind coming up to the library with me?'

'Delighted,' said Horace eagerly.

She led the way through French windows and through a vast yellow and gold drawing-room with faded brocade on the walls and dust covers arranged over the furniture, then through a large dim hall, up a staircase and into a room on the first floor.

'My grandfather's library,' she announced.

Horace looked round the room with acute pleasure. It was a room, from his point of view, quite full of monstrosities. The heads of sphinxes appeared on the most unlikely pieces of furniture, there was a colossal bronze representing, he thought, Paul and Virginia, and a vast bronze clock with classical motifs of which he longed to take a photograph.

'A fine lot of books,' said Miss Greenshaw.

Raymond was already looking at the books. From what he could see from a cursory glance there was no book here of any real interest or, indeed, any book which appeared to have been read. They were all superbly bound sets of the classics as supplied ninety years ago for furnishing a gentleman's library. Some novels of a bygone period were included. But they too showed little signs of having been read.

Miss Greenshaw was fumbling in the drawers of a vast desk. Finally she pulled out a parchment document.

'My will,' she explained. 'Got to leave your money to someone – or so they say. If I died without a will I suppose that son of a horse-coper would get it. Handsome fellow, Harry Fletcher, but a rogue if there ever was one. Don't see why *his* son should inherit this place. No,' she went on, as though answering some unspoken objection, 'I've made up my mind. I'm leaving it to Cresswell.'

'Your housekeeper?'

'Yes. I've explained it to her. I make a will leaving her all I've got and then I don't need to pay her any wages. Saves me a lot in current expenses, and it keeps her up to the mark. No giving me notice and walking off at any minute. Very la-di-dah and all that, isn't she? But her father was a working plumber in a very small way. *She's* nothing to give herself airs about.'

She had by now unfolded the parchment. Picking up

a pen she dipped it in the inkstand and wrote her signature, Katherine Dorothy Greenshaw.

'That's right,' she said. 'You've seen me sign it, and then you two sign it, and that makes it legal.'

She handed the pen to Raymond West. He hesitated a moment, feeling an unexpected repulsion to what he was asked to do. Then he quickly scrawled the well-known signature, for which his morning's mail usually brought at least six demands a day.

Horace took the pen from him and added his own minute signature.

'That's done,' said Miss Greenshaw.

She moved across to the bookcase and stood looking at them uncertainly, then she opened a glass door, took out a book and slipped the folded parchment inside.

'I've my own places for keeping things,' she said.

'*Lady Audley's Secret*,' Raymond West remarked, catching sight of the title as she replaced the book.

Miss Greenshaw gave another cackle of laughter.

'Best-seller in its day,' she remarked. 'Not like your books, eh?'

She gave Raymond a sudden friendly nudge in the ribs. Raymond was rather surprised that she even knew he wrote books. Although Raymond West was quite a name in literature, he could hardly be described as a best seller. Though softening a little with the advent of middle age, his books dealt bleakly with the sordid side of life.

'I wonder,' Horace demanded breathlessly, 'if I might just take a photograph of the clock?'

'By all means,' said Miss Greenshaw. 'It came, I believe, from the Paris exhibition.'

'Very probably,' said Horace. He took his picture.

'This room's not been used much since my grandfather's time,' said Miss Greenshaw. 'This desk's full of old diaries of his. Interesting, I should think. I haven't the eyesight to read them myself. I'd like to get them published, but I suppose one would have to work on them a good deal.'

'You could engage someone to do that,' said Raymond West.

'Could I really? It's an idea, you know. I'll think about it.'

Raymond West glanced at his watch.

'We mustn't trespass on your kindness any longer,' he said.

'Pleased to have seen you,' said Miss Greenshaw graciously. 'Thought you were the policeman when I heard you coming round the corner of the house.'

'Why a policeman?' demanded Horace, who never minded asking questions.

Miss Greenshaw responded unexpectedly.

'If you want to know the time, ask a policeman,' she carolled, and with this example of Victorian wit, nudged Horace in the ribs and roared with laughter.

'It's been a wonderful afternoon,' sighed Horace as they walked home. 'Really, that place has everything. The only thing the library needs is a body. Those old-fashioned detective stories about murder in the library – that's just the kind of library I'm sure the authors had in mind.'

'If you want to discuss murder,' said Raymond, 'you must talk to my Aunt Jane.'

'Your Aunt Jane? Do you mean Miss Marple?' He felt a little at a loss.

The charming old-world lady to whom he had been introduced the night before seemed the last person to be mentioned in connection with murder.

'Oh, yes,' said Raymond. 'Murder is a speciality of hers.'

'But my dear, how intriguing. What do you really mean?'

'I mean just that,' said Raymond. He paraphrased: 'Some commit murder, some get mixed up in murders, others have murder thrust upon them. My Aunt Jane comes into the third category.'

'You are joking.'

'Not in the least. I can refer you to the former Commissioner of Scotland Yard, several chief constables and one or two hard-working inspectors of the CID.'

Horace said happily that wonders would never cease. Over the tea table they gave Joan West, Raymond's wife, Lou Oxley her niece, and old Miss Marple, a résumé of the afternoon's happenings, recounting in detail everything that Miss Greenshaw had said to them.

'But I do think,' said Horace, 'that there is something a little *sinister* about the whole set-up. That duchess-like creature, the housekeeper – arsenic, perhaps, in the teapot, now that she knows her mistress has made the will in her favour?'

'Tell us, Aunt Jane,' said Raymond. 'Will there be murder or won't there? What do *you* think?'

'I think,' said Miss Marple, winding up her wool with a rather severe air, 'that you shouldn't joke about these things as much as you do, Raymond. Arsenic is, of course, *quite* a possibility. So easy to obtain. Probably present in the toolshed already in the form of weed killer.'

'Oh, really, darling,' said Joan West, affectionately. 'Wouldn't that be rather too obvious?'

'It's all very well to make a will,' said Raymond, 'I don't suppose really the poor old thing has anything to leave except that awful white elephant of a house, and who would want that?'

'A film company possibly,' said Horace, 'or a hotel or an institution?'

'They'd expect to buy it for a song,' said Raymond, but Miss Marple was shaking her head.

'You know, dear Raymond, I cannot agree with you there. About the money, I mean. The grandfather was evidently one of those lavish spenders who make money easily, but can't keep it. He may have gone broke, as you say, but hardly bankrupt or else his son would not have had the house. Now the son, as is so often the case, was an entirely different character to his father. A miser. A man who saved every penny. I should say that in the course of his lifetime he probably put by a very good sum. This Miss Greenshaw appears to have taken after him, to dislike spending money, that is. Yes, I should think it quite likely that she had quite a good sum tucked away.'

'In that case,' said Joan West, 'I wonder now – what about Lou?'

They looked at Lou as she sat, silent, by the fire.

Lou was Joan West's niece. Her marriage had recently, as she herself put it, come unstuck, leaving her with two young children and a bare sufficiency of money to keep them on.

'I mean,' said Joan, 'if this Miss Greenshaw really wants someone to go through diaries and get a book ready for publication . . .'

'It's an idea,' said Raymond.

Lou said in a low voice:

'It's work I could do – and I'd enjoy it.'

'I'll write to her,' said Raymond.

'I wonder,' said Miss Marple thoughtfully, 'what the old lady meant by that remark about a policeman?'

'Oh, it was just a joke.'

'It reminded me,' said Miss Marple, nodding her

head vigorously, 'yes, it reminded me very much of Mr Naysmith.'

'Who was Mr Naysmith?' asked Raymond, curiously.

'He kept bees,' said Miss Marple, 'and was very good at doing the acrostics in the Sunday papers. And he liked giving people false impressions just for fun. But sometimes it led to trouble.'

Everybody was silent for a moment, considering Mr Naysmith, but as there did not seem to be any points of resemblance between him and Miss Greenshaw, they decided that dear Aunt Jane was perhaps getting a *little* bit disconnected in her old age.

Horace Bindler went back to London without having collected any more monstrosities and Raymond West wrote a letter to Miss Greenshaw telling her that he knew of a Mrs Louisa Oxley who would be competent to undertake work on the diaries. After a lapse of some days, a letter arrived, written in spidery old-fashioned handwriting, in which Miss Greenshaw declared herself anxious to avail herself of the services of Mrs Oxley, and making an appointment for Mrs Oxley to come and see her.

Lou duly kept the appointment, generous terms were arranged and she started work on the following day.

'I'm awfully grateful to you,' she said to Raymond. 'It will fit in beautifully. I can take the children to school, go on to Greenshaw's Folly and pick them up on my way back. How fantastic the whole set-up is! That old woman has to be seen to be believed.'

On the evening of her first day at work she returned and described her day.

'I've hardly seen the housekeeper,' she said. 'She came in with coffee and biscuits at half past eleven with her mouth pursed up very prunes and prisms,

342

and would hardly speak to me. I think she disapproves deeply of my having been engaged.' She went on, 'It seems there's quite a feud between her and the gardener, Alfred. He's a local boy and fairly lazy, I should imagine, and he and the housekeeper won't speak to each other. Miss Greenshaw said in her rather grand way, "There have always been feuds as far as I can remember between the garden and the house staff. It was so in my grandfather's time. There were three men and a boy in the garden then, and eight maids in the house, but there was always friction."'

On the following day Lou returned with another news.

'Just fancy,' she said, 'I was asked to ring up the nephew this morning.'

'Miss Greenshaw's nephew?'

'Yes. It seems he's an actor playing in the company that's doing a summer season at Boreham on Sea. I rang up the theatre and left a message asking him to lunch tomorrow. Rather fun, really. The old girl didn't want the housekeeper to know. I think Mrs Cresswell has done something that's annoyed her.'

'Tomorrow another instalment of this thrilling serial,' murmured Raymond.

'It's exactly like a serial, isn't it? Reconciliation with the nephew, blood is thicker than water – another will be made and the old will destroyed.'

'Aunt Jane, you're looking very serious.'

'Was I, my dear? Have you heard any more about the policeman?'

Lou looked bewildered. 'I don't know anything about a policeman.'

'That remark of hers, my dear,' said Miss Marple, 'must have meant *something*.'

Lou arrived at her work the next day in a cheerful

mood. She passed through the open front door – the doors and windows of the house were always open. Miss Greenshaw appeared to have no fear of burglars, and was probably justified, as most things in the house weighed several tons and were of no marketable value.

Lou had passed Alfred in the drive. When she first caught sight of him he had been leaning against a tree smoking a cigarette, but as soon as he had caught sight of her he had seized a broom and begun diligently to sweep leaves. An idle young man, she thought, but good looking. His features reminded her of someone. As she passed through the hall on her way upstairs to the library she glanced at the large picture of Nathaniel Greenshaw which presided over the mantelpiece, showing him in the acme of Victorian prosperity, leaning back in a large arm-chair, his hands resting on the gold albert across his capacious stomach. As her glance swept up from the stomach to the face with its heavy jowls, its bushy eyebrows and its flourishing black moustache, the thought occurred to her that Nathaniel Greenshaw must have been handsome as a young man. He had looked, perhaps, a little like Alfred . . .

She went into the library, shut the door behind her, opened her typewriter and got out the diaries from the drawer at the side of the desk. Through the open window she caught a glimpse of Miss Greenshaw in a puce-coloured sprigged print, bending over the rockery, weeding assiduously. They had had two wet days, of which the weeds had taken full advantage.

Lou, a town bred girl, decided that if she ever had a garden it would never contain a rockery which needed hand weeding. Then she settled down to her work.

When Mrs Cresswell entered the library with the coffee tray at half past eleven, she was clearly in a very bad temper. She banged the tray down on the table, and observed to the universe:

'Company for lunch – and nothing in the house! What am *I* supposed to do, I should like to know? And no sign of Alfred.'

'He was sweeping in the drive when I got here,' Lou offered.

'I dare say. A nice soft job.'

Mrs Cresswell swept out of the room and banged the door behind her. Lou grinned to herself. She wondered what 'the nephew' would be like.

She finished her coffee and settled down to her work again. It was so absorbing that time passed quickly. Nathaniel Greenshaw, when he started to keep a diary, had succumbed to the pleasure of frankness. Trying out a passage relating to the personal charm of a barmaid in the neighbouring town, Lou reflected that a good deal of editing would be necessary.

As she was thinking this, she was startled by a scream from the garden. Jumping up, she ran to the open window. Miss Greenshaw was staggering away from the rockery towards the house. Her hands were clasped to her breast and between them there protruded a feathered shaft that Lou recognized with stupefaction to be the shaft of an arrow.

Miss Greenshaw's head, in its battered straw hat, fell forward on her breast. She called up to Lou in a failing voice: '. . . shot . . . he shot me . . . with an arrow . . . get help . . .'

Lou rushed to the door. She turned the handle, but the door would not open. It took her a moment or two of futile endeavour to realize that she was locked in. She rushed back to the window.

'I'm locked in.'

Miss Greenshaw, her back towards Lou, and swaying

345

a little on her feet, was calling up to the housekeeper at a window farther along.

'Ring police . . . telephone . . .'

Then, lurching from side to side like a drunkard, she disappeared from Lou's view through the window below into the drawing-room. A moment later Lou heard a crash of broken china, a heavy fall, and then silence. Her imagination reconstructed the scene. Miss Greenshaw must have staggered blindly into a small table with a Sèvres teaset on it.

Desperately Lou pounded on the door, calling and shouting. There was no creeper or drain-pipe outside the window that could help her to get out that way.

Tired at last of beating on the door, she returned to the window. From the window of her sitting-room farther along, the housekeeper's head appeared.

'Come and let me out, Mrs Oxley. I'm locked in.'

'So am I.'

'Oh dear, isn't it awful? I've telephoned the police. There's an extension in this room, but what I can't understand, Mrs Oxley, is our being locked in. *I* never heard a key turn, did you?'

'No. I didn't hear anything at all. Oh dear, what shall we do? Perhaps Alfred might hear us.' Lou shouted at the top of her voice, 'Alfred, Alfred.'

'Gone to his dinner as likely as not. What time is it?'

Lou glanced at her watch.

'Twenty-five past twelve.'

'He's not supposed to go until half past, but he sneaks off earlier whenever he can.'

'Do you think – do you think –'

Lou meant to ask 'Do you think she's dead?' but the words stuck in her throat.

There was nothing to do but wait. She sat down on the window-sill. It seemed an eternity before the stolid helmeted figure of a police constable came round the corner of the house. She leant out of the window and he looked up at her, shading his eyes with his hand. When he spoke his voice held reproof.

'What's going on here?' he asked disapprovingly.

From their respective windows, Lou and Mrs Cresswell poured a flood of excited information down on him.

The constable produced a note-book and pencil. 'You ladies ran upstairs and locked yourselves in? Can I have your names, please?'

'No. Somebody else locked us in. Come and let us out.'

The constable said reprovingly, 'All in good time,' and disappeared through the window below.

Once again time seemed infinite. Lou heard the sound of a car arriving, and, after what seemed an hour, but was actually three minutes, first Mrs Cresswell and then Lou, were released by a police sergeant more alert than the original constable.

'Miss Greenshaw?' Lou's voice faltered. 'What – what's happened?'

The sergeant cleared his throat.

'I'm sorry to have to tell you, madam,' he said, 'what I've already told Mrs Cresswell here. Miss Greenshaw is dead.'

'Murdered,' said Mrs Cresswell. 'That's what it is – murder.'

The sergeant said dubiously:

'Could have been an accident – some country lads shooting with bows and arrows.'

Again there was the sound of a car arriving. The sergeant said:

'That'll be the MO,' and started downstairs.

But it was not the MO. As Lou and Mrs Cresswell came down the stairs a young man stepped hesitatingly

347

through the front door and paused, looking round him with a somewhat bewildered air.

Then, speaking in a pleasant voice that in some way seemed familiar to Lou – perhaps it had a family resemblance to Miss Greenshaw's – he asked:

'Excuse me, does – er – does Miss Greenshaw live here?'

'May I have your name if you please,' said the sergeant advancing upon him.

'Fletcher,' said the young man. 'Nat Fletcher. I'm Miss Greenshaw's nephew, as a matter of fact.'

'Indeed, sir, well – I'm sorry – I'm sure –'

'Has anything happened?' asked Nat Fletcher.

'There's been an – accident – your aunt was shot with an arrow – penetrated the jugular vein –'

Mrs Cresswell spoke hysterically and without her usual refinement:

'Your h'aunts been murdered, that's what's 'appened. Your h'aunt's been murdered.'

Inspector Welch drew his chair a little nearer to the table and let his gaze wander from one to the other of the four people in the room. It was the evening of the same day. He had called at the Wests' house to take Lou Oxley once more over her statement.

'You are sure of the exact words? *Shot – he shot me – with an arrow – get help?*'

Lou nodded.

'And the time?'

'I looked at my watch a minute or two later – it was then twelve twenty-five.'

'Your watch keeps good time?'

'I looked at the clock as well.'

The inspector turned to Raymond West.

'It appears, sir, that about a week ago you and a

Mr Horace Bindler were witnesses to Miss Greenshaw's will?'

Briefly, Raymond recounted the events of the afternoon visit that he and Horace Bindler had paid to Greenshaw's Folly.

'This testimony of yours may be important,' said Welch. 'Miss Greenshaw distinctly told you, did she, that her will was being made in favour of Mrs Cresswell, the housekeeper, that she was not paying Mrs Cresswell any wages in view of the expectations Mrs Cresswell had of profiting by her death?'

'That is what she told me – yes.'

'Would you say that Mrs Cresswell was definitely aware of these facts?'

'I should say undoubtedly. Miss Greenshaw made a reference in my presence to beneficiaries not being able to witness a will and Mrs Cresswell clearly understood what she meant by it. Moreover, Miss Greenshaw herself told me that she had come to this arrangement with Mrs Cresswell.'

'So Mrs Cresswell had reason to believe she was an interested party. Motive's clear enough in her case, and I dare say she'd be our chief suspect now if it wasn't for the fact that she was securely locked in her room like Mrs Oxley here, and also that Miss Greenshaw definitely said a *man* shot her –'

'She definitely *was* locked in her room?'

'Oh yes. Sergeant Cayley let her out. It's a big old-fashioned lock with a big old-fashioned key. The key was in the lock and there's not a chance that it could have been turned from inside or any hanky-panky of that kind. No, you can take it definitely that Mrs Cresswell was locked inside that room and couldn't get out. And there were no bows and arrows in the room and Miss Greenshaw couldn't in any case have been shot from a window – the angle forbids it – no, Mrs Cresswell's out of it.'

He paused and went on:

'Would you say that Miss Greenshaw, in your opinion, was a practical joker?'

Miss Marple looked up sharply from her corner.

'So the will wasn't in Mrs Cresswell's favour after all?' she said.

Inspector Welch looked over at her in a rather surprised fashion.

'That's a very clever guess of yours, madam,' he said. 'No. Mrs Cresswell isn't named as beneficiary.'

'Just like Mr Naysmith,' said Miss Marple, nodding her head. 'Miss Greenshaw told Mrs Cresswell she was going to leave her everything and so got out of paying her wages; and then she left her money to somebody else. No doubt she was vastly pleased with herself. No wonder she chortled when she put the will away in *Lady Audley's Secret.*'

'It was lucky Mrs Oxley was able to tell us about the will and where it was put,' said the inspector. 'We might have had a long hunt for it otherwise.'

'A Victorian sense of humour,' murmured Raymond West.

'So she left her money to her nephew after all,' said Lou.

The inspector shook his head.

'No,' he said, 'she didn't leave it to Nat Fletcher. The story goes around here – of course I'm new to the place and I only get the gossip that's second-hand – but it seems that in the old days both Miss Greenshaw and her sister were set on the handsome young riding master, and the sister got him. No, she didn't leave the money to her nephew –' He paused, rubbing his chin, 'She left it to Alfred,' he said.

350

'Alfred – the gardener?' Joan spoke in a surprised voice.

'Yes, Mrs West. Alfred Pollock.'

'But why?' cried Lou.

Miss Marple coughed and murmured:

'I should imagine, though perhaps I am wrong, that there may have been – what we might call *family* reasons.'

'You could call them that in a way,' agreed the inspector. 'It's quite well known in the village, it seems, that Thomas Pollock, Alfred's grandfather, was one of old Mr Greenshaw's by-blows.'

'Of course,' cried Lou, 'the resemblance! I saw it this morning.'

She remembered how after passing Alfred she had come into the house and looked up at old Greenshaw's portrait.

'I dare say,' said Miss Marple, 'that she thought Alfred Pollock might have a pride in the house, might even want to live in it, whereas her nephew would almost certainly have no use for it whatever and would sell it as soon as he could possibly do so. He's an actor, isn't he? What play exactly is he acting in at present?'

Trust an old lady to wander from the point, thought Inspector Welch, but he replied civilly:

'I believe, madam, they are doing a season of James Barrie's plays.'

'Barrie,' said Miss Marple thoughtfully.

'*What Every Woman Knows*,' said Inspector Welch, and then blushed. 'Name of a play,' he said quickly. 'I'm not much of a theatre-goer myself,' he added, 'but the wife went along and saw it last week. Quite well done, she said it was.'

'Barrie wrote some very charming plays,' said Miss Marple, 'though I must say that when I went with an old friend of mine, General Easterly, to see Barrie's *Little Mary* – ' she shook her head sadly, ' – neither of us knew where to look.'

The inspector, unacquainted with the play *Little Mary* looked completely fogged. Miss Marple explained:

'When I was a girl, Inspector, nobody ever mentioned the word *stomach*.'

The inspector looked even more at sea. Miss Marple was murmuring titles under her breath.

'*The Admirable Crichton*. Very clever. *Mary Rose* – a charming play. I cried, I remember. *Quality Street* I didn't care for so much. Then there was *A Kiss for Cinderella*. Oh, *of course*.'

Inspector Welch had no time to waste on theatrical discussion. He returned to the matter in hand.

'The question is,' he said, 'did Alfred Pollock know that the old lady had made a will in his favour? Did she tell him?' He added: 'You see – there's an archery club over at Boreham Lovell and *Alfred Pollock's a member*. He's a very good shot indeed with a bow and arrow.'

'Then isn't your case quite clear?' asked Raymond West. 'It would fit in with the doors being locked on the two women – he'd know just where they were in the house.'

The inspector looked at him. He spoke with deep melancholy.

'He's got an alibi,' said the inspector.

'I always think alibis are definitely suspicious.'

'Maybe, sir,' said Inspector Welch. 'You're talking as a writer.'

'I don't write detective stories,' said Raymond West, horrified at the mere idea.

'Easy enough to say that alibis are suspicious,' went on Inspector Welch, 'but unfortunately we've got to deal with facts.'

He sighed.

'We've got three good suspects,' he said. 'Three people who, as it happened, were very close upon the scene at the time. Yet the odd thing is that it looks as though none of the three could have done it. The housekeeper I've already dealt with – the nephew, Nat Fletcher, at the moment Miss Greenshaw was shot, was a couple of miles away filling up his car at a garage and asking his way – as for Alfred Pollock six people will swear that he entered the Dog and Duck at twenty past twelve and was there for an hour having his usual bread and cheese and beer.'

'Deliberately establishing an alibi,' said Raymond West hopefully.

'Maybe,' said Inspector Welch, 'but if so, he *did* establish it.'

There was a long silence. Then Raymond turned his head to where Miss Marple sat upright and thoughtful.

'It's up to you, Aunt Jane,' he said. 'The inspector's baffled, the sergeant's baffled, I'm baffled, Joan's baffled, Lou is baffled. But to you, Aunt Jane it is crystal clear. Am I right?'

'I wouldn't say that, dear,' said Miss Marple, 'not *crystal* clear, and murder, dear Raymond, isn't a game. I don't suppose poor Miss Greenshaw wanted to die, and it was a particularly brutal murder. Very well planned and quite cold blooded. It's not a thing to make *jokes* about!'

'I'm sorry,' said Raymond, abashed. 'I'm not really as callous as I sound. One treats a thing lightly to take away from the well, the horror of it.'

'That is, I believe, the modern tendency,' said Miss Marple, 'All these wars, and having to joke about funerals. Yes, perhaps I was thoughtless when I said you were callous.'

'It isn't,' said Joan, 'as though we'd known her at all well.'

'That is *very* true,' said Miss Marple. 'You, dear Joan, did not know her at all. I did not know her at all. Raymond gathered an impression of her from one afternoon's conversation. Lou knew her for two days.'

'Come now, Aunt Jane,' said Raymond, 'tell us your views. You don't mind, Inspector?'

'Not at all,' said the inspector politely.

'Well, my dear, it would seem that we have three people who had, or might have thought they had, a motive to kill the old lady. And three quite simple reasons why none of the three could have done so. The housekeeper could not have done so because she was locked in her room and because Miss Greenshaw definitely stated that a *man* shot her. The gardener could not have done it because he was inside the Dog and Duck at the time the murder was committed, the nephew could not have done it because he was still some distance away in his car at the time of the murder.'

'Very clearly put, madam,' said the inspector.

'And since it seems most unlikely that any outsider should have done it, where, then, are we?'

'That's what the inspector wants to know,' said Raymond West.

One so often looks at a thing the wrong way round,' said Miss Marple apologetically. 'If we can't alter the movements or the position of those three people, then couldn't we perhaps alter the time of the murder?'

'You mean that both my watch and the clock were wrong?' asked Lou.

'No dear,' said Miss Marple, 'I didn't mean that at all. I mean that the murder didn't occur when you thought it occurred.'

'But I *saw* it,' cried Lou.

'Well, what I have been wondering, my dear, was whether you weren't *meant* to see it. I've been asking myself, you know, whether that wasn't the real reason why you were engaged for this job.'

'What *do* you mean, Aunt Jane?'

'Well, dear, it seems odd. Miss Greenshaw did not like spending money, and yet she engaged you and agreed quite willingly to the terms you asked. It seems to me that perhaps you were meant to be there in that library on the first floor, looking out of the window so that you could be the key witness – someone from outside of irreproachable good faith – to fix a definite time and place for the murder.'

'But you can't mean,' said Lou, incredulously, 'that Miss Greenshaw *intended* to be murdered.'

'What I mean, dear,' said Miss Marple, 'is that you didn't really know Miss Greenshaw. There's no real reason, is there, why the Miss Greenshaw you saw when you went up to the house should be the same Miss Greenshaw that Raymond saw a few days earlier? Oh, yes, I know,' she went on, to prevent Lou's reply, 'she was wearing the peculiar old-fashioned print dress and the strange straw hat, and had unkempt hair. She corresponded exactly to the description Raymond gave us last week-end. But those two women, you know, were much of an age and height and size. The housekeeper, I mean, and Miss Greenshaw.'

'But the housekeeper is fat!' Lou exclaimed. 'She's got an enormous bosom.'

Miss Marple coughed.

'But my dear, surely, nowadays I have seen – er – them myself in shops most indelicately displayed. It is very easy for anyone to have a – a bust – of *any* size and dimension.'

'What are you trying to say?' demanded Raymond.

'I was just thinking, dear, that during the two or three days Lou was working there, one woman could have played the two parts. You said yourself, Lou, that you hardly saw the housekeeper, except for the one moment in the morning when she brought you in the tray with coffee. One sees those clever artists on the stage coming in as different characters with only a minute or two to spare, and I am sure the change could have been effected quite easily. That marquise head-dress could be just a wig slipped on and off.'

'Aunt Jane! Do you mean that Miss Greenshaw was dead before I started work there?'

'Not dead. Kept under drugs, I should say. A very easy job for an unscrupulous woman like the housekeeper to do. Then she made the arrangements with you and got you to telephone to the nephew to ask him to lunch at a definite time. The only person who would have known that this Miss Greenshaw was *not* Miss Greenshaw would have been Alfred. And if you remember, the first two days you were working there it was wet, and Miss Greenshaw stayed in the house. Alfred never came into the house because of his feud with the housekeeper. And on the last morning Alfred was in the drive, while Miss Greenshaw was working on the rockery – I'd like to have a look at that rockery.'

'Do you mean it was Mrs Cresswell who killed Miss Greenshaw?'

'I think that after bringing you your coffee, the woman locked the door on you as she went out, carried the unconscious Miss Greenshaw down to the drawing-room, then assumed her "Miss Greenshaw" disguise and went out to work on the rockery where you could see her from the window. In due course she screamed and came staggering to the house clutching an arrow as though it had penetrated her throat. She called for help and was careful to say "*he* shot me" so as to remove suspicion from the housekeeper. She also called up to the housekeeper's window as though she saw her there. Then, once inside the drawing-room, she threw over a table with porcelain on it – and ran quickly upstairs, put on her marquise wig and was able a few moments later to lean her head out of the window and tell you that she, too, was locked in.'

'But she *was* locked in,' said Lou.

'I know. That is where the policeman comes in.'

'What policeman?'

'Exactly – what policeman? I wonder, Inspector, if you would mind telling me how and when *you* arrived on the scene?'

The inspector looked a little puzzled.

'At twelve twenty-nine we received a telephone call from Mrs Cresswell, housekeeper to Miss Greenshaw, stating that her mistress had been shot. Sergeant Cayley and myself went out there at once in a car and arrived at the house at twelve thirty-five. We found Miss Greenshaw dead and the two ladies locked in their rooms.'

'So, you see, my dear,' said Miss Marple to Lou. 'The police constable *you* saw wasn't a real police constable. You never thought of him again – one doesn't – one just accepts one more uniform as part of the law.'

'But who – why?'

'As to who – well, if they are playing *A Kiss for Cinderella*, a policeman is the principal character. Nat Fletcher would only have to help himself to the costume he wears on the stage. He'd ask his way at a garage being careful to call attention to the time – twelve twenty-five, then drive on quickly, leave his car round a corner, slip on his police uniform and do his "act".'

'But why? – why?'

'*Someone* had to lock the housekeeper's door on the outside, and someone had to drive the arrow through Miss Greenshaw's throat. You can stab anyone with an arrow just as well as by shooting it – but it needs force.'

'You mean they were both in it?'

'Oh yes, I think so. Mother and son as likely as not.'

'But Miss Greenshaw's sister died long ago.'

'Yes, but I've no doubt Mr Fletcher married again. He sounds the sort of man who would, and I think it possible that the child died too, and that this so-called nephew was the second wife's child, and not really a relation at all. The woman got a post as housekeeper and spied out the land. Then he wrote as her nephew and proposed to call upon her – he may have made some joking reference to coming in his policeman's uniform – or asked her over to see the play. But I think she suspected the truth and refused to see him. He would have been her heir if she had died without making a will – but of course once she had made a will in the housekeeper's favour (as they thought) then it was clear sailing.'

'But why use an arrow?' objected Joan. 'So very far fetched.'

'Not far fetched at all, dear. Alfred belonged to an archery club – Alfred was meant to take the blame. The fact that he was in the pub as early as twelve twenty was most unfortunate from their point of view. He always left a little before his proper time and that would have been just right –' she shook her head. 'It really seems all wrong – morally, I mean, that Alfred's laziness should have saved his life.'

The inspector cleared his throat.

'Well, madam, these suggestions of yours are very interesting. I shall have, of course, to investigate –'

*   *   *

Miss Marple and Raymond West stood by the rockery and looked down at that gardening basket full of dying vegetation.

Miss Marple murmured:

'Alyssum, saxifrage, cytisus, thimble campanula ... Yes, that's all the proof *I* need. Whoever was weeding here yesterday morning was no gardener – she pulled up plants as well as weeds. So now I *know* I'm right. Thank you, dear Raymond, for bringing me here. I wanted to see the place for myself.'

She and Raymond both looked up at the outrageous pile of Greenshaw's Folly.

A cough made them turn. A handsome young man was also looking at the house.

'Plaguey big place,' he said. 'Too big for nowadays – or so they say. I dunno about that. If I won a football pool and made a lot of money, that's the kind of house I'd like to build.'

He smiled bashfully at them.

'Reckon I can say so now – that there house was built by my great-grandfather,' said Alfred Pollock. 'And a fine house it is, for all they call it Greenshaw's Folly!'

AGATHA CHRISTIE SOCIETY

If you have enjoyed this book you may be interested to know about the Agatha Christie Society.

The Society was formed in March 1993 to promote communication between the many loyal fans of Agatha Christie and the various media who strive to bring her works to the public.

The Agatha Christie Society is run under the auspices of Agatha Christie Limited, so we can guarantee that all the information you receive through the Society has been gathered by those people who have a commitment to and love of Agatha Christie.

Members receive four newsletters a year, each one packed with information about Agatha Christie. There are interviews with the personalities who have brought Agatha Christie's characters to life on the stage and screen; behind-the-scenes aspects of filming; publishing worldwide; listings of where you can see productions of Agatha Christie plays and much, much more.

These newsletters are very much a two-way operation, and many of the articles are written by members from around the world.

Meetings are arranged from time to time to give members the opportunity to gather together and exchange information about their favourite writer.

If you would like to become a member, please write to:

The Agatha Christie Society
PO Box 985
London SW1X 9XA